"CAPTAIN, IT'S RIGHT OVER US AND COMING!"

The thing was too close to torpedo. It had surprised him, coming at them so suddenly. The computer had identified it as DSRV, a Deep Submergence Rescue Vehicle, but how . . . why was it here?

"Let it in. I'm going aft to see who's come all this way to see us," Captain Lasovic ordered.

He felt the clang of contact as he slid through the engineering room hatch, the chief petty officer behind him with a squad of armed sailors. Pumps began to dewater the channel between *Aspen* and the DSRV. When the ready light went on, two crewmen swung the wheel on the hatch, and it opened with a rush of seawater.

"Tom . . ." MacKenzie almost fell through the trunk, taking in air in great, heaving gulps.

"Mac, what the hell—?" Lasovic bent down beside him, and propped the man's head up.

"Whatever you do, Tom—" MacKenzie had to stop to breathe— "Don't move *Aspen* an inch until we've talked. Full silent."

Mac wanted to explain, but oxygen starvation and fatigue sent him careening over the edge, where everything—the stolen Russian sub, the memory of Justine—was lost in darkness. . . .

FULL FATHOM FIVE

BART DAVIS

BANTAM BOOKS

TORONTO • NEW YORK • LONDON • SYDNEY • AUCKLAND

This book is dedicated to my brothers and sisters:
Brandon, Blair, Rona, and John.
With my deepest love.

FULL FATHOM FIVE

A Bantam Book / May 1987

ISBN 0-553-26205-X

Published simultaneously in the United States and Canada

ACKNOWLEDGMENTS

The author wishes to express his sincere gratitude to those people who have worked so tirelessly and contributed so much to the writing of this book: CMDR John W. Alexander USN, Captain George J. Ellis USN, the Captain and crew of the USS LIPSCOMB, the public affairs staff at Norfolk Naval Base; Mr. Norman Polmar, Brandon Davis, Sharon Davis—and those many members of the U.S. Submarine Force who prefer in all humility to remain nameless.

I am also deeply indebted to Robert Gottlieb and Barbara Alpert. No one could have more, or better, support.

NUCLEAR ATTACK SUBMARINE

Length: 360 feet
Beam (width): 33 feet

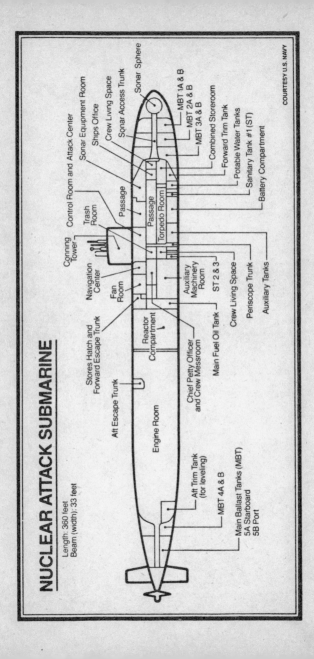

Sonar Sphere
MBT 1A & B
MBT 2A & B
MBT 3A & B
Combined Storeroom
Forward Trim Tank
Potable Water Tanks
Sanitary Tank #1 (ST)
Battery Compartment
Sonar Access Trunk
Crew Living Space
Ships Office
Sonar Equipment Room
Control Room and Attack Center
Passage
Trash Room
Passage
Torpedo Room
Conning Tower
Navigation Center
Fan Room
Auxiliary Machinery Room
ST 2 & 3
Crew Living Space
Periscope Trunk
Auxiliary Tanks
Main Fuel Oil Tank
Chief Petty Officer and Crew Messroom
Reactor Compartment
Stores Hatch and Forward Escape Trunk
Aft Escape Trunk
Engine Room
Aft Trim Tank (for leveling)
MBT 4A & B
Main Ballast Tanks (MBT)
5A Starboard
5B Port

COURTESY U.S. NAVY

PREFACE

The decade-old black Cadillac and the battered pickup truck that followed it appeared to sail rather than ride through the shimmering heat waves on the high plateau. Rebel activity had been reported in this region, so even this far inland a platoon of National Guardsmen manned the border crossing, hardly more than a pair of gate-linked shacks straddling the single-lane road which conscripted peasants had beaten into the dry ground.

The senior Guard lieutenant hitched up the leather harness on his khaki uniform and motioned to the corporal to follow him inside the larger of the two buildings. The corporal would stand guard while the travelers' papers were examined. The remaining two soldiers—an old career man named Sergeant Ortiz and a private named Ortega—unlimbered their rifles and took up positions in front of the barrier.

The driver stepped out of the car and casually smoothed out the wrinkles in his dark suit with long-fingered, aristocratic hands. He wasn't tall, but he was lean and straight-backed. Carlos Segurra moved with all the assurance of a ranking patriarch of a family that traced its lineage back to Spanish nobility. For over a century the Segurras had produced successful traders, landowners, artists, writers, and even a past president of the country. Carlos's own fame, his family stewardship, and his gifted children, had only increased the family's prominence.

"Señor Segurra." The sergeant almost bowed. "An honor."

He was met with a charming smile. "You know me?"

"Without seeing your papers, Señor. I was privileged to attend your concert last month in the capital. Brilliant. A joy."

"You're very kind, Sergeant. But please tell me, what procedure must we follow to cross the border? We have a recital tonight in Tegucigalpa."

"If you please, Señor, the lieutenant will inspect your papers inside. I'm sorry it's necessary," he said, peering inside the car, "but if your children would step out, we must make an inspection of your vehicles. You understand it's routine. . . ?"

Segurra nodded. "Of course. Children? Come out and meet the good sergeant who appreciates our music."

The boys emerged from the backseat. Both were dark-haired like their father, with intense brown eyes and trim bodies. The long-fingered Segurra hands were there too. Segurra pointed to the oldest. "This is my son, Sebastion. At fourteen, he is the family's cellist. And his brother Miguel. The baby of the family. Only nine and he wants to run us all with his violin. Refuses to play the long notes, eh, Miguelito?"

Segurra tousled both boys' hair, and they sidled closer to him, eyeing the Guardsman as if he were a new score to memorize. The sergeant found their scrutiny disquieting, but then his attention was pulled away.

On the other side of the car the passenger door swung open and the final occupant emerged. Segurra said simply, "My daughter, Maria Justiñiana."

The sergeant did not realize he'd stopped breathing. The girl was hauntingly, unbelievably beautiful, with raven-dark hair, and unblemished skin the color of pale honey. Unnerved, he felt himself pulled hypnotically into the dark wells of the child's eyes. Yet neither craft nor guile was the allure; the innocence was obvious. It was more the suggestion of a dreadful pain stirring faintly in the dark brown depths that drew him.

Her nose was narrow and her cheekbones high. The long, graceful fingers were apparent, too, fluttering unselfconsciously across newly budding breasts. She was very thin, almost painfully so. . . .

The sergeant's breath caught in his throat when he tried to release it, and he yanked his head back toward Segurra, fearing a moment's more inspection would offend the father.

"Señor Segurra, please . . . The lieutenant, inside. . . ?"

He was saved any further embarrassment, however, when the driver of the pickup truck ran over to Segurra, complaining bitterly.

"*Patrón!* The instruments! That dolt of a private is

opening the cases. I'm not responsible. I told him of their value. You tell him, *Patrón*. He refuses to listen to me."

Glad of the distraction, the sergeant followed Segurra and his children back to the truck. The tarpaulin that had covered Maria Justiñiana's piano had already been pulled off and both boys' instrument cases were open to the air.

"Everything is ruined!" wailed the driver. "Look!"

The sergeant was not an uncultured man. He knew the value of concert instruments such as these. Visions of demotion to swamp supervision danced through his mind with frightening clarity.

"Private Ortega!" he shouted. "What have you done here?"

The private knew the sound of blame being passed on. He tossed it right back. "But Sergeant, you told me to—"

"Enough!" bellowed the sergeant. "Señor Segurra, this is an unfortunate mistake. The instruments are works of art. If they've been damaged . . ."

Segurra stepped over and lifted out Miguel's violin. He shook his head. "I don't think so, Sergeant. Lucho here is a worrier. He packs them with compounds to absorb moisture lest our tropical climate warp them. But here"— he gestured around—"it's quite dry. The air won't harm them. In fact, your private may have done you a service. Since the cases are already open, if you'd like I will have the children play for you while I attend to matters inside with your lieutenant. Lucho will only have to repack anyway."

The Sergeant was visibly moved. "You would do this? Here?"

Segurra smiled. "We consider it a professional obligation. Children? Lucho, help them."

Lucho provided a stool for Sebastion and brought down his cello. Miguel took his violin and plucked out a few notes experimentally. Lucho lifted Maria Justiñiana up onto the truck's bed. She pulled her bench up to the piano and stripped away the rest of the tarp. Sebastion nodded his readiness, and Miguel lifted the violin to his shoulder.

Carlos Segurra looked deeply into the eyes of all three for a time. Then he lifted his hands into the classic conductor's prelude to beginning. "The Chopin, I think. Yes?"

The children steadied. Segurra's hands flashed up once, then down sharply.

Music burst forth like a river over the mountainous countryside, from Maria Justiñiana's piano in the back of an old pickup truck and from the accompanying instruments wielded by her dark-eyed brothers. It was incongruous here, on the dusty plateau with an armed audience in this war-ravaged region, but the precise, vibrant notes still blended and merged and struck back at the dust and desolation.

The sergeant was entranced. "Ortega!" he whispered fiercely. "Come here and listen. This is something you will tell your grandchildren about someday."

Curious, the private was drawn to his side, soon transfixed by the music as it bounded and grew.

Carlos Segurra cast a final glance at his daughter. It was she, the most sensitive of his children and unarguably the most talented, whom he was worried about most. But she refused to meet his eyes, instead retreating deeper into the hypnotic counterpoint. Segurra sighed softly and walked toward the guard station. Was anything but freedom worth such a price? He made a silent prayer that it should be and stepped into the cooler shadows inside to meet the lieutenant.

Outside, the music continued to swell as each instrument reinforced the others. With mathematical precision notes filled the spaces between running glissandos; time halved, then doubled. Themes emerged and melted away, then reemerged. Miquel got up to stroll around the dry ground like a minstrel, enveloping the soldiers with sound.

But for the raven-haired young girl the music was a refuge she sought but could not totally enter. She tried to wrap the notes around her like a comforter but was too aware of her brothers playing in practiced support and of the soldiers' grinning stares. They all forced her back to her surroundings. She played harder.

The climax she dreaded was now drawing near. She played louder and her technique lost some of its artistry as she forced greater volume out of the stately instrument, striking the keys harder and harder.

The music swelled inside her head. Each passage was

something to concentrate on to block out everything else. She refused to notice when Sebastion's cello dropped from the counterpoint. She did not need to look up from the keys to picture the gleam of the machete's wicked blade as he removed it from the hidden cache within his instrument.

Her brothers were behind the soldiers now. Her ears could not help but locate the sounds.

She played with an even greater intensity when she heard the wind whistle across the blade and the machete bite deeply into the back of the sergeant's leg, hamstringing him while his attention was so completely fixed upon her. She blocked out his agonized scream as the taut Achilles tendon was severed and he fell into the dust, flailing around like a marionette whose strings had been cut. Her ears told her what she could not bear to see—that the other guard had turned in shock, only to be felled by Sebastion with another slashing blow.

She played, pounding through the cadenza, a complicated flourish near the end of the piece, as Miguel laid aside his violin and dropped to the crippled guards, the slender needle that had been hidden in his bow poised in his small, skilled hand. She played so that the melody would pervade her senses; waiting, always waiting, until she finally heard the dreaded but essential pistol shots from inside the shack that meant her father had dispatched the remaining soldiers there.

She played, and for a time there was only the music. Inside her head there was only the sound.

It was her father who finally pried her hands from the keys. She could feel his sadness, almost a tangible thing. His dark eyes were moist. She knew his tears were not for the hated National Guardsmen, but for her. Her eyes remained dry. There was only the music inside. Perhaps, she thought, that was why her father cried.

It was very quiet now. Only the sounds of corpses being dragged along the ground broke the stillness as Lucho and the boys moved them aside. She could see dark stains on the ground. Her hands tried to flee almost reflexively to the keyboard, but her father wrapped them in his own hand and shook his head. *No more, not here.* With his other hand he gently traced the curve of her face, then moved away.

She watched him cross to their car and use the horn as a signal. Two long blasts; then repeated. He settled down to wait. With movements born of long practice at other guard stations just like these, Maria Justiñiana began to cover her piano and pack her brothers' instruments.

Soon the rebel forces began to emerge from cover. Trucks lumbered past the now empty guard station, bringing arms and supplies into the country from over the border. Sunburnt men in jungle fatigues with rolled up sleeves helped with the bodies of the Guardsmen.

Colonel Carlos Segurra conferred with the other rebel officers. Maria Justiñiana could hear concert schedules being discussed. There would be more border crossings.

Anything that could be of use to the rebels was taken from the guard shacks, including the AGR-9 radio—called "angry nights" by the rebels—which could have alerted the capital to send an air strike that would have bombed the supply caravan into oblivion. The capital was only minutes away by air. Maria Justiñiana forced herself to understand; such were the reasons for her father's deception. In recent years everyone fought the tyrant. Leftist, rightist, capitalist, socialist—it had ceased to matter. The alliance was beyond philosophy now; no one could be spared the responsibility of deposing the dictator.

She rejoined her brothers, both so terribly silent in the black car. They waited in the hot interior for their father. After a while he slid into the driver's seat. Soldiers helped to clear the way, pausing only to stare uneasily into the car's interior at the children who had been chosen to pay so much. Some crossed themselves.

Carlos Segurra drove away pondering that cost. Maria Justiñiana's music and Sebastion's pained silence, Miguel's terrible needle. *Oh, mi Dios*, he pleaded. The child was barely nine. . . .

He pressed down hard on the accelerator. There was still music, but only in the mind of the raven-haired, frightened little girl.

The family crossed the border en route to their next performance.

1

Nothing ever went wrong on a submarine individually—it was always a combination of things, Captain Peter MacKenzie thought sourly. And it was always the things no one could have prepared for. . . .

Ahead and slightly below him the Diving Officer cast a worried look back from his gauges. "Depth—eight hundred feet . . . and still sinking, sir." To his credit, the concern on his face did not register in his voice.

"Keep pumping, Mr. Randall," MacKenzie ordered from the control room, hitting the 2MC intercom channel to raise the Engineering Section. "Maneuvering, Conn. This is the captain speaking."

"Conn, Maneuvering, aye. Cardiff here," came back the Chief Engineer's voice.

"What's the status of the power plant, Jake? Don't hedge, I'll take your best estimate."

There was a pause, and MacKenzie could feel the man mentally taking stock. "It's been twenty minutes since the reactor SCRAMed, skipper. We have two more pipe fittings to replace and a big flange. Moisture's fouled the electronics too. Say half an hour minimum."

MacKenzie didn't allow frustration to creep into his voice, but half an hour and the USS *Aspen* would be well below its crush depth. "Keep at it, Jake. Try for twenty minutes." Even that was going to cut it very close.

MacKenzie stabbed at the gray intercom's off button as if it were the cause of the problems on board the *Aspen*, a newly refurbished 688 Los Angeles class nuclear attack submarine. It wasn't; a combination of things were.

Foremost was the crew's inexperience. Some of the men had just graduated from submarine school, and this was their first cruise. The majority of the rest had only recently been assembled for the *Aspen's* sea trials. Only one week out and they weren't yet used to working together. That inexperience, along with several mechanical problems—MacKenzie swore he'd have the Newport News construction boss up on charges—had combined to put the *Aspen* into her present straits.

Things happen suddenly at sea, and the ocean is unforgiving at its best. A space of only twenty minutes separated a successful test cruise from a desperate attempt to stop *Aspen's* murderous plunge below crush depth. A major steam leak had resulted in a reactor SCRAM and left the ship without sufficient steam pressure to operate the main engines. Without those the sub could not achieve enough forward momentum to use the planes to head for the surface. On top of that, a combination of human and mechanical error had resulted in a failure to fully charge the air banks—a group of huge scuba-type tanks used to blow main ballast tanks—so neither was MacKenzie able simply to raise the ship by making it more buoyant.

The battery provided emergency power following the reactor SCRAM, and the electrically driven emergency propulsion motor (EPM) was making a small but perceptible slowing in *Aspen's* plunge, but the lack of reactor power, made conditions in the submarine far more difficult.

Without reactor power to produce electricity, the air-conditioning shut down and the internal temperature rose from a comfortable seventy degrees to over a sweltering hundred. Everyone in the control room was sweating profusely, and MacKenzie had already given the order for the men to shed their shirts. Now, panting sailors with glistening skins sat struggling to keep the ship in stable trim, straining to read their gauges, which were difficult to see clearly in the dim light cast by the emergency lighting. The entire ship had a swampy feel— hot, fetid, and dim.

"One thousand feet," called out the Diving Officer. MacKenzie checked his watch. If anything, they were sinking faster now.

"Take the conn, Tom," he said to his Executive Officer, LCDR Tom Lasovic. "I'm going to see how the work is going."

Lasovic stepped up onto the slightly raised platform on

which the twin periscope tubes stood. "Aye, sir. I have the conn."

MacKenzie moved quickly down the almost vertical stairway. Only an hour before, *Aspen* had been proceeding through the warm waters of the Caribbean Sea on a smooth-running simulated search-and-destroy exercise with her sister ship, the USS *Phoenix*, playing a kind of deadly tag in earnest. *Phoenix* was acting as the Russian submarine, running silent and hiding to evade *Aspen*, or alternately, hunting her to subject the ship's newly installed systems to realistic assaults.

On one such run, with *Aspen* on the defense, sonar had suddenly picked up the *Phoenix*'s sounds close by. What then transpired repeated itself in MacKenzie's mind as he raced aft through the dim corridors to the Engineering Spaces. . . .

"Conn, Sonar. We're picking up what sounds like *Phoenix*, searching. Can't be certain if she's got contact on us yet though."

"Sonar, Conn. How close?"

"Estimate she may be inside four thousand yards, Captain. She's in the shallow zone and searching in a pattern that indicates she's still looking. Wait a second, somebody just kicked her in the tail. Turn count is increasing. She's making roughly twenty knots now."

"That confirms it. She doesn't know we're here. Keep tracking her, Sonar."

MacKenzie thought for a moment. At *Phoenix*'s present speed, both active and passive sonar were inefficient. That meant *Phoenix* had checked her immediate area, found it barren, and was now sprinting forward to another point where she would slow and listen again. That pattern would be repeated until her sonar picked up a target.

MacKenzie smiled. He knew *Phoenix*'s skipper, Commodore Phil Arlin, quite well. He was a methodical, careful man. It would be just his style to continue that pattern at least two or three more times before changing it. With that in mind, MacKenzie thought, perhaps the hunted could outmaneuver the hunter.

"Navigator, Conn. This is the captain. Listen, Frank, assuming *Phoenix* continues her present pattern, give me a course and speed that takes us across her bow at a distance of about five miles. And get us there slowly. I don't want to be heard."

"Conn, Navigator, aye. Can do, skipper. Computing a course and speed now," said the voice of LCDR Frank Lieberman, *Aspen's* third ranking officer and a man who had sailed with MacKenzie before. Each knew the other's style, and both respected their joint commitment to professionalism. They were a good team, one that inspired the junior officers to emulate it.

"Diving Officer, make your depth three-five-zero feet." MacKenzie wanted to bring *Aspen* close to *Phoenix's* depth zone.

"Three-five-zero feet, aye, sir," repeated Mr. Randall, the Diving Officer. "Make your depth 350 feet, three degrees up bubble," was the order Randall passed to the helmsman and stern planesman who sat side by side in front of him, their hands on steering/plane yokes which resembled those in airplane cockpits.

Lieberman's response came back quickly. "Conn, Navigator. Course two-two-zero, speed ten, should bring us across *Phoenix's* track in eleven minutes, Captain."

"Course two-two-oh—speed ten, Conn, aye." MacKenzie looked to the helmsman, "Helm, right fifteen degrees rudder, steady on course two-two-zero. All ahead two thirds."

"Answers ahead two thirds," the helmsman responded smartly.

"Depth at three-five-zero, Captain," the Diving Officer called out.

"Very well," MacKenzie acknowledged as the *Aspen* began a slow turn to the west. *Phoenix* was still heading south. So far, so good. MacKenzie's concentration intensified. Submarines were always on a war footing, never knowing when the exercise might suddenly turn real, often "playing" with Soviet subs equally prepared for the dread call to battle. The fact that his "adversary" was the *Phoenix* had to be forgotten; someday it might not be.

MacKenzie drew in a deep breath. The hunt had started, the most basic reason for all the years of training and preparation. He was planning a tactic that, if it worked—and they would only know that when mission tapes were compared later—would not only add to the crew's confidence and seamanship, but would certainly force Phil Arlin to buy the drinks and dinner when they reached port.

The intercom buzzed into life.

"Conn, Sonar. Contact's slowed. Bearing three-two-oh, estimated range six thousand yards. Still heading due south."

MacKenzie couldn't help the adrenal surge that coursed through his chest. It was time to execute what he had in mind. He opened the intercom channel.

"Sonar, Conn. As we pass across *Phoenix*'s bow, I'm going to execute a high-speed turn and make a 'knuckle' to confuse their sonar and give them a false target to lock on to. Fire Control Coordinator, be ready to shoot as soon as we execute the turn and come to a full stop. Understood?"

"Aye, sir. We're tracking. Should have a good solution for Fire Control following that nifty maneuver, captain."

MacKenzie thought he could see the smile on the Fire Control Coordinator's face. "We'll see, Mr. Talmadge. Prepare a constant fire-control solution on *Phoenix*. We'll simulate shooting two MK-48 torpedoes. Start your tapes now."

"Tapes running, aye."

"Helm," MacKenzie called out.

"Helm, aye, sir."

"On my order, hard right rudder, steady to course oh-nine-oh. We'll pivot around at flank speed, come to all stop and shoot."

"Hard right rudder, steady to course oh-nine-oh, on your order, aye, sir."

MacKenzie hit the 2MC channel again. "Maneuvering, Conn. Prepare to answer all bells. I'm going to want all ahead flank in"—he checked his watch—"four minutes."

"Maneuvering, aye. Whenever you need it, skipper."

"Good, Jake. Watch the big pressure transient when we come to all stop."

It was somewhat paradoxical, but the pressure in the reactor system was not highest, but lowest at full throttle, like a man with his veins opened. A sudden decrease in power requirements stopped the steam flow within the system, and pressure rose rapidly and could rupture steamlines. That was another important element of Mac-Kenzie's maneuver. If the power plant couldn't stand up to real test conditions, it'd be best to know now.

The Quartermaster, on station to MacKenzie's left, spoke up. "Two minutes to turning point, Captain. Still on course two-two-zero, sir."

"Very well," MacKenzie acknowledged, and flipped the intercom switch to 1MC to broadcast throughout the ship.

"This is the captain speaking. In less than two minutes we will be passing right across the southerly track of the USS *Phoenix*, which is engaged in a hunt/kill search of which we are the object. We are going to turn the tables, however, and hunt the hunter. Be prepared for a high-speed turn to starboard to fool his sonar and a sudden all stop to allow us to 'shoot.' Let's all look sharp now. Maneuver commences in sixty seconds."

MacKenzie was ready. He hoped that all the days of work had made both the sub and her crew ready too. It mostly came down to hard work and preparation. The adrenaline surge had worn off by now. This was business. A good captain aspired to professionalism above all else. Heroics only got men hurt.

He reviewed his tactics again. It all depended on whether or not they could pick up the *Phoenix* a third time; if it was where he'd guessed it would be. The atmosphere in the tightly packed control room had grown tense, too, awaiting the results of Sonar's continuing search. In the Conn, packed into a small room whose walls were almost solid gauges and instrumentation, the men were operationally blind and deaf, waiting for Sonar to give them eyes and ears.

"Conn, Sonar," crackled the intercom speaker. "Very faint contact. Bearing zero-zero-zero. I think it's *Phoenix*, sir. Computers agree with the signature. Range four thousand yards."

We've got her! MacKenzie thought as the Quartermaster called out, "Five seconds to turning point, Captain. Three . . . two . . . one . . . *mark*."

"Maneuvering, Conn. All ahead flank cavitate. Helm, hard right rudder, swing her as fast as she'll turn. Steady to course oh-nine-oh. Fire Control, firing point procedures."

MacKenzie's commands were repeated in terse tones. Aft, the main engines burst into life and *Aspen* shot ahead through the water as if slapped by a giant hand. The helmsman swung the ship about hard and men throughout her length had to hold on against gravity's pull. Behind her the churning propellers formed an enormous burst of billions of tiny bubbles—cavitation—which began to collapse almost as soon as they were born. This resulted in sound that traveled through the liquid medium to the trailing *Phoenix*, which responded to the sudden clamor with a sudden pinging sweep of all its active sonar gear, confident of its target.

On board *Aspen*, Sonar heard it all. "Conn, Sonar. Sounds like they bought it, skipper. They're sweeping the bubbles, getting a pretty good bounce too. It's a cinch they think it's us. Wait . . . they're slowing! You got 'em, Captain."

MacKenzie had his knuckle. But there was still the attack.

"Sonar, Conn. Range to target?"

"Three thousand yards, captain."

"Fire Control, open the outer doors," MacKenzie ordered.

"All systems set, Captain. Tapes running. Constant solution plotted."

"Maneuvering, this is the captain. Twenty seconds."

"Maneuvering, aye."

MacKenzie waited. The U-turn was almost completed. *Phoenix* would be dead ahead in just another few moments, moving perfectly into the center of his trap. They had done all they could now. *Aspen* was almost blind at this speed anyway. Ten seconds. Five.

"Captain, steady on course oh-nine-oh," called out the helmsman.

"Maneuvering. All stop! Fire Control . . ." *Aspen* began to slow. Pipes flexed alarmingly under the sudden pressure. ". . . final bearing and shoot."

"Set—Stand by—Fire!"

In the next moment nothing happened. No torpedo leaped out into the surrounding water; only a recording of its projected course for later comparison with *Phoenix*'s position and response registered the fact that the command to fire had been given. But, MacKenzie decided, it felt good. Real good. Until . . .

Moving swiftly along the murky corridors packed with pipes and conduits, all painted white to give the impression of space overhead, MacKenzie remembered the good feeling a well-done, complicated maneuver carried. He was just about to compliment the crew when the first sign of trouble came bursting over the intercom. He could hear the anxiety in Jake Cardiff's normally placid voice.

"Conn, Maneuvering. Major steam leak in the Engine Room! Reactor SCRAM!"

MacKenzie badly wanted to recover the reactor quickly and not leave the ship without power. "Can you isolate the leak, Jake?"

"No good, Captain. It's too far upstream. There's no isolation valve I can use to do it."

"You're certain it's only in the secondary system?"

"Aye, sir. Close to the steam generators. We don't have a radiation problem. But I need at least an hour."

MacKenzie calculated, and stifled an oath. "All right, Jake."

"Engineer, aye, Captain."

Even at that point, MacKenzie reflected bitterly, the reactor SCRAM wouldn't have been critical. Had the sub been in trim and neutrally buoyant, she would have just stayed right where she was until repairs were completed. But *Aspen* was just too heavy. The Chief of the Watch had taken on ballast during the attack run to compensate for the lift created during the turn, and the ruptured steam lines in Engineering added to the weight problem. Without enough forward momentum *Aspen* began to sink slowly, as the Diving Officer worked at the trim pump.

It was always a combination of things, MacKenzie thought. When he'd moved to restore trim, he discovered the uncharged air banks and the faulty pressure gauges. Pulling the gray steel T emergency blow lever to the main ballast tank lever had been totally unproductive.

He entered Engineering. Jake Cardiff and his men were already beginning to repair the ruptured steam line in the humid space, as well as ungagging the steam relief valve. The air was stifling. MacKenzie saw that a whole bank of switches had been shorted out and were being jury-rigged. Cardiff trudged over, looking frustrated and pressured. MacKenzie took him aside.

"What's the time estimate, Jake? I need power and I need it badly."

Cardiff frowned. "With luck, and no test of the system or relief valve, another fifteen to twenty minutes, Captain. This is a big job."

"I can't wait that long, Jake."

Cardiff nodded. *Aspen's* small down angle had not been lost on him. "Maybe I can cut five minutes off that if you don't need full power. But most of the welds will be quick fixes, and I can't say the whole plant won't come apart again the minute we start her up."

"I'll take ten minutes and one-third speed. Can you give me that?"

Cardiff looked at him steadily. "It's make or break, isn't it?"

MacKenzie nodded. "Ten minutes, Jake. I'll be waiting."

The struggle to hold depth was still in progress when MacKenzie got back to the control room.

"I have the conn," he announced, taking back his place. "Stay close, Tom," he said to his exec, then, "Diving Officer, I want full rise on the planes on my order. Keep the rudder amidships. Mr. Randall, what is our depth?"

"One-six-zero-zero feet, sir."

MacKenzie winced internally. They were very deep; there was no margin for error. Already systems were nearing the buckling point. Pipes could rupture any second. There was a steady groaning and hull popping all over the ship.

"Conn, Maneuvering," came Jake Cardiff's voice. "The reactor is critical. We'll be ready to answer minimum bells in sixty seconds, Captain."

MacKenzie invoked a silent prayer. "All right, Jake. Answer bells on the main engines and give me all you can."

"Aye, Captain."

MacKenzie stood steady. He was fully aware of the bunched muscles in the sweat-shiny backs before him. They knew. Make or break . . .

"All ahead one third." He paused. "Full rise on both planes. Chief, keep the trim pump at top speed." Silently he urged *Aspen* to respond.

"Full rise both planes, aye, sir."

"Trim pump is running at full speed, sir."

"Answering ahead one third."

Now, thought MacKenzie, as the sudden surge of power vibrated through the steel stanchions he held onto. "Depth, Mr. Randall! Call it out." The effect would be close to immediate . . . or not at all.

"Depth at one-seven-zero-zero . . . one-seven-zero-one . . . one-seven-zero-two . . . one-seven-zero-two . . . Captain! One-seven-zero-two . . . she's holding! One-seven-zero-zero . . . one-six-nine-nine . . . one-six-nine-seven . . ."

MacKenzie was hard pressed to hold in a sigh of blessed relief. "Maneuvering, Conn. Well done, Jake, and spread that around. How's she holding?"

"No problems so far, Captain. We'll do some testing once we surface."

"Mr. Randall, prepare to surface."

After a few moments MacKenzie gave the order, "Surface the ship."

"Surface the ship, aye," the Diving Officer repeated happily.

MacKenzie turned. "Chief, get the low-pressure blower on main ballast tanks as soon as the sail clears the surface and commence charging all air banks. Have the Electrician replace all the gauges on your board. No repeats, eh?"

The chief grinned ruefully. "No repeats. Yes, sir."

Full lighting came on suddenly and ribbons began to flap against air-conditioning grills. A collective sigh of relief emanated from the now-smiling men around the conn, echoed by everyone else on board.

A captain spent his working life concerned with details and planning for contingencies, MacKenzie thought, and a good cruise was generally one without incident. Underwater the unexpected would always be anathema.

He felt the weariness of post-crisis fatigue settle over him. His ship and crew were safe. Repairs would take place quickly, he hoped, and he could leave that in his executive officer's competent hands. His thoughts turned to *Phoenix*'s captain. Arlin would have been "watching" all this while, his listening gear deciphering most of *Aspen*'s problems. MacKenzie decided he should let him know that all was okay and file an additional report with COMSUBLANT.

He turned the conn back over to the XO, Tom Lasovic, whose warm respect communicated itself eloquently enough with a simple grin and nod of the head. They had been friends for a long time, and MacKenzie had specifically requested the broad-shouldered, black Annapolis graduate on this cruise.

There were plenty of grinning faces as MacKenzie made his way to his cabin. Word spread quickly in a three-hundred-sixty-foot tube. MacKenzie waved most of the praise away graciously, preferring instead to acknowledge those individuals who had reacted well.

The captain's cabin was a six-by-six-foot miracle of things built into walls, and the only one with its own head. MacKenzie stole inside gratefully, suddenly needing a few moments alone in his only sanctuary. He stepped into the head and filled the stainless steel sink with cold water, dipped both hands in and splashed it appreciatively onto his face, his hair, and his neck.

The face in the mirror caught his attention, and he watched the water roll down its craggy planes. It was a forty-one-year-old face, one whose Scottish features were deeply lined from too many years of water and weather. He ran his fingers through his black hair, still surprised that after days like today he didn't spot more gray. He stripped off his uniform, consciously inspecting the lines of his body, satisfied that his frequent workouts still kept it trim and hard.

He leaned nearer to the mirror, scrutinizing his face more closely. He saw the lines and tight creases that responsibility had engendered around his eyes and mouth. No one in command ever escaped its peculiar, steady erosion for long—just as no one carried the weight of all those other lives without the fear-worm frequently wriggling hot and unbidden inside the deep-secret places in one's own guts.

MacKenzie looked at the weary face in the mirror, suddenly in sharper focus. Facades were penetrable at this distance. He forced himself through the familiar but still unpleasant task that most men scrupulously avoided, seeing in simple, straightforward fashion—without illusion—precisely what was underneath.

Commanding one of the fastest, most powerful attack subs in the Navy was a height to which he had aspired with single-mindedness, a trait he knew was a large part of his basic character. And though there were higher ranks possible, no assignment or duty would ever again have the challenge, the immediacy and—he had to be honest—the damn *sexiness* of commanding the powerful *Aspen*. Even the cost in doubt, dread, days like this, and the continuing and often enervating self-examination, was worth it. Especially, he reminded himself, when he won.

He'd won today. Practice and training and competent officers had gotten them through the crisis. But he was still sharply aware of how close it had been. Had Engineering been ten minutes longer . . . Rather than push that away, he began to make mental notes to revise training schedules and equipment tests. He'd speak to Tom about it. Professionalism—that was still the key.

MacKenzie grabbed a towel and pressed it to his face. His pale eyes peered over the white linen and watched their own depths in the glass. *Aspen* had been at risk and he'd pulled her out. Despite any other concerns, that felt damn good. He could feel the fear-worm subside for a time and a relaxed exuberance slowly take its place. For a long moment he experienced a clarifying sweetness. The corners of his mouth twitched upward, surprising him. He tossed the towel aside, showered quickly, and pulled on a fresh uniform. The costs for such sweetness could be borne, he decided.

The face in the mirror grinned back in agreement while he combed his hair.

MacKenzie took ten minutes to code the messages he wanted to send and then headed back to the conn.

2

Phillipe Barrista, the Sandinista Minister of Defense, sat stiffly behind his desk and shook his head. "I'm sorry, Miguel. But I won't go over the same ground again. I need the information your brother has in his head."

Miguel Segurra started to argue but thought better of it. He looked down at the carpet. "Is Sebastion hurt?"

Barrista got up and drew the shades on his office windows, cutting off the bright yellow sunlight slanting across the room. He peered intently at Miguel through the ensuing dimness.

"Your brother's forces attacked a fuel storage depot early this morning fifty miles inland from the Costa Rican border. Successfully, I might add. Over half a million barrels went up in smoke. Christ, Miguel. Enough to run an army, gone in one moment. Troops arrived as Sebastion was attempting to make good his escape." Barrista paused. "I will say this for him. The bastard hadn't lost any of his nerve. He still leads his troops himself."

"Just as he once did under you," Miguel prodded gently.

"Yes, well, that was a different time. Anyway, his jeep was blasted out from under him by an army machine-gun emplacement and he was tossed out. He's been badly battered and in all probability the army wasn't very gentle getting him here either."

"Sebastion was one of the revolution's finest military commanders," said Miguel with growing anger. "I've even heard you say so. He shouldn't be treated this way."

"Sure. And I shouldn't have spent two years in the stinking pits Somoza called jails, being beaten up by some of the same men now massing on our northern border ready to attack us," Barrista shot back. "Things change, Miguel. Your brother isn't on the same side as we are anymore."

"He's not with those men either. You know that," Miguel insisted.

"But what about your sister? Can you make the same claim for her?"

Miguel shook his head. "Justine is—"

"Justine is CIA," Barrista said flatly, "and a major figure in their contra organization. At least Sebastion, misguided though he may be, acts independently."

"He always did." Miguel smiled ruefully. "I don't wonder he hasn't changed."

"When did you speak to him last?" Barrista asked.

"Over three years ago. About the same for Maria Justiñiana . . . Justine."

Barrista's forehead furrowed in thought. "Changes come quickly in wartime. Yours was one of the country's great families, your father a national hero. He was killed when?"

"Ten years ago," Miguel said. "I was nineteen."

"A sad day," Barrista acknowledged. "And it's sadder still to have the three remaining Segurras all on different sides—Justine with her CIA-backed rebels in the north; Sebastion still leading his own personal crusade against us from the south; and you, Miguel, a leading member of the legitimate Sandinista government."

Miguel managed to summon up some spirit. "Let's be honest, Minister. Any number of people dispute our legitimacy."

Barrista eyed him narrowly. "But do you, Miguel?"

Miguel hesitated, feeling even his small defiance evaporate. "No. But sometimes I wonder if it's my voice that's valuable to the government or just my name."

"Cynicism does not become you. Of course your voice is heard. I hear it."

"Yes, I know that."

"Then let me continue to guide you." Barrista leaned closer. "Speak to Sebastion, Miguel. Reason with him. If he tells me what I want to know, I'll see he's shipped quietly out of the country. There are very good hospitals back in Costa Rica. He can be back there in a day, handed over directly to his troops."

Miguel twisted uncomfortably. "He won't listen to me, Minister. The last time we spoke he called me a traitor to the revolution and a filthy Marxist. Among other choice epithets," he added.

Barrista's tone grew darker. "Try anyway. This is a serious time, my young friend. You've read the intelligence reports I've given you. The American maneuvers in Honduras, the Naval ships in our harbors. You've heard the things the American President has called for. It's in the air, Miguel. And soon. An all-out invasion of Nicaragua. Maybe the American Marines will lead it, or maybe they'll just sit back and let the contras and fools like your brother do it for them. We don't know, Miguel." He paused for emphasis and bore down harder. "But Sebastion does. I have to have the details of Washington's plans and their timetable. Grenada was the signal. We can't count any longer on their post-Vietnam vacillation. They're coming, Miguel. And your brother knows how and when."

"I . . . I'll try, Minister."

Barrista stood up. "Good." He pressed a button on his desk. The office door swung open almost at once and a uniformed officer entered. Barrista steered Miguel forward. "Go with the captain. He'll take you to Sebastion."

"Minister. I . . . ." Miguel hesitated.

"Yes?"

"I have your word he'll be set free after he tells you?"

Barrista smiled serenely. "Of course. My word on it." A moment later the door closed and Barrista was alone again.

It was shocking really, Barrista thought, the lengths he had to go to just to placate the boy. He returned to his desk and sat down, pulling out some correspondence. Miguel was a rare phenomenon. Twenty-nine, and he'd been an accomplished killer for over two decades. Barrista disliked looking too directly at him. There was a kind of desperation deep in those dark eyes that disturbed him. What visions of inner hell did they recall? Stories about the Segurra family during the early days of the revolution to overthrow Somoza were almost legend. God only knew the full effects of such a childhood on all of them.

Miguel seemed, at least, normal enough on the surface. But he was frequently at a loss emotionally, as if he had fewer internal guideposts to reckon by. Another thought struck Barrista. Maybe Miguel had even more complicated guideposts. No matter. He had used the boy regardless. Shamelessly. The Segurra name was a valuable trump card in a country where tradition played such an important role. Despite everything the communists had done to change that, names like Segurra still meant legitimacy in the people's minds. So he had cultivated a strong father-son relationship with Miguel. The boy needed that desperately. In return Miguel was almost slavishly loyal. Barrista had even turned him against his brother and sister, and in the years since, had used Miguel to kill for him over and over again. The boy was a unique weapon, the perfect assassin. Barrista often wondered if old Carlos had ever truly understood what he was forging.

Now Sebastion was back in his ex-comrade's hands. This was a great stroke of good fortune—holding one of the men who had broken from the Sandinistas, charging them so publicly with a betrayal of the revolution's democratic principles. Barrista sighed. How unworldly he and the others like him had been to believe that the communists would not break from the alliance as soon as real power was won. Did they expect the East/West tensions to resolve themselves any better in Nicaragua than anywhere else in the world?

But now, with armies poised to strike above and below the country, the other Sandinista leaders were shitting in their pants to find some leverage to use against the hated United States. Castro was trying to help, but everybody knew his success was a fluke. Still, the fat old man persisted in mouthing revolutionary platitudes as if he had a direct line to God and not just the Russians.

Maybe Miguel could open his brother up. The timetable could then be used to embarrass the U.S. government publicly. Any revolutionary worth his salt had long ago grown astute in the ways of manipulating American politics through public opinion. Simply challenging the leaders on abstract moral grounds was still the fastest way to induce paralysis in half the elected officials in Congress. Especially the Democrats.

In any event the rebel leader was as good as dead the minute he'd come back into Sandinista hands. Somoza wasn't the only one in this country who understood how to stay in charge, Barrista thought.

Naively, quite a few forgot that.

Miguel Segurra followed the captain down flights of stone steps, feeling the indentations countless feet had worn in the rough blocks. It grew cooler as they descended into the subterranean levels, and Miguel realized they were passing the floors of jail cells. He remembered the day years before when they had liberated this place. Pale, skeletal figures in rotting rags had stumbled out into joyous comrades' arms. It had been a great day indeed, all those empty cells. Now they were full again.

He understood; it had all been explained to him. They were enemies of the revolution. But sometimes he wondered if he and all the others had gone through so much just to replace one group of poor, suffering bastards with another. Different names; same suffering.

Such speculation, however, was useless. No one had the answers. He could believe only in the revolution itself. Men come and go; his father had taught him that. Only the fighting was forever.

The captain led him into a small room with rough stone walls on the building's lowest level. It was an antechamber, with a second door and a metal grill set into the far wall. Miguel could see through the latticework that there was another room beyond. The captain motioned him forward and then left the way they'd come in. Miguel stepped up to the steel mesh and peered through. Sight and sound came to him clearly.

It was an awful room beyond, a place of nightmares. Featureless gray walls broken only by an exit door surrounded a raised stone table. A naked man was strapped to it. His prison uniform and a couple of blankets lay crumpled in the corner. A drain in the floor was covered with a metal grill. There were spigots for water, and black hoses lay coiled underneath like waiting snakes. A charcoal brazier stood near the table, instruments of unmistakable design protruding from the ashes.

The man on the table was his brother Sebastion, and he was not alone.

On that long ago day when this place had been

liberated, Miguel and all the others had sworn that rooms like these would never be used again. There were enough one-eyed cripples in the country. But the man with Sebastion, a stick-thin, sallow-looking person, was obviously under no such pact. He was dressed in an army uniform and was speaking.

". . . to picture this, Señor Segurra, because in the end it may save us time, and pain—you must not forget that. Always pain. So listen . . . and think.

"You can see these. A simple pair of scissors. Shears, perhaps. But I don't think them so big, really. So, scissors. For cutting paper. But sometimes meat. Imagine that, a warm slab of meat. One nice and red, with veins of white fat. A good steak, maybe, a fine roast. You should see how the scissors cut off little pieces. Every snip and an inch or so of raw, red meat falls to the cutting board. Piece after piece, Sebastion. Like toes. One piece at a time. The scissors go snip, and the tiniest bit of red meat is sliced off. Warm meat is the easiest. It compresses so nicely before the blades pass through. Think about it, Sebastion. You can save yourself that. Nothing fancy; just pain. I ask you again to tell me what I want to know."

The sound of Sebastion's voice was older and gruffer than Miguel remembered. And more tired too. "Did you know," he said to his tormentor, "that I was one of the first to liberate this place with my brother and sister years ago? I suppose I've now seen it from both sides."

Miguel smiled behind the grill, pleased that Seabastion remembered as he had. Memories still shared from so long ago . . .

"What are you telling me?" demanded the torturer.

Sebastion's voice was a hissing sneer. "That you will suck your own mother before I tell you anything, *mierdoso*."

The man didn't react for a long moment. He just blinked a few times and lifted Sebastion's foot. The scissor snipped air twice. "Little pieces. Very little pieces. A brave man is composed of so many little pieces. . . ."

Miguel went through the door by the grill and stepped into the room. The torturer looked up sharply, his face flushing with disappointment. He tried to put the blades to Sebastion's toes.

"Enough," Miguel said sharply. "Go now."

"But—"

"Go *now*," Miguel repeated.

The man finally shrugged and stole out the door.

Alone with his brother for the first time in years, Miguel felt himself strangely at a loss for words. Sebastion was still strapped to the table, his head held firmly against the stone. Miguel didn't think he could have seen who had entered.

He stood silently for a while, emotions hotly coursing within him. His brother's body was a mass of fresh abrasions and bruises. Burns scored his chest and arms and must have been very painful. There was no evidence of medical treatment.

"Miguel?" It was Sebastion's voice. "It is you, isn't it?"

So he knew. "Yes, it is," Miguel answered after a while. "How are you, Sebastion?" he asked at last, because nothing else came to him.

Sebastion's laughter was like a sudden torrent, fresh from an old, familiar stream. The sound enclosed Miguel. In spite of himself he grinned.

"I've been better, Miguel. Almost everywhere," came Sebastion's good-natured response.

"Do your wounds hurt?"

"A bit."

"You must be cold."

"Yes, that too."

Miguel suddenly relaized that he was just standing there stupidly. Finally his clumsiness galvanized into action. "Here, let me . . ." He released Sebastion and helped him to a sitting position. He picked up the blankets and wrapped them around his brother's shoulders.

"Thank you, Miguel. That's better."

Miguel looked at him. Sebastion was his big brother, his protector. Four years older—that made him thirty-three now. They were still easily recognizable as related, even though Sebastion's hair was a mass of dark curls where his own was straight, and Sebastion was a bit taller and more stocky. He was darker, too, from the sun, and his muscles were taut and ropy from years of jungle living.

Sebastion said, "It's good to see you again, Miguelito."

Miguel's face changed. "Don't call me that!"

Sebastion's brow furrowed. "I don't understand . . . Miguel?"

"Papa always called me that. Always before . . . or after. So don't, Sebastion. Please. All right?"

"Of course, Miguel. Of course. It was unthinking of me. I'm sorry."

Miguel nodded. He said, "I only heard you were here a few hours ago. Minister Barrista confirmed it."

"You still work for him?" Sebastion's distaste was evident.

"He's a good man. A true revolutionary. You have no right to criticize him."

"No one has the right to criticize anything in Nicaragua any more. What happened to the free press, Miguel? Why can't your true revolutionaries tolerate opposing opinions?"

"Because they are used to subvert the people."

"How good of you to do their thinking for them." Sebastion sighed. "And free elections?"

"We held elections," Miguel said adamantly. "And the Sandinistas won overwhelmingly."

"That's not so hard when you also run the newspaper, the television, the radio, and the army, and no one can really run against you. Please, Miguel, won't you see that they've become exactly what we fought to get rid of? Let them be part of Nicaragua, to be sure. They've rightly earned that. But they can't be allowed to be *all* of Nicaragua. That's still tyranny."

"Someone has to govern."

"Of course. But we were democrats. When did pluralism die so hard a death?"

"Phillipe says—"

Sebastion turned away. "Spare me."

"You see? You never listen."

"To what? Are Barrista's Internal Security Forces any different from Somoza's National Guard?"

"Of course. Entirely different."

Sebastion smiled ruefully. "Look at me, Miguel. And look at where I am. Then tell me how different they are."

Miguel shifted uncomfortably. "This is something else. A special case."

"It always is. But can you really believe they brought that loathsome menace with the scissors out of retirement just for me? Those hoses are well worn, Miguel. So are the irons in the brazier. I'm not the first here."

Miguel turned away. "Enough, Sebastion. You're still too good at confusing me. I could never argue with you. But please, let me help you. I do want to. Tell me what Phillipe wants to know. I have his word that you'll be given safe transport back to Costa Rica."

Sebastion looked at him with sad affection. "I'm sorry, little brother. I couldn't, even if I believed him."

"Stubborn jackass! I can't protect you."

"Miguel, I know you mean well. But I was a dead man the minute I was captured. Only a fool would let an enemy commander go in wartime. And the Sandinistas are no fools. Especially Barrista. Look at what he's done to you."

"I am my own man."

Sebastion said nothing.

"I am!"

"All right, Miguel. You are. So let me go."

Miguel made a strangled sound deep in his throat. Finally his shoulders sagged. "I can't."

Sebastion was silent for a while, then said, "Miguel?"

"Yes."

"Let's not do this anymore."

"I don't want to, Sebastion."

"All right then. We'll speak of other things."

Miguel reached over and pulled the blankets more securely around his shoulders. "There were happier times. Look, I don't know how much longer we have, but I can try to get you some food. You must be hungry."

"That would be nice. Maybe some rum too?"

Miguel grinned. "Do you remember the time we took the cask of rum we'd liberated from the Chief Magistrate's house and shared it with the Martinez sisters?"

Sebastion's curls shook with sudden laughter. "I remember."

"And Justine was angry because we gave the girls her last silk underthings?"

"She chased us both out of the camp."

"And the time when we thought she was sleeping with

Calvanos, so we moved him and his sleeping bag over the red anthill?"

Sebastion smiled warmly. "I remember that too. Some good times, Miguel."

They continued to talk for a while, closer, regardless of their surroundings, than they had been in years. Differences narrowed, repealed by long-held affections. Miguel's expression changed to concern when a harsh tremor shook Sebastion's frame.

"You need a doctor. I'm going to find one."

"I'll be all right."

Miguel shook his head. "Just rest. No one will hurt you. I promise. I'll be back in a few minutes."

Sebastion's color was fading rapidly and the planes of his face were more gaunt. Miguel cursed his own preoccupation. The wounds must be hurting badly, he thought, and turned to go. But Sebastion reached out a hand and caught his shoulder.

"Little brother?" he said softly. "Tell me. Do you ever play anymore?"

Miguel could not meet his brother's eyes. In memory there was pleasure; but there was also great pain. He shook his head slowly. "I lost the music, Sebastion. Years ago, I don't know. Somehow I just lost it. You?"

Sebastion nodded. "The same. It got all confused for me. Death and beauty; all upside down. I felt . . . perverse. And there was no escape in it."

"Or from it," Miguel added somberly.

"That too."

"I'll be back, Sebastion."

"And I'll be here."

Miguel took one last look at Sebastion and left by the door he'd come in through. Conflicting emotions warred inside him. Loyalties pulled him in irreconcilable directions. Like so many other times throughout his life, he felt unsure, unable to establish guiding principles. What mattered most?

Alone in the small, stone antechamber he could not decide. Could he free Sebastion? What *did* he believe in? Barrista. Barrista would help him decide what to do. In a moment of clarity he hated his dependence on the man. But just as clearly he knew that without Barrista he was as unable to navigate as a ship without a rudder. God help me, he thought.

The self-loathing only increased as he left the room, finally hating himself just a little bit more . . . for locking the door behind him.

3

HONDURAS

The light, single-engine aircraft circled once in the cloudless blue sky and began to descend. Word of its arrival spread quickly through the straight rows of army-green tents, and soldiers in camouflage-colored jungle fatigues began to emerge into the warm air and gather together in small groups.

In the command shack, the only other wood-frame building besides the officers' quarters, Colonel Manuel Torres ordered his aide out to the small landing strip to accompany the plane's occupants back. Then, with the unpredictability he had a growing reputation for, he changed his mind, ordered his jeep brought around, and went to meet the plane himself.

The camp housed over a thousand soldiers of the Nicaraguan Democratic Force; contras, everybody called them. As Torres drove, he was pleased to see that his CIA-trained troops were performing their duties with military discipline. Lines of land vehicles were tended to carefully, aircraft were serviced under canopied tie-downs. If American aid kept coming, he thought, the group would continue to function as capably as any army unit in the world; better, in fact, than most.

The plane came in low over the treetops and bounced hard onto the unpaved runway, kicking up clouds of dust. It lost speed quickly, turned, and taxied back to where Torres had parked his jeep. He stood beside it, waiting.

The plane's engine died with a sputtering cough and jungle sounds quickly returned to fill up the silence.

There was only one passenger. She climbed down off the wing with an ease that demonstrated physical agility, and strode over to the waiting colonel.

"How goes it, Manuel?"

"Well enough, Doña Justine." He paused, courtesies over. "But whoever dreamed up this idiocy better be prepared to do some fast explaining to me."

Justine Segurra tugged off her windbreaker and loosened the fatigue vest underneath. She tucked her hair under an army cap and produced a bandanna which she rolled and tied around her neck to blot up the moisture the hot sun brought instantly to her skin. "The overall planning came straight from the Deputy Director's office. The specifics are mine and a few others. What more do you need explained?"

Torres bridled under her challenging stare. He'd worked with her—*for* her, actually—for years now, and still hadn't adjusted to her forthrightness. Or the woman herself, he had to admit. She was more than just good-looking. Her physical presence hit you like a punch to the chest. Had a sculptor carved her likeness, he would have been called a fraud—nothing could be so perfect. Yet Torres had never once seen her let down her guard, or pick up a drink, or show him or any other man the slightest inclination to enticement. Once, he'd put a hand on her. A test. He knew well enough that she had sufficient training in unarmed combat to hurt him if she'd desired. But she hadn't moved. Just looked at him as if she were inspecting a much lower form of life. He withered. Such a look would freeze the semen of giants. He hadn't tried again.

"I don't want to fight with you, Justine, but this raid is going to be costly. More than you imagine."

"Not if it's carried out properly."

"That's bullshit too. Nothing's ever carried out properly except in the wargames room. A lot of men are going to die just to get your brother out. I don't think it's worth it, frankly."

Justine's response surprised him. "You'll get precious little argument from me on that score, Manuel. Sebastion's theatrics are a constant source of annoyance to everybody concerned. He allies with no one, refuses assistance from everyone but his own private backers, and usually achieves little more than to muddy up the international waters. In the normal course of events I'd let Barrista toss him in jail for a while and trade for him or buy him back outright later on."

"So the logical question is, why don't we?"

"One of Sebastion's backers got hold of the invasion plans. And what he has, Sebastion has too."

Torres cursed fluently.

Justine held up a hand. "I know. I already told you I agree with you. But it means Sebastion's got to come out before Barrista wrings everything out of him. Granted?" Her tone was conciliatory.

"Granted." Torres sighed. "All right. Let's get back to camp. What else have you got for me?"

Justine handed him two sealed packets. "Letters from your family. A commendation from the Director. Some banking stuff. The other has the satellite photos."

"Good. Thank you."

They climbed into the jeep as the plane took off again and drove back to the operations shack. Inside, one wall was devoted to maps, another to file cabinets, and in the center of the wood-plank floor twin desks manned by clerks sat side by side. Justine followed Torres into his office. The colonel's senior officers were already waiting.

They welcomed her warmly. She was one of them. "Doña Justine, it's good to see you," said one major.

"The word is good from Congress?" asked another.

Justine spread her hands. "Who really understands the Americans? If they gave us half as much as they spend to feed their dogs, there wouldn't be a single Cuban left in Central America. But we can make do."

"The day is soon? We hear rumors, even here."

"Soon enough," she answered. "In part it's why we have to go in tonight. But I know the colonel has explained all that to you."

"I have," Torres cut in mildly. "But orders and not explanations run an army. Yes? Fine. See here, Doña Justine. I want to go over this with you."

They gathered around a table covered by a relief map of Nicaragua, and Torres spread out the photos Justine had brought. They were looked over carefully. "Please notice these points," Torres said. "Here, and here. We have good intelligence on the routes, and the satellite photos seem to concur. There is no troop activity in the sectors that concern us. And the overland route we'll be taking afterward seems to be clear. Anyone see anything different?"

No one did. "*Dios*," said one officer feelingly. "What we could have done during the revolution with photographs like these."

"Be thankful they're not being used against us," reminded another.

Justine was pleased. Torres and his men had done a good job. The details of the raid planned in Washington had been translated into its practical elements with care and precision. They would enter Nicaragua by the usual overland routes and all sections would rendezvous outside Managua. There, the primary force would launch its raid on the Defense Ministry—where Sebastion was being held, their intelligence reported—while a second unit struck at the Central Bank as a diversion. If they could actually get out with some money, so much the better. In any event both units would join up again and draw the army northward into the jungle, where a third contra unit would be waiting in ambush. Justine, Torres, Sebastion, and a small, select group, however, would be long gone. They would feint east, over the central mountains, to the Atlantic coast, where a submarine would pick them up.

Justine was satisfied and said so. Torres and his men were ready to turn the Sandinistas' old tricks right back on them.

"We'll leave an hour or so before dark," Torres said. "I'm glad you're satisfied, Doña Justine. Any other questions?"

"None."

"Good. Then you'll want to get some rest before we go. Captain, escort la Señora Segurra to her quarters."

"Thank you, Colonel. Gentlemen."

Torres bowed politely as Justine left. A funny thought struck him. He always refered to her as la Señora, yet he really didn't know if she was married or not. He'd heard she was, once; but it wouldn't have surprised him to discover she liked women instead. In fact his ego would definitely have preferred it.

Torres brought the conference to a close, issuing final orders to his officers, who filed out to implement them.

Alone in the office he sat down and slit open the packet Justine had brought him. It did contain personal letters, financial statements, and a pleasing but wholly worthless commendation. But it contained more.

A letter from his second son. Torres pushed aside the rest of the correspondence and took up that one. He read it carefully. Things were nice, it said. He was thanked for the new bicycle and baseball mitt. Certain words caught his attention. He reached for the codebook.

Torres didn't have a second son. Only one, and two girls. Clearly Justine didn't know that, nor did she know the extent of his additional orders, transmitted in this fashion directly from the Deputy Director. He decoded it and began to relax. Someone at last was thinking practically.

In a sense the mission was still to get to Sebastion Segurra before the Sandinistas had a chance to pump him dry. But the new orders gave him a lot more leeway than Justine had.

It was felt that Justine didn't need to be burdened by any possible guilt involved in dealing realistically with her brother's situation. Torres grinned at that. How unselfish of them.

His orders were clear. If there were even the slightest possibility that Sebastion could not be successfully extricated from the Sandinistas, or that he might fall back into their hands, Torres was to kill him at once. There was even the suggestion that if Sebastion didn't make it out, more than a few people would be relieved. Torres understood. Hadn't even Justine said her brother was increasingly a pain in the ass? The odds on Sebastion's survival were fast becoming increasingly small.

Thank God for the pragmatists, Torres decided. He destroyed the letter carefully and then left to get some sleep before night fell.

In the room she'd been given, Justine stripped down to her underwear, grateful to be out of her clothing for the

first time in over thirty-six hours. She took her things from
the duffel bag she'd brought and placed them on the old
bureau, alongside the wash basin and clean towels.

She felt better after she washed. Her hair was matted
from being crammed under her cap. She brushed it out,
spreading the black tangles with long, tapered fingers.
When that was done she lay down on the bed and drew a
cool, clean sheet over her.

She was almost home, again. And it had shaken her.

She frowned at the ceiling, unhappy with herself. One
had to have achieved an equilibrium, a firm steadiness to
do this kind of work. Long ago she'd given up screaming
slogans and put aside the righteous anger that fueled
most freedom fighters. Only the dispassionate lived very
long in this region. Too many shouting men had died
during the revolution and too many idealists had been
imprisoned by the Sandinistas immediately after. That still
stunned her. Had no one been watching? How could the
revolution itself have been stolen from them so easily?

She'd been away in Europe on a concert tour designed
to raise money and political support for the fledgling
government. When the tour was over she returned to
Nicaragua, only to find Sebastion self-exiled to the south,
Miguel fawning over Phillipe Barrista, and the whole
country under the kind of rule most had fought for years
to eliminate.

She had to admit, though, that for a time they had
succeeded in fooling her, too, with their promises. This
restriction will be lifted soon—it's only temporary. This is
an emergency measure—just a little bit longer. . . . But
every day more Cubans and Russians landed in the
capital, and soon the newspapers had censors and the
jails began to fill again and certain political parties were
declared illegal. . . . She sighed. How could she and the
others not have seen it coming?

It came to a head for her when the government
requested she give a concert series. She agreed, albeit
reluctantly, but thinking that trends were only temporary
and that there was still hope for change.

She would never forget the tight-faced, dour woman
who came to see her. She had the title of Cultural
Coordinator, and an officious, self-righteous attitude. She

arrived at Justine's apartment shortly after the musical selections were announced.

"Señorita Segurra," she began politely enough. "The Ministry of Culture requests that the Copland piece you're planning to play, well . . . it's felt that the selection is inappropriate. Would you reconsider playing it?"

"Inappropriate? In what way?" At the time, her naiveté still left her responding reasonably. She was genuinely confused.

"It is felt that the piece is much too regressive. Decadent. And the composer . . . he is an American. We would be pleased if you'd consent to play something else."

Justine still hadn't seen it. She resisted politely but firmly. "I'm sorry, but I'm planning on the Copland. I've gone to a lot of trouble to reorchestrate it. You'll see. It will be well received."

"I'm afraid you don't understand. You *can't* play that piece."

Justine looked at her blankly. "Can't?"

"This composer is proscribed for the masses. A political decision has been made."

Justine bristled. "Artistic judgment pays very little attention to politics."

"From now on it will have to."

"The Copland stays!"

"We have decided otherwise. The concert will be canceled if you persist."

Justine saw it then, in the woman's eyes, an obscene arrogance combined with a bitter hatred that anyone could be so . . . individual as to know her own mind—and worse, to have the internal moral strength to act on it. No; *we* have decided against you. *Our* mind over yours. Why?

Because *we* are always bigger than you.

She understood then who was running the country. No other signal could have been clearer. The following day she fled Managua, joined Sebastion in the south, and started the fight all over again.

Oddly enough the Copland piece—the one they refused to let her play—was called *Fanfare for the Common Man.*

She twisted on the bed, facing more difficult memories. Seeing Sebastion again, assuming they could get him out, was going to be painful. They had been very close, but he'd never forgiven her for leaving his small, brave army of idealists and joining the Americans. But she had refused to fight any more losing battles. Who else besides the United States had the resources and the commitment to defeat the Sandinistas?

She'd had it with idealists. Like her father, she thought, they all left you wanting.

The CIA had trained her and given her the means to wage an effective fight. Effective—that was the highest value. She knew they valued her name and the credibility it gave them. Fair enough. Let the perfectionists debate endlessly over ways and means. She felt that motive was just an illusion anyway.

Sebastion had told her she was wrong. He claimed the revolution had to be kept pure, like a wife. She must not be dirtied with other lovers. If she were, she would end up being only a whore.

She shook her head sadly. Like all romantics, Sebastion never understood that you could purchase only what you had money to pay for. In the long run if you had very little money, the real difference between a wife and a whore was that the whore was cheaper.

Poor Sebastion. Her big brother, but such a brave, damned fool. She wondered if he'd changed much. Inside Nicaragua his reputation had grown to almost mythical proportions. *Commandante Cero*, they still called him—his old rebel title. When communicating by radio, zero had always been the leader; one, the second-in-command; and so on. She shook her head ruefully; Commander Zero, locked up in a Sandinista prison that he'd once liberated.

But other images slipped into her mind. Sebastion of the warm laughter and of the glossy curls wet with river water. He was always the one she'd run to when the dreams came again. She missed him still. . . .

It was darker now. Almost time. Light from the window had turned a sullen red. For a long while she lay there remembering, waiting and hoping for sleep to come.

4

CARIBBEAN SEA

LCDR Tom Lasovic rapped on the open door to the captain's cabin. "You wanted to see me, sir?"

"Come in, Tom," MacKenzie said, motioning him to sit. "We just received this from COMSUBLANT. I'd like your opinion on *Aspen*'s readiness to comply."

Lasovic hunkered his big frame past MacKenzie and perched on the bunk. Reading the communication, his brow furrowed. "Since when do attack submarines run pick up and delivery missions, skipper?"

"I was thinking along the same lines," MacKenzie admitted. "The merchandise must mean an awful lot to somebody."

"I'll have to look at the coastal charts," Lasovic said thoughtfully. "But offhand, I don't remember a whole lot of depth in that area. It could be fairly tricky getting close in. We could get caught without enough water to hide in."

"*Phoenix* has been enlisted for this one too. She'll cover us. The antiship Harpoons can take out any surface ships."

"No submariner could relish getting that close in," Lasovic objected. "Why do you think they're not using some quick in-and-out amphibian aircraft?"

"The Sandinistas have the new Russian coastal defense radars, same as Castro. Maybe no one wants to risk running that, or providing the kind of strike to neutralize them. But that's speculation. Can we do the job?"

Lasovic nodded vigorously. "Absolutely. Engineering reports that all repairs are completed, and we've gone over the conn instrumentation so many times I'm beginning to feel like I designed it myself. That was a tough series of accidents before, skipper, but it's not going to happen again."

"Good." MacKenzie's single syllable was heartfelt.

"If you don't mind my saying so, and I will even if you

do"—Lasovic smiled warmly—"you did a real fine job before, Mac."

MacKenzie's face creased into a grin. They made a good team, he and Lasovic. The exec had a stronger background in engineering and the more technical aspects of submarines than MacKenzie—who was by training the superior tactician. They'd known each other for over ten years and had served on the same sub once under another captain. When MacKenzie got his own command, he lost no time in having Lasovic transferred. This cruise was their third together, Lasovic's first as exec.

Tom Lasovic was a superb XO, deeply committed to the same kind of professionalism as MacKenzie. Also, he was a fine teacher, liked and respected by the men, who all knew that he would go out of his way to help those seamen dedicated and ambitious enough to be studying for higher ratings. For MacKenzie nothing could be more reassuring than to make a decision and know that the big, quiet, competent Lasovic was tending to it.

"I appreciate that, Tom. But between you and me," MacKenzie responded dryly, "sweat wasn't the only thing staining my shorts when I took them off."

"Yours weren't the only ones, I'll wager."

"Probably not. What do you propose as a new package of training schedules?"

"If it's all right with you," Lasovic said, "I'd like to make some changes in the rotations. . . ."

For a while they discussed the crew's performance and made decisions which would be augmented at the next meeting of the department heads, the senior officers. They could use the time it would take to reach the Nicaraguan coast to drill and drill again.

"Let me know the status of our rubber rafts, and the weapons locker, too, Tom. We may have to send a party in to get these people."

"Aye, sir."

"I think that's all then. We'll be getting under way shortly. Thank you."

"Pleasure, skipper."

Lasovic left and MacKenzie locked the codebooks and papers in his safe. As he left his cabin he noticed the Weapons Department Head in the wardroom and stopped to compliment him on the performance of his people in Sonar and the Attack Center earlier. A cup of coffee and some good-natured discussion later, MacKenzie left the officers' dining area and headed up to Conn.

Submarines had come a long way since WW II diesel boats, he thought, as he walked past the spotless, stainless steel galley and up the steeply pitched stairway. Formica wood-grained paneling lined the stairwells, giving the illusion of space. The nuclear power plant provided sufficient power for air-conditioning, VCR's, Coke machines, and ice-cream makers. The menu would have made an old sub captain swoon.

But no one should ever make the mistake of thinking that a nuclear attack submarine was anything less than a man of war, too, he thought. Always ready and on a war footing, MacKenzie believed that *Aspen* and her sister ships were the single strongest deterrent for the growing Soviet naval fleet. They might not be awe-inspiring, like the huge carriers, and no one was going to use the small black sail sticking up out of the water for power projection—the old-time showing the flag—but silent and deadly, they prowled the oceans, and not a thing the Soviets could build would match *Aspen's* ability as a warfare device.

He entered Conn and relieved the officer of the deck, preferring to take the sub under himself.

"Thank you, Mr. Casey. I have the conn."

"Aye, sir." The lieutenant stood by, waiting.

MacKenzie surveyed the control room and felt the expectant atmosphere. "Maneuvering, Conn. Answer bells on the main engines."

MacKenzie swung his gaze over to the Chief of the Watch, the man in charge of ballast. "Chief, status of rig for dive?"

"The ship is rigged for dive, sir. Bridge is clear, last man down, and hatch secured. Straight board, sir."

"Good. All ahead one third."

Aspen began to slice forward through the blue-green water, her sail awash, dividing the water like Moses as she passed. MacKenzie smiled inwardly, feeling the power vibrate through her. He spoke calmly, but with clarity and precision,

"Diving Officer, make your depth one-five-zero feet. Let's take her down smartly, Mr. Randall."

"Aye, sir." Randall relayed the command as the diving horn sounded throughout the length of the ship.

"Fifteen degree down bubble, aye," responded the Stern Planesman. Aft, the big stern planes swung accordingly.

"One-five-zero feet, aye," answered the Helmsman, pushing forward on the control column. The deck tilted.

Navigation gave the desired course to MacKenzie, who spoke directly to the Helmsman. "Helm, come left to course two-seven-zero."

"Come left to two-seven-zero, aye."

Years before, as officer of the deck on his first watch, a phrase had popped into MacKenzie's mind as he took his first ship down, then he had to stifle the sudden mischievous desire to come out with it. Through the years it often reoccurred, an odd stimulus-response arc that had been created that day. Now, with *Aspen* spearing through the water in perfect harmony with her crew, MacKenzie felt the old desire rise again. But he was captain now.

"And away we go. . . ." he whispered softly, with supreme reverence.

Aspen slid under the waves.

5

MANAGUA

Miguel didn't care for the Cubans. It was mostly their attitude—they thought they were in sole possession of political truth. He wanted to remind them that plenty of others had died for the cause too. But he couldn't get past the jargon that spouted out of their mouths like water from fountains under too much pressure.

Neither of the two men had said an original thing in the several hours he'd spent in their company. Miguel was sure they resented being pressed into service by him. On loan from Castro's internal security apparatus, they were some of the myriad "technical advisers" Barrista had brought in. They fancied themselves ambassadors; Miguel saw them as robotic. Push this button, get this response.

But there was no other way to prevent Barrista's ordering the torturers to return. One of the Cubans, the doctor, was supposed to be highly skilled with his drugs, and the political officer with him was billed as an expert in interrogation techniques. They were the only compromise Phillipe would accept.

Sebastion was again strapped to the stone table, this time unconscious from the doctor's drugs. But at least some elementary attention had been paid to his wounds, and he was modestly covered with a white sheet. I.V. tubes ran from his ropy veins to bottles of clear fluid on stands beside him.

The doctor, whose name was Nogueras, finished inserting a second set of I.V. tubes and connected them to a pair of hypodermic syringes. "We're almost ready," he said to Miguel.

"I'm going to stay."

Nogueras shrugged. "Then please remember this is a very subtle operation. The line is very fine between semiconscious states, and he's going to be moving in and out of them for hours. The drugs we use are to modulate these states and make him pliable for Major Limos's hypnotic suggestions."

Limos was a short man with a hairline mustache, slick hair, and the face of a rat. He had already set up a cassette recorder and microphone, and now pulled up a low stool near Sebastion's head. "It could be valuable you're being here, Miguel," he said. "Some of your brother's responses may need interpretation, or maybe some of the memories from your shared past will help with the illusions I create. You'll help me?"

"If you need me to." Miguel found the idea of invading Sebastion's psyche deeply disturbing. But the thought of the blades poised against his toes made even this preferential.

The doctor took up both syringes. "With these I can bring him up towards consciousness or push him deeper down toward sleep. Brakes and accelerators. The trick is to balance him somewhere in the middle. Major?"

"I'm ready. Bring him up."

Nogueras exerted pressure on the plunger of one syringe and liquid flowed down the tube into Sebastion's arm. Just seconds passed before he began to stir. Limos started speaking in a calm, soothing voice.

"You are on a journey, Sebastion, a journey of complete relaxation where no one can hurt you or harm you and where you are perfectly safe. Safe and relaxed and secure. Totally safe . . . totally relaxed . . . totally secure. You will listen to the sound of my voice as if it were your own. My voice. The sound of my voice. My voice is your guide. Only the sound of my voice is important, only the sound of my voice matters. Nothing else has meaning, only the sound of my voice and feeling totally safe, totally relaxed, and totally secure. Totally safe . . . totally relaxed . . . totally secure . . ."

One of Limos's hands was extended out where Nogueras could see it. Throughout his patter he cued the doctor with its motions. Deeper, deeper . . . hold . . . hold . . . up a bit. Good. Drugs were administered accordingly. They worked as a team, together stringing Sebastion's mind out on a line between them. Slowly Sebastion's muscles relaxed and his head began to nod in time with Limos's cadence.

". . . feel the soft raft under you, supporting and lifting. No pressure, no pain; nothing but softness under you, holding, lifting, supporting. Slowly, the raft moves down a river. You are on a river flowing smoothly forward. A journey awaits. You feel pleasant. Relaxed. Totally safe, totally relaxed, totally secure . . ."

Miguel watched, fascinated in spite of himself. He could spot the technique in Limos's patter. There were hidden suggestions, small increments of control to which Sebastion began to respond. Limos insinuated himself behind deeply held defenses. In Sebastion's mind it must have been like his own internal voice speaking.

". . . to speak freely, to speak comfortably, to speak without restraint or hesitation. The river flows. You are safe. Alone and secure. Without fear . . ."

Miguel shuddered. It was an ugly thing in reality. Like a

worm in your sleeping bag. For over an hour they kept it up, asking for nothing yet, just insinuating themselves deeper and deeper, further and further, on and on. . . . He shook his head. It was contagious.

He checked the time. Almost midnight. It had taken a long time to round up the Cubans. But he was pleased with himself. He'd navigated a successful course through difficult waters. He'd helped Sebastion while still being loyal to Phillipe. No one need suffer. He was glad he didn't have to make a real choice between them. He still wasn't certain what it would be.

"Miguel!" It was Limos.

His head snapped around. "Sorry, I was daydreaming."

"Your brother was a musician, yes?"

"Yes. Once."

"His instrument?"

"He had several. Violin, viola, and cello, mostly."

"Tell me about one. One he cared about."

Miguel almost choked on the words. "There was a del Gesù . . . a beautiful thing. His violin, less . . . less . . ."

"Come on, Miguel."

". . . less carefully finished maybe than the instruments of Stradivarius, but bolder in design and tone. My . . . our father gave it to him on his tenth birthday. Sebastion loved it."

"That's good. Thank you." The patter droned on.

Later, "Miguel. An old girlfriend. One who hurt him, maybe. Unrequited love always opens a man."

"Graciella . . . Maria Graciella. He was sixteen."

"Good. Now Sebastion . . ."

Miguel hated being drawn in further. He was suddenly an accomplice in the psychological rape, and it repulsed him.

Nogueras moved swiftly to change empty syringes and check the tubes. Limos looked up, pleased. "We're close," he said. "I think we'll have it soon enough."

Sebastion was talking freely now, as if he were alone. Miguel felt like a voyeur—an *entendeur*, more accurately; an eavesdropper. These were private things which embarrassed him, things he would rather not have heard. The air began to grow oppressive. Finally, when Sebastion began talking about how much he loved his little brother and sister, Miguel fled the room.

He sought refuge in the cool, stone antechamber, sprawling out spread-eagled on the rough floor. His physical and emotional universes were reeling, and he needed something solid underneath him. In the other room his only brother lay helpless while a pair of vampiric spiders perched over him, draining his mind's blood.

And Miguel had put him there.

He twisted in pain and curled up like an embryo on the hard floor. Reason tried to assert itself. Phillipe had to know what Sebastion carried in his head. Sebastion had chosen his own side; he had no right to expect sympathy.

He told himself this over and over again, trying to harden his heart.

Alone in the stone room, he failed utterly.

6

MANAGUA

The night air was warm and moist and clung to Justine's skin as they waited in the idling army jeep. She felt the chest-tightening adrenal surges raise the tempo of her pulse, and her fingers pressed harder against the grip of her Uzi machine-pistol. The street they were parked on was unlit and empty, the buildings abandoned since the '74 earthquake. Around them were nothing but hollow shells with crumbling walls covered with scrawled revolutionary slogans and silhouettes of the original Sandino in his huge cowboy-style hat.

She caught Torres's look, sent from his perch on the second jeep. Steady, relax. She knew it was barely five minutes since she'd last checked her watch, so she used her refusal to check again as a means of self-discipline. The second force had left an hour ago. They would hit the bank as soon as they were in position. The first explosions would be Torres's signal to go.

Behind her one of the soldiers jostled the jeep by leaning against the .55 caliber machine gun on its fixed tripod. There were five jeeps in all, twenty soldiers including her and Torres. Most were familiar with the Defense Ministry, and there were only three levels Sebastion could be being held on anyway—the two floors of jail cells and the bottom level reserved for physical torture.

She craned her neck toward the area of the city where the bank was located. Her feet tapped an impatient jazz rhythm in their army boots. The mugginess made her sweat under the black ski cap covering her hair, and she reached up to rub it but stopped, not wanting to smear off the blackface.

Abruptly a portion of the sky turned glowing red and a deep, bass "pfumph" reached them. She turned to Torres, pointing. It was unnecessary. He saw it too. There was a sudden series of sharp clicks as weapons were cocked. Transmissions were slammed into gear.

Torres tapped his driver and nodded. The jeep shot ahead, throwing up a shower of dirt from the unpaved roadbed. Justine's driver followed. The remaining three jeeps fell into line caravan-style, and they all roared forward.

Wind whipped at their exposed faces as the jeeps sped past burnt-out rubble toward the populated areas. Already sirens were screaming balefully over the city. Every available army unit would soon be racing to the bank. Twenty minutes was all Torres could allow to get to Sebastion. More, and no one was getting out tonight.

This late the streets were empty. The jeeps bucked and bounced over deep ruts and potholes, finally fishtailing onto the paved roads. They turned and headed for the downtown area, covering the remaining blocks at high enough speeds to kill them all if they overturned.

The Ministry of Defense suddenly loomed up before them, and Torres's jeep drove right up the wide front steps. The .55 caliber opened up immediately, raking the building's guards and jerking them up and back like insane marionettes. A satchel charge blew out the front doors and covered the immediate area with twisted steel and shards of glass.

Justine was already out of her jeep and running. A

driver and a gunner stayed with each jeep, backing them in towards the building to form a .55 caliber screen. The remaining eight soldiers formed up on her and Torres and followed them inside.

Justine stopped in the lobby for a moment to get her bearings. She pointed. "That way. The stairs down."

"Paco, Diego. Hold the lobby. Everybody else come with us," Torres ordered.

They ran down the main corridor, past darkened offices on both sides. At the first corner Torres poked his head around the bend gingerly. Shots picked plaster off the wall over his head in response.

"Three," Torres said curtly, "behind some overturned furniture. Twenty yards. Jorge, a satchel charge. Fernando, with me right after."

The charge was primed. Jorge bent low, ducked into the corridor and tossed the flat package. It went sliding along the polished floor, and answering fire erupted. But Jorge was already back.

A bright flash and a hard, low sound filled the corridor. The blast tore along its length. Torres and Fernando ran right into the cloud of dust it created, weapons firing. Only one soldier had survived the explosion, and he did not survive Torres's gun. The colonel left two more men to guard the position and the remaining four followed him.

Justine ran. Every darkened room was a potential death trap but they couldn't stop to check them all. Too much time. They were moving fast. Careless, she thought, but she ran.

It happened all at once. From one of the rooms soldiers came spilling into the corridor. Justine turned and fired all in one steady motion, disregarding the sudden biting pain in her arm. Two men went down. Torres turned angrily. His weapon barking along with hers, they cleared the corridor.

But two of their own were lying in pools of blood. Justine bent down over them. Torres raced over. She shook her head. His face grew tighter. They were at the stairway now but time was fast being eaten up. He posted his remaining two men at the entrance and ran inside with Justine.

"Wait a second," she said, stopping him. "You're bleeding."

"So are you."

Justine saw that her green shirt was black with blood. She cursed with a range that brought a smile to Torres's lips as she shoved a medi-pad against his wound.

"Let me return the favor."

"Forget it, Manuel."

"Shut up. There. Finished."

"Let's go," she said impatiently.

He looked at his watch. "We've got time problems, Justine."

She thought quickly. "Forget the cells then. Let's gamble on Sandinista expediency and go straight to the interrogation rooms."

He nodded. "All right. Carefully."

They padded down the stairs.

Miguel heard the first explosions from inside the antechamber. A firefight had a distinctive rhythm, like point and counterpoint. He knew the building was under attack the moment he heard the staccato answering fire.

Whoever they were, they were coming toward him. His well-trained ears picked up the sounds and analyzed them like sonar. In the next room the Cubans were still pumping Sebastion. They'd gotten what Phillipe wanted, the rest was for intelligence reasons—propaganda and blackmail. He left them there and went through the back door and up the private stairs.

The smell of explosives and powder was stronger as he ascended. The main corridor was blocked by contras; he knew them at once. Going higher was pointless except to hide. He'd better get the Cubans and Sebastion. He could do nothing else. He had no gun and certainly the phone wires would have been cut. He went back down.

He reentered the antechamber. They'd all be safe on the upper levels, he thought, even if they couldn't get out of the building. He reached for the connecting door.

But in the same moment his hand touched it, he heard the sound of wood splintering and the breathless voices of men bursting into the interrogation room beyond.

Miguel pressed his face to the grill and saw two armed contras. The Cubans were standing bolt upright in shock.

"You," the contra colonel demanded. "Who are you?"

"I . . . I am Dr. Nogueras, and this is Major Limos of the Cuban Free Militia." He tried to summon some dignity. "We are here as guests of the Nicaraguan government and demand—"

"Demand something else and I'll shoot your tongue off," said the colonel sharply. He gestured at the unconscious patient. "What's wrong with him?"

Nogueras moved forward. "Nothing. I swear it. In fact, just let me—"

But the other contra soldier came rushing around him to the stone table. "Sebastion!" the name was wrenched out with an anguished cry. "Just what the hell have you bastards done to him?"

Justine! Her voice called to Miguel from across a gulf of years. . . . He could no more mistake it than a middle C. So this was *her* raid. Of course, she'd come for Sebastion.

"Bring him around," Justine demanded hotly. The colonel covered the Cubans.

"Yes, yes. Absolutely," said Nogueras unctuously. Limos didn't move a muscle to protest.

The doctor made fast work of removing the I.V.'s, and Sebastion began to stir within seconds of the "up" drug being administered. But he was too groggy and disoriented to move.

"What were these tubes for?" Justine pointed.

"Please. Just vitamins. To help him."

She shook her head and gestured with her gun to the tape recorder. "Manuel?"

"I see it, Justine."

The sound of the colonel's gun going off was almost deafening, even in the antechamber. The Cubans smashed back into the walls whose only feature now was their blood. Manuel understood. Whatever Sebastion told them could not be permitted to be retold. The echoes began to die away.

Justine turned back to her brother. "Sebastion! Wake up. C'mon, lazy. Get up. I've come to—"

It was as far as she got. The contra colonel hit her with a sharp, savage chop to the back of her neck and she sagged to the floor. Miguel watched, confused by the suddenness of it all.

"I'm sorry, Justine," the colonel said softly. "But they really don't want him back." He came around the table and popped the cassette out of the recorder. It went into a pocket that he snapped shut.

Miguel knew what was coming. Justine would never allow Sebastion's murderer to live very long, and if this colonel knew her at all, he knew that too. If he killed Sebastion, he'd have to do Justine as well. Just like the Cubans.

But this did not concern him, Miguel told himself. In the revolution there were no biological brothers and sisters, only ideological ones. Phillipe had taught him that. These people were his enemies. Let them kill each other and all be damned. How many loyal Sandinista troops were already dead upstairs?

The colonel raised his weapon. His back was still to Miguel. Just do nothing and the problem will be solved, he thought. Besides, the colonel will probably never make it out of the city. It wasn't his personal problem. it wasn't!

He was trembling as the needle slid into his hand. He moved forward, urged on by an unbearable pressure. The connecting door swung open noiselessly, presenting the colonel's back like a still target. A strain of music began somewhere that he knew no one else could hear. In his head, Chopin . . .

The colonel straightened bolt upright, as if he'd been hit by a million volts, when Miguel's needle slid into the base of his brain. Every joint stiffened, and the gun dropped from nerveless fingers. It clattered to the floor. With a practiced motion Miguel had the needle back out before the colonel toppled like a felled tree to the floor.

Miguel bent over his sister and stroked her face tenderly. Even in repose she was still so sad and beautiful. "Justine?" She began to stir.

Quickly he retrieved the cassette and slid it into a pocket of her blouse. Up on the table Sebastion, too, was coming awake.

Miguel cast one long, last look at the only two people in the world he could truly say he loved, and left the room.

Returning to the grill, he watched Justine awaken. She looked around and saw the colonel. For a moment nothing registered. She ran a hand over her scalp, pushing off the black cap, releasing her hair. A stray thought came to Miguel. The past few minutes were the first time they'd all three been together in the same room in over five years. Visions of a pickup truck slipped in and out behind his eyes. Border crossings . . .

One of Justine's hands ranged over the spot where the colonel had hit her. The other tugged her clothing into place. Miguel watched her find the cassette. Her brow furrowed more deeply.

She bent over the contra colonel and felt for vital signs. There were none. But neither were there marks. He watched confusion cross her face again. She turned the body over.

Miguel knew he should leave now. But he could not tear himself away.

Justine found the mark. He saw recognition change her face. She knew; even though she could not have truly known.

"Miguel?" she said aloud, searching.

He could not answer.

"Miguel!" she called mournfully. Louder, "*Por favor.* Please, Miguel!"

The pain in her voice tore at him. He backed away from the grill, tears turning his vision kaleidoscopic.

"Miguel. . . !"

He ran, bursting from the antechamber into the private corridor, leaving them both behind. Pursued by his own private demons, he ran up the steps, all the way to the roof. Justine's voice reached for him, calling. He ran.

The night air was thick and sweet and he filled his lungs with it. Ghosts screamed at him, but he blocked their voices. Music began again inside his head, but he refused to hear.

Deeply shaken, he walked to the edge of the roof and peered cautiously over its edge. Several stories below, a circle of jeeps stood guard, waiting. Tiny figures stood inside, pointing tiny guns.

The army was nowhere in sight. But there was a red

glow to the west. The bank was in that area, and the grain silos. A diversion? Probably.

More tiny figures came running out of the building, one supported by others, several carried. The jeeps were filled quickly. He heard Justine giving orders. One by one the jeeps peeled off and sped down darkened streets.

Miguel pulled back and listened to them go. His eyes remained tightly clenched until the last sounds of their leaving faded back into the night.

7

CARIBBEAN SEA

Aspen made good time. They were just off the Nicaraguan coast according to the inertial guidance system whose accelerometers constantly recorded the ship's movement in every direction and fed that information to the computers, which translated the cumulative movement into their exact position. Exactness was critical since, in the case of a missile being fired, an error of less than a quarter mile in plotting the sub's position would result in an error of over half a mile off target.

With the *Aspen* ready to proceed to periscope depth, MacKenzie ordered, "Make your depth six-zero feet, Mr. Randall."

Aspen rose. MacKenzie called for a surface radar sweep as soon as they reached ordered depth. He already had sonar scouring the area but it had failed to hear anything but fish. But he knew it never hurt to be doubly safe.

MacKenzie was uneasy in these shallows. Most of the unique advantages a submarine possessed were nullified under these conditions. Combat tactics required the vast reaches of the open sea for the deadly sober and highly sophisticated games of "hide and seek" and "tag" routinely played with Soviet boats.

Most people forgot that the primary targets for attack submarines were other submarines themselves, to prevent their being deployed against one's own shipping. Deep, open water was their element. Here, a simple patrol boat and a few hand grenades could possibly damage *Aspen* before MacKenzie could move her out to sea. Even *Phoenix*'s close presence was less than fully comforting.

"Six-zero feet," the Diving Officer reported.

MacKenzie brought his thoughts back to the business at hand. The area was all clear of close contacts. He ordered, "All stop."

"All stop, aye."

"Raise number-two scope and the communications antennas."

The optical scope, largely unchanged since WW II in its basic principles, rose upward smoothly on its hydraulic lift. Should MacKenzie have wanted it, there was a second scope rigged for television transmission and video recording. It stood directly behind the optical periscope, which stopped with a sharp click, fully extended. MacKenzie wrapped his hands around the twin handles and pressed his face to the rubber eyepiece.

They were about a mile offshore. The coastline was a black line against a dark gray sky. It was over an hour till dawn, and thick clouds obscured the moon. There wasn't enough light to separate objects yet, but MacKenzie could see that a harsh wind was whipping up the surface. He hunkered the scope through a full 360 degrees. The choppy water was clear as far as he could see.

He swung back to the coastline. A turn of the handles raised the power of the scope's magnification. He made out a small strip of beach backed by thick undergrowth and scrub forest.

"How close to contact time?" he asked Lasovic.

"We're past it now, sir. Communications started listening as soon as we got a mast up."

"Rubber boats ready?"

"Yes, sir. Parties assembled, armed, and ready to go."

"It should be soon, Tom, inform them."

Lasovic left Conn. MacKenzie stilled his own impatience. "Sonar? Where's *Phoenix*?"

"Still on our stern, Cap'n. A mile in back of us. Like a wagging tail."

MacKenzie smiled. He liked the image.

"Conn. Radio. Incoming message, sir."

"Our pick up?"

"Yes, sir. Looks like it. Right frequency, right code."

"You got authentication?"

"Authenticated, Cap'n."

MacKenzie had a moment of misgiving. Codes had been broken before. On the surface they were a sitting duck. He shrugged the feeling off.

"Take her up, Mr. Randall. Let's get those folks on board and get out of here."

Aspen's rolling motion increased as her sail broke through the surface. She was more subject to wave motion now. It would be felt all through the ship. Aft, under Lasovic's taut direction, crewmen broke open the steel deck hatch behind the sail and brought the black, rubber boats out on deck.

Choppy water was breaking over the black, steel deck plates. The crew dragged the boats into the water and sailors clambered in, bobbing up and down. The putt-putt sounds of muffled outboard motors blended with the slaps of the low waves against Aspen's hull as the boats sped away into the growing wind.

The hatches were sealed again, a fact that showed up on the Chief of the Watch's instrument panel. He reported the "straight board" to MacKenzie.

Lasovic called in, confirming the departure. "Boats away, Captain."

"Cap'n? We've got some weather moving in," Radar reported.

MacKenzie frowned. "How quickly?"

"Fast, sir. From the south. Maybe half an hour, maybe less for the leading edge."

"Keep tracking it."

"Yes, sir."

If he had to wait, MacKenzie decided, it was going to be underwater. "Submerge the ship, Mr. Randall. Make your depth six-zero feet. Sonar, Conn. Report all contacts."

"Sonar, Conn, no contacts, sir."

"Good. Stay alert. Another half hour should do it."

"Sonar, aye."

With enough water overhead to conceal his ship's

presence, MacKenzie settled in to wait for the boats to return.

The contra sergeant pulled back from the edge of the woods and ran over to Justine. "They're coming," he said quickly, moving to help transport Sebastion's limp form from the back of their latest vehicle, an old pickup truck.

They were five all together: Justine, Sebastion, the sergeant, a corporal who had driven, and a Miskito Indian who had served as their final guide. The trek over the mountains was difficult, and they were forced to change vehicles twice and cover a good part of the distance on foot. A group of Miskito Indians, no lovers of the Sandinistas after their forced and often bloody "relocations," had met them on the Atlantic side and led them here.

The rising wind was churning the sea into whitecaps and flinging beach sand around like buckshot. Justine helped support Sebastion's weight as they slipped out of the woods. She was worried about him. He'd never regained full consciousness, and not for the first time she worried that the Cuban doctor had been able to do further damage before Manuel killed him.

Manuel . . . There was no time now to figure out just what had happened in the interrogation room. One second she was looking at Sebastion; the next, she was waking with a sore head and a dead companion. And where did Miguel fit in? It had to be Miguel. The needle mark was as distinctive as a fingerprint.

They settled Sebastion down on the sand and sheltered him from the caustic spray. She could see the rubber boats, three in all, coming in over the mounting waves.

A harsh, pelting rain began as the first of the boats slid onto the beach with a grating sound. Armed sailors leaped out and took up defensive positions, guns at the ready. A sandy-haired, young officer approached her.

She held out her hand. "Justine Segurra. I'm sure you understand that 'Evil is as evil does.'"

The sailor grinned. "Yes, ma'am. In that case, 'Evil to him who thinks evil.' Lieutenant Casey, ma'am. Pleasure to know you."

"Thank you, Lieutenant." Justine gestured around them. "We should be off, I think."

"As quick as we can, ma'am. Our ship's about a mile offshore. We'll have you warm and dry in no time."

The other two boats ground into the beach and more sailors swarmed out. Casey raised a two-way radio to his lips and confirmed contact. He was told to haul ass, the weather was coming in fast.

The contras had already been helped into one of the boats, and Casey waved them on. They pulled their boat into the water and lowered the motor back in. They shot off across the swells.

Casey looked at the unconscious man. "Wounded?"

"Drugged," Justine called over the wind. Together they slipped a life jacket over his arms and lifted him into Casey's boat. Justine donned one as well. They dragged the boat down to the water's edge.

The Miskito Indian and the rest of the crew piled into the last boat and shoved off into the frothing sea. They were lost to view within seconds.

Casey started their motor and headed back towards the ship. By the time they were only a few hundred feet off shore, he, Justine, and Sebastion were bobbing up and down like apples in a basin. There was little light and it was hard to see. Walls of water began to crest higher than their heads. The rubber boat slid up and down the steep walls, sometimes skewing crazily as the propeller bit into nothing but air.

They were drenched by the rain and the spray, now whipped by the wind and indistinguishable. The first lightning crawled jaggedly across the sky, and thunder boomed almost immediately after. Their clothing was plastered to their bodies and cold water pooled in their life jackets. Justine tightened the straps across Sebastion's chest.

Casey had lost sight of the other boats minutes before. His hand was steady on the boat's tiller, steering doggedly and aiming for where he figured *Aspen* to be. The sky was a shade brighter now, and a weak, pale light suffused the storm as dawn broke beyond the clouds. He strained to see through the rain. Where the hell was the ship?

Justine leaned forward precariously over the bow. Her hair was a matted tangle, and she pushed it angrily out of her eyes. She clung to the ropes laced across the boat's skin, protruding out like a wooden figurehead straining out into the storm.

"There!" she called suddenly, pointing.

Casey saw it too. Like a whale breaching the gray water, *Aspen* was breaking through the surface. White foam trailed off her sail and down her sides. She was maybe half a mile away. Casey swung the boat towards her.

The storm was a hellish thing. Justine felt the first wave of nausea clutch her stomach and she threw up violently, clutching at the ropes to keep from falling in. Another sudden lurch and she had to throw herself across Sebastion as he pitched forward. She vomited again, this time over both of them.

Casey's own stomach was heaving, but he got a hand around Sebastion's ankle and hauled him back. He could not leave the tiller even for a second. The smallest time in those deep troughs would swamp them. He cursed the surface and everything in it.

Justine found purchase and pushed herself back to a sitting position. She peered into the wind, trying to find the submarine and guide Casey. All she saw was water. Steel-gray undulating walls came racing at them. There were already a few inches of water on the bottom of the boat. A new fear assailed her—that the boat would fill and capsize.

A wave crested, and suddenly they were suspended for a split second at the top. She caught sight of the sub. The other two boats had made it and were being hauled on deck. She turned anxiously and caught Casey's nod. He'd seen it; his wistful look was clear enough.

The thunder was loud enough to deafen when it burst over their heads. Justine bent low, digging her fingers into Sebastion's sodden clothing beneath her. The lieutenant was hurling forth a steady stream of invectives. She turned to see him slapping at the engine housing with a look bordering on desperation.

"This sea's too much," he yelled. "We might lose it!"

Justine craned her head up when they crested over the next wave. Only a few hundred yards separated them from the sub. But the storm's violence had grown worse. She thought she saw figures peering forth from atop the sail, and waved frantically to attract their attention. But they slid down again and were lost to her view.

They lurched forward. Casey was hitting the motor with a closed fist. Justine heard it sputter again, then catch, only to fail again after just seconds. The fight to mount each wave grew longer as they lost momentum. But *Aspen* was closer now. She could almost see it continuously. Her wave was returned; they saw her too. Less than a hundred feet remained.

They might have made it if the motor had lasted. A few more waves to slide up and over were all that remained. But just as they roared up the curve of one sheer gray wall of water, the engine died with a final, coughing gasp.

The boat caught in the curl of the wave as it began to fall. The raft was flipped over backwards, as if a giant hand had flung it. It speared into the sea. Justine's fingers were torn from the ropes and she tumbled headlong into the water.

A terrible gray-green silence engulfed her. She fought to right herself, flailing around helplessly. Saltwater rushed into her throat, burning and choking her. She was thrown about like a rag doll. She kicked up hard, struggling to reach the churning surface.

She broke into the air and gulped long, noisy pulls of oxygen into her lungs. Spitting and choking, she looked around, desperate to find Sebastion. Water broke over her head, smashing her under again. She came back up, lost in the maelstrom and unable to spot either land or the sub.

She panicked, thinking the sub must have gone under after seeing them capsize. Already her legs were weakening and the wound in her arm burned wickedly from the saltwater. The first sense of despair flooded through her. She could see nothing but the water. Sebastion and the young lieutenant were long gone. Thunder roared overhead. She was alone. The wind's scream was her own. All at once she knew.

She was going to die.

With white-knuckled hands MacKenzie gripped the steel wall around the bridge cockpit on top of the sail and peered into the storm that had attacked them with such viciousness. He'd seen the boat go under and was putting *Aspen* as near as he could to that spot. The rain was driving directly into his face but he would not turn away.

It was getting too dangerous to stay on the surface much longer. The sub's roll was more and more pronounced. Casey had been very lucky. He was spotted just as MacKenzie was getting ready to clear the deck. Even though the sailors were tethered to the deck, the storm was getting violent enough to drown them if they were swept overboard.

How Casey had ever held onto the unconscious man was a mystery. But the crew had gone in for them both. They were being treated now. MacKenzie had a team waiting just below deck and ready to go should they spot the girl, but it was a long shot.

The order "Right full rudder" was passed to Lieberman, the Officer of the Deck in the control room, through the wireless headset he was wearing. The OOD and the helmsman had on matching sets. *Aspen* came about, turning in as tight a circle as possible.

The waves were bastards, and already many of the men would be sick below. His best judgment was telling him to forget the girl. All right; enough. He decided to abandon the search.

He looked out over the surface and saw nothing but waves. The well-worn, old trick hadn't worked. No last minute reprieves after the bell rang; no mischievous god turned the tide at the last minute. No cavalry came. . . . Shit. He was being foolish. One more minute? One more. That was all, he thought sadly.

He saw the girl as he was reaching for the hatch.

"Control, Bridge. I have her in sight. Left twenty degrees rudder, steady one eighty. Tom, get those men back on deck. Tether everyone. All stop!"

MacKenzie bolted as soon as he heard the replies. He slammed the bridge hatch down over his head and sealed it, shouting at a seaman to get out of his way as he slid down the ladder and ran aft.

Lasovic had the steel hatch open and was already on deck with the rescue gear. More men were waiting in the corridor below. MacKenzie grabbed a tether, hooked it to his life jacket, and clambered up the ladder.

The storm's fury was unabated on the unprotected open deck. The rain lashed out like shrapnel. Lasovic was staring hopelessly out into it. He looked to MacKenzie and spread his hands.

"I saw her," MacKenzie insisted. "Over there. I spotted the jacket."

Lasovic was using his own tether like a guy wire, holding him in place as the deck pitched wildly. He shook his head. Water washed over them in sheets. Their uniforms were sodden messes, their faces drenched.

MacKenzie spat back at the storm. It was getting to be personal. The girl was close by; he'd seen her. He wasn't about to lose her now.

Suddenly a bright streak showed against the gray.

"There!" MacKenzie said triumphantly. He fed speed and course changes to the OOD through the wireless headset and the phone talker. *Aspen* drew closer to the bobbing figure. She was facedown in the water. Lasovic tossed him a worried stare.

The storm seemed to take on a new potency. The wind heightened and lightning lit up the sky in almost continuous flashes. Faces became nightmarish as sailors stared wide-eyed. The waves grew bigger, slamming against *Aspen*'s hull like angry fists.

"Captain!" Lasovic yelled. "Look out!"

The wave that tore them off the deck was a cold, green hand that brooked no disobedience. MacKenzie had barely enough time to yell for Lasovic to see to the men before he was himself dragged deep under the surface. He refused to panic. The line was holding. What mattered now was time.

Lieberman was a good officer; too good to let *Aspen* be swamped. If MacKenzie and the others weren't back on deck within minutes, Lieberman would have to take *Aspen* down to protect her.

MacKenzie tore off his shoes and kicked for the surface. His headset had been torn off. The life jacket propelled him upward and he broke into the air gulping down lungfuls and wiping at his eyes. A quick glance as the waves crested and he saw *Aspen*'s familiar black shape. His ship was still safe. He struck off for the spot where he'd last seen the girl.

It was like swimming in a boiling caldron. Noise blotted out all direction and waves picked him up and threw him over their rolling crests. He slid up and down like a puppet on a chain, tethered by a single strand to *Aspen*, grabbed and pummeled by a maniacal sea.

He searched for the girl every time he could break the surface long enough to see. Once, the brightly colored vest flashed by but he couldn't reach her. He kicked out again. It *was* personal. He was damned if he was going to lose her now.

He slid over a wave and saw her. She lifted her head weakly and water poured out of her nose and mouth. She had no strength to swim. MacKenzie realized she was functioning on instinct alone. She had no idea he was near. He swam toward her with a determined stroke.

Her head snapped back and bile erupted out of her. Too much seawater. He had to get her out of this soon. He increased his kick. Oddly, the distance between them increased. What was. . . ?

All at once he realized that Lasovic must be pulling him in! He should have known they wouldn't abandon him while the tether held. They couldn't see how close he was to the girl, see he needed just seconds to get to her.

He pulled against the line frantically like a fish fighting the fisherman's pull. He twisted and turned in the cold water, desperate to get to her. The back pressure increased. He gritted his teeth and swam for all he was worth. It was no use. The backwards pull was inexorable.

Another few seconds and the girl would be gone.

MacKenzie released the tether.

He shot forward and the wave motion brought him surging past her. He clasped tired arms around her gratefully, pulling her to him. He got his hip up against her back, turning her, and looped his arm around her chest. He had to conserve strength now. Get back to the ship. Solid kicks; one after the other. Keep her head up.

Where was the ship? Forget it. Kick. Keep on kicking. Find the ship. Breathe; kick. He swallowed water and retched. He kicked harder; stroking, stroking.

Aspen's dull black shape swam out of the rain at him and he wanted to cry. He did cry, in great heaving gasps that wracked his body in time with his desperate, weakening kick.

Sailors were in the water now, all around him. Hands grasped his shoulders. He felt the weight on his back lifted away. For a moment he'd forgotten it was there. Lightning illuminated Lasovic's drenched and weary face as MacKenzie was pulled on board. He couldn't hear the XO's orders over the thunder.

MacKenzie didn't care. All he could do was lie shivering on the rolling deck, retching. He was helpless before the convulsions. Strong arms lifted him finally, but he couldn't see any faces through the sting of the salt in his eyes. He only vaguely felt himself passed through the hatch into more waiting hands.

He felt even less as he slid down another corridor, this one darker and of his own making. Fatigue and exhaustion swept over him.

As the diving klaxon sounded its raucous cry and the OOD yelled, "Dive, dive," *Aspen* plunged to safety in the black depths below the surface.

MacKenzie sank into another comforting blackness, this one all his own.

8

MANAGUA

The small square near the Constituent Assembly meeting place was one of Miguel's favorite spots. From one of its stone benches he could see the church's twin bell towers and the fountain and bright flower gardens the nuns still tended on either side.

The Assembly's incessant arguments had given him a headache. The sum total of every motion seemed only to ratify what the ruling council had already done. A creative idea, or even more rare, a real disagreement, was getting as difficult to find as bread in stores.

He sat quietly, letting the hot sun bake his face. It turned his closed eyelids orange red. Sounds came drifting over to him, carried on the warm air. A unit of the civilian militia raced double-time across the square; a group of dejected women clicked across the flagstones, bemoaning the wait at yet another store where the endless lines took hours to get through; a member of the neighborhood's Defense Committee, handing out ration books, reminded citizens about the mandatory political lectures. Miguel sighed; the sounds of the new Nicaragua.

Miguel himself was neither hungry nor required to attend any political indoctrinations. Members of the Assembly, like members of the rest of the government and the military, were considered politically educated and thus were exempt from reeducation classes. They were also allowed to buy at the "dollar" stores set up to attract hard currency. In the Soviet Union the elite were called the *Nomenklatura*. Suddenly Nicaragua had its own class of special citizens.

Miguel shrugged and turned his head to bake his other cheek. Was it so different before the revolution? Necessity, that was always the key. And power. Put one man in a room with a whole cow for food and one kind of system developed. But put *two* men in that same room and watch another kind of system evolve. A hundred men had to create yet another.

He had always believed that the main difference between capitalism and communism was the way the former seemed to accept—even revel in—inequities as a natural order in the universe. Now, however, there were the Sandinista stores, and he wasn't so sure. Was there any real difference after all? Maybe. In America there were no lines.

The sound of one recognizable tread of footsteps prodded him like a recurring melody. He did not move, but tensed internally instead, gathering inner resources for the meeting he'd been dreading since last night.

Another body settled in beside him. Miguel didn't trust himself to speak first. He waited.

"You know, of course, that your brother was taken out of our hands by the contra raid," Barrista said quietly.

Miguel nodded. It wasn't a question.

Barrista went on. "It was very professionally done. A diversion at the Central Bank, a quick strike at my

Ministry, a run up north. We lost quite a few troops following them."

"You forgot our old tricks, Phillipe."

"Don't be coy with me," Barrista snapped. "I want to know what happened in that interrogation room. You were there. I saw your mark."

Miguel said tiredly, "I did what I could. I had no gun. How could I stop them from taking Sebastion? The contra colonel stayed behind to kill the Cubans. I was able to kill him."

"That's all?"

Miguel knew his face was being searched closely. He held it impassive. "No. It's not." He opened his eyes. "They made a tape. The Cubans. They really were as good as they claimed. Sebastion was opened up like a ripe fruit. I heard it all from the other room."

Barrista's interest quickened. "Why didn't you come to me at once?"

Miguel looked back into the sun, squinting. "The contra colonel. Afterwards . . . I needed to sit in the sun for a while. You begrudge me that, Phillipe?"

The other man's hand found his shoulder. Barrista's voice softened. "No. I suppose not."

Miguel turned to him. "You were right, Phillipe. They *are* coming. It's a clever plan too. The contras take over a small area of the country on the Honduran border, just enough to claim territoriality and set up a provisional government. That makes military aid to them legal under American law. We attack to recover the land because we'd have no choice but to respond. The situation escalates, Honduras claims we've crossed their border to attack them and America must respond under the terms of the OAS charter. Sum total. . . ?"

"Invasion," Barrista concluded.

"Just so. They won't permit another Cuba."

Barrista said sharply, "We're not Cubans."

"You don't have to raise your voice to me, Phillipe. I'm not deaf. And I'm not blind either. But there are increasingly few differences."

"I don't like this talk, Miguel."

"Obviously. Three quarters of the content of the opposition paper seems to fall into the same category. *La Prensa* looked like swiss cheese this morning."

Barrista averted his eyes. "Paper shortages."

Miguel said nothing.

But Barrista was not to be outflanked for long. "We have reports that a woman led the raid last night. Would you know anything about that?"

You bastard, Miguel thought. You play me like a fish on a line. As tonelessly as he could, he said, "A woman?"

Barrista knew he had the upper hand now. He took his time answering, fixing his attention on the people passing through the square. Signs of the military were everywhere. Opposition to the draft was still widespread and a serious problem, but they were putting the screws to the church and the priests were exercising greater caution in counseling young men to evade it.

"Phillipe? You were saying?"

Barrista had known Miguel would weaken first. It was a victory of sorts, the kind that let the boy know who was still in control.

"I was saying that a woman led the raid. Good-looking, the report said. Black hair. Spoke like a native. Sound like anyone you know?"

"Should it?"

Barrista's snort was derisive. "The soldiers who were only wounded said the woman was with the contra colonel when he went towards the interrogation chamber. You didn't see her?"

"No one . . ." Miguel managed.

"You couldn't fail to recognize your sister, even after a few years."

"Phillipe, I swear. She wasn't there!"

"You should have killed her, too, Miguel. You know that."

"I didn't see Justine."

"She is as dangerous to us as any contra colonel. An important enemy."

"I know, but—"

"You should have killed her, Miguel."

"I couldn't!" It was torn out of him. His composure evaporated. A plaintive sob was torn out of him and he buried his head in his hands. "She's my sister. I . . . I just couldn't."

"Did she see you?"

Miguel shook his head. That was not quite a lie. "She left before the colonel. Honestly, Phillipe, I couldn't have taken her unarmed even if I wanted to. The colonel, though—that was good, wasn't it? Phillipe?"

The sunshine felt good today, Barrista thought. He reached out and stroked the boy's neck, parting the fine hairs at the nape. "Yes, Miguel. That was good. Getting the plans was good too. You heard the date?"

"One month from now. August first."

"Excellent. But letting Justine go was wrong. You know that now. She remains our adversary. You must remember that."

"I will."

"So if you ever see her or your brother again . . ." He dug a nail into Miguel's skin.

"All right, Phillipe. I understand."

"That's good. Now come. We have to make a report to the council."

"Will you tell them about Justine?" For a moment Miguel was genuinely frightened for his life.

Barrista looked at him. "Of course not. In fact, they want to reward you for the colonel. He's further proof of American complicity. Great propaganda value."

"Thank you, Phillipe."

"You're welcome, my boy."

Barrista rose and signaled to his driver, who brought his car to a stop in front of them. "Cheer up, Miguel," Barrista said expansively, opening the door for him. "Don't I always take care of you?"

Miguel slid into the car's dark interior. Barrista got in beside him.

"You do, Phillipe. It's just that, well . . . I'm so confused sometimes. So many sides, so many gray things. How do you know what's right so easily?"

"Principles, Miguel. Adhere to those and you will always be guided. But relax now, we'll talk later. You'll come home with me?"

"If you want."

The city streets whirled past the car's windows. It was

still early in the day, and the lines were growing at every shop. Miguel caught a brief glimpse of a militia patrol as it marched by. Most of the soldiers couldn't have been over fifteen. He sighed.

Principles.

There were nine members of the ruling Sandinista council, all men who had fought Somoza for years, many of them trained in Moscow and Cuba.

Miguel found himself examining the hard faces again and thinking, not for the first time, that idealists did not win wars. The men at the long oval table were hard pragmatists who had long ago shrugged off any pretenses. They were followers of Marx and Lenin, and links forged with Moscow were constantly being strengthened. The United States was the villain, the slave master, the creator of Somoza and Batista, Duvalier and Pinochet. Several of the nine had spent time in prisons constructed by some of those men.

Miguel couldn't blame their animosity. America had been involved in Nicaragua for over a century and over the course of that time had supported increasingly repressive measures to keep its puppets in power. Even the vaunted American generosity became stilted and self-serving, tokens provided for publicity value.

Miguel remembered the time the U.S. had sent a medical team out of Fort Hood in Texas to Managua after the devastating earthquake in 1974 which leveled much of the city. The U.S. team operated out of a barbed-wire enclosed compound in front of Somoza's residential palace. On the surface a benevolent gesture, surely. But the Cubans sent a team too. They operated in the packed Managua barrio of Maximo Jerez. The result was that the 185-man American team treated less than 250 patients a day, while the fifty man Cuban team treated over one thousand.

Somoza himself, meanwhile, was busy reselling the blood plasma supplied by the Red Cross for victims' relief back to the international black market.

Miguel saw. Time and time again the word freedom was used as an excuse for hunger or sickness or illiteracy. It had to be stopped somewhere. People had to eat first, have their wounds tended and their children in schools. Call the rulers whatever name pleased you. He would ally with the ones who did that first.

But what did you do when the hospital builders began to build an army instead? And closed down the papers, and indoctrinated—rather than taught—in the bright, new schools? He shrugged. You grew confused.

He saw that the nine were seated now. Most were dressed Castro-style in simple gray army tunics and trousers. One, the priest, wore his Roman collar. They all listened as Barrista gave the details of the contra raid. Ortega, the president, gave a short speech when Miguel's heroism was praised. Miguel stood to receive their accolades and then retook his chair.

Barrista began to speak again. "So now we know for certain. In less than a month we face the combined military might of the United States and its Honduran and contra sub-forces. Sebastion Segurra's army will attack from the south, catching us in a neat pincers movement. So I tell you this. Regardless of the size of our army, regardless of our Soviet weaponry, regardless of our own guerrilla training, and regardless of our valiant Cuban allies . . . " Barrista paused for emphasis, studying their faces. They expected stirring words from their Minister of Defense. Well, he would give that to them. He tossed the bombshell calmly in their laps. "My brothers, regardless of all that, we are surely going to lose."

"Unthinkable!" The president was on his feet.

Another, one of the old guerrilla fighters, was up and shouting, "We'll go back into the hills! The mountains are ours!"

Barrista stood his ground. He waited for the anger to subside. Take to the hills indeed. "Idiocy," he said flatly. "And all of you should know it. We aren't prepared for a retreat into the mountains again. Who among you fancies living in a cave? Our entire organization is urbanized, and the infrastructure that existed during the revolution doesn't exist anymore."

"The revolution still continues," Ortega chided him.

"Of course. But as an idea. Where are the arms caches? Supply lines? Communications? It's absurd to think we could fight a rearguard action against the American army."

He held up a hand. "I know what you're thinking, but

this isn't Vietnam. Supply lines are air minutes away for them, and Costa Rica, Honduras, and El Salvador are their allies. Where would we retreat to? No, don't talk to me about falling back to the hills. Save that nonsense for the troops."

Miguel was fascinated. Barrista insulted them and even tore down cherished beliefs. Yet every face was riveted on him and no one challenged his assertions.

"We aren't unmindful of American power," said Ortega. "But are you suggesting we simply lay down and die?"

"Not at all. We are here and here we stay. But I am saying that conventional warfare against the Americans in their own backyard is suicide. Grant me that?"

Ortega glanced around the table. "Granted."

"Then my second proposition is that guerrilla warfare against them won't work either. No more Vietnams is their slogan now. El Salvador is a good example. In spite of our continued assistance the guerrillas there have been reduced to mere urban terrorism just to keep their memory alive. Eliminate us and the whole region becomes untenable for them. Besides, even when such tactics do succeed, as in our own case, the state becomes particularly vulnerable to economic sanctions and precisely the same covert guerrilla harrassment that brought the state into power in the first place. Hence, the contras. Look, I know how painful it is for the old campaigners to admit it, but grant me also that guerrilla warfare is equally out of the question."

Ortega took a longer time to read the faces around the table, but in the end he nodded. Barrista plunged on.

"All right then. Ruling out both conventional warfare and guerrilla tactics, we are left with only one type of warfare which is impossible for the U.S. to defend against, is cost-effective—and may I remind you all of how little is in our treasury; we've been printing *cordobas* like they're going out of style—and is the only effective equalizer against a country with such a superior military-industrial base."

Barrista took a deep breath and stared around the table before continuing. Some, he saw, were already nodding in understanding.

"I propose," he said, "that the sole strategy capable of

protecting us from an American invasion is a nuclear one."

"They would never stand for it," said the priest. "They'd be here faster than the Israelis took out Iraq's plant."

But Ortega was pensive. "I don't know. Once operational, wouldn't the weapons be their own defense?"

Barrista pounced on that. "Exactly! The threat of mutually assured destruction prevents a U.S./Soviet conflagration. Why wouldn't it be sufficient to prevent a U.S./Nicaraguan one? In fact we have a greater advantage. The Americans might risk much for Moscow, but would they really risk the loss of New Orleans, Houston, or Miami—all of which are less than fifteen hundred miles from us—just to take Managua?"

"Unlikely," the priest agreed.

"It's clear to me that the U.S. policy on non-proliferation of nuclear arms is *not* designed to prevent nuclear war. It's to prevent the equalization of arms between large and small nations. Remember, regardless of the differences in size between men, a good pistol equalizes them. Comrades," Barrista said simply, "we need an equalizer."

Miguel watched the idea take hold. One after the other they caught the fever. Faces glistened with the possibilities. Miguel saw the silent communion that passed between Barrista and the other members of the circle. God, he thought, what a performance.

"Assuming we accept your theories," Ortega said carefully, "have you solved the procurement problem?"

"Not quite," Barrista admitted. "But I do have some ideas in that direction."

"We would be pleased to hear them."

Barrista again spoke at length. When he was finished Ortega summoned his secretary into the council chamber.

"Please tell the Soviet ambassador we would be pleased if he would join us as soon as his schedule permits."

The aide departed. Ortega looked back to his Minister of Defense. "Please, Phillipe. Let's have it all once again, shall we?"

Barrista said, "Of course." He took a sip of water from the glass at his elbow. "The problem of procurement is actually a three-fold issue. . . ."

Sometime later the secretary returned to announce that the Soviet ambassador was on his way.

9

MANAGUA

The Soviet ambassador walked into the council chamber with an air of confident informality that would only be assumed by a trusted ally. Miguel had met Viktor Kalnikov many times at Embassy gatherings and had spoken to him at length. As soon as Kalnikov entered, Ortega, Barrista, and the rest of the council rose to greet him warmly, ushering him into a chair placed at the table by Ortega's secretary.

Appearances before the council were common occurrences for the ambassador, a skilled diplomat with years of experience in the region. He understood hemispheric politics and had an excellent grasp of the ever-changing nuances involved in dealing with the United States. Kalnikov was wearing a well-cut, gray business suit with a white shirt and tie. His only jewelry was a Swiss watch, and he wore gold-rimmed glasses which extended back into the gray hair which grew on the sides of his head. Kalnikov had a pleasant face, Miguel thought, round and full-cheeked, with intelligent eyes.

"We've received some extremely disturbing information," Ortega began, "and felt you should be made aware of it as soon as possible." He caught Kalnikov glancing questioningly at Miguel, still sitting outside the circle. "The vehicle for this information," Ortega explained.

Kalnikov nodded and turned his attention back to Ortega. "And this information is?"

The president paused for a moment, studying the mural of Sandino on the far wall before replying. "It seems," he said slowly, "that our northern neighbor plans to invade us on the first of August."

Kalnikov blinked rapidly for a few seconds. "Your information is reliable?"

Ortega explained its source. "I don't see how we can doubt it."

"No, nor do I. But the audacity of it is staggering. They're risking a major social split."

Barrista spoke up. "They obviously feel secure enough. It's a very different political climate there now."

"But an out-and-out invasion?"

Barrista shrugged. "As opposed to aiding the contras, it has the virtue of honestey and forthrightness, two prized American beliefs."

"Along with the implicit assumption that they'll win," added Ortega, "a very big third."

"Will they? Win, I mean."

Barrista looked hard at the Russian. "Of course they will. You know to a man the strength of our troops and the nature of our weaponry. But," he added slyly, "the picture changes dramatically if your country would intervene."

Kalnikov shook his head. "Direct confrontation between nuclear powers is unthinkable. We both know what escalation could mean. I'm sorry. It's quite out of the question."

"Why? The nuclear threat has kept them out of Cuba," Ortega interjected.

"A special case. One that nearly brought us to the brink though. Afterwards, an understanding of sorts was reached."

"Then arm us with the same weapons, to help us reach the same understanding." Barrista put both hands on the table and leaned toward the ambassador. "The council stands as one on this issue. The only way to prevent this invasion is to threaten the United States with nuclear retaliation."

"They'd bomb you into dust."

"Not if they were going to lose several states in the process."

Kalnikov altered his expression to careful neutrality. "I am a specialist in diplomatic alternatives, not nuclear weapons. Let me contact my government and we can apply other measures first."

"We have increasingly little faith in Russian diplomatic initiatives," said Ortega. "You couldn't prevent Grenada and you're barely holding on in Poland. Even East Germany, of all places, is making overtures to the West."

"Merely the ebb and flow of global relations," said

Kalnikov smoothly. "Look, you mention Cuba. That island costs us over ten million dollars a day in hard currency. Do you have any idea of the strain on our reserves that sum accounts for? We have counseled you over and over again to learn to live with the United States. Use them. Rebuild your economy, reconstruct the country. Our ties will remain firm and grow stronger. In time many more things would become possible. You could be a showcase for socialism. Instead you're being nibbled to death by contra raids, trade imbalances, and runaway inflation."

"So prevent it," demanded Ortega.

"How?"

"Arm us," Barrista said flatly. "Land-based missiles. Enough to protect us, with our guarantee that they will never be used in first strike as long as our borders are secure."

"Out of the question."

Barrista was angry now and his voice was hard-edged. "You are more like the U.S. than you can admit, even to yourselves. You both want to keep the weapons that really matter out of the children's hands lest they threaten the adults."

"Think about what you're saying," Kalnikov said, trying to soothe. "Would you want such weapons in Khomeini's hands?"

"I don't care for the comparison," Barrista objected. "We're not fanatics."

"I gave you an example, not a comparison. And it remains one very good reason for containing nuclear arms."

It was Ortega who lifted a hand to still Barrista's retort. "You're still failing to state your government's real reason, comrade. I'm surprised at you."

"I don't follow."

Ortega's tone hardened. "You're frightened, Comrade Ambassador. Frightened of our request because it uncovers your real concern."

"Which is?"

"Afghanistan."

Kalnikov tried to hold Ortega's gaze. "I don't know what you mean."

"Come now. The entire Politburo knows that the day you adequately arm us is the same day the U.S. arms the rebels in Afghanistan with a whole lot more than rifles and grenades. That scares the old men down to their souls. How many troops do you have bogged down in those mountains, one hundred thousand? One hundred fifty thousand? You know what shoulder-fired anti-aircraft missiles would do to your precious MIG's. Fifty-million-dollar jets taken out by a few hundred dollars of explosives. Flying through those mountains, they'd never even see them coming. And low-yield nuclear devices would fry your troops and tanks on the ground. The U.S. knows how paranoid you Russians are about your land ring of satellites. They cost you billions. One step in our direction and the U.S. will escalate the war in Afghanistan till it bleeds you drier than the bones you toss us."

"You must see this situation in more global terms—" Kalnikov started.

"We see it in the only terms possible—our own. It's time to change the rules of the game if we can't survive under the present ones."

Kalnikov stood up. He was far less composed than when he'd come in. "I can only relay your request to my government."

Ortega stood also. "When will we have a response?"

"Within a day."

"Thank you, Comrade Ambassador. We'll be waiting."

Kalnikov gave a short bow, but it was much too stiff, Miguel thought. The strain on his face was evident. Ortega had ripped off the mask and revealed the pretenses hidden underneath.

Ortega returned to his seat after the ambassador left. He turned calmly to Barrista. "Well, Phillipe, you were right. They'll refuse to help us. As you said, we are just too far away, and Afghanistan and Poland are too close."

"The charade was necessary though. We had to ask," Barrista acknowledged. "It also would have saved us a great deal of trouble if they'd agreed to help."

"What now then? You'll proceed?"

Barrista nodded. "Yes, as we discussed. Our consciences are clear. Survival nullifies morality. All I need is your formal approval."

"All in agreement. . . ?" Ortega asked.

One by one, seven other hands were raised. Ortega put his own up. "Approved."

"Thank you, comrades," Barrista said. He was anxious to begin.

"Very well, then, Defense Minister," Ortega said. "You have your mandate. Whatever you need will be provided on a first priority basis. When shall we meet again?"

When the hurly-burly's done, when the battle's lost and won. Barrista's mind supplied the tail end of the quote from the forgotten play, the response to the witch's question. *In thunder, lightning, or in rain . . .*

He said simply, "When I've stolen the submarine."

Ortega ended the meeting and the council stood, leaving one by one. Barrista was the last to rise, and Miguel followed him out.

10

CARIBBEAN SEA

MacKenzie woke from a deep sleep, feeling rested and vaguely self-satisfied. It took him a moment to remember what the feeling meant, till the memory of rescuing the girl returned.

Stretching lazily on the narrow bunk, he realized he wasn't in his own cabin. The sounds were wrong, the feel of the bed different. Lasovic must have put the girl in his cabin, he thought, the only place to accommodate her with any privacy. He rolled to one side, finally deciding to open his eyes, and received the disconcerting shock of staring into the dark eyes of a stranger in the opposite bed.

"Hello, Captain."

"How do you do," MacKenzie responded politely. Both of them were wearing only undershirts and briefs. For that, the salutations seemed a bit formal.

"Sebastion Segurra," said the man, holding out his hand.

MacKenzie took it and could not fail to notice the muscular arms. "Peter MacKenzie. You're the man Casey dragged on board, right?"

"I don't remember it, but that's what Justine told me."

"Justine?"

"The one *you* dragged on board. My sister," he said, smiling.

"Oh, I didn't know her name. Jesus, that was a miserable storm. Would have been a milk run without it."

Sebastion was silent for a moment. "She would have drowned. Your executive officer said you released your hold on the ship to get to her. What do they say in your services . . . above and beyond?"

"More like thick-headed obstinacy." MacKenzie reached up and scratched his stubble sheepishly, "A captain leaving his command is in violation of so many codes and rules, I'd be hard pressed to name them all. It's best forgotten."

"There are higher codes than Navy regulations," Sebastion said. "Regardless of what you say, I think you subscribe to them. Thank you for saving my sister's life, MacKenzie."

MacKenzie nodded. Suddenly a memory asserted itself. "Now I know. It took me a minute to place the name. Segurra. Commander Zero, right? I remember now. You fought with the Sandinistas till they went Marxist, then took up arms against them from the south."

"Costa Rica. I was captured during our last raid. My sister led the action that got me out. Funny, for days now I've been getting knocked out in one place and waking in another. The battlefield, the prison, this submarine. Very disconcerting, I'm afraid."

"I would imagine."

"The great irony, though, is that Justine and her friends rescued me."

"Why? You're on the same side."

"First of all, there are many sides. We're not exactly on the same one. I operate independently, at least, as independently as I can. Justine works, well, with a special branch of your government."

It was MacKenzie's turn to smile. "The CIA's covert aid to the contras is no secret, nor are your feelings about that aid. May I ask you why you object to it?"

"Yes, but the answer is simple. Self-interest."

MacKenzie frowned, "I don't follow."

Sebastion lay back against his pillow and took a moment before answering. "I find something curious. Justine calls me an idealist. In fact that was her reason for leaving me and joining the contras. But I see myself as more of a pragmatist than any of them. I accept the world as it is, and self-interest rules it. Americans, Russians, the contras, the Church, the Sandinistas—all act according to their own interests."

"Including you?"

Sebastion thought that over. "Maybe. I'd define it a little differently. But in the final analysis only the Nicaraguans have the best interest of Nicaragua at heart. Everyone else wants their piece."

"The Sandinistas are Nicaraguans," MacKenzie reminded him.

"Surely. And I suppose in their own way they're acting for the country too. I oppose their politics, not necessarily their basic motives. Put another way, I differ with them on issues of democracy, pluralism, allies, and government; not love of country."

"Those issues are sufficient for you to kill them?"

"Look around you, Captain. Why else does such a ship as this exist, if not for the need to kill those of opposing ideologies? I regard my country as under occupation."

"I understand that. Look, protecting my country is not only my career, it's my life's work and my most basic obligation."

"Accepted. But because of that, I maintain that your commitment to Nicaragua, or any place like it, will always be secondary to the strategic interests vital to protecting your country. That's why I can't accept your presence either. Self-interest governs the United States' choices as well."

MacKenzie shook his head. "Too black and white, Segurra. We have a common enemy and a shared goal. *Mutual* self-interest. What else is any alliance?"

"So Justine claims. But what always strikes me as odd is

that I argue reality and get called an idealist. You and she call yourself pragmatists and argue ideals. Anyway, call me Sebastion."

MacKenzie lay back thoughtfully. He was about to reply when Justine Segurra's voice asked for permission to enter.

"Come in," he called out, pulling the covers up over him.

It was his first good look at her minus the bile, the tangled mat of hair, and the churning sea. It actually stopped his breath for a second.

"Good morning, Captain. Sebastion. How nice to see you both up."

She was wearing a gray sweat suit with USS ASPEN printed on the back of the hooded sweatshirt. One of the smaller crew members must have volunteered a pair of sneakers, MacKenzie decided. Her hair was lustrous, dark and straight, pulled into a thick braid that hung halfway down her back. MacKenzie noticed that her trim, athletic figure pulled the sweat suit in directions that none of his crew ever had.

"*Buenos días, Justiniaña*," Sebastion said.

"Good morning," MacKenzie responded, feeling more than a little awkward lying half undressed under the sheets. "Please forgive my appearance."

Justine gave a little laugh and said, "Given what I must have looked like when you pulled me out of the sea, no apologies are necessary."

It was an odd gathering at this time and place, MacKenzie found himself thinking. The female CIA operative—female alone being enough to cause tremors in an all-male closely confined ship—the sunburnt guerrilla fighter, and the submarine captain. Interesting, too, was the fact that each owed his life to the other: Justine rescued Sebastion, MacKenzie had rescued Justine. He wondered if the others were as conscious as he of the unlikely interconnections.

Justine said something in rapid-fire Spanish to her brother and listened to his response. Then she turned to MacKenzie.

"Sebastion says he already thanked you for pulling me out of the sea. Please, you must also accept my heartfelt gratitude personally. The storm . . . I'd never been in anything like it. I was convinced I was going to drown. I think I must have panicked. I don't remember much else."

"You were still fighting pretty gamely to stay afloat when I finally got close to you. I don't think you were anywhere near fully conscious, but you were still struggling."

"I don't remember it."

MacKenzie said kindly. "You were operating on will alone. It was a very brave thing to see."

"Or just very stubborn."

"Perhaps." His next words were out of his mouth before he actually realized he was going to say them. "But I was touched anyway."

She looked at him strangely. "By a puking, waterlogged, drowning mess?"

"By a fighter."

The atmosphere in the small cabin had grown awkward, and MacKenzie cursed himself for being its source. Justine was studying him closely and he could not avoid her glance. He looked back. For the briefest of instants their eyes locked and something coursed along the connection. The small room suddenly grew smaller, warmer. Then it was gone. Justine backed away. MacKenzie cleared his throat.

Sebastion spoke into the stiff silence. "The very kind Mr. Lasovic tells me that there are some guitars on board. Justine? Will you accompany me tonight?"

Justine had recovered her composure by now and shook her head. "It's been too long since I played, Sebastion. And the guitar was never my favorite instrument anyway. Nor was it yours, if I remember correctly."

"You do. But pianos and violins don't adapt very well to the jungle. Come, we owe this ship something. What else can poor people offer?"

Justine hesitated. "Captain?"

MacKenzie thought it over. "You could play in the crew's mess, I suppose. It's the biggest space on board. And we could pipe it throughout the ship on the intercom for the rest of the crew." He sighed. "It's been a trying cruise. Might be good to have a little diversion."

"What will we play, Sebastion?"

"We can work that out. We owe ourselves to play on at least one happy occasion."

"Unlike—" She stopped herself abruptly, and MacKenzie saw a dark look pass between them.

"Unlike so many things, sister," Sebastion filled in the gap. "We'll actually rehearse. This afternoon, if the captain can arrange it."

"Done," MacKenzie said.

Lasovic's voice sounded clearly from the corridor, "Is this a private party or can a working stiff join in?" His head poked around the doorway.

MacKenzie smiled. "Come in, Tom."

Lasovic could only lean into the room. He settled his big frame in the doorway. "Glad to see you up, sir. How are you feeling?"

"Fine, Tom. I'll be up and around as soon as I've cleaned up. Give me a status report, please."

"We're running at flank speed, sir, straight for Guantanamo. Orders from COMSUBLANT. We should arrive, at the latest, tomorrow afternoon. They'll provide air transport back to the mainland for our guests. Incidentally, a well-done has been sent."

"Very good. Then if you'll see to Miss Segurra's needs . . ."

"Mrs. Segurra," Justine said automatically.

MacKenzie felt an odd feeling in his stomach. ". . . Mrs. Segurra's needs, I'll be getting up now."

"Yes, sir. Mrs. Segurra? This way, please."

"And Tom?"

"Yes, sir?"

"A very well done from me too. Pass it on. And a personal thanks for hauling my tail out of the drink."

Lasovic grinned. "Had to. Too much damn paperwork explaining where the skipper went if we didn't."

He stepped back out of the cabin, followed by Justine. MacKenzie sat up for a moment, savoring the steady drone of the engines, the right feel of a tautly run ship. He threw off the covers and stood up. Not bad. Only a little stiffness in the legs and lower back. The hot water in the shower loosened both up. He shaved and dressed, then made way for Sebastion to do the same.

Mackenzie got a good look at the collection of old scars

and fresh wounds on Sebastion's body when the man stepped out of the shower. *Aspen's* medical corpsman must have treated them as best he could, he thought, but Sebastion needed more care than the ship's dispensary could provide. It occurred to MacKenzie that Sebastion must be in considerable discomfort.

"If you'd like," he said, "I'll have one of my officers give you a tour of the ship. Certain areas are classified. I'm sure you understand. But even what you can see is fascinating. Ever been on a sub before?"

Sebastion was slipping very carefully into a pair of coveralls. "No. I'd be very interested."

"Perhaps we can spare Mr. Casey for an hour or two."

"Just the man I had in mind," Sebastion said. Abruptly his mood changed. "MacKenzie? Can I ask you a personal question?"

"Shoot."

"You're not married."

"That's not a question. But no, I'm not. Why?"

"My sister. I can see."

"That's impertinent."

"Nevertheless, that's my question."

He was looking at MacKenzie very seriously. MacKenzie had not felt so uncomfortable since adolescence. He didn't like the feeling.

"Impertinent questions don't deserve answers," he said, glowering.

Sebastion stood up. He was smiling again. "I'll accept that as answer enough."

"As you like," MacKenzie said stiffly. He turned toward the doorway and stepped into the corridor.

Sebastion's voice called after him. "MacKenzie?"

"Yes."

"Justine . . . the *Mrs.* she uses?"

Funny, there was a surprising warmth in Sebastion's voice. "Yes?"

"She's a widow."

MacKenzie walked away without replying, but not before he caught the twinkle in Sebastion's eyes and felt a sudden elation that lifted him up all the way back to the conn.

11

Only one third of a submarine's crew is on duty at any one time. Of the remaining two thirds, half are training and half sleeping. Word of the performance, however, had altered the schedule somewhat, with everyone trying to juggle his time to be in attendance.

They gathered in the crew's mess, an area about twenty feet by ten, bordered by the hull on one side and the stainless steel galley on the other. A Coke machine and ice dispenser were set into the outer galley wall, and a television/VCR stood in the far corner. The Formica tables were bolted down in close rows, as were the benches alongside them.

Submarine informality extended to seating as well, with officers and men sitting where they could. It was a sign of the men's increasingly good feeling about their captain, though, that MacKenzie, who never would have ordered it, was saved and offered a front-row seat.

The gesture wasn't lost on MacKenzie. During a sixty-day cruise, where few of the men ever saw daylight, any diversion was prized. The crew understood he was responding to their common need. The seat was one way of telling him they appreciated it. MacKenzie was a superior officer. He knew that the crew that worked for you willingly, because they felt you were worthy of their best efforts, was the hardest working crew you were ever going to have.

Captains like MacKenzie were a large part of the reason, over and above superior hardware, that the Russian navy, with its ironbound, oppressive discipline, its constant political interrogations, and its refusal to allow any individual initiative, would never be the equal of the American navy.

The galley by now was filled to overflowing, and men perched on tabletops and stood three deep in the corridors. Justine and Sebastion sat against one bulkhead with their guitars across their laps. A pair of microphones hastily wired by an electrician's mate stood in front of them.

Justine was still dressed in the gray sweat suit and Sebastion in his coveralls, but each radiated the highly intense energy of consummate professionals. MacKenzie caught Sebastion's nod of readiness and put up a hand to still the crowd.

"My name is Sebastion Segurra," Sebastion said into the microphone, "and beside me is my sister, Justine. We hope the crew of this fine ship will accept our small offering in appreciation for all you've done for us. With special thanks, the first piece is dedicated to your captain."

There was a burst of applause and whistles. MacKenzie waved it off, privately pleased nonetheless. The outburst released the final anticipatory tension, and the men settled down to listen.

From the first notes the men seemed to realize they were hearing something special, something no one could have anticipated. Sebastion played the melody boldly, fingering a strong central theme. By itself it would have been startling. But it was Justine's performance that lent it depth: brilliant, intricate harmonies that wove in and around his notes.

It didn't seem possible there were only two guitars. There was too much sound, too many notes. The melody reached out hauntingly, daring one to define it. It teased at the outer reaches of perception, never quite finishing its plaintive phrasing. Only after several minutes did MacKenzie recognize the classic malagueña in their unbelievably complex and deeply moving version.

Tempo changed. Their fingers plucked at the settings as if each were a hot coal, the briefest of notes doubling and tripling in time. The effect was dazzling, machine-gun staccato, each note bounding and rebounding off the others.

MacKenzie found himself leaning forward, half out of his seat. Others edged forward too. The men were in awe. Tempo changed again. The Segurras played their audience like an instrument, drawing them out and pulling them back with sudden, lunging melodic progressions.

The duet slowed suddenly. It became more intimate, more loving; and yet, in some way, sadder. Sebastion released his hold on the melody and Justine took it. Her fingers produced a mournful, haunting sound that pulled MacKenzie and everyone else toward her like a call from a frightened child.

She drew out the melody. Pain and sadness lingered in the intervals between notes. Tears welled up in the corners of her eyes. For just a moment she looked back out from her solitary, inward-staring gaze and found MacKenzie's eyes.

This, he understood she was saying, *is what you'll find if you reach for me. This is the wellspring you'll tap. Can you want such pain? Can anyone face such despair?*

MacKenzie took it all in and didn't look away. It was a warning, to be sure, but didn't that also make it a sign of caring, to send when no such concern should have remained? He wouldn't release her eyes. Did the melody then change subtly, as something like wonder crossed her face ever so briefly? But the piece moved on and she was no longer playing just for him.

Sebastion rejoined her. Faster and faster the music swelled to its conclusion. Justine flicked at the guitar's face with rapid-fire slaps while Sebastion raced on around her. Chords clashed, resounded, resolved. Once, then again, then a final time. One last, full-throated chord of awesome beauty strummed with all the force that hope and triumph could produce.

Then silence.

Sailors leaped to their feet, applauding wildly. They whistled and slapped each other on the back. The applause was unrestrained, a tribute to what everyone realized they'd heard—beyond technique, in some unknowable fashion: honesty.

MacKenzie found himself standing with the rest. Justine would not meet his eyes but he was certain she was aware of him. He was also certain that Sebastion had arranged all this quite deliberately to let him see what turmoil brewed inside Justine, and to see if it would matter. He looked at Sebastion, politely bowing with Justine's hand in his, and waited till he turned his way. The sly, subtle look on his face was all the confirmation MacKenzie needed.

The applause was continuing unabated, and finally MacKenzie had to turn and gesture for everyone to return to their seats. Sebastion announced the next selection.

Halfway through the second piece MacKenzie was urgently summoned to the control room.

Lasovic had the conn when MacKenzie arrived.

"Sonar's got something, skipper. Jim's not sure yet, but I thought you should take a look. Lieberman's on his way too."

MacKenzie nodded. The atmosphere of the conn was a marked contrast to the emotional turbulence he'd left behind in the mess. But he'd had to leave it behind. He knew that whatever might or might not have been taking place between himself and the puzzling Justine Segurra had no place here. He walked into the sonar room with only *Aspen* on his mind.

Sonarman first-class "Bear" Bendel was hunched over his instrument table with his headset on and an absent, faraway look on his face. In actuality his senses were far away, extended, at least auditorily, several miles around the sub through the passive sonar listening devices mounted in *Aspen*'s bow and down her sides. *Passive* was used in the sense that the awesomely sensitive sound-gathering devices collected incoming signals like huge ears. Active sonar was the familiar pinging sound probe originating on the submarine, and like its analogue in radar—Radio Detection And Ranging—sonar, *sound* detection and ranging, was used to locate or "range" a target.

Standing over Bendel was his division officer Lieutenant Jim Kurstan, who directed MacKenzie's attention to a flickering screen similar to an oscilloscope as soon as he entered.

Bendel continued to make adjustments on the instrument panel, eyes half closed, and the sputtering curve grew steadier.

"What have you got, Jim?" MacKenzie asked.

"A routine sweep of the area picked up what we believe is a Russian Alfa, skipper. Bear logged the contact and taped the signal signature for verification by Norfolk. Routine. But then Mr. Lasovic remembered that the boys in the SOSUS section have been more than a little unhappy with the way the Alfas have been popping up around here without our picking them up. This is far from their normal cruising area. So we slowed to listen. We're staying pretty far out because of the racket we're making. But here's the thing, skipper. Ten minutes ago Bear picked up a second and third sub. Mr. Lasovic thinks maybe we found ourselves a running route."

"If it is, it's damn fine work, Jim. Keep listening. I'm going to kill the noise and take us in closer."

MacKenzie stepped back into the conn. "Mr. Lasovic, rig ship for Ultra Quiet and man battle stations. The concert's over. Convey my apologies to our guests but they are to remain in their quarters. I want a conference in the wardroom with you and Frank in ten minutes. Bring the charts for this area."

"Aye, sir."

"The captain has the conn," MacKenzie announced, feeling the familiar feeling of expansion as *Aspen's* senses and sinews became his own. "Give me a sounding."

"Sounding, two hundred fathoms," said the Quartermaster.

"Maneuvering, Conn. Make minimum turns. Mr. Randall, make your depth eleven-zero-zero feet. We will be close to the bottom. Stay alert."

"Aye, sir."

"Sonar, any close contacts?"

"Conn, Sonar. Nothing close."

"Quartermaster, what does the contour chart show here?"

"Captain, there's a gradual flat five-degree slope without any charted projections. Slope increases sharply in one-point-five miles, though."

MacKenzie looked up, curious.

"The Cayman Trench, sir." He was referring to the long, deep gash in the ocean floor that cut right through this area. It began off Cuba and extended several hundred miles.

Things were beginning to fit into place, MacKenzie thought.

"We're at ordered depth, Captain."

"Very well. Gentlemen, we are going to put *Aspen* on

the bottom. Maneuvering, all stop. Watch your seawater suctions closely. I don't want to lose vacuum in the condensers. Chief, watch the trim. I want to settle in very slowly." With the utmost care MacKenzie brought *Aspen* down the remaining hundred feet till her keel settled in firmly on the bottom. He felt her rock slightly, then hold steady.

"Maneuvering, Conn. Answer bells on the Emergency Propulsion Motor. Spin the main engines only as necessary, Jake. Keep everything as quiet as a church. Sonar, Conn."

"Sonar, aye."

"I want your best operator on the console. Stay alert and give me your best estimate of bearings and bearings drift so we can get a quick depth, course, and speed of everything that pops out of there."

"Aye-aye, Captain. Petty Officer Bendel is our man."

"Mr. Randall, you are relieved of Dive. You have the conn. I'll be in the wardroom."

MacKenzie left the control room as soon as Randall took his place. He made his way along the now-silent corridors, towards the officers' dining area—the wardroom, directly across from his cabin. At every station he passed, men were sitting without speaking, poised at their instruments, silent chiefs overseeing it all. Until MacKenzie gave orders otherwise, *Aspen* would continue to be as silent as a grave.

Lasovic and Lieberman were already sitting in the blue vinyl booth that surrounded the single round table that took up most of the room's space. The walls were paneled with wood-grain Formica. MacKenzie accepted a cup of coffee from a mess specialist and settled in opposite the senior wardroom officers.

"I think you've got it dead right, Tom," he said without preamble. "Let me see it on the charts."

Lieberman spread out the hydrographic maps on the table. "Here, skipper," he said, pointing to a spot just south of Cuba. "This is the approximate start of the Trench. And this is the end, which is roughly twenty miles west of where we're sitting. If you had the Trench mapped right, and could make the depth, a sub could dive in here"—he pointed to the Cuban end—"run at high speed, and emerge two thirds of the way to the Panama Canal without ever having so much as raised anybody's eyebrows. The depth would mask an enemy sub even from the Orions."

MacKenzie was forced to agree with that assessment. The P-3C Orion aircraft were land-based, anti-submarine search-and-destroy platforms. Using an array of sophisticated detection devices such as Magnetic Anomaly Detection—which measured changes in the earth's magnetic field caused by the huge metallic mass of a sub—and able to launch sonobuoys to further isolate a target, their vertically mounted tubes for launching MK-46 torpedoes could make short work of a sub unlucky enough to come within their range. But the great depth of the Cayman Trench could hide a sub from its long reach.

"So what we've stumbled on," MacKenzie concluded, "is a running route that can bring Russian subs out of Cuba and allow them to progress at high speed to within missile range of the entire Central American land mass, including the Canal, up till now without the slightest risk of detection from us. Jesus!" he swore.

"That's how I make it," Lasovic agreed. "the Alfas have the deep diving capability and the speed."

"With this arrangement they also have a tactical advantage in this entire area," Lieberman said, musing out loud. "In a pinch you could dive for the Trench, leaving your pursuer behind, run, turn, and fire almost with complete impunity."

"You figure they've got the route wired?" asked Lasovic.

Lieberman thought about it for a moment. A series of limited-range, low frequency transmitters could be used to direct a submarine's inertial guidance system under computer control to any desired course. "It's possible," he finally replied.

"Pass the word to Sonar to look for an underwater signal," MacKenzie said.

"How long do you plan on staying here?" Lasovic asked him.

"Not very. We should notify Norfolk as soon as possible, and we can't do that from here. Let's verify that we've got what we think we've got and then scoot. Someone else will have to come back to do the surveillance."

That would be boring duty, MacKenzie reflected. Days

on end of interminable quiet, listening to the comings and goings of enemy subs, trying to get a fix on the route.

Interesting concept, a route. Take an area full of sharp obstacles and gingerly pick your way through it. That became the Route. Then practice it over and over again till you could run it at top speed without a hitch. Imagine the advantage it would be possible to achieve anytime an enemy came into that area or could be drawn into it. While he slowed to a minimum or blundered into the obstacles, you danced lightly along at top speed into a perfect firing position and made the kill. Or you could use the Route in reverse, to disappear. Ballistic missile submarines had very little offensive weaponry, and survived mostly by stealth. They could hide under the ice packs, or in thermals . . . or deep in the Cayman Trench.

". . . those depths mask most of the Alfa's noise, and that was always their greatest weakness," Lasovic was saying.

"I agree, Tom. We've uncovered a major trouble spot. We'll give it another twelve hours and slip out quietly to report. I think the SOSUS lads are going to be doing somersaults over this one."

Project SOSUS—Sound Surveillance Underwater Systems—was responsible for planting the arrays of passive sonar listening devices, bottom-mounted hydrophones, across areas of the oceans that Soviet subs pass through to reach the major oceans, an area such as the Bering Straits. A sub's noise was picked up and electronically transmitted to a Navy satellite overhead, then relayed to the giant computers in Norfolk. The sub's specific signature was isolated from myriad background noises, identified, and its position plotted. In such a way most of the Soviet fleet could be accounted for. But an area like this, MacKenzie knew, where they could escape detection, was one more hole that needed to be plugged.

He said to Lieberman, "I want you to work closely with Tom on this. There may be any number of entrance and exit points. Let's get as much as we can while we're here."

"Okay, skipper."

"Christ, Tom." MacKenzie whistled, thinking over the implications again. "You've earned a commendation for this one. I'm very pleased."

"T'wernt nothin'," Lasovic deadpanned, but his pleasure was evident.

"We'll keep this shift on for the additional time," MacKenzie decided. "Less movement, less noise. We can adjust the rotations when we're under way again."

"Good idea, skipper."

"Any other suggestions?"

Both Lasovic and Lieberman shook their heads. Lieberman said, "We're covered, skipper. A nice quiet afternoon of sub watching."

"Won't beat the ball games we've got on tape, or that concert either," joked Lasovic.

"It was quite a recital while it lasted, wasn't it?" MacKenzie mused. "Nice for the men."

"They appreciated it too," Lieberman said. "I caught it over the intercom and it still blew me away. Imagine what they'd sound like in a real concert hall?"

MacKenzie was half listening, his thoughts drifting back to those moments he'd held Justine's eyes. Had he really seen what he thought he saw?

"Skipper? You with us?"

"What? Sorry, yes, I'm here. What were you saying?"

Lasovic said, "Duty rosters. But it's okay. I'll see to them. You looked a million miles away."

Much less, thought MacKenzie. Maybe twenty feet— the distance to his cabin, where she waited. "Lost in thought, Tom. Nothing to worry about. Anything else?"

"We're set, skipper."

The conference was at an end. Lieberman folded up his charts and Lasovic left to confer with the chiefs about the duty assignments. MacKenzie sat for a while, savoring the moments of solitude.

He leaned back against the cushions, letting his mind empty. Even the usual throb of *Aspen*'s engines was absent. Finding the Russians' route on top of a successful, if a bit hairy, pick up of the Segurras, was a nice cap on a cruise that had begun almost disastrously. It showed you that sailing the oceans—on top or below them—was still as capricious a task as it had ever been. Only the ships changed.

Only? Maybe men changed too, MacKenzie thought, and wondered if he could reorder the habits of a lifetime.

Premature, some inner voice warned. And that was correct. For now only *Aspen* could matter. But after they reached port . . .

Who could say?

12

HAVANA, CUBA

The State dinner held in Barrista's honor had ended some time earlier and he, Miguel, and some of Cuba's elder statesmen had retired to the adjoining library for brandy and cigars. A warm evening breeze wafted in through the open window, which helped to pick up and dispel the satin-gray cloud of tobacco smoke by swirling it up toward the ceiling fan. The men reclined in leather wing chairs.

"I tell you, Phillipe," said Jorgé Cruz, the Foreign Minister, "we were pretty damn worried for a while. God help us the day the imperialists care more about Cuba than world opinion."

"It's coming closer," Barrista said. "And it was the Soviets who gave them the way in. A precedent, if you wish, with Afghanistan and Cambodia."

"Cambodia's a Vietnamese problem," observed Fidel Castro, knocking a silver ash off his cigar. He propped a booted foot up on an ottoman.

"Of course," Barrista said with gentle sarcasm. "Just like Angola is a Cuban one. Come, Fidel. The children have all gone home. Moscow still runs the show."

Castro examined the tip of his cigar. "Indeed."

"The contras are still giving you a hard time," Cruz commented. "It would be nice if the American congress got them off your back for you."

"Keep raising moral issues," Castro instructed. "Confuses the hell out of them."

"We are trying to, Fidel. Among other things."

Castro nodded wisely, still looking at his cigar. He said,

"I hear you hired an American public relations firm. You got image problems, Phillipe?"

Barrista accepted the barb in repayment for his remark about Angola. "As you say, Fidel, public opinion matters there."

Castro shook his head in wonder. "It's unbelievable, really. Can you imagine any other country that would allow the hiring of one of their own businesses by the very people they're at war with?" He made a motion by his ear. "Crazy."

"I think they call it freedom of speech," Miguel said quietly. "You remember, Fidel."

Castro's eyes grew cold and for a moment the jungle fighter of old looked out. "*Hombrecito,* you could be breakfast here."

"He thinks he's defending me, Fidel," Barrista said hastily, shooting Miguel an angry calm-down look. "Besides, you probably knew his father quite well. Carlos Segurra?"

Castro's features opened wide with pleasure. "This is *his* son? In that case, I forgive you. Loyalty is still a good thing. But so are manners, eh? I remember your father. A very good man."

"He spoke of you as well."

"An old and honorable family," said Castro. "I drink to it." All the others lifted their glasses too.

Miguel said, "Thank you, Fidel."

Castro turned to Barrista. "What is it you need, Phillipe? I'm assuming you came here not only for our cigars, but with your hand out."

Barrista flushed but controlled himself. "We've got serious supply problems, as I'm sure you know. The American navy watches every inch of our coast, and they guard the Gulf of Fonseca like it was their own. We're having more and more trouble supplying our friends in El Salvador. Our coast guard is old and inadequate. I've got a commitment from the Soviets to supply us with a half-dozen new high-speed patrol craft, but I need a cadre of officers to train my own force. Experienced men."

"Why not ask the Soviets?"

"There are too many Russians in Nicaragua as it is. More would be like waving a red flag, you'll excuse the pun, at the Americans. Their president loves nothing better than to point his finger at the Russian advisors as proof of conspiracy."

"He points to our presence too."

"Fellow Latins are far more acceptable. Especially to the Contadora nations."

Castro sat back and blew a smoke ring. "Jorgé?"

Cruz shrugged noncommittally. "It's not a major problem. We're due to rotate home a sizable construction crew. Sending over a few naval officers wouldn't affect the balance adversely." He finished with a look that said, It's up to you.

But Castro was still pensive. "It could be construed as military support, no?"

"We can pick men with backgrounds that support the fiction of an engineering mission," Barrista argued. "If you'll help us, we can be at Cienfuegos in the morning, go through the files, make our selections, and be home by nighttime. We need this, Fidel. When we need something as badly as this, we come to the master. We need you now. Don't let us go back empty-handed."

Castro finally arrived at a decision. Smiling expansively, he said, "In that case, you can have the men." He lifted his glass again. "Salud!"

"Salud!" came the response from his men.

Got you, you fat, insufferable prick, thought Barrista to himself. He lifted his glass.

"Salud, Fidel."

The naval station at Cienfuegos on Cuba's southern coast is the Soviet's submarine base and naval-training center in the Western hemisphere. Only by the most delicate of interpretations, however, did the docking of nuclear submarines there not constitute a breach of the unwritten agreement with the United States never to put nuclear weapons on Cuban soil. Stable for over twenty years, the situation would remain that way as long as, in the American view, the vital elements of control and ownership remained solidly and irrevocably in Russian hands.

Outside the base's administration building, where Miguel and Barrista had spent the morning poring over personnel files, the ocean and sky were the same deep azure blue. Castro's imprimatur on the project had given them access to everything they needed.

After a brief meeting with the senior personnel officer they were left alone in a conference room to read, with clerks bringing them any material they requested. In a few hours an initial group of over two hundred qualified officers had been narrowed down to thirty men; twenty in one group to fill the ostensible purpose of their visit, ten other possible candidates to meet their real need.

Miguel had conducted a thorough inspection of the room to make sure they weren't bugged. He was satisfied they could speak freely.

"What do you think of the first group?" he asked the Defense Minister.

"They're fine. Who knows? As long as we've got them, we may even start a training program. It's the least we can do now that Fidel's been so generous."

"Brandy and cigars," observed Miguel, shaking his head. "Long way from the jungle."

"As far as we are from the mountains, no? You shouldn't be so narrow-minded. Even revolutionaries prefer to take a crap indoors."

Miguel shrugged and picked up a file. "What do you think of this one? Lieutenant Jesus Castalzo. He's trained on Russian heavy crusiers. Antisubmarine experience too. No actual time on subs though."

"He's useless without that. But even that's not everything. We're looking for a particular type. An angry man, angry enough to go renegade. Look for the officer who's been denied rank or one who's been broken down a few notches. Look for negative ratings by his superior. You can't expect to turn a man who loves his service and is loved in return. Find me the odd man out, the one who never quite fit in."

Miguel picked up another file. Barrista turned back to the one he was reading. Several more officers had the requisite experience but none had the necessary personality. Over several more hours they were all rejected. Barrista called for more files.

"What about this one?" Miguel said, looking over one from the new group. "Captain Luis Santillo, born here in

1945 in the town of Antilla. He has experience in submarines, mostly diesel, but did one tour as a very junior officer on a Russian nuclear attack boat."

"What's his service record look like?"

Miguel turned a few pages and his eyes widened. "Christ, Phillipe. It doesn't look like there's anyone this guy didn't alienate. Listen to the adjectives—capable but erratic, impertinent, undisciplined, sometimes brilliant and incisive but lacking in self-control. . . . It goes on from there."

"Where is he now?"

"Captaining a tug in the harbor at this base."

Barrista's interest quickened. "That's no position for a man with his experience."

"Somebody must have shunted him aside. Let me see."

"San-tee-yo." Barrista stretched out the syllables. "Anything else?"

"This is probably it. The stated reason for his being passed over was his 'ideological incorrectness.' Apparently he doesn't love the Russians. He's quoted as resenting their influence here. Called Cubans second-class citizens."

"The Russians must have loved that," Barrista mused. "And Santillo's had years to stew over what they did to him."

"So we see this one?"

Barrista took the file. "Absolutely. He'll probably need to be flattered, someone to cater to his bruised ego. If necessary, can you summon up sufficient anti-Soviet sentiment to appease him?"

"I'll have to dig way down for it."

Barrista sighed. "I wish you'd be less sarcastic."

"It's more difficult these days. But relax, Phillipe, if it plays that way, Santillo will find me in perfect sympathy."

"Good. But if I've got him pegged right, we may not need it. Let's go. I want to meet him." A thought struck him. "Let him know we're coming. His reaction ought to be interesting."

Miguel called in a clerk and made the arrangements. The clerk hurried out. Minutes later another clerk came in to tell them that a car was waiting to take them to the dock. A launch would be waiting there.

Miguel put the folders back into piles. "What will you offer him?" he asked.

"What he's always been looking for and never found here." Barrista put on a pair of sunglasses and tucked Santillo's file under his arm. He seemed supremely confident.

"You never met the man," Miguel protested. "How do you know what he's looking for?"

"I know."

"How?" Miguel pressed.

"I'm surprised at you. Read the file. I should think it's obvious."

"I hate when you do this."

"Well, think. Santillo was given great opportunity but was never happy or satisfied. Why do you think that was?"

"According to him, he resented not being treated as an equal by the Russians."

Barrista's expression was one a father might wear when a favorite child still missed the obvious. "Miguel, a man who argues incessantly about everybody else's position is usually most concerned about his own. It wasn't that the Russians didn't listen to the Cubans, it was that they didn't listen to Santillo. He never wanted equality. That he could have earned. He wanted superiority, to be in command, a chance to show up everybody, Russians and Cubans. So that's what we'll offer him in one short step—superiority. I think he'll see it coming and jump at it."

"That's why you want him notified we're coming out to see him."

"Yes."

"You're malevolent."

"I prefer manipulative."

"Tell me, Phillipe, do you play me this well too?"

Barrista looked hurt. "You should know better. You mean . . . more."

"I . . . I'm sorry."

Barrista patted him on the shoulder. "All right. Forget it was said. Let's see this man and cater to his ambition. Come. You'll see I'm right." He walked away.

"You always are, damn you," Miguel whispered.

Barrista didn't hear him. He was already out the door.

* * *

The harbor tug was a soiled old scow. Different shades of wood patched her sides and the wheelhouse needed a painting. The launch waited about a hundred yards back till the tug disengaged from the barge it was nudging into a slip, then the pilot brought them across the intervening water and sailors from the tug reined them in against it.

Barrista was the first over. "Captain Santillo?" he asked the first man.

"In the wheelhouse. I'll bring you."

Miguel followed them around the wet, wooden deck. The sailor opened the wheelhouse door and indicated they were to go in. They passed through into the dim interior.

"Good afternoon, comrades," said a pleasant voice.

They had their first good look at Captain Santillo. He was an ascetic-looking man with a loose-jointed way of swaying with the boat's roll. His uniform was sharply pressed, his neat appearance in marked contrast to his boat. *I am not of this,* was the message, Miguel decided. He held out his hand.

"I am Miguel Segurra. Allow me to present the Sandinista Minister of Defense for all Nicaragua, Phillipe Barrista. I am his First Deputy. We appreciate your seeing us on such short notice."

Santillo nodded. "Comrade Minister, Comrade Deputy Minister. Welcome to my boat." He shook hands with both.

Miguel noticed how large Santillo's hands were when he rewrapped them around the wooden wheel; like long, gnarled pieces of some dark-grained wood. They were somehow at odds with the man's neat precision.

"I trust you were informed we were coming," Barrista said, speaking for the first time.

Santillo indicated the tug's radio. "I was. Will you tell me why?"

Miguel began to see it. Not so much an arrogance, but a straightforwardness that denied traditional humility. He was too direct for a subordinate. Gods from on high had arrived and he didn't even blink.

"I can only tell you we have it from the highest Cuban authority that you are free to come with us, and that your time on this garbage scow is over if you wish it to be,"

Barrista said. "Is that inducement enough to put off explanations till later?"

Santillo put a latch cord over a spoke and released the wheel. "Julio!" he called out. A man poked his head through the hatch from below. "Si?"

"You're in command."

"Si, Capitán." He climbed into the small cabin and took the wheel.

Santillo looked at his visitors. "Comrades?"

Barrista nodded and turned to go. Santillo followed. Miguel watched Santillo's departing back. That easily? Without even a second thought the man walked off with them? He applied Phillipe's logic. It began to make sense.

They'd chosen the right man. Captain Santillo would go with the side that promised him his place in the sun—the place he felt he deserved. The Defense Minister of Nicaragua had to be offering something better than this miserable tug. Destiny waited, walking in Barrista's form.

No wonder, then, that the arrival of the gods hadn't really surprised Santillo.

He'd been expecting them sooner or later all along.

13

U.S. NAVAL BASE, GUANTANAMO, CUBA

A Navy tug nudged *Aspen*'s bow through the clear, blue water into the waiting slip, and crewmen along the sub's length caught the heavy lines thrown from the dock and secured her to the pier. Supervising the operation from the bridge, MacKenzie brought his ship to stand-down and felt a small release of internal pressure once they were formally moored in safe harbor.

Several cars were waiting on the concrete pier. As soon as *Aspen* docked, a junior lieutenant carrying a file folder emerged from one of them and trotted down the gangway. The supervising officerr accepted the folder, and seconds later it was in MacKenzie's hands. He read the contents and summoned Lasovic.

"Get Frank and tell him we're wanted at the base commander's office. And inform the Segurras that a car is waiting for them. Wait. Cancel that. You just see Frank. I'll take care of the rest."

Brushing by the curious look on Lasovic's face, MacKenzie climbed down from the bridge. He made his way aft and knocked on his cabin door.

"Yes?"

"It's MacKenzie. May I come in?"

The door opened. "Of course, Captain," Justine said pleasantly. "After all, it's yours. Are we docked yet?"

"A few minutes ago." MacKenzie sat in his desk chair and Justine folded herself back on the bed. "I came to tell you there's a car waiting for you and your brother."

"You're kind to come yourself."

MacKenzie shifted uncomfortably. "Justine, I came because I wanted to see you before you left. When you walk off *Aspen* I may have no way of reaching you again. That felt, well . . . unsettling, I suppose."

"That's an odd word, Peter."

MacKenzie leaned closer. "A good word, though, because that's what your being here has done to . . . you called me Peter?"

"Non-crew privilege." She was smiling.

"Justine, I'd like us to talk if we can find the time later. Over some coffee maybe." He said it seriously. "Okay?"

She hesitated, then reached out and put a long finger on the back of his hand. "All right."

He straightened. "Good. You know, it occurred to me before that I never even showed you around the ship."

"You were busy."

"Not very romantic, I guess."

She laughed. "Did they make submarines to be?"

"No." He liked looking at her. "They don't usually include that."

"I may have to fly to Washington," she said abruptly.

"Tonight?"

"It's possible. Depends on who's come down here. If they're of sufficient rank, I may not have to go back."

"Let's hope," he said earnestly.

"Yes."

"We have to go now. You have everything?"

She nodded. "Everything. Which means only what the storm left me, what I'm wearing."

He looked towards the XO's cabin. "I haven't seen Sebastion."

"He went forward. Walking takes kinks out of his legs. He's still in considerable pain."

"The base hospital will do a lot more for him than we could. I enjoyed our talk. He gave me quite a bit to think about."

"That's the usual result of a talk with Sebastion," Justine said.

"He watches out for you, you know."

"He tries to anyway." She sighed. "He always has. But the two of us, well . . . we have our differences."

"He told me. But can they be so deep if you could play music together like that?"

Her eyes grew sad for a moment. "It's funny, Peter. Most people grow apart because they have too much time between them. I think Sebastion and I have too much music. That night was an interlude only."

"I don't follow."

"There's no way you could," she said sympathetically. "Maybe sometime I can explain it."

"Maybe later?"

"Maybe."

"Try and leave word where you are." MacKenzie said, standing.

"Yes, Peter. If I can."

"If I don't see Sebastion, wish him good luck for me."

"I'll tell him. He'll appreciate it. He likes you."

MacKenzie's face went mock serious. "That's nice. But it's his sister I'm concerned about."

Justine got off the bed, a sudden glint of laughter in her eyes. "Don't be," she said. "His sister likes you too."

"Later then?"

"Later," she agreed.

MacKenzie left the cabin and made his way out to the pier. Lasovic and Lieberman were already in the car. He got in and opened the windows to savor the warm, flower-scented air, so sweet after the days of confinement. The driver wheeled out and headed for the base commander's offices.

Admiral Benton Garver studied the charts Lieberman had spread out on the table and said happily, "So that's how the bastards are doing it."

MacKenzie pointed out the more detailed hydrographic surveys on the wall-mounted, computerized video display and grimaced. "They caught us napping, sir. Look at that survey. The Cayman Trench is a virtual blank."

"It was never a feasible avenue for us," said Lieberman. "The Alfas dive much deeper than we do. Sure, they're noisier than hell, but that's their design trade-off. No one figured the Trench for a practical route, much less one that's deep enough to eat the Alfa's sound. And why spend the time mapping what no one's going to be using?"

"We'll have to now," said Garver, a stocky man with a jowly, bulldog face. "Probably have to plant hydrophones and mine it too."

"In a pinch you could catch quite a few titanium fish in that net," observed Lieberman, his reference to the material of the Alfa's hull. Titanium was enormously expensive, but the Soviet Union had large reserves, and it was far stronger than steel. The cost, though, limited its use to the single class of attack subs.

"That's a lovely thought," Garver agreed. "What do you say, Mac?"

MacKenzie's eyes were on the video display. "I'd station a sub here." He used an electronic marker to make a point on the display glow. "She'd lie dead silent and listen to the traffic. Once we got a fix on what was coming through, I'd put a SOSUS array across here and here." More points glowed. "The mines across here and here."

The display looked like strings of Christmas lights. Garver nodded. "We'd have to use a DSRV to do the real deep mapping, and one of the specially built SOSUS subs to lay in the 'phones."

"Say two weeks for the surveillance sub," Lasovic added.

"When will a DSRV be ready?" asked MacKenzie. The Deep Submergence Rescue Vehicles were actually rescue submarines which could be transported anywhere in the world a submarine disaster had occurred. Carried by special aircraft, the DSRV's looked like long, fat torpedoes. They were capable of diving down to over five thousand feet, and when mated to a mother sub from which they dove, returned, recharged batteries, and dove again, transferring a full complement of officers and crew off a downed sub in approximately seventeen hours.

Garver said, "They're using *Mystic* off Pearl for salvage work, and *Avalon* is being refitted. We should have her back in a week or so."

"The whole job could be done in less than a month then," Lasovic concluded.

Garver looked at the VDT and punched in a command to the desktop keyboard. The view drew back to include the entire region. "Christ, almost a tunnel straight to the canal, and we didn't even spot it. Turn your fucking hair gray. How close can they get?"

Lieberman answered. "Maybe four hundred miles."

"Goddamned Tomahawks could do that in a few minutes of flight. Radar would never see them. Their cruise missiles aren't as good, but almost. One shot and *poof*, no more canal."

"In an emergency we'd also have their attack subs all over this area covering our southern tanker routes," MacKenzie added. "Make the North Sea during World War Two look like a mill pond."

"Shit, yes," Garver agreed. "Well, let's all pat ourselves on the back, then, for being so damn vigilant it's never going to happen. Privately, you should know there are a whole lot of brass very happy with *Aspen*'s findings. Our collective asses could have been in some very hot water over this one."

"Tom gets full credit," MacKenzie said firmly. "If he hadn't waited by the Trench, it would have been chalked up to just one more contact in a big sea. If that's not stated clearly, Admiral, I'll want to write an addendum." He added graciously, "With your permission, sir, of course."

"Don't bully me, Mac. And don't steal my goddamned thunder. Tom has already been cited for the find, as you requested, and a string of commendations go along with it. Maybe his own command too. What do you say to that, Mr. Lasovic?"

"I'd say fine, sir. Real fine. Thank you."

"You're welcome."

"But it was Mac here who should get the credit for—" Lasovic began.

Garver cut him off. "Captain MacKenzie, will you please take this mutual admiration society out of my office before I get ill?" His face relaxed. "You all did a good job. Now get out of here and feel free to do some serious drinking. *Aspen*'s not going back out till we decide what to do about the Trench. We may even have to do a quick refit."

MacKenzie's mind turned to other agendas with the speed of his sudden release from responsibility. He was halfway out the door when Garver called him back in tones only an admiral could muster. "MacKenzie!"

He stopped short. "Sir?"

"You're not in your goddamned submarine now, mister. Remember to salute, damn you."

"Yes, sir," MacKenzie snapped, flipping his hand to the peak of his cap smartly. Then he was out the door.

Terrence Holmes was the senior CIA liaison officer in the region, and he had known Justine for several years. In a nondescript meeting room he sat across from her at a gray steel table with only a tape recorder and a phone on its surface. Holmes was a large, florid man, forever sweating in the tropical heat. He had a keen mind, and knew the intrigues of the region better than any man short of the senior chiefs of the Latin desk.

"Then it was the Cuban doctor who took out Torres?" he asked.

Justine had honestly reported all the other details of the contra raid but Miguel's suspected presence in the interrogation chamber. She shrugged. "Manuel got careless. The doctor had a hypo hidden in his hand, and I was concentrating on Sebastion. Manuel got stabbed when he turned away. He fired as he fell and took out both Cubans."

"You hefted your brother up the stairs yourself?"

"Some of the way. He was semi-conscious at that point and helped somewhat. The soldiers at the top of the stairs heard us and took him from me. I got the jeeps loaded and got us out of there. I've already told you about the trek over the mountains and the storm boarding the sub. That's all."

"Too bad about Torres," Holmes said. "Otherwise, it was a good mission."

"We got Sebastion out," Justine said hotly. "That's what we went in for. It's still a good mission."

"Agreed. Odd though. Torres wasn't a careless man."

Justine fixed him with a hard stare. "Not twice anyway."

"True enough," Holmes said. His *camiseta*, the cotton shirt worn outside one's trousers, was wet, stained in half-moons at both armpits. He took a crumpled handkerchief out of a pocket and wiped his face. "Your brother's still a problem, you know."

"Not mine," Justine said flatly.

"Since when are there *your* problems and *our* problems?"

"When they concern something I have no power over. I can't control him any more than you can."

"We'd very much like him to place himself under our umbrella."

She laughed. "So would I, but he won't. Besides, I thought the consensus was that he still makes our opposition to the Sandinistas more credible regardless. The 'if he left them, they might just be as bad as the untrustworthy CIA says they are' school of thought."

"That does have its value, true. But there is a growing concern that his independence might threaten the military operation. This isn't a tea party you come to when you please. There are goals and objectives, timetables. We need very close cooperation."

"Why tell me this?"

"I want you to speak to him again."

Justine sighed. "It's pointless, I tell you."

"We lose nothing by asking," Holmes insisted. "And he is in our debt now. He might listen to reason."

Justine frowned. "Tell me something, Terry. I may be getting stupider in my old age, but even for me the mists begin to clear. Wouldn't you have been just as happy if Sebastion hadn't made it back?"

"I can't truthfully deny that. Your brother is a willful prima donna."

She looked closely at the man opposite her. "Manuel had the terminate order, didn't he." It was no question.

"No. He had the same brief as you did—get the man out to prevent the information in his head from getting to the Sandinistas. That's a fact."

"And if we couldn't get him out?"

It was Holmes's time to turn hard. "He would have been expected to do exactly what you would have been expected to do. But that's not the point. Come on, Justine, we sent in a rescue team, not a hit squad. For Christ's sake, we sent *you* in."

Justine let up. "All right, Terry. I'll speak to him."

"Thank you."

"And afterwards?"

"We'll play it by ear. But remember, this is no Bay of Pigs. No back outs are possible. We can't let these people down. On August first we go in."

"Where do you want me till then?"

Holmes mopped his face and wished, not for the first time, that he'd studied arctic history rather than Latin American. "You still have the apartment in Miami?"

She nodded.

"Take Sebastion there. Do what you can. Use the rest of the time to take it easy and heal. Get well. How's the shoulder?"

"Stiff. I'm not sure about the arm either."

"Stay here for a day or two, then, and get in some time at the gym. I'll need you in the contras' camp a few days before the first. You'll be in planning sessions till then."

"You're coming up to Miami?"

"Close enough. We're setting up an operations center at Homestead Air Force Base."

"Who's taking over for Torres in Honduras?"

"Major Ramirez. He led the raid on the bank for your diversion."

"I remember. A good man. No hothead; no Somocista either."

"I'm glad you approve. He's sent you his regards and the hope that Doña Justine will be with them when they enter Nicaragua. That symbol is very important to them."

"I'm just a person, Terry, no symbol of anything."

He shook his head. "The girl who led the Angel's Choir at nine and fought beside her father and brothers for fifteen years is more than just a person, Justine. A bus driver is a person. So's a butcher. You're more than that. Heroines have to be."

"There were no heroines, only very frightened children. And I'd rather we didn't discuss this further, if you don't mind."

She'd grown pale, and Holmes had no desire to hurt her more than the memories already had. "As you wish. By the way, the Director sends his compliments. You really did do a fine job. Please take care of yourself. I'll see you in a week." He stood to go.

"Good-bye, Terry."

"Adios, Justine."

After Holmes left, she sat for a while by herself. Patriotism, she decided, should be noble speeches and grand entrances, not uncertain, ordinary people planning questionable deeds in small, barren rooms. But these were the people to whom it had fallen. Ramirez was a good choice to replace Torres. He was a moderate, and they were going to need moderates after August first. At least everybody had learned that much, the American president and the CIA included. Security lay in like-minded democrats, not strong-armed tyranny. No more Somozas, just dedicated, rational men who believed in pluralism, who knew that America was the last, great hope of achieving human freedom, and were its allies by choice.

She picked up the phone and told the special operator to reserve time for her with the base instructor at the gym, as Holmes had suggested. She left word for Sebastion at the base hospital that they would be leaving for Miami in the next day or so. As usual he would stay with her for a day or so, then contact his expatriate backers and fade back into the shadowy world of Latin exiles. They would get him back to his troops. She'd offer anyway. He'd seen the force she could muster; maybe it would change his mind.

And MacKenzie? A surprisingly warm feeling accompanied the mental image. Maybe it was just gratitude for saving her life. Or maybe someone had finally struck a responsive chord in her, she thought. There was complexity to the man. He was tenacious and competent and she valued both qualities. At the same time he was attractively vulnerable, as if he, too, came at his emotions with some difficulty.

A mischievous gleam appeared in her eyes. She picked up the phone. While she played on the sub she'd shown him a very private part of herself. But lest he think that was all there was to her, maybe another kind of performance was necessary. If he was going to be frightened away, she wanted to know now. She wasn't easy—never that.

Let's see what the man does, she decided. She called the Base Commander's office and asked to speak to Captain MacKenzie. He was out, but could be reached. Did she wish to leave a message?

She left word he could meet her at the gym in half an hour.

14

                              GUANTANAMO NAVAL BASE
MacKenzie got Justine's message in the tidy, little efficiency apartment he'd been assigned to for the duration of his stay on the base. Off duty, he pulled on a pair of jeans, rolled up the sleeves of a loose-fitting white shirt which he left untucked, and slipped into a pair of tennis sneakers. The gym was only a few blocks away. He decided to walk.

The summer air was a balm. Navy jeeps scurried back and forth to the docks like fat beetles. Beyond the rows of buildings, out of his sight, were the electronic eavesdropping devices that monitored Cuba's radio traffic. Beyond those were the perimeter fences, the barbed wire, and the no-man's-land that separated American territory from Cuban.

MacKenzie headed into the gym. Most personnel were working this early in the afternoon, so the building was fairly quiet. A few men were lifting in the weight room, and MacKenzie passed two sweaty joggers on the inside track, but the basketball courts and the apparatus rooms were empty. Justine had said the gym, hadn't she?

He went downstairs. This level had rooms whose floors were covered with thick rubber mats. The lights were out in all but one, and sounds were coming out of that one. MacKenzie went to the door and looked in.

It had the same rubber mats on the floor, but this room was much bigger than the others and had rows of bleacherlike seats for spectators. One wall was mirrored and had a stretching bar across it. The rest were uniformly white.

Justine stood in the center of the room. She was dressed in a black, sleeveless body leotard that left her arms and legs bare. MacKenzie could see one arm still had a pressure bandage on it, tightly secured. Her hair was pulled back into a tight bun, and she looked for all the world like a ballerina getting ready to perform. She was moving in a slow circle, alternating a series of kicks and stretching movements. But they were too sharp and forceful for ballet. Justine continued her movements in front of the well-built man crouched about four feet away.

MacKenzie sat down quietly on one of the benches. He made no move to call to her, knowing the attention of both *karateka* was centered only on each other for the duration of their encounter. *Kumite*, the ritual combat—his mind delivered the word from his own training years before.

The man facing Justine wore the traditional karate uniform, a loose white cotton tunic and trousers tied around the waist with a colored belt; in the man's case, a black belt, the highest rank of the traditional system of colors—white, yellow, green, brown, and black.

Legend held that the earliest initiates conducted their workouts on grassy fields and began with belts of pure white. As training went on, the novice's belt, which unlike the uniform is never washed, began to grow dirtier and dirtier from uncountable kicks and spills and falls, first turning dirty yellow, then grass-stained green, then grimy brown. Finally, when the belt had been in use long enough to have turned black, a master had been created. To this day, in honor of that tradition, *karateka* never wash their belts.

MacKenzie was fascinated. He judged the man to be in his late forties, and he had the advantage over Justine of at least sixty pounds in weight and six inches in height. He fought out of a cat stance—crouched back and turned slightly sideways, with most of the weight on the back leg. The front leg remained lightly balanced on the ball of the foot, ready to snap out a kick. His hands were extended halfway in front of him, moving slowly, curled open and ready to block, punch, or grab.

Justine's stance was more unconventional. She was bouncing quickly and lithely, shifting her weight from side to side in a kind of boxer's rhythm. She seemed quicker than the man and would have the advantage of speed. But she would have to be quick indeed to negate his superior strength. Judging from his physique, she was going to have to be very good to beat him.

The black belt suddenly drew himself up and bowed from the waist. Justine's head came up quickly and took in MacKenzie's presence. Then she bowed as well. The man nodded, and they began to circle in earnest.

Their first moves were exploratory. Justine threw a short front kick which the black belt blocked, continuing into a turnaround side kick to her midriff in return. Justine danced out of the way and kicked for his head with a snap roundhouse, but the man ducked out of the way and she connected only with air as he moved past her.

They faced each other again in fighting stance. It was the black belt's turn to be more aggressive. He leaped forward with a back fist to her head, his hand snapping out like a flicked towel. Justine had to fall back. His leg shot out in a thrusting side kick that she barely blocked, and he continued on in with a second side kick delivered jump-style. It caught her in the stomach and almost drove her over backwards, but she found her balance and countered with a neat spinning turnaround back kick that the black belt had to drop to the mat to avoid.

Sweat began to shine on both their bodies. Justine was breathing harder, controlling her exertions. The black belt was in superb condition. He moved lightly back into cat stance, springing forward, carefully balanced to keep his three weapons—both hands and his front foot—on the forward line of his attack.

He came at her hard, pressing her back with a series of hard, straight punches followed by one jumping side kick after another. Again he connected, and this time Justine went down on her back. He was on her in a flash, his hand slicing downward, straightened into a knife-edged, stiff-fingered weapon right for her exposed neck. A final *"Ke-yi!"*—the explosive cry of total commitment to the blow—and it was clear she would have been finished had not he stopped the strike a fraction of an inch from her skin.

She got up and bowed. He returned it. MacKenzie saw his eyes flick to the side and saw her nod. A few sets of safety kicks and safety gloves hung from the bar. If they were going to use them, it meant they were increasing the degree of contact. Head shots that connected were now acceptable. Punches and kicks could connect more fully.

The gloves extended over the back of the hand and covered the knuckles, but left the palm free to grab or block. The kicks were similar, covering the top of the foot, the heel, and the toes. The ball of the foot was left free for balance.

They bowed. This time, though, the action was faster. Justine had learned her lesson too. If she allowed him to gain too much forward momentum, his size and strength made him too much to stop. She had to press first, gain the upper hand, and swiftly move in for the kill.

She threw a snap front kick to bring his hands down, and he did just that, trying to block it. She leaped in with a spinning back fist to his head and partially connected, but the force of the blow was diluted by the gloves and his turning out of the way. He got his hands up and punched at her body, augmenting it with a thrusting side kick to back her off, but she blocked the kick neatly, moved in past it and delivered a straight punch right to his jaw.

It was a well-timed inside move, and regardless of the gloves, snapped his head back. She side-kicked him in the chest and drove him over backwards. He fell to the mat, where Justine delivered the final head stomp which he could not have avoided if she had truly been committed to the blow. She *Ke-yi*'ed and moved away. A smile crossed the black belt's face in acknowledgment. He executed a shoulder spring and was up facing her as soon as she backed away.

She bowed, this time challengingly, and the black belt's smile increased. He let her come at him. Again she drove forward, her leg snapping up at his face. But he wasn't about to be taken in by the same tactic twice. He let her come, blocking and parrying her blows, each time increasing the distance between them. Justine began leaning forward to make it up and lengthening her moves. It was her undoing. Suddenly the black belt leaped into the air with both legs thrown forward in a flying V. Justine threw up her hands, but his body sailed past her unsteady block. He landed with both legs astride her shoulders, straddling her head. He locked his legs and twisted his body as soon as he hit, and Justine was flung to the mat like a rag doll grabbed by the neck. She lay helplessly pinned under him as he delivered the final strike and rolled off.

MacKenzie was amazed. He'd never seen a fighting technique incorporate a standing jump like that. Often black belts worked out special personal moves that were unique to them. This must be one, he concluded. In any case it had taken Justine completely by surprise. For many the defeat would have been humiliating. In Justine he saw the look of redetermination appear on her face. She bowed with genuine respect, then put up her hands and gestured for a final encounter. The black belt dropped back into stance.

Both were being cautious. Neither would win with the same technique again. They threw a few kicks and punches, more to study timing than anything else. They circled warily, looking for an opening.

Justine was breathing heavily now. Her chest heaved and her kicks had less force behind them. The black belt saw her flagging and began to move in. He dove in behind a back fist and launched a kick to her middle. She narrowly sidestepped it and launched a weak front kick to his stomach. The black belt saw it coming. Here was the opportunity he'd been waiting for. Plenty of time to grab her foot and wrench it high over her head to dump her over backwards. He opened his hands and reached down . . .

With perfect balance Justine pivoted on her back foot and brought the kick in mid movement up and around his extended hands, driving it up and over his shoulder in a beautiful roundhouse kick to the side of his head. The black belt was caught fully extended and taken totally by surprise. The ball of her foot crashed into his head just over the ear. As fluid as a dancer, Justine stepped in and grabbed his arm, pivoting again and executing a perfect leg sweep.

The black belt dropped to the mat as if a scythe had cut his legs out from under him. Justine stepped over the arm she still held, and brought it up sharply behind her knee, which acted as a fulcrum against the elbow. She straightened slightly and partially executed the breaking move. The black belt slapped the mat in surrender. She delivered the final partial blow to his head and stepped neatly back. She was breathing quite normally.

The black belt vaulted up and bowed. MacKenzie saw genuine admiration on his face. Justine also bowed, and they both fell forward into a fond embrace, the man slapping her on the back.

"Wonderful, Justine. Just wonderful. I fell for the fake front kick hook, line, and sinker."

"And you?" She shook her head in wonder. "I never saw a move like that flying scissors. Almost broke my neck. I don't know ten men who could do it. Where did you come by that one?"

The black belt grinned. "An acrobat friend of mine. We thought it might be suitable. He worked out the variations." He tossed her a towel.

"Thanks for testing it out on me," she said dryly. She looked over to the bleachers. "Peter? Come on down. I'd like to introduce you."

MacKenzie loped down from his seat and extended his hand. "What a pleasure to watch you both," he said.

Justine made the introductions. "Captain Peter Mac-Kenzie, Dr. Les Triola, the best code expert in the Navy and the quickest hands in this section of Brother Fidel's island paradise."

"Pleased to meet you," MacKenzie said. "Again, that was wonderful to watch."

"There are too few with Justine's ability on this base," replied Triola in acknowledgment. "I can never pass up the opportunity to have my head kicked in when she's here." He rubbed the sore spot ruefully.

"You've known each other for some time then."

Justine said, "A few years. We work out whenever I pass through. This time I wanted to see if my shoulder could take the stress. Get out the kinks."

"It appears to be fine," pronounced Triola wryly. "I'm going to have to teach my students that move."

"With my compliments, Les." She wrapped the towel around her neck. Her damp skin was beginning to cool and form goose bumps as the sweat evaporated. "I've got to shower. Peter, give me twenty minutes? I'll meet you outside."

"Just enough time for me to rustle up a jeep."

"Great. Thanks again, Les. See you next time I'm in." Triola bowed deeply. *"Arigato, Justine-san."*

She trotted off to the shower.

Twenty minutes later MacKenzie decided that the woman who climbed into his jeep couldn't possibly be the same one who'd just beat up the feisty black belt inside the gym. She had on a yellow print strapless sundress and low white heels. Her skin was deeply tanned, and she'd brushed her hair straight so it flowed freely past her strong shoulders. Simple gold earrings hung from her lobes, settling happily against the pulse beat in her long, graceful neck.

"You look lovely," he said, honestly moved. "But I know you came on shore with nothing more than the clothes on your back."

She settled into the seat beside him. "Mercifully, this corner of the island is civilized. A new innovation called stores."

"Oh."

"In a pinch," she said conspiratorially, "we could have smuggled in a dress or two with the local top secret stuff."

"Might be more effective."

"It probably would be."

"Hungry?"

She nodded. "Famished. I gave up lunch to shop. And though the food on that ship of yours was pretty good, now I'm ready for fresh fish, candlelight, and champagne. I want flowers on the table, Peter."

"You can't eat atmosphere."

"Since when?"

"Formica probably. But anticipating your need for refueling after beating up that poor defenseless code expert, the Admiral's Club is waiting to receive us. All the flowers and water view you can eat."

"Peter?"

"Yes?"

She leaned toward him. "Don't I scare you? Even a little?"

"In what way?"

She gestured toward the gym. "Not very ladylike, unarmed combat. And when you fished me out of the drink, I'd just come from an assignment where I ended up having to shoot a fair number of men. I'll probably have to go back there too."

"I thought you CIA guys said terminate."

"Rarely. On the other hand, you've heard me play. I was a concert pianist at the age nine. I've traveled around most of the world performing, and someday, God willing, I may even play professionally again."

MacKenzie took all that in. "So?"

"So some men would be intimidated."

"Ahh," he said.

"Ahh?"

"Ahh. Like in, I see."

"Do you?"

"Sure. You're a woman of many talents. But can you tie a double half-hitch or spot a granny from a square knot?"

"No, but—"

"Or touch your wrist with your thumb?"

"No, but—"

"I can. Double jointed," he said proudly. "Someday I may tour with it."

"Peter?"

"I could have sworn you'd say terminate at least once. Neutralize, maybe?"

"Peter!"

"Yes?"

She was leaning forward, and the bodice of her dress fell more open. Her skin was soft beige, the color of a faun. "We could always skip dinner," she said softly.

He suddenly wanted to reach out and touch that palette of skin more than anything else in his life. His throat was very dry. "You can't eat atmosphere," he said.

She smiled. Her long legs moved under the yellow print. "We can try."

"Ahh . . ." he said.

Late afternoon sunlight slanted across the bed. The sundress came off in his hands. She wore only white bikini briefs underneath, and they slid down her legs like oiled rings. She pulled at his shirt, suddenly insistent, and buttons popped. She yanked it down his back.

His jeans followed. She pulled him towards her but he held back, wanting just to look at her for a moment. Her face was soft in the honeyed light but her mouth was hungry. Proud breasts jutted up from her heaving chest. Her belly was a taut concavity, and the black triangle at the junction of her legs was already moist with desire.

She ran her fingers across his chest, intertwining them in his chest hair. He felt the pain as she pulled him towards her by those dark curls, but it was the kind that didn't hurt. He put his hands on her and she arched her back like a demanding cat.

He kissed her, reveling in her taste and smell. Her breath aroused him. He took her by the throat and kissed her again. Her body pressed up into his. He waited, drawing his lips gently over hers. He let his mouth wander slowly down her neck to her breasts, and heard her gasp. Her hand found him and began to caress. A groan escaped his lips. She twisted out from his grasp and her mouth moved over his body. His hands entwined in her hair, and she dug her fingers into the firm muscles of his buttocks.

She released him and came up on her knees. Her hair was a wild halo around her head. Sweat beaded in the hollow between her breasts. She took his hand and pressed it between her legs. He felt her open to him, grabbed her then and pulled her close, so her chest was soft, full against his. She brought his hand up and put his fingers in her mouth, sucking greedily.

When they finally joined together, it was only just ahead of the cresting wave that had taken them over. Her velvet smoothness engulfed him. He was one central core of fire inside. Rhythms took over and the cadence of need locked in. She wrapped her legs around his back, and he pinned her arms to the bed with his hands. She writhed madly. He covered her mouth with his. They reached the edge together and fell over as one. Once, twice, and again, agonizing stunning eruptions took them both.

She cried out the last time. He buried his face in her hair. Their final sounds intermingled. Breathing began to still into a gentler rhythm. Ending, their motion subsided.

The room was very quiet. A trickle of sweat ran down his side and pooled on her belly. Her lips found a soft spot in the hollow of his neck and nuzzled there. The colors of dusk turned the bed ember red.

They slept.

15

THE CARIBBEAN

The plane carrying Barrista, Miguel, and Santillo swung westward over the island and headed back towards Nicaragua. They were flying into the setting sun. The steward pulled the green shades over the cabin windows, leaving the interior cool with muted light.

Captain Santillo was obviously more pleased with his new surroundings than his old ones. He held his wineglass delicately poised between thumb and forefinger and studied it with relish. To Miguel's careful inspection, he seemed for all the world like a man who had finally come home.

They were sitting in what was almost a living-room type grouping of padded airline seats set around a marble cocktail table. The plane had once belonged to Somoza, so all its appointments were opulent, from the gold-plated faucets to the private bedroom in the rear section. Though it was an obvious affront to Marxist principles, no one had yet seen fit to change a thing.

Miguel caught Barrista's gesture. He wanted Santillo to reveal more of himself so a clearer picture would be generated. This was ultimately in Santillo's best interests. If he learned of their intentions and proved unsuitable for the role, he was going back to Cuba in slightly less luxurious fashion than he had left: inside a body bag.

"It amazes me every time I go back to Cuba," said Miguel, "just how much the Russians have done for Fidel."

Santillo looked over at him. "I'm surprised to hear you, of all people, say that."

"Why so?"

"Because there was never a Russian who did anything for anybody who didn't offer them the greater profit. Nicaragua is a prime example."

"Aren't the Russians our friends?"

"You'd be better off with your enemies," Santillo said flatly. "Besides a few lousy helicopters and a host of advisors, what have they really done to ensure your security? Look at Israel, or El Salvador for that matter. At least when the U.S. arms someone, they have some strength."

"You're pro-U.S.?" Barrista questioned him.

Santillo's face darkened. "I know you're both testing me, Minister, so I'm trying to answer honestly. I think that's why I'm here. But even you must be made aware that I lost good friends on Grenada. Too many for me to want to do anything to the U.S. but see it blown to bits. They are just as bad as the Russians."

"Why would we test you, Captain?"

"I don't know exactly. But your deputy deliberately provokes me. I know you must have read my file. It is no accident I was captaining that scow. If you want me to speak my mind, all you have to do is ask."

"Tell us then."

Santillo's voice grew deadly serious. "Nations like ours are nothing more than pawns in the contest for influence between the superpowers. It will be even worse when China comes into the play. I believe our only hope is to see them all fall."

"How would you accomplish this?"

Santillo sighed. "Unfortunately, I don't know. If anyone offered the answer, I would have joined them years ago. I tried to raise the issue, and for my pains on behalf of my country I was put where you found me. You, I hope, will have a sounder strategy."

Miguel asked him, "Why do you assume we have one at all?"

"Why else would I be here? When you want fish, isn't that what you order? My beliefs are on record. I assumed they were what brought you to me."

"That, and other things," said Barrista.

"Will you tell me what they are?"

"Your knowledge of submarines, for one. Russian submarines, specifically."

Santillo's eyes widened. He was quick, Miguel saw. Already he glimpsed the truth of it. Shadowy, to be sure, but the glimpse was enough. "I knew it!" He pounded his fist into the arm of his chair. "I knew someday my words would fall on the right ears, ears belonging to powerful men. You're after a Soviet sub! I tell you, it can be done. It most certainly can."

"Tell us how," prompted Miguel.

"It's true then? You're really planning to steal one?"

Barrista nodded. "We would appreciate your thoughts on the matter. How many men would it take?"

"Fewer than you think. Most of the officers are asleep at any one time. I'd need a Chief Engineer, a Weapons Officer, and a good Sonar man. Maybe one other to act as second-in-command. There are any number of men in the Cuban navy who would fit the bill and feel the way I do. Do you have the power to arrange their transfers?"

"We do. But where would you find the rest of the crew?"

"We could use some of your men, but the best bet would be to use the sub's own crew. Russian seamen are like trained dogs. They'll follow anyone with a tone of command in his voice. If you substitute one of your own men as Political Officer and he quotes enough Lenin, they would kiss his shoes if he ordered them to. The main thing is replacing the officers. They're the only ones left with some capacity to think."

Barrista nodded slowly. This was the right man. His own plans grew clearer, more distinct. But Santillo was still speaking,

". . . nuclear-tipped cruise missiles. The Russian subs in this area all carry them. They were put in after the U.S. deployed the Pershings in Europe." His eyes were bright. "You could start a fine war, Minister. Both sides would think it was the other. They'd have to respond. If the—"

Barrista cut him off coldly. "You misunderstand, Captain. That tired old scenario will never take place. No one survives a nuclear war, especially not the countries a few hundred miles from the superpowers' borders. There will not be a single shot fired. No war. No conflict. In fact that's what we propose to prevent."

"Why do you need a sub then?"

"Nuclear blackmail, Mutually Assured Destruction, call it what you like. We are targeted for a U.S. invasion. The retaliatory power of a nuclear sub will prevent it."

The light in Santillo's eyes was back. "I see. It's brilliant. They wouldn't dare attack if you could respond in such a way."

"But there is a problem," Miguel said. "Assume we steal the sub. What's to prevent them from attacking it, dropping a nuclear bomb on it, or just hunting it down with their own subs?"

Santillo grew thoughtful. "A trip wire," he said after a while. "That would prevent it."

"Explain, please," requested Barrista.

"Well, you know what a trip wire is, Minister—a line stretched across a trail or around a perimeter. It's attached to a grenade or a gun emplacement, and anyone tripping the line activates the weapon automatically. No recall. Just trip it, and boom. We would have to set one up, a trip-wire defense."

"How do you do that in the ocean?"

"You use an imaginary line, just what latitude and longitude are. Set up an area of . . . interdiction, let's call it. Somewhere around a few thousand square miles. Extend your sonar out to that limit and be ready to launch the second anything crosses into that zone. Anything by air or sea, on it or under, would trip the wire. They wouldn't dare to cross it. Inside the zone you patrol on a random course. There's no weapon made that wouldn't give you at least enough warning to launch. They'd know that. They'd have to back off."

"A standoff," Miguel said.

Santillo nodded. "Actually a real launch-on-warning situation. By the nature of the threat they'd have to assume you were willing to die. That's what makes it credible."

"Are you?" Barrista studied him. "Ready to die, I mean."

"Rather than go back to that tug," Santillo said fervently. "But if this is set up right, no one has to die. No president is going to go after you if it means losing Houston or Miami."

Barrista looked to Miguel. Santillo's ideas fit perfectly into their own. A sub was a self-contained, totally independent launch platform. No external support was necessary. The nuclear fuel was good for many years. All the telemetry and guidance was computerized and built into the sub. Parts could be extorted later, as the need arose. In one single step Nicaragua would become the world's newest nuclear power. It was dazzling in its simplicity. He saw confirmation in Miguel's eyes.

Santillo spoke up. "Excuse me, Minister. May I ask a question?"

"Of course."

"The Russians guard their subs with a caution that borders on mania. How do you intend to get on one, much less take it over?"

Barrista's smile was enigmatic. "I can't explain it all to you now, Captain, but suffice it to say we are going to take a lesson from the very first revolutionary."

"We're talking about Sandino? Guevara?"

"Neither. Long before them. I'm talking about Jesus Christ."

"He's going to help you capture a sub?"

"The fisher of souls. Yes, He is. In that very way."

Santillo's face grew wary. "You're toying with me."

Barrista shook his head. "Not at all. Miguel will tell you. Do you know your bible, Captain? I had it pounded into me by some very strict, rod-carrying nuns from the time I was five. Matthew five, verse eighteen. 'As He walked by the sea He saw two brothers casting their net into the sea, for they were fishermen.' Miguel? Finish it, if you please."

"'And He said to them,'" Miguel intoned, "'Follow me and I will make you fishers of men.' Verse nineteen, Captain. Do you see?"

Santillo was no one's fool. He nodded slowly, "Yes, I think I do."

"Welcome to the disciples, Captain Santillo."

"Thank you, Deputy Minister."

Barrista said, "Amen."

16

GUANTANAMO BASE

Justine had a small efficiency apartment similar to Mac-Kenzie's, and she was moving around it now, rummaging through cabinets to find the makings for coffee. She was wearing only a kimono robe that came to mid thigh, and a happy expression.

MacKenzie was content to watch her from his vantage point on the rumpled bed. He liked the fact that she was humming. It was dark out, and he had swtiched on one of the lights. He had a pleasant feeling of isolation with the drapes drawn. For a time the rest of the world would continue along quite nicely without them.

"Damn," swore Justine mildly. "Nothing here but old tea bags and some sugar. That will have to do."

"Tea's fine," he said. "Come back to bed."

"Let me get the heat on."

MacKenzie tried leering at her.

She looked at him quizzically. "What's wrong with your face?"

"I'm leering at you."

"You look all bug-eyed."

"I'm communicating sexual desire."

She laughed. "I've already gotten the message." She stopped for a moment to look at him warmly. "It was lovely, Peter. That's my message."

He smiled. "You're the only one who calls me that, you know."

"Lovely?"

"Peter. Everyone else calls me Mac. I think I hate Peter. Not as much when you say it, but usually."

"Really? Why?"

He shrugged. "What I really hate is Pete, or Petey. People also seem to find Peter impossible to pronounce. It's always Peder, or Pee-tah. Nobody mispronounces Mac."

"No one mispronounces Jocko, either, but it's equally as inelegant."

"Maybe. You can use Peter if you want."

She put the cups on saucers and added sugar. "We'll see. I'll use both and decide which one I like best. Mac makes me feel like I'm talking to some Navy drinking buddy."

MacKenzie looked at the bed's disarray. "We must have really tied one on."

"Fool."

He grinned. "You were the one who suggested skipping dinner."

"You're sorry?"

"You're kidding."

She smiled too.

The teapot whistled and she took it off the flame. She filled the two cups with the steaming water, brought them over to the bed, and sat down cross-legged next to him. He put a pillow behind his head to prop himself up and balanced the saucer on his chest.

"Sebastion called you another name. What was it?" he asked her.

"Justiniaña. My full name is Maria Justiniaña Segurra Carera. Carera was my mother's maiden name. She died when I was seven. A peaceful woman, very loving.

Sebastion remembers her better than I do. Miguel barely knew her."

"Miguel?"

"Oh, I forgot. Sebastion and I aren't the only Segurras. Miguel is our younger brother. I haven't seen him in years . . . at least not directly." She paused. "He is a committed Sandinista. The Deputy Minister of Defense under a ruthless man named Barrista."

MacKenzie was surprised. "I thought there was just you and Sebastion. I guess it's like he said, there are Segurras on every side."

Justine nodded sadly. "Wars split people, families. We couldn't agree on anything at the end. Sebastion left Miguel. I left Sebastion. It goes on still."

"What did you mean when you said you haven't seen Miguel, at least not directly? On television?"

"No. He's not one of the ruling nine." She told him about the contra raid. ". . . when I woke up, Torres was dead. Since he'd already killed the two Cubans, there are only two possibilities. Whoever knocked me out killed him, but that makes no sense because anyone who would have killed Torres would have killed me too. Or Torres himself knocked me out and someone killed Torres to protect me, and Sebastion, maybe."

She paused to take a sip of tea. "It's no secret that my superiors would have been just as happy to see Sebastion fail to return as long as his knowledge died with him. Believe me, it would solve quite a few problems. Torres may have decided to do a good deed for them."

"So whoever took out Torres did it to protect Sebastion and you both. Did Torres know you well enough to know you would have avenged your brother's death regardless of the consequences?"

"Yes." She looked at him sharply. "I'm surprised you do."

"Captain's stock-in-trade. All in all, though, it sounds like a brotherly thing to do. Is that your point?"

"Yes. Miguel. I believe it more strongly every time I think of the mark on Torres. It was Miguel's."

"The needle puncture?"

She nodded. "It was his weapon, like the piano was my

instrument. He was a deadly little mosquito. So small, so afraid. Only nine and my father taught him how to kill."

MacKenzie's face was grim. "I may be way out of line on this, but your father was a fanatic to do that to a little boy."

The comment aroused her. "Maybe. But what do you call a fanatic about freedom? Maybe all idealists become fanatics. All we knew is what he fought for. But what do you know about it, Peter? You were born in a country where all you ever had to do for your political convictions was vote. It's considered a real commitment if you contribute a few dollars to a campaign or hand out a few leaflets in the shopping center. Of course a man like my father would seem fanatical to you."

"But Justine, a child of nine?"

"What would you expect of your children if the U.S. were occupied?"

"I wouldn't turn them into killers. Nothing justifies that."

"No?" The teacup had begun to clatter against the saucer. There was pain in her eyes. "Winning justified it. You wonder why Sebastion doesn't trust the United States? Whose weapons do you think armed Somoza? Which government kept the tyrant in power? Do you think we would have had to live like animals in the hills all those years if the United States, the light of democracy, had just once taken a look at Somoza being something besides an anticommunist? Sure we fought. Everybody fought. There were no exemptions."

"All right. I can understand. But even assuming it was justified, look what it did to you."

Her voice was suddenly very small. "It killed me, Peter."

He took the teacup out of her hands and drew her down to him. Her head lay against his chest and her hands were pressed to her mouth. The words came out in a torrent.

"I started at nine, just like Miguel, but a few years before, because I'm older. It never seemed to affect Sebastion quite the same way as it did Miguel and me. Sebastion's stronger in some important ways. Or maybe he was just older, or the first son. I don't know. But I could see it twist Miguel and me into horrible knots.

"Up north the guerrillas had to work the fields by day,

so they buried their weapons underground. Word of an approaching patrol was carried from farm to farm by the swiftest runners. It was a terrible sorcery, the invisible army forming, digging up their rifles like corpses and silently moving into position along the trail.

"We children were part of it, and so we moved with them. I was one of the leaders because my father was one of the commanders. It was expected of me. They called us *el coro de los ángeles*—the Angel's Choir. We were a tactic, Peter, to confuse and frighten the enemy to even the odds. At the commander's signal the children would start screaming at the top of their lungs all up and down the trail. On both sides. Can you imagine how terrifying that was for men whose nerves were already stretched to the breaking point that far out in rebel territory? It was a chilling sound, a horrifying sound. We stood there in the steaming jungle screaming and crying and hissing when our throats were too raw to do anything else . . . all those children shrieking at the top of their lungs while our men opened fire and cut the panicked government forces to pieces. . . .

"There was this one soldier, Peter, God knows what he was doing in the Guard because he must have been a basically kind man. I remember him most. It was on a very clear day that we ambushed his patrol. When the children started to scream, he thought—oh, God, forgive me—he thought *we* were in trouble, that we needed help. The rest panicked but he dropped his rifle and started yelling for us not to worry, that he would be right there. He stumbled through the bush just as the men opened fire. He took a bullet in the chest but still kept on coming, still thinking we were in danger, still yelling not to worry, children, not to worry. . . ."

"Justine, stop. Justine!"

"He got shot again but it didn't stop him. He saw me. I was just standing there and I couldn't stop screaming. I was so frightened. I saw a confused look come over his face. He must have been dying, but he looked around and finally realized what a fool he'd been. The look on his face was . . . unspeakable. He started towards me. I couldn't stop screaming. My father must have been watching for me. He shot the soldier a third time. The man cried out and fell against me and the blood gushed out and stained my shirt. Papa came, but I couldn't stop screaming. I couldn't stop . . . I couldn't . . . that man . . . his face . . ."

MacKenzie threw his arms around her and pressed her to him. She struggled, crying breathlessly and shaking her head bitterly back and forth. He refused to let her go. "I'm here, Justine. I'm here. Shh, I'm here. Oh, Justine . . ."

"I didn't understand," she cried. "Only nine. How could I understand?" The words came out between ragged breaths. "My father managed to get us back to the city. He was a popular musician and Somoza didn't know of his rebel connections. We gave concerts in Managua, then all over the region. Each time we traveled, it had to be of use to the rebels. At border crossings I had to distract the soldiers by playing so my father and brothers could kill them. Miguel's needle. Chopin. Too much music, Peter, and the screaming. Always the screaming. This time it was the border guards. Oh, my God, Peter. Oh, my God!"

He held her while she cried, rocking her in his arms insistently. "It's all over, Justine. All over. No one to hurt you now. No one. Just rest, that's all. Rest."

He held her while the sobs wracked her body. He felt the heat rising from her. She wept with deep, gasping breaths that tore at her chest. He held her, crooning gently that he would never let her go.

She began to quiet. Her robe was open and her skin warm and wet where they touched. He stroked her hair.

"You weren't to blame," he said quietly. "My poor little love, you're not to blame."

"I killed them," she insisted. "All of them."

"You did only what your father told you to do. You led a choir, played Chopin. Nothing more."

"But that man . . . he hated me."

"He hated what he must have finally understood, dying in such a place."

"Not me?"

He shook his head sadly. "No. Not you."

"You can't know that."

MacKenzie couldn't see, because tears had turned his own eyes into a thousand refractions. "No one blames the children, Justine. A man who tried to protect them must have surely known that."

"Who else could he blame?"

"The country, the world, politics, anything and everything. But not the children. Tell me, what did you see on his face?"

He felt her forehead crease, remembering. "When I picture him, he looks so very tired. And at the same time so sad."

"That's not a look of hatred."

"No, it isn't," she said.

MacKenzie groped for the right words. "You blame yourself so you put your own recriminations on his face. But when you actually remember it, he looks very different."

"Tell me why, Peter."

"Because what you saw on his face was a look, a . . . realization, I suppose, that no nine-year-old could possibly understand. We're all victims, Justine, beginning with the children. He must have known that, and if he did, I don't think he could have hated you. He could only have felt tired, and sad . . . and died."

He felt her press into him, taking that in, thinking. Her arms encircled him. Her breathing was almost normal now but he could hear the fatigue in her voice from the emotional exhaustion. "Wise old submarine captain," she said in a tired, grateful voice.

He shrugged. "We have different jobs, you and I. Different skills. You don't do armchair therapy—"

"Bed therapy," she corrected him, and he was encouraged by the first sign of a lighter mood.

"You don't do bed therapy," he said accepting the correction, "and I won't do fake front kick, roundhouse-kick, leg-sweep combinations."

Her hand appeared in front of his face. "Deal."

He turned it over and kissed it.

"You're a nice man, Peter." She was getting tired, her voice slurring with sleep.

He said, "Thank you."

"And a good captain too."

He smiled. "Thank you."

"You're welcome." A few seconds passed. "Peter?"

"Yes?"

"Thank you for loving me."

He looked at her. He was having trouble seeing again. "How long have you known?" he asked.

She smiled sleepily. "From the beginning, darling."

He was quiet for a time. "You?"

The smile deepened. "The same."

His was a long pause. "Thank you."

"You're welcome," she murmured. In another few seconds she was fast asleep.

MacKenzie held her for a long time. Almost till morning.

17

MIAMI

From the cabin window of the Navy transport plane, Justine watched the base at Guantanamo—Gitmo, everybody called it—dwindle in size till it blended in with the rest of the island and was lost to view.

She settled back in her seat, experiencing a rare feeling of well-being that was, she knew, largely attributable to the previous night. The intensity still hadn't worn off, and part of her was still with MacKenzie. They'd said good-bye in the morning after more talk and love-making. That, too, was special. The memory made her loins tighten. Plus the fact that he would be able to meet her in Miami. He had leave till *Aspen* was reassigned.

She never told anyone the things she told MacKenzie, or shared feelings on so deep a level. A great catharsis resulted from that, and she felt more lighthearted than in years.

"You're smiling pretty serenely," observed Sebastion from the seat next to hers. "The sub captain?"

"You're too nosy."

He laughed. "I thought so. Good choice. I like him."

Justine rested her hand on her brother's shoulder affectionately. "He said that about you too."

"I'm glad. This is no one you can push around, you know. Not like that Dodo bird you last married."

"He wasn't a Dodo bird, Sebastion. Only a little unwise at worldly things."

Sebastion made a rude noise. "He walked into an ambush a ten-year-old would have spotted. Lost a lot of good men. Sometimes I think you married him because you knew he wouldn't last long. Perfect for you. Intense, tragic, and brief."

"You're being facile. I cared for him."

"Maybe. I like this one a lot better though. In his own way he's tougher than you. Less cynical too. So watch your step, little sister, or you may find yourself married, pregnant, and driving a package-loaded station wagon instead of an army jeep. And all the nasty skills you learned over the years are of very little use in suburbia. I hear they frown on killing supermarket clerks."

"Who said anything about that kind of permanence?"

He looked at her. "I know you too well, Justine. You're an all-or-nothing person. I saw attractive, sophisticated men all over the world make passes at you when we were performing. Your affairs were few and far in between."

"I don't open up easily, Sebastion."

"I know that," he said gently. "I'm glad you're able to with him."

"Me too." A sudden look of amusement crossed her features. "As I remember, however, you never had any such trouble."

"I remain open to the world," he said expansively. "A sexual democrat."

"You have the morals of a cocker spaniel."

"You're beginning to sound like Miguel."

"Miguel is . . . otherwise." She sighed.

Sebastion fell silent. "I wish I could see him again. Just once, to talk," he said finally.

"I feel the same way." She hesitated. "There's something I didn't tell you. For a while I wasn't sure, but Miguel saved our lives in Managua. It doesn't make sense any other way." She explained her convictions about their brother.

Sebastion listened, nodding when she was finished. "It makes sense. Torres could have wanted you to die elsewhere. All of us in that room would have been too much to explain, so he knocks you out first, takes care of me there and you somewhere else later. You say you called out to Miguel? He knew you'd talk?"

"I pleaded with him. If he could hear me, he knew I meant it."

Sebastion grimaced. "I hate that he's with the Sandinistas."

"I do too," she said. "Barrista especially."

"Do you understand the hold he has on Miguel?"

"I . . . forget it, Sebastion. Miguel is where he wants to be."

"I suppose." He decided to switch topics. "MacKenzie's coming to Miami?"

"For a few days. Until he's reassigned. The apartment's large enough. I hoped you might stay too."

He shook his head. "Can't. I have to get back. My plans revolve around August first also, you know."

She looked at him, still so proud and independent. The years hadn't changed him. He treated his aloneness as a virtue. But was it? For the first time she wondered if he escaped their childhood as unscathed as she once believed.

"A word of caution then," she said. "You're walking a very fine line. No one with any sense of responsibility for what's to happen on August first will let you muck it up."

"What does that mean, exactly?"

Her tone was serious. "It means that they've already got one Segurra. They don't really need two."

The plane banked sharply and began to descend.

"I'll remember that," he said.

"Look, why not come home with me. Even for a little while. I'll make us a meal. We'll talk . . ."

"I'd like to, Justine, but I can't. I'm sorry."

She leaned back in her seat. She knew better than to argue when he'd made up his mind. She turned and watched the strips of building-bordered beaches flash by, turning into low buildings and crowded roads on the mainland. They flew over block after block of pastel-colored houses, skipped over a last few rows of palms, and finally settled down on the tarmac of Miami International Airport.

He got up to go when the plane taxied to a stop. "Thanks for the lift, little sister."

She leaned over and kissed him. "Remember what I said. Take care, Sebastion."

It was hard not doing what Justine asked, Sebastion thought to himself as he walked through the glass-and-steel airport exit doors in search of a taxi. But hers wasn't the only hold on him.

He carried no luggage. The tan, tropical suit and cordovan loafers he wore had been purchased at the base. His light blue shirt was open at the collar, and Justine's people had thoughtfully provided a leather billfold for the cash and papers they gave him.

There were some advantages to working in accordance with CIA wishes, he had to admit. The last time he entered the States he had to jump off a Honduran freighter. Now that he was a trusted ally, he came and went as he pleased.

He picked up a taxi and gave the driver an address in the city. They pulled out of the airport. It was always a funny feeling to be back in this country. What did the people here really know about hunger or suffering? Enough to avoid them, answered an inner voice. He decided maybe that was enough.

He spotted the tail car on his third routine check. He shrugged. So much for the *trusted* ally part. It was a white Toyota with Dade County plates.

"Driver? Forget that address. Make it 1273 Forty-ninth Street instead."

The driver nodded, abruptly swinging into the left lane to turn in the new direction. Sebastion looked back. The Toyota followed.

Forty-ninth Street was badly in need of someone to care about it. Black mildew stained the whole block of one-story stucco buildings, and torn curtains only partially obscured dirty windows. The driver glanced in the rearview mirror at Sebastion's suit. "You sure thees what you want, señor?"

"Yes, it is. Here. Thank you."

"Gracias, señor."

"De nada."

Sebastion got out and the driver pulled hastily away. The smell of garbage left too long in the sun hung in the air. Sullen eyes peered out from behind some of the windows. At the end of the block a few hard-looking boys with bandannas tied around their heads eyed him as potential prey. As Sebastion watched them, the Toyota came around the corner and parked on the other end of the street.

Number 1273 was a low, pink building with its windows tinted almost completely black. Hand-lettered words on the door said CLUB 49. There was refuse in the alley on one side and a chain-link fence encircled a sparse, sandy lot on the other. Behind it were old, wooden-frame houses with clotheslines strung across the alley in back like threads of spittle.

Sebastion closed his eyes and waited outside the door to 1273. He knew he'd be virtually blind if he walked in from the bright sunlight, and he was not so careless.

The street remained silent. He could hear the boys down the block teasing each other, plucking up the courage to approach him. Not today. He pushed open the door and walked inside.

A dozen round tables and chairs stood inelegantly in front of a long wooden bar. It was cold from the air conditioner set high up on one wall, next to a Budweiser clock with the wrong time. Most of the men were playing *naipes* with a Spanish deck. A few were seated at the bar. Two whores with fat thighs and double chins were doing their nails.

Conversation quieted as he walked to the bar, closed-in faces tracking him like laser sights. Sebastion didn't know the bartender. He put a bill on the pitted wood. *"Cerveza, por favor."*

The bartender was a beefy man in tee shirt and apron. He looked at Sebastion narrowly and put a bottle down in front of him. "If you doan got no business here, señor, this is not the place for you. Drink your beer and go, okay?"

Sebastion felt the stares on his back. "I got business, but I don't know you."

"If you had real business, señor, you would know me. No trouble. Just drink and go."

Sebastion took a long pull at the bottle, then a second, savoring it. It was so cold it hurt his throat. "You Cubans think you own the city," he said pointedly. "I'll go when I'm ready. It's still a free country, no?"

The bartender's tone was acid. "We are all from Nicaragua here, señor. Nicaraguans, not Cubans."

Sebastion caught his quick nod of the head. He took another long pull and emptied the bottle, listening carefully. Soft, shuffling footsteps. Two, maybe three. A sharp click. Switchblade . . .

He grabbed the bottle by its long neck and turned sharply. One man was in a crouch, the knife in his extended hand. Two more were behind him. Sebastion took a quick step forward, surprising the knife wielder as he moved in and smashed the bottle sharply into the point of the man's elbow. There was a sudden, confused cry of pain and the knife dropped from nerveless fingers. Sebastion plucked it out of midair. He placed it on the bar and turned back to the other two.

"Reconsider," he suggested pleasantly.

One did, the other didn't. He brushed his comrade out of the way and kicked viciously at Sebastion's groin. Still holding the bottle, Sebastion caught his ankle in an X block formed by overlapping one forearm over the other, and trapped it there. Once more the bottle came up sharply, this time smashing into the side of the man's knee. He howled in agony. Sebastion released him, and he foolishly tried to put his weight on the injured leg. He sprawled headlong onto the floor and dragged himself away.

The club was deathly quiet now. Others rose. Sebastion turned back to the bar and drew a small circle in the moisture that had condensed there. The bartender watched him curiously.

"Cero," Sebastion said. "I need to get to Sanchez. The white Toyota outside watches me."

The bartender's eyes widened. He leaned closer, studying Sebastion's face. "Cero!" he said excitedly. "Of course, I should have known you. Commandante Segurra, I fought with you north of Ocotal. Dios, I should have known you."

"It's been a long time since Ocotal." Sebastion shrugged apologetically. "I'm sorry for the testing but I had to be sure who was here. Will you help me?"

There was a low buzz in the room as Sebastion's name passed from mouth to mouth. The beaten ones lost their hangdog look—no shame to be taken by this one. Cubans indeed. A good joke. Someone went to the front window and looked out.

"The car is there, as he says."

The bartender nodded. "We are yours, Commandante. Eduardo, your car is in its usual place?"

"Si, I can drive him."

"Good. This way, Commandante. Eduardo will take you out the back way."

Sebastion reached out and shook hands. "When we're back in Managua, I promise to buy the first round."

"I accept. Good luck."

Sebastion followed Eduardo into a storeroom packed with cases of beer and liquor. Eduardo opened the back door and looked out. He pulled his head back in quickly.

"One there." He thought for a moment. "Wait. I'll be back."

He returned in a few minutes. Pushing Sebastion to the door, he opened it a crack. "Watch," he instructed.

A man in a dark suit was waiting in the alley between the club and the old houses behind it. A low stone wall separated the properties. The man had a two-way radio in his hand and was alternately looking at the club and at the curtainless windows, trying to peer at the shadowy forms inside.

Something suddenly caught his attention. A girl of seventeen or so moved into view. She began to take off her dress. The man went to the wall and actually tried to climb up a ways for a better view. She had pert, young breasts that rose as she pushed her hair under a shower cap. The man strained higher.

"Hey, asshole!" called out an angry, accented voice. "What the fuck you think you're doing?"

The man almost fell into the alley. He jumped hastily

down as the group of boys from the corner surrounded him. They had hard, unforgiving eyes.

"Look, I meant no—" He raised the radio.

One of the boys knocked it out of his hands. They grabbed him and spun him around. "You get out of here, asshole," they jeered.

The man's hand reached into his coat but he thought better of it. He backed off, trailed by the boys like a pack of angry hounds.

Sebastion and Eduardo stepped into the alley.

"Just like the jungle, eh, Commandante? We made a diversion," he said happily.

Sebastion looked around at tired, old buildings and the piles of garbage. The steamy heat settled in outside of the air-conditioning. He looked at the other man. "Just like the jungle, Eduardo. We go now?"

"Sure. This way."

Sebastion followed him up and over the wall.

Just below the Coconut Grove section of the city, where yuppies and artists were trying to create Greenwich Village South, thereby boosting property prices tenfold, is an area of stately mansions whose red, terra-cotta roofs look down on swimming pools, tennis courts, and half-acre lawns bordered by Royal Palms.

The home of Victor Sanchez was a twenty-room, sand-colored hacienda entirely surrounded by a high wall. Guards with trained Dobermans patrolled the grounds, and the weapons cache in the basement could have equipped a small army.

Sanchez was the oldest surviving member of a family older than the Segurras. They were in mining mostly, with sidelines in timber and coffee. Victor's father, the family patriarch, had died in the late seventies from a stroke. He was a true autocrat, a supporter of Somoza, and was opposed to any reform that conflicted with his philosophy of naturalism—that is, the strong always ate the weak and always would.

The elder Sanchez attempted to raise his son Victor in the same tradition and would have succeeded save for one mistake. In 1950, after a privileged upbringing of hunting, private schools, family influence, and almost unlimited funds, he sent Victor to school in the United States.

The magic there was perspective, and the terrible change it wrought in Victor was a respect for the middle class. His aristocratic attitudes were tempered by the values of his friends and by the obvious success of their society. Victor became a democrat.

He returned to Nicaragua after college and reorganized the family businesses along more modern functional, financial, and humane lines. His success resulted in greater profits and less labor strife. Over the next two decades the businesses grew rapidly. It was their profitability that finally attracted Anastasio Somoza's attention.

Through a series of government regulations passed by the dictator's tame Assembly, Sanchez found his affairs increasingly hampered by harsh and repressive restrictions. Added to the strong arm of the National Guard, they left him with no recourse but to sell his companies to the tyrant for a fraction of their value. His father's stroke was a direct result of the Guard's harassment. Reluctantly, Victor moved what was left of his family and fortune to the United States and returned to Nicaragua to join the revolution.

When Somoza was ousted the temporary government was receptive to Victor's requests, noted his record, and returned his various properties. Victor was an older, harder man after years of fighting, but he put down his rifle and returned to his former occupation. Once again he showed that an intelligent, humane employer could turn a profit.

But by now the Sandinistas had consolidated their hold on the government. Sanchez, almost fifty, had his fervent pleas against nationalization fall on deaf ears. Marx ruled. For the second time Victor's companies were taken away from him, for reasons he regarded as no less illegal.

This time, however, with his family still safe in the States, and being somewhat of a hero of the revolution, he felt safe to protest. Somoza was long gone. The Sandinistas arrested him for counter-revolutionary agitation, tried him in one of their "people's" tribunals, and sentenced him to ten years in prison. He had to be dragged from the courtroom.

Prison changed him. His left leg was broken during a

swamp reclamation project and never given proper attention. The result was a permanent, pronounced limp. He lost over fifty pounds and his eyesight was adversely affected by the malnutrition. The democrat who once believed in legality and due process became an embittered old man filled with anger and the need for revenge.

Twice the powerful had taken everything from him. This time they were killing him too. Slowly. He told himself that if he ever got out, they would pay. His ideology was reduced to that.

During the third year of his imprisonment, Sebastion Segurra's small band of anti-Sandinista rebels raided the prison and freed the over three hundred ill-fed and overworked political prisoners. Amidst his gratitude Sanchez recognized the guerrillas' dire need for funding as soon as he saw their camp and meager supplies. He sought out the famous Commandante Cero. There were others besides himself, he told Sebastion, who would contribute to an alternative to the northern contras. Would Sebastion accept this support?

A secret agreement was made. Sanchez wanted no disclosure of his role. What was left of his fortune was in American companies and he wanted no trouble from the U.S. government. He returned to Miami where, like so many other Latin emigrés, he felt at home, and began a network of Nicaraguan exiles who would work for Sebastion. The name of the benefactor was closely guarded. The club Sebastion visited was one of the few routes to Sanchez kept open.

Eduardo's ancient Pontiac left him at the iron gate, where he was searched and his identity checked. It was over a year since Sebastion had seen Victor. The guards escorted him up to the house and a uniformed servant, who Sebastion knew was heavily armed, took him into the library.

Sanchez came into the book-lined room, using his black, ebony cane as deftly as a sword. "Sebastion, how good to see you."

"And you, Victor." They embraced warmly.

"Sit, please. A drink?"

"Something soft," Sebastion said. "I've had enough medicine in me to make alcohol a lethal beverage. But feel free."

Sanchez called for a servant to bring the drinks. He lowered himself into an armchair opposite Sebastion's chair and set his cane against the arm. He was still gaunt and sunken-cheeked, as if no amount of fine food could fill out his frame. Perhaps, Sebastion thought, the very cells underneath his skin were dead.

The servant brought the drinks and left. Sanchez eyed Sebastion speculatively. "You look stiff. Were you hurt on the way out?"

"On the way in," Sebastion responded. "They got my jeep with some heavy fire and I was tossed out when it exploded. I woke up in one of Barrista's interrogation rooms with a zombie who threatened to cut me up or dice me, whichever I preferred."

"They are desperate. They sense the U.S. government's impatience to act."

"They wanted what I knew very badly," he agreed.

"We tried to open negotiations as soon as we found out you were alive. They stalled, and no amount of hard currency enticed them. We were exploring other options when we found out the CIA was going in after you."

Sebastion was surprised. "You have someone there?"

Sanchez nodded. "A very useful situation. Saves on duplication of effort. In this case they had the resources and we did not, so we made no move to interfere. If you made it out, you would find us when you could." He paused. "I am personally very happy to see you safe. The Sandinista jails are no hotels, as I well remember."

"No, they aren't."

"I hear your sister led the raid." Sanchez's eyes looked elsewhere, picturing her. "Doña Justine. She must still be very beautiful. Is she still as unhappy?"

Sebastion smiled. "Less so, these days."

"I'm glad to hear it. I would dearly love to have her with us again. Do you think there's any chance of it?"

"Actually, we came in on the same plane and she broached the opposite notion to me. Join them. I told her we remained unallied—no Soviets, no CIA."

"What was her response?"

"A warning not to screw up on August first. She said her people already had one Segurra. Two might be deemed superfluous."

Sanchez looked pensive. "An interesting notion. Are you concerned?"

"About them assassinating me? No. Look at all the trouble they went to getting me out. Although," he said, "there is some question about that." He explained Justine's theory about Torres. "But I'm not worried," he concluded. "Now that I'm here, they'll want me just where I'm supposed to be, commanding the southern prong of the attack."

"It may be another matter when you get to the capital though."

Sebastion shrugged. "I'll worry about that then. When do you plan to return home yourself?"

"As soon as the Marxists are rounded up. I'd like to be a part of the provisional government. You certainly will be. I also have assets for which claims must be filed."

"I have no knowledge of those."

"You don't have to. But please remember that supporting your army hasn't been inexpensive. I need back what was taken from me. Once back in power, I expect you to remember your friends."

Sebastion's eyes narrowed. "I'd like it a whole lot better if you expected me to remember my principles."

Sanchez spread his hands. "It's the same thing."

"Not always."

"Here, it is. I can prove what the Sandinistas took from me."

"In that case," Sebastion said firmly, "you don't need my help."

"All right, Sebastion. There's no pressure in this. Christ, you are a hard man sometimes."

"I never said differently." His face softened somewhat. "Don't worry, Victor. How soon can you get me back?"

"To Costa Rica? A weapons shipment is leaving port the day after tomorrow and you can be aboard if you like. Give you a few more days to rest. Or we can simply book you on an Eastern flight direct to San José. Since our working arrangement with CIA, you're as free to leave the country as to enter it."

"I'll take the flight."

"Very well. I'll make the arrangements."

Sebastion stood. "Thank you, Victor. Now, if you don't

mind, I'd like to get some rest. We'll have dinner together?"

"Of course." Sanchez took his cane and rapped it on the tile floor. A servant entered.

"Take Señor Segurra to his rooms. And tell Aura I wish to see her."

"Si, Don Victor."

Sanchez put his cane across his lap and looked up at Sebastion, noting his stiffness and fatigue. "The Sandinistas will fall," he said grimly, "for what they've done to all of us."

"Their time is coming," Sebastion agreed. "But not because of what they've done to us—because of what they've done to our country. It would do you some good, I think, to remember that, Victor."

"Of course." Sanchez's tone was carefully neutral. "How good of you to remind me. Good day, Sebastion. Sleep well."

Sanchez curled his hands tightly around the cane and fought for control. He wanted to sling the ebony stick through a window. How dare Sebastion speak to him that way. He had to exert control over his breathing to slow it. The fury began to ebb. Better. Control, not passion, produced victories. He was in command again when the knock sounded on the library door.

"Come in."

Aura Vasquez was as un-Hispanic looking as cherry-vanilla ice cream. Blue-eyed and blond-haired, she was model thin, and her one-piece, gray shift fell over boyish hips and exposed her long, lean legs. She was the daughter of a Nicaraguan businessman and his French mistress, and had first come to Victor's attention when he shared a cell with her father, also accused by the Sandinistas and thrown in jail. The two men endured much hardship together. Just before Aura's father died from malaria he contracted in the swamp, he made Victor promise to look after his daughter should he ever escape from their mutual hell. The girl had been sent to the U.S., but her father lost contact with her during his imprisonment.

Like revenge, Victor took his promises seriously. After

his return to the States he traced the daughter to a high-class brothel in Houston, Texas. He bought her contract and gave her a choice. She could go free with a sum of money sufficient to last until she "retrained" or found a husband, or she could come work for him.

"You look very nice, my dear," he said. "A new hairstyle?"

"A few weeks old. Thank you though. You wanted me, Uncle?"

Sanchez nodded. He was fond of the girl and permitted her the use of the familial title. "Justine Segurra is in the city. I believe you know her."

"My father knew her father. Justine and I met at a few parties, restaurants, places like that. We never liked each other."

"Can you keep track of her?"

She thought for a moment. "If I can use Packard, it should be no problem. He's part of Terry Holmes' unit. If she'd involved in the August first planning, as I assume she must be, they'll have intersected there."

"You may use him. I may want her picked up."

Aura pursed her lips. "Uncle, I don't mean to overstep, but if you would let me in on your plans, I may be able to do a better job for you. Putting men in place at the last minute always raises the possibility of screw-ups. It's up to you, but please consider it."

Sanchez did. "You've proved yourself very capable in the past, my dear. And I don't like last minute hurrying either."

"May I sit?"

"Please." He gestured to the same seat Sebastion had occupied minutes before.

He watched the dress slide up her legs as she reclined. She made no move to cover herself, another subtle acknowledgment of his ownership. "Something Justine said to her brother," he began, "started me thinking. She warned him to be careful because her employers might decide they had sufficient Segurras for credibility's sake without him."

"Does that place him in real jeopardy?"

"It could, but that's not what interests me. Consider what's going to happen after the Sandinistas fall. There's going to be a power vacuum like none before it. Everybody politically significant is either dead or in exile. There is virtually no opposition left inside the country. Who is going to catch the people's attention? Obviously the Segurra name will have great drawing power, enough maybe for a bid for the presidency."

"Won't the CIA want Justine in that role?"

"I would think so. Just the fact that she's female should be good for half a dozen congressional appropriations before anyone even thinks to look at her politics. Now here's the question: What would happen if Justine isn't available?"

Aura looked at Sanchez and admiration slowly spread over her face. "They would have to come to Sebastion and hope to hell he could be controlled afterwards."

Sanchez looked at his star pupil proudly. "Exactly my thinking. Therefore, Justine cannot be allowed to lead the contras into Nicaragua. Creating a modern day Joan of Arc only pushes Sebastion back into the shadows."

"How far do we go? An ordinary car accident would lay her up long past August first."

"Not enough. She would be back and they could still count on it. It's got to be more."

Aura's hand toyed with the hem of her dress. There were no outlines of undergarments. "As she herself said, Uncle, one Segurra is enough."

"I think so," he agreed. "Ours. See to it."

"Yes, Uncle."

The upstairs bedroom was dark and quiet. Aura sat down softly on the bed.

"Sebastion?"

He was naked under the sheets. He turned groggily. "Wha— Oh, it's you, Aura. Long time, little one, since I saw you last. Victor still treating you well?"

There was a rustle of the covers and a pale, sleek body was suddenly pressing against his. "Well enough to keep me." She giggled. "Too long, old man. You still got the strength?"

He turned over. "My heart is pure."

"The only part, I'll wager." She bit him.

"Ow!" He grabbed her hands and held them behind

her back. "Aura, I feel like several tanks ran over me. Gently, precious, or I toss you out of here on your slim little tail."

"Yes, Sebastion," she cooed. "How is Justine?" She reached down.

"Hmm? Just fine. But I didn't think you two got along."

"All in the past."

"She's probably soaking right now in that big tub of hers in that fancy bathroom."

"Alone?"

Sebastion put a finger on her lips. "Not your concern."

"She still has the same apartment, though, in the Hamptons?" Her motion increased.

"A bit lower," he sighed.

"Sebastion, Justine has the same place?"

"Ahh, right there, Aura. Yes, yes. Same place." He opened one eye. "You came here to talk? I had enough talk with Victor."

Her lips were soft and wet, hovering above him. "No more talk, darling. Not now anyway."

He arched like a man hit with a cattle prod when she took him into her mouth. She delighted and drained him totally.

Much later he woke up to find he'd slept through dinner.

18

MIAMI

Justine's apartment was in the luxury Hamptons high-rise in North Miami. The white, landscaped building sat on the intracoastal waterway and looked out over the million dollar private homes on Golden Beach, a mile-wide stretch to interconnected islands which made up the opposite bank. The blue-green ocean lay beyond that, giving the impression that Golden Beach had been placed there solely to give the view from her eighteenth-floor apartment some visual perspective and to create the illusion that the Grand Bahamas were just below.

MacKenzie lowered himself into the sunken Roman bath and twisted the hot water jets so that they played over his shoulders. The bathroom was all marble, with Italian porcelain fixtures. Justine reclined against him and lazily soaped her body. Both had finally risen, after spending the afternoon in bed.

"That was very nice," MacKenzie said. If he'd been any more relaxed, he mused, he'd be sleeping. "But you never said 'Welcome to Miami.'"

"Deeds outweigh words." She stretched happily. "And if memory serves me, there wasn't much time. I'm the one who should be thankful you didn't say 'Thank you, ma'am.'"

"You can't say that when it lasts that long."

"Well, I accept my share of the blame."

He put his hands on her breasts. "I missed you."

"I missed you too. Even if it was only a few hours," she said. "How much time do you have, Peter?"

"Three days. Then *Aspen* goes out again, and I go with her. I'll catch a ride back to Gitmo with the same Navy flier who brought me over."

"Oh."

He found the feel of her slick, wet skin intoxicating. "You're angry."

"No."

He pushed himself up to a sitting position. She sat cross-legged opposite him. "We were going to have to talk about some things sooner or later and I guess now is as good a time as any," he said. "Justine, you and I aren't kids. We're both well beyond legal age and lead full lives. Realistically, if I wasn't going out again in a few days, how much more time would you have? A week? Two?"

"Even less," she admitted sadly. "And comes, well . . . next month, I'll be away for some time."

"Back to Honduras?"

"I can't say, Peter. But that's close enough."

The notion that their lives were beyond their control was so alien to MacKenzie that he rejected it outright. He thought for a while, aware that her silence meant she was doing the same thing.

"The way things work in the Navy," he said slowly, "is that sea assignments rotate with land postings. My tour on *Aspen* will be over in about a year. Then it's back to shore for a staff assignment and probably advanced schooling. Can we think about fitting us into that?"

"I don't know," she said honestly. "I can't see myself pushing around a laundry cart at some base while you're away a year at a time."

"You could work. I think you have what are called 'transferable skills.'"

She paused for a moment. "I want you to understand something, darling. I am where I am for one specific reason—to see my country freed from a dictatorship. This may sound harsh, but once that's been achieved, I'm out. All the way. No switch to Naval Intelligence or DIA or some consulting firm. No desk job sending others out or planning obscure missions or unraveling Soviet conspiracies. I hate this work. I hate this life."

"I know that."

"Besides," she said, "do you think a government salary pays for this kind of place?"

"I assumed family money."

"There's some left, but not a lot. The far greater segment was saved from concert tours, and I still receive royalties from some of my recordings. Peter, I gave up Paris and Rome and Vienna and a dozen other cities to kill people in stinking jungles for a reason I thought compelling enough. So did my father and my brothers. The little girl waiting at home with the light in the window just isn't."

He wished he didn't understand so easily. "Loving isn't the only issue, I know that. But—"

She touched his face tenderly. "But at the same time you should know this, dear: Any thought I could possibly have of home or children or permanence only makes sense when I envision it with you, Peter."

He stroked her neck quietly. "There are lots of people who do it," he said. "I've got some friends in Washington. A posting in New York or someplace like it would let you play. You could travel when necessary. . . ."

She inclined her head. "Perhaps."

"A year from now," he insisted. "Let's give it that. We

might both be in a place by then that allows for options we can't see right now."

"No laundry carts?"

He laughed. "You can afford a maid. My salary can pay for the cleaning supplies. How do you feel about kids?"

Sebastion's words rang in her ears. "Unsure," she admitted.

"That could be a deal breaker," he said honestly.

"My own childhood gets in my way."

"It doesn't have to. Think of all you could give, all you could do differently. No Angel's Choir, no border crossings, just a cute little Scottish-Spanish kid to teach the piano to."

"Scottish Spanish?"

"Sure, he can say 'hoot, hombre.'"

She had to smile. "Peter, will you accept a very frank 'possibly'?"

"Yes, and when the time comes—"

The doorbell rang.

Justine cursed and pulled herself out of the tub. She wrapped an oversized towel around her. "Just a minute, darling. I'll get it."

MacKenzie lay back and let the fantasy roll out on the picture screen in his mind. Home could be more than the officers' quarters at whatever base he was assigned to. Family responsibilities; not a burden, a rejuvenation. Maybe they wouldn't live in a luxury building like this one right away, with tennis courts and doormen and security intercoms and . . . a sudden thought struck him. No one came directly to the front door in a building like this one. Why hadn't the front desk buzzed for permission to send the caller up?

He bolted out of the tub and tugged a towel around his waist. She wasn't in the adjoining bedroom or the living room. He began to panic. He stumbled into the tiled foyer, sliding on wet feet. The front door was ajar.

The hallway outside was empty too.

Justine was gone.

The security guard at the delivery entrance paid only token attention to the kerchiefed Hispanic lady pushing the laundry cart and speaking in loud, rapid-fire sentences to the man in the dirty coveralls walking beside her. They were clearly a low-class pair, and the guard frowned, thinking that on the beach side of the city the spics were everywhere, attracted to dirty laundry and car washes likes bugs to an outdoor meal.

The laundry van they had backed up against the loading dock was as disreputable as they were, but their passes and work orders were genuine. Still, he was keeping an eye out for them, just to be sure. He was happy they were leaving.

"Bueno," he said. "All finished?"

"Si, jefe," said the woman. "Gracias."

The guard bent over the cart. Never hurt to check. Some little television or something from the lobby could easily walk out of here with these two.

"Jefe. . . ?"

"Just checking. My job to, right?" He moved a few pieces of soiled linen aside. Something brown appeared. He moved some more. A leg. What?

He reached for his gun but it was far too late.

"Sorry, chief," said the man, and shot him in the face with a silenced automatic. The guard crumpled to the floor bonelessly.

Aura Vasquez said, "Shit." Victor was going to call it sloppy. Well, nothing to be done about that now. She turned to Marvin Packard, Justine's CIA colleague—whom she'd counted on to get Justine to open her door without undue reticence or suspicion—and pointed to the corpse. "Dump him in too. And get the van open."

Packard did as he was told. He rolled the cart into the van and slid the doors shut.

"Can she still breathe in there?" Aura asked him.

"What's the difference? The guard's enough for mandatory life if we're stopped. One more won't matter."

Aura paused, thinking of how easily the Segurras looked down at her. Sebastion used her like a whore, Justine treated her like one.

"Wait till we get there," she said.

"Why?"

She slid into the driver's seat and motioned for him to get in. "Because I want her to know it's me." She paused. "Because I want to watch."

Packard looked at her uncomfortably. "That's really weird, Aura." He grimaced as she started the engine.

"I know," she said complacently, and gunned the van out of the dock.

19

CARIBBEAN SEA

The Nicaraguan freighter *Corazón* put out from Bluefields, a port on the Atlantic coast, just before dawn. It was almost ten A.M. now, and Miguel was drinking another cup of coffee, waiting next to the vessel's captain. Both were gazing out the bridge's wraparound windows at the open sea. They were almost a hundred miles from shore.

The intercom buzzed. Captain Mercado picked it up and listened for a moment. "We're ready, Deputy Minister," he said to Miguel. "You wish us to begin?"

"The radio operator is certain of his instructions?"

"Yes. The appropriate transmissions will go out."

"And the fishing boats?"

"They are within ten miles of us, according to our last check."

"Good. Proceed then."

Mercado nodded and left the bridge. Crazier orders he'd never had in his career. Only two days before, he was ordered to unload his entire cargo and make ready to sail. Then a team of workers from the Ministry of Defense arrived and did things to his poor ship that made him wince.

But who could argue? He took orders, not gave them. He slid down the ladder into the big stern hold and roused the men there. "This is it. Be ready. Are you all set?"

The man from the Defense Ministry patted the odd-looking, bell-shaped steel housing almost eight feet in diameter at its widest point, which was welded to the hull just at the waterline. "Any time, Captain."

"The Deputy Minister has given the order. You are to proceed."

"Want to watch?"

Mercado thought of the limpet explosives attached to the hull inside the bell and shuddered. "No thank you. I'll be on deck."

The man flicked a switch. "As you like. It's armed now. Thirty seconds."

Mercado was back on deck in half that. He counted silently. At thirty he braced himself.

The explosion shook the ship violently. Mercado felt the heavy deck plates vibrate and saw dark smoke rising. He ran to the railing and peered over the side.

There was a gaping, jagged-edged hole in the hull wide enough to sink the ship. And so it would have, had not the bell housing welded onto the inside formed a protective seal around the breach, preventing water from entering the hold like a blister in reverse. With all the blackened steel it looked like a genuine hit.

Mercado looked to the gang of men aft, above the hole, and waved them into action. One touched a torch to three barrels of oil. They ignited at once and thick plumes of black smoke poured out, drifting up into the sky.

Mercado opened the door to the radio room. The operator sat in front of his rig with his headphones on and a pad in front of him. He looked up.

"We're okay, Captain?"

"Just fine, son. You have your signal ready?"

"Yes, sir."

"All right. You can send it now."

"Yes, sir."

His hand went to the sending key and began to transmit.

The Soviet Victor III nuclear attack submarine *Kirov* was working its usual patrol route of the southern access corridors to the Panama Canal when it picked up *Corazón*'s distress signal. The radio officer frowned repeatedly as he read the transmission, then hurried forward to Captain First Rank Sergei Gorskov in the control room.

"Comrade Captain?"

"Yes, what is it?"

"We just received this distress signal from the Nicaraguan freighter *Corazón*, and I thought you would want to see it immediately."

Gorskov ceased his inspection of a valve that had been intermittently leaking fluid and wiped his hands on a towel. He was a stocky man with a large, shaggy head resting on square shoulders, with almost no neck in between. A white turtleneck sweater obliterated the rest. He said, "Read it to me, Mishkin."

"Comrade Captain, the *Corazón* says it has been attacked by an American submarine. It's taken one torpedo aft and is on fire. It signals all ships."

Gorskov's eyebrows rose. "Can this be? Let me see the transmission." He took the paper and called his navigator over. "Pavel Ivanovich?"

"Yes, Comrade Captain."

"Check these coordinates. How far are we?"

The navigator consulted his charts. "Less than two hours, Comrade Captain. Shall I plot a course?"

Gorskov thought it over. "Yes. And proceed at top speed. I want to look this situation over. It's incredible, really. But maybe the Americans have stepped up the hostilities. First the embargo, now this."

"Yes, Comrade Captain."

"Mishkin, give me your pad. Fleet Command will want to know about this. And I'm certain they'll want visual and photographic confirmation." He wrote for a few seconds. "Send this and the *Corazón*'s signal."

"Yes, Comrade Captain. Any reply to *Corazón*?"

Gorskov shook his head. "I don't wish to advertise our presence. Every ship in the area will be steaming for her. Let's see what we find when we arrive."

Gorskov hit the alarm for battle stations as Mishkin left. Men moved into position and weaponry was readied. Gorskov decided to make a personal inspection. The current political officer demanded so much lecture time, it was difficult to get in sufficient training. Best to see to everything himself. He hit the intercom.

"Sonar, this is Captain Gorskov. We are entering an area where at least one hostile American submarine has been reported, and there could be more. I want your extreme vigilance."

"Absolutely, Comrade Captain. For the motherland."

For your asses, Gorskov thought sardonically. Let's get those home in one piece first. "Pavel Ivanovich, maintain course and speed."

Gorskov left the control room to make his rounds.

Over seventy fishing boats, some barely larger than sailing skiffs, others as big as yachts, sailed through the low chop less than five miles from the *Corazón*. They had left port about an hour after the freighter and were now close enough to see the long black trails of smoke that emanated from her stern.

The *Caimán*, the largest boat in the fleet, surged ahead under full canvas. The other vessels scattered around it looked like colorful corks tossed out over the sea.

The regular crew of the *Caimán* was removed the day before and were now sitting back in port getting drunk on government-provided liquor. The replacements were all regular navy but were wearing the loose-fitting garments of working fishermen. Three stood in the rear of the boat, trailing what looked like fishing lines into the sea. Like the fishermen, however, neither were these lines what they appeared to be.

They were in fact waterproofed coaxial cable, and at the end of each line was a highly sensitive hydrophone. The cables trailed back into the wheelhouse, where they fed into an electronic sorter and amplifier. Attached to this by means of a set of headphones was Captain Luis Santillo.

Santillo's eyes were dreamy and half focused. His second-in-command kept the course. Santillo listened to the undersea noises, occasionally reaching out to turn a dial and filter out the constant hiss of seventy keels slicing through the sea.

"Two miles to the *Corazón*," his second called out. "I can see her, Captain."

Santillo nodded without looking up. "Put us in between the hole in her side and the open sea. They'll have to get in close to see it."

"Aye, Captain."

Sounds filtered into Santillo's ears as the boats around

them altered course to stay abreast of the *Caimán*. He'd been working with the equipment for days and could recognize the creak of a wooden rudder from a dolphin's high-pitched squeal. Had not all the boats around them, including the *Caimán*, not been traveling under sail, and the *Corazón* not dead in the water, the noise would have been impossible to sort through with equipment of this size. But he had only one engine to listen for.

Santillo took a quick look out. The *Corazón* was burning like a smudge pot. He could vaguely make out the hole in her side. They were broadcasting continuously, and twice American recon planes had overflown the area. Fifty miles east an American heavy cruiser out of Guantanamo had radioed it was on the way. He saw that the fishing fleet was almost in place.

The race had begun.

On board the *Corazón* Captain Mercado turned to Miguel. He held the signal just passed to him from the radio room. "The American ship will be here in less than two hours. What do we do if it offers assistance?"

"Bluff," said Miguel. "Order them off using the state of relations between our two countries as pretext. But hope that it doesn't come to that. We'd have to—"

"Captain!" an excited voice called down from the flying bridge. "Periscope five hundred yards due west. Circling."

Miguel felt the first flush of adrenaline kick at his heart. Even Mercado had an admiring look on his face. Miguel clapped him on the shoulder.

"The devil up from full fathoms," he said softly, nodding. "Captain, signal the *Caimán*. Send, Strike One."

"Captain Santillo, message from the *Corazón*. Strike One."

Santillo nodded. The confirmation was welcome, but he'd been hearing the cavitation noises for several minutes. Still, it was good to be certain. He looked at the range dial on his equipment. "One mile due north of us," he said out loud. "Course westerly. She should be coming around for a look any minute now. It has to be this way. Launch the red flare. Five minutes to action."

His second loaded the Very pistol and pointed it up into the sky. A sudden hiss and a loud "phumpf" and the flare shot upwards, bursting over the fleet and trailing a glowing red light.

In seventy boats men made ready.

Captain Gorskov hunched over the periscope and looked at the burning freighter and the assemblage of fishing boats around it.

"The *Corazón*'s been holed by something," he said. "Sonar, are you picking up anything in the area?"

"No, Comrade Captain. All is clear."

"And the American cruiser?"

"Its last active transmission has it over thirty miles east. It is not yet within our range."

"So," Gorskov mused, "no subs, no cruiser. The freighter doesn't look in danger of sinking, and anyway, there are enough boats around her to take the crew off if it begins to. A ruse of some kind?"

"The sub could be long gone," suggested the navigator.

"Or the explosion was the *Corazón*'s own fault and the captain blames it on a convenient enemy. In either case I want pictures. The experts at home can study them and determine cause." They had almost finished one circuit around the freighter. The fishing boats floated in between them and the ship.

"Turn to course oh-one-oh, ahead one third. Down scope till we're through them. All stop one hundred meters from the *Corazón*."

Gorskov opened a locker and removed the heavy Zeiss camera from within. Fitting the special collar to the periscope's eyepiece, he began to mount the camera to it.

"Course oh-one-oh, Comrade Captain."

"All ahead one third," ordered Gorskov.

A smile lit Santillo's face. "That's it. That's it! Turn, you inquisitive bastard. Get in closer." The sounds in his ears grew sharper, louder. He could visualize the sub's big propellers churning on their shaft. He checked the range dial. The needle stood almost at zero. Sounds increased. The sub was almost directly under the fleet.

"Now," he ordered. "The white flare. Now!"

The second flare shot up from *Caimán*'s deck and hissed across the sky. In every fishing boat men bent to their assigned tasks. Length after length of tough, coarse netting was thrown overboard. Much of it was strengthened with steel wire and weighted with stones. The netting hit the water with a flat splash and slid underneath with a brief hissing noise.

Santillo listened to the blizzard of netting fall. The sub's prop noise was loud enough to deafen him but he clamped the headphones more firmly over his ears and concentrated.

"Send to *Corazón*," he ordered. "Strike Two."

Captain Mercado accepted the radio signal and read it to Miguel, who put down his binoculars and pointed out to the fleet. "Yes. I can see it. Start the recorded message."

Mercado gave the order.

"Comrade Captain? Sonar. We're receiving strange sounds . . . never heard these before—"

"Identify them," Gorskov snapped.

"Yes, Comrade Captain. But—"

The first patter of stones falling against the *Kirov*'s hull jerked Gorskov's head up as if he'd been struck. "What is this?" he demanded, confused. His forehead furrowed deeply. The "rain" continued in a random pattern. Slithering noises began, trailing down the sides of the ship.

"Sonar!" he demanded again. "Identify."

Gorskov felt the first stirrings of alarm. He looked around, but no one on the bridge offered any explanations. More thunks. He turned sharply as the radio officer ran in.

"Comrade Captain, we're picking up short-wave radio communications from the fishing boats. Some claim to have spotted a whale, others a school of giant tuna. Comrade Captain—" He winced as something else clanged against the hull. "Is it possible they mean us?"

Whale? Tuna? Gorskov blanched. Those sounds. Nets! "Engine room, all stop. *All stop!*"

With a sudden sinking feeling in the pit of his stomach, Gorskov knew it was too late even as he gave the order. The *Kirov* gave a sickening lurch and began to slow as the netting tore and wrapped itself around the propeller and its shaft. The hull shuddered.

"Comrade Captain, the bow planes! They won't move."

The *Kirov* began a slow downward drift, and Gorskov was powerless to stop it. The nets fouled the big stern planes as well, and he lost depth control even as he thought to dive out from under the deadly, cloying rain.

"Steer course . . ."

"Comrade Captain, the helm refuses to answer."

"Control room, this is the engine room. The power plant is losing vacuum. We must disengage. We're in danger of losing power. Comrade Captain, do you hear me?"

"Disengage," Gorskov said bitterly.

There was nothing else he could do. The strain had certainly fouled the main shaft, so it was useless to send out divers to try and cut the netting. And they were sinking, with the bottom too far down to come to rest safely.

"Blow emergency ballast," he ordered, and there was a deep and terrible lethargy in his voice. "Prepare to surface."

Kirov began to rise.

Santillo heard it all—the tortured sound of engines trying to twist their shafts out of their bearings, the power shutdown, and finally the tremendous whoosh of compressed air forcing tons of water out of the ballast tanks as the crippled sub headed for the surface.

For the first time in hours he pulled the headphones off his ears and stared out to where the black sail of the Russian sub was breaking through the surface. He knew it was a Victor III as soon as he saw the distinctive teardrop-shaped sonar pod on the top rear fin. Very good, he thought, the Victors carried nuclear-tipped cruise missiles.

Miguel Segurra would be on the radio by now, talking to the sub's captain and offering his protection as Nicaraguan Deputy Defense Minister inside Nicaraguan territorial waters. He would be apologizing profusely for so terrible an accident befalling an ally come to help. Port repair facilities at Bluefields would be provided as an honor of the Nicaraguan government. Happily, the damage to the *Corazón* had been repaired. It could limp back to port. A tow could be arranged.

The Soviet captain was no fool. He was embarrassed and helpless. A sudden storm could sink him, and Cuba was too far away to get a tender to him in any reasonable time. Finally, the American cruiser would be on his screens by now. He would accept *Corazón's* offer.

"A fisher of men," Santillo said, eyes bright.

"Captain?"

Santillo shook his head. "Nothing. Just a stray thought. Signal to *Corazón*. Send, Strike Three."

The Russian sub, *his* sub, was within reach.

20

MIAMI

MacKenzie fought to keep calm while his call was routed through Admiral Garver's office at Guantanamo, with Garver arranging the pass-through connection to the resident CIA officer. He drummed his fingers impatiently on the night table.

He had no experience with kidnapping. It was grim and terrible. His first reaction was to chase after someone. But after whom? Years of command situations compelled him to think his actions through. This much was clear—he needed help. Justine's debriefing officer on Gitmo was the quickest way he knew of to get to her people.

"This is Terrence Holmes," came the voice over the receiver. "Captain MacKenzie?"

"Here. Look—"

"This isn't at all the way we do things, Captain. So first, your serial number."

MacKenzie gave it, stifling an oath.

"And your posting before the *Tarpin*?"

"*Aspen*. Before that, NMPC Detailer, Submarine Squadron Eighteen, Charleston."

"Please, proceed."

MacKenzie clamped a lid on his emotions and held his voice steady. "Justine Segurra was just taken forcibly from her apartment by someone or ones who came to the front door. There are no signs of struggle. I didn't hear a thing from the next room. She's just gone."

"Justin taken? Look MacKenzie, isn't it possible she just went for a walk?"

"In a towel?"

"I see. Where were you?"

MacKenzie felt anger stir. "Waiting for her to come back to the hot tub. I got out when I realized the desk should have rung up about a visitor. The front door was open. That's all. She's gone."

"Fuck. All right, I'm going to alert our people in Miami. Hold on."

The dampened sound of being on hold filled MacKenzie's ear. He wasn't an easy man to rattle, but this shook him severely. He felt impotent and ill-prepared. The menace in Justine's shadowy world had suddenly become real, and it scared him in a way that the sea never had.

"MacKenzie?"

"Here. What's going on?"

"We'll have a team over there in ten minutes. Here's a number to call if anything breaks meantime. You stay put."

MacKenzie didn't say anything. Holmes continued, "We have to move quickly in situations like these. Too much time—"

"I want to call in her brother," MacKenzie said.

"Absolutely not." Holmes's voice was harsh. "For all we know, Sebastion's people are behind this. One less Segurra concentrates the power of the name."

"I've seen them together. You're way off base. He would never allow any harm to come to her."

"Maybe. And maybe Sebastion's people don't tell him everything they do."

"All the more reason to let him know. Where is he now?"

For the first time, he heard embarrassment in Holmes's voice. "Unfortunately, he's gone. He came in on the same plane as Justine but they separated at the airport. Sebastion went to a Latino club on Forty-ninth Street, a hangout for ex-revolutionaries. City's filled with them. So many goddamned exiles you can hire a spy or a mercenary easier than a maid."

"If she's been taken by one of those groups, it's another argument in favor of calling in Sebastion. Who knows the politics better?"

"I do," said Holmes flatly. "I'll be there in less than an hour. We want her back, too, Captain. Just sit tight."

"I don't think—"

"If necessary, I'll have Admiral Garver make that an order."

MacKenzie knew he couldn't disobey Garver's order, so he decided to leave before it was given. He dropped the phone in a not-so-gentle manner.

"MacKenzie? MacKenzie!"

Justine's car keys were on the dresser. The number of her garage space was pressed into a metal ring attached to the keys. Holmes's voice was a small, tinny thing far away.

"MacKenzie, goddamn it . . ."

It took less than three minutes to find the gun he was sure she kept. It was underneath the night table, a .38 caliber Police Special secured to the wood by a metal clip. He slipped it inside the belt of his jeans and covered it with his light cotton windbreaker.

He went back to the phone. The line was dead. That was okay too. He had nothing more to say to Terrence Holmes.

MacKenzie took the elevator to the basement. No one could have taken a near-naked woman through the front lobby. If she was put in something, it would have to have come out this way also.

There was a uniformed security guard by the rear entrance. He had a walkie-talkie pressed to his mouth and looked concerned. ". . . I don't know, Sarge. He's just not here. . . . Nope, no note . . . I *did* check the john. He's not in there either. . . . Okay . . . Okay . . . Wait a second." He looked at MacKenzie. "Yes, sir?"

"You're the guard usually stationed here?"

"No, sir. He just stepped away for a minute. Is there a problem?"

MacKenzie frowned. The missing guard and Justine's disappearance were too much of a coincidence. "Is there a sign-in log or something for the past few hours?" he asked.

The guard pointed to the desk. "Sure, but— Hey, you can't take that!"

MacKenzie almost went for the gun, but thought better of it and reached for a twenty dollar bill instead. The guard looked shy for a second, then pocketed the money and moved a few paces away.

There were log entries for the entire morning, and three within the last hour. The first and third were drop offs from local markets. The second was a van from a cleaning service. He turned to the guard, "This cleaning company," he pointed to the entry. "Why send a van?"

"They pick up all the building staff uniforms."

There was a notation next to the entry; M & FH. "What does this mean? Here."

"Male and Female Hispanic," the guard responded. "We have to know who's in the building, right?"

MacKenzie thought it out. The van arrived only fifteen minutes before Justine was taken, and there was no record of the man and woman ever leaving. But the van was gone, and so was the security guard. It didn't take a police detective to reason that events were connected.

"I need a phone," he said to the guard.

Apparently the twenty went a long way. He was handed the desk phone. "Dial nine for an outside line."

MacKenzie called information and got the cleaning service's number. Their dispatcher was obliging. No, sir, no pick ups at the Hamptons today. . . .

"Which way to the garage?"

"Down this corridor, second right."

Holmes's voice rang in MacKenzie's head as he walked. *For all we know, Sebastion's people could be behind this.* The kidnappers were Hispanic. Was Holmes right? Or could it be some new, rival group? Doubts assailed him. He pushed them aside.

He found Justine's car, a late-model Camaro, which started on the third try. He yanked it into gear and sped out of the garage, pausing only for the exit barrier to be lifted. He accelerated rapidly out to the main highway along circular Country Club Drive and was over the speed limit in seconds, heading south.

The occupants of Club 49 looked up with undisguised hostility as MacKenzie walked into the room. He stepped up to the bar, acutely conscious of being the only Anglo in the place. The bartender looked at him with a frown. "This is a private club, señor. You drink somewhere else, okay?"

"I didn't come here for a drink. I have to find Sebastion Segurra. He was in here yesterday morning. This is extremely important. Urgent. My name is Peter MacKenzie. Captain Peter MacKenzie." He held out his Navy I.D. "I'm a friend," he finished lamely. "Please."

"That name isn't familiar. Your friend hasn't been in here."

"I know he's been here. He wanted to avoid the surveillance he was under and you helped him. Look, his sister's been . . . taken. He's got to be told. If you won't take me to him, call him. Tell him I'm here. He'll tell you I'm his friend."

"How can I call someone I don't know, señor?"

MacKenzie felt a frustrated rage building. He wanted to grab for the gun and make some demands of these people. He almost went for it; men were closing in behind him. But if he pulled the gun, he was surely going to have to use it. He was not so inept as that—everything he knew about controlling men told him that was not the way to do it. He deliberately relaxed his shoulders. When he spoke, it was with a captain's voice, calm and certain and used to command. He ignored the men behind him and looked directly into the bartender's closed-in face.

"I'm going to tell you a story about a nine-year-old girl," he began, "and you're going to listen." His eyes never left the bartender's. "I know what no one who isn't a friend of the Segurras could know, what you only hear about as rumor and legend. When I'm done you'll call Sebastion and tell him I must see him. Understood?"

He moved and the men behind him jerked back abruptly. MacKenzie waited. He felt them crowd back angrily, but the bartender held up a hand—wait. Tempers were hot and high.

"There was a way for the rebels against Somoza to make the Guard afraid. When the soldiers came into their area the children were put along the roadside to scream at the top of their lungs just before the start of the attack. This ungodly sound sent the soldiers into a panic and they could be picked off easily. It was a terrible chorus—the Angel's Choir.

"Justine Segurra was one of the leaders of the children because her father was one of the leaders of the men. She saw a soldier die in front of her. Even her father couldn't stop her screaming. He took her away. Carlos was a fine musician. So were his sons and daughter. They went back to Managua and became Somoza's favorites, then betrayed him every time they crossed a border."

The bartender was watching him closely, caught up in the narrative. Heads bobbed slowly up and down around the room, responding to a deeply felt cadence.

"Every border crossing," MacKenzie said, "Justine would play while her father and brothers killed the Guard."

"Doña Justine . . ." whispered one man. The bartender was nodding again.

"Sebastion's machete." MacKenzie urged them to remember. "Miguel's needle."

"I was there," said another. "It was just as he says."

"That little girl is a grown woman now. My lover," said MacKenzie, with hope and fear in his voice. "She's been taken. I must tell this to her brother. You must tell him for me if I can't. That's all I'm asking."

He stood alone and no one made a move to touch him.

"One moment, señor," said the bartender. He searched the others' faces and read the same message on all of them. They believed.

MacKenzie said, "Where can I find Sebastion?"

The bartender told him.

MacKenzie pulled the car off the road after his third circuit around Victor Sanchez's house. He regarded it with a skeptical eye. The wall could be climbed, but what was he going to do about the guards and dogs?

Time was pressing him hard. Over an hour and a

quarter since Justine was kidnapped. But there was just no way to break into this place. He drove over to the gate.

The guards eyed him suspiciously. One came over to the car.

"Please tell Sebastion Segurra that—"

The guard shook his head. "No one here, señor."

"I know he's in here. This is—"

The guard cocked his rifle with a disconcerting *snick-chuck-click* and pointed it at MacKenzie's head.

MacKenzie reversed the car and pulled out of the driveway. He parked again, searching for another way. An abrupt thought came to him. What was that about Joshua and the walls of Jericho?

He made a screeching turn and headed back into Coconut Grove. He found an electronics store within minutes and a lot of cash changed hands.

Less than half an hour later MacKenzie was back, parked across the road from Sanchez's mansion. He flipped the amplifier switch to on. A light glowed on the silver chassis which was connected to the power supply through the cigarette lighter. He picked up the microphone on its coiled cord,

"*Sebastion Segurra, this is Peter MacKenzie. . . . I need to talk to you. . . . Justine is missing. Sebastion Segurra, this is Peter MacKenzie. . . . I need to talk to you. . . . Justine is missing. Sebastion Segurra, this is Peter MacKenzie. . . .*"

His voice boomed out of the speaker on top of the car. Police used a similar hookup, so did election candidates. He turned up the gain and made sure the horn-shaped speaker was pointed at Sanchez's house.

"*. . . I need to talk to you. . . . Justine is missing. Sebastion Segurra . . .*"

He kept it up. People from neighboring houses were beginning to walk down their long driveways, staring. A guard slipped out from Sanchez's gate and came running across the road.

"*. . . I need to talk to you. . . . Justine is missing.*"

The guard poked his head into the car and began screaming. "You better"—MacKenzie stuck the microphone into his face—"*get out of here or Señor Sanchez will make you into*—" he stopped abruptly, mouth snapping shut angrily. He reached for the amplifier, and MacKenzie shoved the barrel of the .38 against his temple.

The man retreated carefully. MacKenzie picked up the mike again.

"Sebastion Segurra, this is Peter MacKenzie. . . . Justine is missing. . . ."

Sebastion heard the racket. He opened a window. He could hear clearly now. MacKenzie? How could he have found him here? But the rest of the message made that unimportant. He raced out of the room and down to the main floor.

The house was in chaos. Guards were running in for Victor's instructions and the servants were crowding to the windows. Sebastion pulled the guard commander over.

"Bring the man here," he ordered, "and see that he isn't hurt."

The guard hesitated.

"At once!" Sebastion snapped.

"Si, señor." He relayed the order.

"Have him brought to the library. Where is Señor Sanchez?"

"In the vineyard, señor."

"Get him too."

Sebastion turned towards the library. Justine missing? Internal warning bells began to ring a strange knell. Was there danger here he hadn't suspected? A guard was running for the door. Sebastion sidestepped clumsily and the guard ran right into him. They almost fell, but Sebastion steadied the man and patted his clothing back into place.

"You okay?"

"Si, Commandante."

He sent the man on his way with a hasty apology and slipped the gun he'd lifted from him into the waistband of his pants, under his shirt.

"Sebastion!"

It was a very worried-looking MacKenzie accompanied by a pair of house guards. Sebastion waved them off and steered MacKenzie into the library.

"Where's Justine?" he asked as soon as they were inside.

"She's gone, taken by someone." The rest of the story came out in a rush. "So I came to you," MacKenzie finished. "I don't know who could be responsible. You might. Who comes to mind?"

"One alarming possibility. You alerted CIA?"

"First thing. Terrence Holmes set the wheels in motion. Look, Sebastion, if CIA's not behind it—and it makes no sense that they are . . . Christ, the contras worship Justine—no one but your group would profit by her disappearance."

"That's what alarms me. The only other force to profit from her loss are the Sandinistas themselves, and they don't have the reach for this." He grew pensive. "She just opened the door? No struggle?"

"I would have heard it. At least one of them must have been someone she knew."

"I agree. And someone she could reasonably assume could have bypassed security."

"No tradesman then."

"No, but another agent, maybe. She opens the door for a familiar face, thinking it's business, and gets hit with a hypo or gas."

"Do we call Holmes?"

Sebastion shook his head. "He'll have figured all that out already. There's a shorter route to finding the turned agent. The security log said one was female?"

"Yes."

"I have a very bad feeling that—"

The door opened and Victor Sanchez came in, leaning heavily on his cane. He was accompanied by two guards with drawn pistols.

"Search him," Sanchez commanded, pointing to MacKenzie.

"What the hell is this?" MacKenzie protested angrily as the .38 was taken roughly from him.

"Captain Peter MacKenzie, meet Victor Sanchez," said Sebastion. He was composed and somewhat distant.

Sanchez hefted the .38. "Why do you come to my house with a loaded gun, señor? Besides creating a terrible disturbance in the street, upsetting my neighbors?"

MacKenzie started to speak but Sebastion cut him off. "Victor, Justine is missing. Kidnapped from her apartment."

"This is terrible!"

"I'm glad you're concerned. It will make it easier for you to give me the name of your man inside the CIA."

Sanchez reacted to Sebastion's remark with a shocked look. "My man? I don't know what you're talking about."

"Come on, Victor. It works out that way. It was someone she knew, someone on her side. But he was working for someone else. You have someone like that, Victor, just like that. You told me so yourself. And later, Aura's questions. A man and a woman." He took a deep breath and let it out slowly. "All right. We get her back, I can learn to forget. If not . . ." He shrugged.

"You threaten me in my own house?"

"We're talking about my sister. What do you want, Victor, the only Segurra? A guarantee of your property returned? Tell me. I get Justine back, it's a deal."

Sanchez's face changed sorrowfully. "I think it's too late for that," he said. "You don't really hate enough, Sebastion. That's always been your problem. It limits you. But I hate them enough for both of us. Three years in a swamp. This." He pointed to his leg. "I made a road to power, to a place where no one could ever do that to either of us. After August first you would have been the only choice, the people's salvation. President, if you liked. But not with Justine around."

"My sister, Victor. Where is she?"

"Such a small loss. Don't you see? You have to be the one. Not her. You."

"Not me, Victor."

Sanchez looked like that eventuality genuinely distressed him. "I don't want the contras in charge of the country, Sebastion. If you don't want the power, I'll find someone else. Better that than your sister the CIA puppet."

"She would never be. You don't know her at all if you think she could. Let her go and I'll be your man."

Sanchez shook his head. "I may not know her, but I do know you. You don't forget or forgive, or bend even a little. Sadly, I miscalculated."

"Where is she?"

"She was taken to the ranch. I'm sorry." Sanchez motioned to the guards. "Take them." He looked at his watch. "Aura's a very smart girl. She knew your weaknesses. They'll almost be there by now. I am sorry it came to this, Sebastion."

"Me, too, Victor. Truly." His hand fluttered for a second in front of him, and suddenly there was a gun in it. He shot Sanchez in the head first, then the wide-eyed guard before the man even had a chance to take a step.

The sound of the gun's explosions was thunderous in the tiled room. The second guard turned from MacKenzie and fired at Sebastion almost as Sanchez was falling. But MacKenzie was already moving. He bowled into the man and slammed him back against a glass bookcase. Shards rained down on them, and the gun flew from the guard's hand. MacKenzie hit him with a closed fist once, then again. The man slumped to the floor.

He turned to Sebastion. "What now?"

Sebastion retrieved the weapons and handed him the .38. He thrust his chin at the door. "I think the others will listen to me. Sanchez wasn't the only backer, just the main one. The coordinator. The others will clear this up."

"Where's the ranch?"

Sebastion picked up the phone and dialed a number. "North of here, and west," he said while he waited for the connection. "They'll go up Ninety-five and cut across Eighty-four. Alligator Alley."

"I know it."

"Just a minute. Elias? Bueno. Sebastion . . . Si." He spoke in Spanish for a few moments. "Si . . . Bueno, adios." He put down the receiver, lifted it again, and looked to MacKenzie. "You have a local number for Justine's people?"

MacKenzie gave it to him. "It's been two hours, Sebastion. We need fast transportation."

"I know. Wait. Hello? This is Sebastion Segurra. Yes, MacKenzie is with me. . . . Yes, we can take you to Justine. . . . Yes, agreed . . . No, pick us up first. . . . Absolutely." He gave Sanchez's address. "In back, a grassy lawn. It's big enough. . . . Fine. Good-bye." He turned to MacKenzie. "All set."

"Helicopter?"

Sebastion nodded. "Ten minutes."

"Let's go."

In the main room guards and staff stood about aimlessly. Sebastion addressed them in Spanish. Outside, a black limousine was coming up the drive. "My people," he said to MacKenzie. "They'll take care of things here. Come."

In back the grass stretched down to the gardens that bordered the walls. White wrought-iron benches sat under the trees by the house.

"This ranch, Sebastion—what's it doing in the middle of the Everglades?"

Sebastion shielded his eyes and peered into the sky. The *woop-woop-woop* of helicopter blades reached them.

"There." He pointed.

"You haven't answered me. What kind of ranch sits in a swamp?"

"The kind that raises alligators," Sebastion said, and MacKenzie felt fear and sickness twist his guts.

"My God, Sebastion."

The helicopter dropped out of the sky and hovered an instant before touching down. A man poked his head out. "Terrence Holmes. Segurra? MacKenzie?"

"Right."

They climbed into the craft. The blades picked up speed again, till the airwaves flattened grass and shrubs. For a second they were poised only feet above the ground. Then they leaped into the sky and swung north.

21

THE EVERGLADES

The swamp was a patchwork quilt of greens and blues and deeper greens seen from the air; small stagnant lakes and moss-covered trees. Their helicopter was a good-sized Sikorsky, and they'd made good time. Holmes was already filled in, and in back, a platoon of Marines in battle dress cradled automatic weapons and waited for the signal to go.

"Five or six miles," Sebastion called up to the pilot. "Twin lakes together like a figure eight. The ranch is on the northern shore in between."

The pilot gave him the thumbs-up sign and dropped lower.

"Any suggestions for a landing site?" Holmes asked.

"The main pens are on the water. About fifty yards back are the growth sheds and the main house. In between it's mostly grass and scrub and a few smaller pens. Behind the house is the skinning and butchering shed."

"Butchering? Someone eats those things?"

"The tails. Gourmets consider them quite a treat. Tastes like veal. Obviously, the skin's the main thing. The animals are brought to the shed behind the house for both. If I was in charge, I'd land in back there, take the main house first, then fan out in twos to the other buildings."

"I'll tell them."

"One other thing," Sebastion said. "You'd better tell the Marine CO these ranchers are all ex-soldiers, loyal to Sanchez. If they see an armed man, they assume he's hunting them."

"Okay."

Holmes went back to the Marines and Sebastion pulled MacKenzie towards him. "Some advice?" he said into his ear, over the engine noise.

"Sure."

"This isn't the kind of fighting you're used to. No hide-and-seek tactics, no technology, no precise commands. Look and fire, that's all. Stay by me. We'll go in together."

"All right."

"Last thing. If we find her, we get her back to the copter. Let the Marines do the rest. No grudges, no excess. Just get her out and back."

MacKenzie nodded. The .38 lay snug against his waist again, and he'd added an automatic weapon, the kind used by the Secret Service. Its boxlike shape and short, vented barrel sat comfortably in his lap. The clip was full. He'd lost the extra ammunition for the .38, but an extra clip for the automatic protruded from his back pocket.

"There." Sebastion pointed.

The copter pilot saw them too. Twin lakes with a group of buildings in between. He hit a button over his head and a buzzer sounded back by the Marines. The CO gave the ready sign. They packed together, huddled by the exit door.

MacKenzie picked up his weapon. A silent rage was building up, and he took deep breaths to control it. He was very frightened. Too many visions of what they might find filled his mind.

They hit the ground and the Marines were already moving. Shots crashed into the helicopter. Two men with scowling faces and dirty hair went down under the Marines' fire. The shots stopped. But there was sudden fire from the house. One Marine fell. The rest covered the others and moved in.

A grenade took out the front door. The Marines' fire steadied. A man fell out the second-floor window. One tumbled out the side porch. Two Marines made it to the front door and ducked inside, weapons firing steadily.

"This way," yelled Sebastion to MacKenzie.

They ran across the sand to the first outbuilding. Sebastion raked the entrance with a sustained fire and then rolled in low and fast, MacKenzie covering his back. They stood in the shed breathing heavily, wary of movement. Around them were low-walled pools filled with writhing green hatchlings. The air was fetid and foul.

Sebastion saw the soldier out of the corner of his eye even as he realized he was too far from cover. The man's gun came up . . . and MacKenzie's fire spun him around like a crazed dancer. He sprawled backwards into one of the pools and was covered in an instant by squirming, snapping reptiles. Sebastion let his breath out and moved off.

MacKenzie forced himself to look into all the pools. The next shed was empty but for more hatchlings. Mercifully, the pools contained nothing else.

There were still sounds of fighting from the direction of the main house. Sebastion pointed to the butchering shed and they ran across the scrub grass.

"Sebastion, look!"

"I see it." A van marked Klean-Rite was parked outside the shed. It was empty. MacKenzie's heart was racing. They slowed and moved quietly along the cinder-block wall toward the doorway.

"On three," Sebastion whispered. "One, two . . . *now.*"

They burst into the long open room . . . and stopped dead.

"Nothing rash now," warned Aura Vasquez in a commanding tone. "Hold off. We're going to talk deal."

It took a full second for MacKenzie to take it all in. The girl was standing on the rim of an open pit that contained a pair of seven-foot alligators. Suspended over them lengthwise, in a canvas sling attached to the ceiling by lengths of chain and pulleys, was Justine. She was conscious, but her hands and feet were bound and she was gagged. Her eyes were wide with fear. Below her the bloody-mouthed lizards nudged the remains of a man. Their long jaws opened and shut like drawbridges. The stench made MacKenzie gag.

At one end of the pit was a cage, and at the other, a low steel table with a guillotinelike affair on it. *They eat the tails,* MacKenzie remembered Sebastion saying. The reptiles were brought to the pit in cages, killed, and transported to the table by sling. There they were skinned and the tails removed. But this woman let the reptiles into the pit alive.

"I can lower her down," she threatened. Her left hand rested on a switch. "You can see past results."

"There are Marines here, Aura," said Sebastion. He stood unmoving, not wanting to provoke her. "And Justine's friends are outside. You know *them.* They frown on this sort of thing. They don't like it at all." He frowned. "Neither do I."

"I don't care what you like, Sebastion. I don't even care how you got here so quickly. You're here, and we've taken out some insurance. You get her back if we walk out of here."

"We?"

A man stepped out of the shadows. He was armed. "Both of us," he said simply.

"Ah, Victor's man," Sebastion said. "You know Holmes?"

The man nodded. Sebastion said, "He's outside. You can go if you want. You and he might talk—"

"He stays with me!" Aura said quickly. "Packard, do you

hear me? Victor will get us out of the country." The man hesitated for a moment, and clearly the possibility of some accord with his former employers crossed his mind. But the hesitation lasted only a few seconds. There was no going back. He moved closer to Aura.

MacKenzie forced himself to wait. There was no opening yet. With Justine over that pit he could do nothing. Promise them anything, he urged Sebastion silently. Just get that woman's hand off the switch.

"Get rid of your weapons," Aura commanded. Sebastion took MacKenzie's automatic and his own. "In that drum there," she directed.

He saw what she meant. A fifty-five-gallon drum filled with a dark, foul-smelling fluid stood nearby. He dropped the weapons in without protest. "Go now, Aura," he said. "All we want is Justine."

Aura edged toward the rear door and pulled it open without her hand leaving the switch. Packard disappeared outside. "You'd be a better liar if you had more practice," she said to Sebastion. "But even you can't come after us if you're too busy."

"No! Aura!"

But she slapped the switch as she was turning, and ducked neatly out the door as the sling began to drop. Neither man's attention was on her, though, as the chains slid through the pulleys and plummeted for the floor. It hit the bottom of the pit with a sickening thud.

MacKenzie was over the side before conscious thought impelled him. He vaulted the low wall and landed in a crouch, aware only of fear so deep and terrifying he was amazed he could still move.

The .38 was in his hand as the first alligator saw him and advanced. The reptilian eyes tracked him, and the tail flicked back and forth like a bullwhip. MacKenzie fired. He put two bullets into the creature's head but it still kept coming. He pulled the trigger again and again. The animal kicked over on its side, turning and twisting almost into a circle and slamming its tail down into the concrete till finally it died.

Justine was struggling to get out of the sling. He started towards her.

"MacKenzie! Watch out behind you!"

It was Sebastion's voice, and MacKenzie leaped without hesitation. He heard the wet slap of jaws closing behind him so close he could feel the wind on his legs. Fear shot up his spine, tightened his groin. He turned. Tail undulating like a wave, the second alligator charged him.

"Get Justine!" he yelled, aiming the .38 and pulling the trigger in the same instant. The blast jerked the creature's head around, but it shrugged it off with an almost human gesture of disdain. It came on again with its short flexing legs sending it forward. MacKenzie pulled the trigger again. Nothing—the gun was empty.

He threw the gun at the reptile and ran to his right, trying to keep out of its way but desperate to draw it away from Justine. Peripherally he saw Sebastion cutting at Justine's bonds, pulling her out. But he had no time for any help. The alligator lunged at him, and only chance and the bloody remains at the bottom of the pit saved him.

He slipped in the gore and went down as the reptile charged. All at once the scaly hide was on top of him, twisting and trying to get its jaws on him. He yelled in pain as the weight hit him, but the head was past and he pushed with his legs, frantic to shove the hissing monster off him. Pain shot up his legs. It rolled over him and slithered away.

MacKenzie tried to stumble back to his feet, but the sudden pain in his legs overwhelmed him. He fell back. He tried to crawl, unable to support his weight. He slipped in the muck again and it suffused his nose, his eyes. He wiped at his face to clear the awful slime from it . . . just in time to see the alligator turn back to him, its frightening eyes locking on to its helpless prey.

He panicked, clawing at the concrete and trying to crawl away. He imagined his legs in the lizard's mouth, gobbled up piece by piece, and prayed to God. But his legs just wouldn't hold. He cried, turning to see the razor-sharp rows of teeth that lined the jaws, knowing it was over, praying. . . .

Sebastion hit the creature like a runaway truck. Its jaws snapped shut in momentary confusion and the ugly snout turned aside. Sebastion grabbed one of the creature's legs in a vain attempt to turn it over, but he hadn't counted on its weight. The body lifted but wouldn't overturn. The great tail thrashed wildly, knocking Sebastion over backwards. His feet slid in the gore, and the alligator slithered away.

It stopped. Harsh eyes watched Sebastion retreat, then refocused on MacKenzie. It fixed on him for what he knew was the last time. He couldn't climb out of the pit. Sebastion was searching for a weapon, but there were none. MacKenzie was too heavy to be lifted out, and the alligator would be on them in seconds if they tried.

The slithering creature hissed angrily and came straight for him. . . .

MacKenzie would never be certain afterwards how much of what he saw next was altered by fear and pain and how much was real. In later days he would discount the shining light and the silver glow to her naked, blood-spattered body as delusion, but beyond that he would never forget Justine racing past him with the guillotine table's long, sharp blade raised high in her hands and the terrible rage that drew her features into a rictal mask as she brought the blade slicing down savagely into the alligator's spine with all her strength.

The kind of scream he'd heard in the gym tore from Justine's throat as she wrenched the blade loose. The reptile twisted madly, snapping its jaws, but she leaped aside and brought the blade down again in the same spot. Blood spurted from the mortal wound. Justine slammed the blade home again, just managing to dance away from the frenzied, lunging creature. Hissing madly, it bucked away, crawling forward, dying slowly. Its legs gave out on the other side of the pit and it sank to the floor, motionless.

Sebastion came and put his arms under MacKenzie's shoulders, and he and Justine dragged him out of the pit. There was a hose near the cages, and Justine took it and played it over herself, then MacKenzie and Sebastion. MacKenzie motioned to Sebastion to give her his shirt. Justine took it, smiling bemusedly, and wrapped the sodden garment around her. Better than nothing, MacKenzie's stern look said, as Marines came running in.

MacKenzie felt himself lifted and placed on a medic's stretcher. Outside, the light made him blink, but the fresh air dispersed the awful stench. He was grateful. Over to the side were two bodies laid side by side on the sandy ground.

"Yours?" asked Holmes, coming up alongside.

MacKenzie looked at Aura and Packard and shook his head. "Not mine," he managed. "Yours?"

Holmes nodded. "The man. Pity."

MacKenzie thought about the pit inside. No pity at all. Good job, Marines.

The pain in his legs was moving behind his eyes, and the need for sleep was a physical hunger. People were speaking but he paid little attention. Justine said something, then hunkered down beside him and lifted his head onto her lap. That was nice. He didn't even protest when someone stuck a very sharp needle into him.

She was back.

They carried him out smiling.

22

NICARAGUA

Colonel Nikolai Renkov of Soviet Naval Intelligence looked at the primitive airfield from the exit ramp of the jet that had brought him from Moscow. The heat caught him at once. The collar of his white shirt seemed suddenly too close fitting. He was a middle-aged man of medium height, with clear gray eyes and closely cropped salt-and-pepper hair. He fished out a handkerchief and mopped at features that were solidly Great Russian. He walked down the ramp and extended a hand to the Nicaraguan official who had come to meet him, having to transfer the attaché case he was carrying to his other hand.

"Comrade Renkov," said the official, "I am Miguel Segurra, Deputy Minister of Defense."

Renkov shook hands politely. "Thank you for coming to meet me. We'll go directly to the submarine?"

"First to the Minister of Defense. He wishes to meet you, to extend our apologies personally."

"But I was told—"

Miguel steered him into the car. "There is nothing to be concerned about, Colonel. The *Kirov* is being refitted under the watchful eyes of your Captain Gorskov, and repairs should be completed this afternoon."

This seemed to relax Renkov somewhat. "That is good news. Where is the crew?"

"In the city on shore leave. They'll be back by dusk. With any luck at all your sub will be under way by midnight."

"My government is grateful," Renkov said. "You can imagine the concern—a fully armed nuclear submarine. Besides, the embarrassment of having to be towed in." He shook his head ruefully.

"The published reports spare you any blame. Everyone is aware of the unfortunate incident with our fishing fleet."

"What is true and what the foreign press can build into what isn't are two different things. The indignity of wallowing in the sea with American reconnaissance planes buzzing by is, well . . . difficult for us, at the very least. We are very anxious for *Kirov* to sail. Who handled security?"

"Why, I did myself," said Miguel. "No one was allowed on board unsupervised. Your captain checked every repair, and our Chief Engineer Santillo even completed the initial damage inspection and the final certifications with him present."

"That was very conscientious."

"We tried to be thorough. The ship is perfect, quite up to your standards. It was the least we could do."

Renkov considered that. "Perhaps," he said, "this talented Chief Engineer would like to be a candidate for advanced training in one of our technical institutes. A year or two and he would return a master."

"We're very pleased with him now."

"Of course. But consider it."

Miguel said he certainly would.

Santillo eyed the computers in the Sonar room with undisguised admiration. They were the latest additions to

Kirov's fighting array. Gorskov knew Santillo's being here was a violation of security, but the man was so interested in everything. Besides, given his job crawling around *Kirov*'s insides, keeping him out of places was next to impossible anyway. Finally, Gorskov stopped trying. Moreover, he found Santillo an intelligent listener, and had actually begun to enjoy explaining some of the more technical items. He could rarely speak so freely, but it was a long way from Moscow, and the political officer wasn't on board. Gorskov grinned, thinking of him running frantically around the small, apparently quite decadent city surrounding the port here, hopelessly trying to shepherd the crew through a place where liquor and women seemed to be everywhere.

"These, then, can filter up to that wavelength *and* identify separate targets?" Santillo was asking.

"If you patch across the Ural-70 and run the ABSOLVE program I told you about."

"But wouldn't that limit the range?"

"Not if you compensate with the Borslav. It's a new wrinkle, but it works."

Santillo's face lit up. "I see. What a clever innovation."

"We believe it to be."

"Well, Captain, I think we're ready to conduct deck trials. Do you want to rotate the main shaft now?"

"Yes, I think we should." He called down to the Engine Room and gave the orders. They waited. Soon they felt a steady throb through the deck plates. "Bring the engines to half power," Gorskov commanded. "Three minutes." The vibration increased to a level expected for half power.

"Everything is running fine, Comrade Captain," said the Chief Engineer's voice over the intercom.

"Fine. shut them down," Gorskov said. He clapped Santillo on the back. "Even officers deserve a reward at the end of a long labor. Come, there's a bottle in my cabin waiting for us. Real vodka, Russian vodka."

"I'm honored, Comrade Captain," Santillo said, meaning it.

"Good. We'll drink to a successful voyage."

"I'll happily drink to that."

* * *

The *Kirov's* political officer was very unhappy. For the last hour he'd been searching for stray crew members and couldn't find any. This worried him. There were always strays.

He walked down the empty main street—an average-sized avenue with two- and three-story wood-frame buildings down most of it—and was forced to admit finally that everybody must have taken the buses back to the temporary barracks.

"Pardon, señor?"

He turned towards the voice. A Sandinista army officer was coming out of the police station, beckoning and speaking to him. Since he spoke only Russian and a little English he had no idea what the soldier was saying. He tried to communicate that fact.

The soldier smiled. No problem. He pointed and beckoned again. *"Kirov?"* he said questioningly.

The political officer decided one of his men might be inside, perhaps in custody for some petty crime. He nodded, smiling, too, and followed. The soldier led him into the building, past a few local constables seated at cluttered desks, to an area in the rear. The cells were here, mostly empty.

But one was full. It took the political officer a full second to recognize the rest of the *Kirov's* officers, so unexpected was the sight.

"Mishkin? Pavel Ivanovich? What. . . ?"

Heads swiveled toward him and mouths opened to warn, but the soldier had the cell door open and pushed the political officer inside before there was even time to react. He stumbled into the other men, now all standing, and they pushed him back upright. He turned furiously, fuming at the outrage, dancing around like a jerked puppet while quoting Lenin. He demanded his rights as a Soviet officer.

The guard seemed genuinely interested, until he abruptly walked away. Removing the audience had little effect on the political officer though. The tirade continued unabated.

It was Mishkin who finally looked at the others tiredly, aware that such idiocy could go on for hours. He took in their Spartan surroundings with a wry gesture.

"All this," he said, "and lectures too."

"Shit," said Pavel Ivanovich.

Kirov's crew, for the most part, were still slightly hungover, quite happy with their liberty, and somewhat less than overjoyed about having to return to the rigors of duty. They were also wondering what the rows of chairs facing the podium in this building they'd been brought to were for. As obedient seamen, however, they took the seats without protest, aware that debate often proved dangerous.

There were almost a hundred men, and they watched the navy officer who entered the room dressed in full dress uniform of the Nicaraguan High Command march up to the podium and tap the microphone to see if it was working. His voice abruptly boomed out in pretty good Russian.

"Comrades, I am Lieutenant Eduardo Perez of the Nicaraguan Navy and the newly formed joint Russian-Nicaraguan International Command. I am here to congratulate you on being selected for a glorious honor and to be part of an historical mission that will be spoken about for generations. The crew of the *Kirov* has been chosen to serve on the first international Communist naval ship in the world. Our two countries are partners in this daring enterprise. Sadly, only some of you will be selected. Happily, the rest will be going back to the glorious worker's paradise to serve on other ships. For those selected, additional pay and benefits, however, will soften the blow of not returning to the motherland so soon."

There was already a murmur in the crowd. Who wanted to go back?

"In order for our personnel experts to determine those among you ready and able to serve on such a venture, I ask you now to step one at a time into those cubicles at the far end of the room, where you will be interviewed and a decision rendered.

"Good luck to all of you. This is an historic moment for worldwide communism, and one which you can be proud of. Someday you will be known as the crew that sailed the *Kirov,* the first ship of its kind.

"Good luck to all of you. You may begin lining up now, comrades. Good day."

No strangers to lines, the sailors began a steady shuffle back to the cubicles. There was some discussion of this strange turn of events, but most were careful not to have an opinion. That was always safer. However, some did think it strange, and as time wore on, rumors began to circulate that the new captain wouldn't be a Russian. Very odd. But another rumor held that the cook wouldn't be Russian either. This meant the food would improve. A fair enough trade, most figured.

All of the interviewers were trained Internal Security officers. It took them less than two hours to weed out anyone who figured differently.

Barrista's limousine turned onto the pier and pulled to a stop beside *Kirov*. Soldiers opened the door for the Minister of Defense and his party. The green waters in the slip lapped quietly against the sub, and the tall black sail rose high overhead. Barrista was the first to cross over the metal grating to the sub, followed by Miguel and Colonel Renkov. One after the other they descended into the corridor underneath.

The empty sub had an odd feel, like a party before the guests arrived. It discouraged conversation. Renkov had probably had enough conversation anyway, Barrista thought, since he'd been kept occupied for almost three hours. No stranger to the Victor III's, Renkov was finally able to move without the Minister of Defense at his side, and he took off for the captain's cabin.

The sounds of muted conversation reached them before they arrived. Renkov called out, "Comrade Captain Gorskov?" More followed in Russian, sharp commands.

Gorskov came hurriedly out of his cabin and saluted sharply. "Comrade Colonel," he said stiffly. "I can report all work is done and *Kirov* is seaworthy again. Allow me to present Comrade Engineer Santillo, who oversaw all the repairs."

Renkov inclined his head. "Your Minister speaks most highly of you, comrade. We appreciate your effort in our behalf."

"Nothing, really," Santillo said. "It's a very good ship."

"We think so too." He turned to Barrista. "With your permission, Minister, I would like to speak with Comrade Captain Gorskov in his cabin."

"Of course."

Barrista, Miguel, and Santillo moved down the corridor as the door to Gorskov's cabin closed.

"Gorskov has the firing keys?" Barrista asked Santillo quietly.

"In the safe," Santillo replied. "In a situation like this a very senior person is always dispatched to investigate. Gorskov's been expecting someone like Renkov. He'll turn over all the control data, firing keys, and codebooks, and Renkov will command the sub and bring it back to Cienfuegos."

"You're ready?"

Santillo looked around. "As ready as I'll ever be. I've been over every inch of her, and Gorskov was kind enough to explain what I didn't understand. How many of the crew could you keep?"

"Seventy out of a hundred," Miguel replied. "Enough for two shifts. Anyone the slightest bit edgy or overly inquisitive was culled out."

"Leaving only the dullards," Santillo said realistically.

"Dull ones don't question orders though," Miguel suggested.

"True enough. Are the officers ready to board?"

"Whenever you say."

"There's no reason to delay. Minister, I . . . Minister?"

Barrista didn't answer for a moment. He seemed far away, and touched the bulkhead as if to reassure himself the dream was indeed real. The power in this slim, black hull . . .

"Phillipe," Miguel prompted gently.

"Yes? Oh, yes. Let's do it now."

Renkov emerged from Gorskov's cabin with an efficient expression on his face, carrying the attaché case close to him. He stepped into the corridor . . . and several soldiers surrounded him and took the case out of his hands.

He spun around, sputtering indignantly. "Minister, what is this?"

"I'm sorry, Comrade Colonel, but for some very complex reasons my government is taking possession of this submarine. You, the captain, and the senior officers will be sent home shortly. No harm will come to any of you. Please relax. The crew will be released as well—that is, those who have elected not to sail on the first International Communist submarine."

"What is this nonsense?"

Barrista handed him a thin leather case. "Please see this gets to the General Secretary. It will explain everything. Perhaps he may even decide we aren't on different sides on this after all."

"You are stealing Soviet property in defiance of every treaty and law governing . . ."

Miguel was watching Gorskov. He was edging back, preparing to bolt. But the soldiers were too quick. They stepped in and clubbed him down neatly. Renkov took the opportunity to break for the ladder, but he got no farther than Gorskov. The soldiers lifted the unconscious pair, and Barrista directed them to be taken to the rest of the officers.

"Luis?"

Santillo had the case open. "All here. Give me a minute to study them and change uniforms and I'll be ready. You can bring the officers on with the crew. Give them all a feeling of arriving together."

"Lieutenant Perez is with them. I'll let him know," said Miguel. He climbed back up the ladder.

Barrista went forward. It was done. The control room was ready to be occupied, the ship all set to sail. The months of planning had come to fruition, and placed a force capable of destroying half a continent into his hands. *His* hands.

The newest nuclear power in the world was just born. Now it would burst forth from the sea.

Unbidden lines from another half-remembered play swam into his mind. The sea . . . strange . . .

> *Full fathom five thy father lies.*
> *Of his bones are coral made,*
> *those are pearls that were his eyes.*
> *Nothing of him that doth fade*

> But doth suffer a sea change
> into something rich and strange.

Something rich and strange . . . For a moment Barrista stopped hating the old nuns for what they represented and heard again only the magic of the English poet's cadence. Full fathom five; the sea changes everything.

He thought, In a few days it was going to change the world.

23

NICARAGUA

Kirov's radio officer, Mishkin, strained to get his chin above the window ledge set so high into the cell wall. The weapons officer under him grunted as Mishkin's boots dug harshly into his shoulders.

"Can you see anything?" asked Pavel Ivanovich, the navigator.

"It's Gorskov!" Mishkin exclaimed. "They're carrying him in along with another. Looks Russian. Both are unconscious."

Pavel Ivanovich looked to the Sonar officer, who was still scraping grease off the cell door hinges and smearing it on the floor outside. "That's all we have time for," he said.

The Sonar officer pulled his arm back through the bars and returned to his bunk, wiping his hands on the bedding.

"Watch me," Mishkin said to the others, clambering down. "When I go, we all go. Then it's every man for himself."

They all nodded. Down the corridor the steel door opened and two pair of guards came in, carrying the unconscious men. One shifted the weight to put the key in the doorlock, another reached for his pistol. The door began to swing open and the guards drew back.

Mishkin leaped off the bed and rammed the door with his shoulder, putting as much of his weight as he could manage into it. The door banged back into one startled guard who tried to turn out of its way, slipped in the grease, and went sprawling into the others like a bowling ball. The guard with his pistol drawn had no clear shot, and he went down too.

"Follow me!" Mishkin yelled.

The Russians stampeded out of the cell and ran for the main corridor. Shots rang out overhead. A few stopped. Mishkin put his head down and ran for it. Alarm bells began an unholy racket. Guards from the front raced in, tackling any seaman they could get their arms around. More went down.

"Pavel, in here!" Mishkin called, racing down the length of the room like a broken-field runner and bursting through a doorway.

The navigator followed him, but it was a poor choice indeed. They both stopped. Pavel Ivanovich looked around the bathroom sadly as Mishkin ran from stall to stall in vain search of an exit. But the green painted room held none.

Mishkin faced him ruefully. "Not such a good move, eh?"

Pavel Ivanovich shrugged. "We tried. You can take a crap while we wait, at least. That's something."

The sounds of the melee on the other side of the door were dying down. The escape just wasn't going to work. Mishkin sat down, depressed, but Pavel Ivanovich was still looking around.

"Mishkin?" he said. "Up there. You're the skinny one. Can you get through that window if I hold you?"

Mishkin squinted. "It's worth a try."

Pavel Ivanovich laced his fingers together and vaulted the radio officer up the wall.

"Almost! Higher, Pavel."

"Mumpf . . ."

"What?"

Pavel Ivanovich spit. "Your boot was in my mouth."

"Higher!"

"I'm trying."

"Almost, yes, wait . . . there."

Suddenly the weight was off Pavel Ivanovich's shoulders. Had Mishkin said good-bye? Probably; he just hadn't heard him. He looked around the empty bathroom. It was lonely without Mishkin.

He sat down to wait for the guards to find him. They had to wait for him to finish when they came.

24

CARIBBEAN SEA

The *Kirov* was traveling smoothly under the warm waters of the Caribbean, looking for prey. Her new officers were now used to the unfamiliar systems and to the difficult task of relaying orders through translators stationed in each area. It was helpful that many of the Nicaraguan and Cuban officers spoke English, as it turned out that many of the crew did also. Ironically, it proved the most common language and was used for much of the communications on board the first "International Communist ship."

Santillo's officers were still continuing the fiction that this was a training cruise. Lieutenant Perez was the navigator; Lieutenant Cordova commanded the attack center; and Lieutenant Villega was in charge of the sonar crew. Santillo had his men working smoothly. Drill after drill fused officers, men, and machinery into a working unit.

On the fifth day they began to hunt.

"Comrade Captain, Sonar. Target bearing oh-nine-oh, drawing left, estimated range fifteen kilometers, speed thirty kilometers per hour."

Santillo replied, "We'll take a look. All ahead two thirds, come left to oh-three-oh."

Kirov swung northeasterly.

"Proceed to periscope depth."

The Russian scope was heavy, and the crosshairs on the scope head window were sometimes lost to glare, but the image of the tanker churning low and fat through the water came clearly to him.

"Track her," he ordered Perez, "but take no hostile action and remain undetected. You're in charge till I return."

"Yes, Cap— Comrade Captain."

The Defense Minister and his Deputy were in the officers' mess, engrossed in a discussion over an array of charts spread out on the table. Santillo coughed politely.

"Yes, Captain?"

"We've picked up an oil tanker. Just the kind of thing to make an impression. It's fully loaded and well within the Zone. What do you think?"

Barrista and Miguel both wore the same gray coveralls worn by both officers and crew. Barrista looked at the clock thoughtfully.

"In less than an hour the American president will be told about us. I want this timed right. Surface and circle the tanker. Be sure they see us. As soon as we get the word from the council, we'll attack. What's her nationality?"

"Saudi."

"Perfect," Barrista said.

Santillo returned to the control room. "Prepare to surface." He looked at the clock. Less than an hour. The battle stations alarm was a fat red button over his head. He ached to slam it on.

"Right full rudder. Slow to one third."

Kirov began circling the tanker.

President Andrew Fletcher walked into the Oval Office with his Chief-of-Staff, Mark Dellman, beside him. Both wore dark business suits, but had discarded jackets and ties and rolled up their sleeves, which was a tribute to the steamy Washington summer lurking just beyond the windows.

"What does Arguello want?" Fletcher asked, frowning.

"I don't know," Dellman responded. "But he mentioned August First."

"Shit."

"He did something else that bothered me. Asked me to

set up an appointment with Ambassador Belov. Urged me, in fact."

"Christ, Mark. If there's been a leak on this . . ."

Dellman, a middle-aged scholar who'd been discovered to have a surprising flair for foreign affairs, internecine politics, and racquetball midway through a brilliant academic career, had come to work for the man who first convinced him to accept a posting at the United Nations and leave Harvard. He pressed a button on Fletcher's desk and a secretary answered at once. "Let me know as soon as the President's one o'clock gets here. Make sure he and the Soviet Ambassador are separated. No contact at all."

"Yes, Mr. Dellman."

Fletcher sat down on the couch and loosened his collar. Dellman kept his office running like a fine Swiss watch.

Dellman said, "There couldn't be any leaks on this. No way. We were assured Segurra was gotten out before he could tell them anything."

"Then what does the Nicaraguan Chief of Intelligence want here? He knows our position. The entire council knows it."

Dellman shrugged. "I don't know what he wants. But here's what convinced us to bring him in." He handed Fletcher a manila envelope. There were eight by ten enlargements inside, and markings on the back indicated CIA analysts had already been through them.

"Us? You said convinced us?"

"Myself, Becker at CIA, Admiral Merton. A few other technical specialists."

Fletcher went through the photos. Details were fuzzy, the images heavily grained. "What am I looking at?"

"According to the analysts, the interior of a Soviet Victor Three class nuclear-attack submarine."

"Victor Three? That's the kind that got fouled up off Nicaragua."

"Yes, it is. The scary thing is that we have nothing like this on file. Even deliberately overexposed, as CIA thinks they've been, these are an Intelligence coup."

"And Arguello's just handing them to us?"

"You can see why I agreed to the meeting. Something's going on. The Russians are visibly agitated, have been for days. Ambassador Belov sounded like he'd been waiting for my call."

Fletcher looked unhappy. "I don't want to walk into this blind, Mark. What links the Russians, Arguello, and an attack sub?"

"We just don't know. Satellite reconnaissance says the sub was repaired and sailed almost a week ago."

"Could they want a hard currency deal—military specs for dollars?"

"Unlikely. They wouldn't expect us to undercut our own sanctions."

"Well, put the whole interview on tape. We'll go over it later."

"Yes, sir." Dellman lifted a hinged plate on the President's desk and touched a switch. An LED glowed as the wireless, infrared relay activated sound-video cameras in the walls. The seal in the desk was invisible.

The intercom buzzed. "Yes?"

"The one o'clock is in the outer office."

"Thank you. I'll be out. Mr. President," Dellman said. "Arguello's here."

Fletcher was already fastening his tie. Dellman helped him into his suit coat.

"Tell him he's got five minutes and that I'm none too happy about seeing him in the first place," Fletcher said. "Tell him I'm hoping to hear something new."

"Okay."

Fletcher took the photos and stared at them for a few seconds before shoving them into his desk. He chose not to display his disquiet, even to Dellman, knowing the ex-scholar treasured the fiction that Fletcher was the most self-assured man on earth. He thought about the photos again. Self-assured people weren't supposed to believe in bad omens.

But if Fletcher had learned anything in over forty years in politics, these pictures were about as bad as omens could be.

"Mr. President, thank you for a meeting on such short notice."

"Señor Arguello." Fletcher didn't stand or offer his hand. He gestured politely for the Intelligence Chief to take a seat. "Mr. Dellman deserves your thanks. He seems to think you have something to say to me."

"I do. If you will allow me to speak freely . . . ?"

Fletcher smiled. It moved his whole face; the kind of smile people work to see. He couldn't resist the opening. "Everyone is allowed to speak freely here. I believe that's one of our main differences."

Arguello's face tightened but he said nothing. That bothered Fletcher. There was nothing obsequious or boastful about the man. That bothered Fletcher even more. He knew a confident look when he saw one.

"Mr. President, as of five o'clock Eastern time today, the Soviet nuclear submarine *Kirov* is under the control of the ruling council of the government of Nicaragua. We are aware of the intentions of the United States to invade our country and of the pretext you plan to use to justify it. I am required by my government to list three salient points.

"First, the *Kirov* is armed with SS-NX-21 nuclear-tipped, long-range cruise missiles. These missiles' range are in excess of twenty-five hundred kilometers.

"Second, any attempt to intervene militarily in Nicaragua will be repelled with all the forces at our command, including the *Kirov*. I must remind you that virtually every one of your southern coastal cities are within that twenty-five-hundred kilometer diameter. We ascribe to the same policy of Mutually Assured Destruction that has prevented combat between yourselves and the Soviet Union for decades. You may count on the release of the *Kirov*'s weapons should you initiate any attempt to coerce my government by force.

"Third, in order to safeguard our platform a second strategy has been put into place. The *Kirov* will be sailing with the SS-NX-21's fully armed and on ready-to-launch status. The *Kirov*'s patrol area will be a roughly circular area of the Caribbean Sea between Cuba and the Latin American land mass that extends from longitudes eighty to eighty-five degrees west and latitudes seventeen to twenty-one degrees north."

Arguello slid a slim portfolio across Fletcher's desk. "The precise coordinates are spelled out in these documents."

"*Kirov*'s defense is quite simple, Mr. President," Arguello continued. "The perimeter of her patrol area will be regarded as, in effect, a trip wire. Any attempt to cross that perimeter to engage *Kirov* will not, I repeat *not* result in engagement, but in a release of missiles instead. Therefore, in the interests of safety, you are required to clear *Kirov*'s zone of any merchant or military craft. Within one hour any ship not clearly on a course carrying it out of the Zone will be sunk. Any craft entering the Zone from that point on will trigger our response.

"There is no weapon available to you, including your P-3C Orion aircraft, LAMPS helicopters, attack subs, radar-guided missiles, or even low-yield nuclear bombs that can destroy *Kirov* before it can release its missiles. We regret such an action has been taken, but our position is clear. You can destroy the Sandinista government, but in our death throes we will take approximately one third of the United States with us. We feel sure that to prudent men such an outcome will be unacceptable."

Arguello stopped speaking. Fletcher could not miss the defiant look that crept over the other man's face. He leaned back and whistled softly. "Well, I've got to hand it to you. That is something new."

"Blackmail, that's what it is," said Dellman angrily. "And that's not new."

Arguello looked pacific. "*Nuclear* blackmail is. We hope you will see you left us little choice. Wasn't it your own Westerners who referred to a specific type of handgun as a Peacemaker? Think of the *Kirov* in the same way."

"What part did the Soviets play in this?" asked Fletcher.

"None. The submarine was stolen from them. Liberated, might be a better word."

"I like stole," Fletcher cut in grimly.

Arguello shrugged. "As you wish. But the Russians are certainly as surprised as you are."

"Spare parts, refueling, satellite telemetry, and the like . . ." Dellman said. "Where do you get those?"

Arguello leaned forward. His expression was that of a teacher whose pupil has failed to comprehend. "You're making an elementary mistake here," he said. "We aren't building a navy. We are well aware we can't fight a conventional war with you. The *Kirov* is to *prevent* that. It's a self-contained nuclear missile-launching platform.

That's all. Its nuclear fuel will last for years, it possesses internal guidance, and spare parts needs are months away. These aren't the rules of engagement as you're used to them. Just stay away or we fire. That's all."

"We require greater proof than just your word," Dellman said.

"In the portfolio," Arguello gestured. He checked his watch. "Further proof will be on the radio . . . say, in an hour or so. The first reports should have come in by then." He stood. "Thank you for this meeting, Mr. President. My government has nothing more to say at this time."

Fletcher studied the man for a while, then nodded to Dellman to let him out. Arguello left stiffly. Formally.

"Have him watched," Fletcher ordered when he'd gone. "Arrest him if he tries to leave the country. Well, what do you think, Mark?"

"I think we're in big trouble if they've got what he claims they've got. A stolen Russian sub. Jesus!"

Fletcher handed him the portfolio. "Get this to CIA. Then, very quietly, assemble the Joint Chiefs, National Security Advisor, liaisons from State and Defense and . . . no, we'll inform the congressional intelligence committees later on. Get Admiral Merton to bring over his top submarine men. You've got about an hour to prepare an initial briefing. Get them all into the situation room— slides, the works. I want to see one of these Victor Threes."

"Yes, sir."

Fletcher picked up the phone. "General Keller." The special operator had him connected in under five seconds. "General? . . . Yes, fine, thank you. But there's something upcoming. I want to heighten the alert status of our southern bases on the very, very quiet. Additional aircover against low-flying subsonic objects. Call it a smuggling operation, maybe. . . . Okay, that's good. Do it. Mark Dellman will be in touch within the hour. . . . Fine. Good-bye."

"What do you want to do about Ambassador Belov?" Dellman inquired.

"Stall him. He's not to leave the building. I'll talk to him, but after we've thought this one out a bit. I've seen contingency plans on everything from war in Europe to plague. But a stolen sub? Never."

Dellman picked up the portfolio and hurried out to arrange the briefing. Fletcher was tired and more worried than his expression showed; angry too. He walked over to the bar concealed behind a portrait of his long dead wife and poured himself a stiff brandy. After all these years he still didn't really think of her as gone. He wished she were here now.

"Millicent, my dear," he toasted the pretty, southern image. "We just took it up the ass." He drained the brandy. "I don't like the feeling, Millicent."

She demurely refrained from comment.

Arguello's car passed through the White House security gate, watched by a man across the street. As it went by, the lights flashed on and off twice. The watcher took note of this and walked away. Turning down a side street, he walked a few blocks to a restaurant he ate at frequently. Inside, he ordered a meal and went to the rear to use the phone.

"Operator? Long distance to Managua, Nicaragua." He gave the number and the operator repeated it back. The way she rolled the R's in Nicaragua, he knew she was Hispanic. It took a few minutes to make the connection, but his party answered on the first ring.

"Si?"

"The message was delivered," the watcher said.

"Gracias." The phone went dead.

The watcher went back to his table and ate what he'd ordered. The food was surprisingly good here. He sighed contentedly. He loved America—they made it so easy.

Aboard Kirov the radio officer, Lieutenant Ramos, had been waiting with the radio mast extended for the better part of two hours. The frequency was preset for this time of the day. Knowing its importance, when he received the transmission from Managua he brought it forward himself. He still didn't completely trust the flat-faced Russian sailors under his command.

"Captain?"

Santillo stepped away from the navigator's table. "Si, Ramos?"

"This just in. From Managua."

Santillo took the paper. There was only one word written on it and it made his heart jump. It read: PROCEED.

"Back to your station, Ramos," he ordered. "Thank you." His hand hit the Battle Stations alarm. A harsh bleat filled the control room, galvanizing the crew.

"Submerge the ship. Make your depth twenty meters," Santillo ordered. "Steady to course oh-one-oh."

The helm responded. *Kirov* turned north, leaving the tanker behind, and submerged to ordered depth.

"Attack Center, track and maintain a firing solution on that tanker. Torpedo room, verify tubes one and two are loaded with long-range torpedoes set for surface targets."

Tubes one and two were the only tubes available for torpedoes. The rest were loaded with the cruise missiles. But two torpedoes should be more than enough for a fat old tanker, Santillo thought, swinging the periscope around. They were almost at the northern perimeter of the Zone, and he'd placed the tanker just south of them, still inside it. He planned to turn back to the south, shoot, and proceed past the tanker, leaving it as a grim marker of their boundaries. Then he'd take the *Kirov* into the Zone and clear it of anything left inside.

"Right full rudder. Steady on course one-eight-oh."

The tanker was a lovely black hyphen poised on the horizon. So far *Kirov*'s crew was performing very well. "Radio room, broadcast a warning to the tanker's crew. Advise them to abandon ship. Inform them they have less than ten minutes before we destroy her."

"Yes, Comrade Captain."

Santillo waited, peering through the periscope. No lifeboats were launched. Pity. "Range to tanker," he called out.

"Eleven hundred meters, Comrade Captain."

"Status of tubes one and two?"

"Tubes one and two flooded and outer doors open, Comrade Captain."

"Range to tanker," he demanded again.

"Five hundred meters."

"We will shoot tube one, check bearing, and then shoot tube two."

Santillo waited. He felt the crew's anticipation. Good. This was a moment they should remember. He could see men gathering on the tanker's deck.

"Final bearing and shoot tube one. Set—stand by—fire!"

"Torpedo tube one away, Comrade Captain."

"Final bearing and shoot tube two. Set—stand by—fire!"

"Torpedo tube two away, Comrade Captain."

He couldn't have torn his eyes away from the scope for anything on earth. Twin wakes sped from *Kirov*. He tightened his grip on the periscope. Steady . . . steady, he urged.

The torpedoes hit the tanker in her main storage holds, and the explosives ignited them in a blinding paroxysm of fury. Flames shot a hundred feet in the air and thick, black smoke trailed into the sky like deadly plumage. The remaining holds blew out, and steel plate buckled like paper. The tanker broke into pieces, each burning furiously. There weren't any figures left he could see.

Santillo slapped the handles against the scope. "Down scope," he said happily. "All ahead one third. Make your depth seventy meters." That slow and deep, no one was going to spot them easily.

But if they did, the cruise missiles loaded in the remaining tubes would be a fitting eulogy. Mushroom clouds. Fire and smoke. Devastation.

A eulogy of fire and smoke. He liked that.

25

THE WHITE HOUSE

Another slide clicked into place, and the picture of a submarine on the surface of a choppy sea filled the screen in the darkened Situation Room.

"This is a Victor Three class nuclear-attack submarine," Dellman said in his best lecture voice. He was quite comfortable here; the academic was no stranger to the podium.

"Its submerged displacement is over 6300 metric tons and the propulsion system is nuclear. It carries a full complement of torpedoes—SS-N-16 antisubmarine rockets, and the newest SS-NX-21 nuclear cruise missiles, which the Victor Three has been modified to accept."

Another slide clicked onto the screen, a sub under way, her sail awash. "Introduced in 1979, the Victor Three has improved capabilities and technologies and is larger in size than the Victor One, with greater weapons capability. Like all Soviet subs, the diving planes are hull-mounted, rather than sail-mounted like ours, which gives them advantages in under-ice maneuvers. We, incidentally, are switching over."

"How does this sub compare to our Los Angeles class?" Fletcher inquired.

Dellman flashed another slide on the screen. "The Victor Threes have more power and greater depth capability, but the Soviets have to accept a whole lot of noise to get those. Heavier cooling pumps, bigger reactors—all mean we can locate them more easily. Unlike World War Two engagements, where speed and maneuverability on the surface counted heavily, today the important thing is silence and speed submerged. I've got a lot of technical explanations to follow, Mr. President, but perhaps Admiral Merton would care to condense it for us?"

Joe Merton was a tall, willowy man with a lined face devoid of beard, and piercing blue eyes. He was an old carrier man, and understood antisubmarine warfare—ASW—from long experience. He stood and brought a hand to his chin. "What Mr. Dellman is saying, sir, is that we've learned a lot about the way sound behaves in water since World War Two. Even if our sorting capability and our electronics hadn't evolved as rapidly as they have, that would still have given our antisubmarine warfare program a tremendous advantage. We know now what different-temperature waters do to sound, how thermals operate, why sound travels upward under ice, and so on. Now, when you add that knowledge to modern computers that can sort through billions of ambient sea noises, and electronics that extend our sonar range, you've got a whole different scenario than the run-and-fire boys of that era. That's why we've opted for fast, but stress the more silent subs. In ASW what can be heard can be located and destroyed. The Russians are just learning that."

"So what about the *Kirov*?" Fletcher asked after the lights came on. "Can we destroy it?"

Merton was cautious. "The L.A. class boat is the best in the world, sir, but the situation Mr. Dellman has described is outside any of our planning. I can order a squadron into *Kirov*'s zone and guarantee you that submarine will be destroyed within hours. But before it launches—that I cannot guarantee."

"So we're at the mercy of these terrorists?" Fletcher said, appalled.

"Sadly, sir, that may be the case for right now. The suicide bomber or terrorist who cares nothing for his own life makes a frontal attack unworkable. The Nicaraguans don't fear reprisal like the Soviets. We value New York; the Russians value Moscow. Both sides know that the value is too great to ever look at any type of nuclear exchange as anything but unthinkable. So we compromise. We each count on the other's restraint. But for Managua?" He shrugged. "I think they'd launch, sir."

"What about our ASW aircraft?"

"Same problem. As soon as the sonobuoys hit the water, the *Kirov* would hear them. One possible alternative would be a nuclear strike. The explosion would vaporize the cruise missiles even after launch."

"Wouldn't we be then doing to ourselves precisely what it is we wish to avoid?"

Dellman answered, "Initial calculations indicate the resultant tidal wave from a bomb big enough to do the job—not to mention the blast damage, firestorm, radiation and injuries—would cause property damage in the islands in the billions, kill hundreds of thousands, virtually wipe out several of the smaller Caribbean islands, rule out fishing and oil exploration for decades—"

"Thank you, Mark," Fletcher cut in. "The point is well taken. For the time being we're going to have to play for time till we work this one out. A nuclear strike is unacceptable. Roll back the plans for August First until we've cleaned up this *Kirov* mess. Admiral, cordon off the requisite area to all shipping."

"A question, sir," Merton said. He gestured to the other Chiefs. "There are other policy issues here as well. The sub is theoretically Russian property. They may insist on their right to go in and get it back. What do we do if they try and cross into *Kirov*'s Zone?"

"Stop them. The cordon includes all shipping, Admiral. I'll deal with the Soviets through diplomatic channels. They may listen to reason. But the policy is still clear. All shipping is to be kept out of the Zone. Use what you have to, but enforce that to the limit."

"Understood, sir."

Fletcher turned to the others. "Gentlemen, I'm grateful for your counsel. Set up a joint management team for this one and have some suggestions to me within a day. Mark will liaison. Whatever you need, you get." He paused. "Needless to say, I want this out of the papers. Anyone leaks this, I'll track him down and shoot the bastard. That's all."

The President walked back upstairs. Dellman grabbed for his papers and followed him.

The Soviet ambassador to the United States, Valery Belov, knew what his long wait in the White House was caused by, and it worried him deeply. He was an atypical Russian, a gifted man with artistic sensibilities that had not been totally eroded by the Soviet system. Belov was also a survivor; his career in the foreign service stretched back over fifty years, second only to Gromyko himself.

He remembered the day he first met Andrei Gromyko, then just a fast-rising member of the Foreign Ministry. Belov was a researcher assigned to the American department, with a few notable successes to his credit, including an analysis of the post-war elections which was very favorably received. It was Gromyko who called him into his office to discuss the report. After a fairly academic discussion Gromyko seemed to loosen up a bit, demanding more personal observations from Belov.

"Tell me, Valery Alekseiovich," Gromyko prompted, "What do you think the purpose of the diplomatic corps is?"

"Why, to implement the directions of the Foreign Ministry, whose policy is formulated by the members of the Politburo," he said carefully.

"Yes, yes, I know that answer. It is correct thinking, of course. But I want to know what *you* think."

Belov was not accustomed to taking such risks, but he sensed he had to take one now. "I think, Comrade Gromyko, that diplomats exist to prevent powerful nations from resorting to arms. War comes when men stop talking."

"And we have seen too much war, you imply."

Belov pulled no punches. "Twenty million of our comrades urge us to think so."

Gromyko absorbed that, seemed to think for a while. Abruptly, he changed topics. "You are a painter, I'm told."

"In my spare time."

"What is art?"

"The dictates of Socialist Realism provide for—"

Gromyko was angry. "Don't be dull, Valery Alekseiovich. What is your art?"

"A standard," Belov forced himself to reply honestly, "of what men could be."

"All men?" asked Gromyko. "Not just the new Soviet man?"

Belov nodded firmly. "All men. Neither painters nor diplomats can afford to blind themselves, Comrade Gromyko. The motherland can only profit from clear-seeing sons, I believe."

Gromyko considered the slightly younger man before him. "All right, Valery Alekseiovich. But just be certain your clear-sightedness continues to expose the weaknesses in our enemies more so than in ourselves. We'll talk again. Go and continue your work."

Three days later Belov was promoted. Additional schooling followed, a transfer, his first posting. As Gromyko's star rose, so did his. Gromyko himself had made Belov ambassador to the United States five years before.

Belov was older now than in those first heady days. Wiser, too, in the ways of upper echelon politics. But the same inner man peered out from hazel eyes under the high domed forehead. Hair now only grew in white tufts on the sides of his head, and his waistline was threatening to take him yet up another size. But his sense of standing between men-at-arms had never lessened.

"Mr. Ambassador?"

It was Dellman, the President's Chief-of-Staff. Belov liked the man's keen intellect, a trait he valued over most. Probably left over from his own scholarly training, he mused. They shook hands.

"I'm sorry you were kept waiting," Dellman said, "The President can see you now."

Belov followed him into the Oval Office. Fletcher was seated behind his desk and made no move to get up. A bad sign. "Good day, Mr. President," he said.

"And to you, Ambassador Belov. Please, be seated."

"Thank you." Belov hesitated. "Your Mr. Dellman was quite insistent we meet today. What service can I render?"

Fletcher walked around his desk and sat in a chair opposite Belov's. "That depends."

"On?"

"On what your government has to say about its submarine, the *Kirov*."

"Ah," said Belov. "I see. The Nicaraguans have been here."

"You make it sound like a fraternity, but yes, they have. How long have you known?"

Belov reached into his jacket pocket and brought out a sheaf of papers. "These were given to one Colonel Nikolai Renkov three days ago by the Nicaraguan Minister of Defense, Phillipe Barrista. It is everything we have. I assure you, we had no part in this . . . this criminal act."

"Why didn't you tell us about this sooner?"

"And run the risk of your thinking we played a part in it? No, we are victims too."

Fletcher's fingers formed a steeple. He gazed over the tip at Belov. "Some of the experts are a bit doubtful the Nicaraguans would alienate their strongest ally. Your thoughts on that?"

It was Belov's turn to be diplomatic. "I can say this much, Mr. President. A request for, ah . . . advanced weaponry was made to my government. But we adhere to treaties. The request was refused. We believe this business is the result."

"Yet you've done nothing so far."

"What would you have us do? To approach *Kirov* with one of our own subs might trigger an incident you'd hold us responsible for. That is an unacceptable risk. But we certainly condemn it as strongly as you do."

"Then you'll help us?"

"If we can. What do you want?"

Fletcher looked to his Chief-of-Staff. Dellman moved closer and said, "I could be more subtle about this, I suppose, but most of the cards are on the table already. What we want are the military specifications for the Victor Three class submarine. Everything: sonar, weaponry, ASW tactics, the whole ball of wax. I'm told that having these, we may find a way to take the *Kirov* out before it can launch. Other than that, keep your shipping out of the area. We don't want a confrontation, but if you try to enter the Zone, you'll be turned back. We can't allow anyone to trip the wire."

"I can tell you this," said Belov slowly. "Your requests will be relayed home, but what you want is so . . . antithetical to our notions of security that I personally have trouble believing it is possible."

"Don't tell me what is or isn't possible," said Fletcher angrily. "This is your sub. You're responsible for it."

"Not when it isn't under our control, and we didn't put it there," Belov reminded him gently.

"One doesn't mismanage a weapon of this magnitude and escape responsibility," Fletcher insisted. "Make sure that's understood. This kind of situation has unforeseeable consequences. It's clearly to everyone's advantage to limit it as quickly as possible."

"There we certainly agree," said Belov.

"Good." Fletcher rose. "That's all, Mr. Ambassador. Good day."

Belov stood as well. He made one more effort to soften the angry emotions the meeting had produced. "Mr. President, we are truly concerned about this. You must believe that. We are every bit the victims also."

Fletcher's face did not soften noticeably, but Belov thought he detected a lessening of tension when Fletcher said, "A fine sentiment. Adding actions to it will do much to convince us you mean it."

"I'll do what I can."

Fletcher nodded. He watched the ambassador leave. The man's reactions had told him a lot. Getting military information out of those aging paranoids in the Kremlin, he thought, was going to be almost impossible. Most of them would love nothing better anyway than to see the U.S. involved in a nuclear accident like this, and the backlash from public opinion could hamstring arms policy for decades. Nuke-free zones, impossible restrictions: the Soviets would be in propaganda heaven.

Fletcher knew that the rest of the politics were just as tricky. A lot of people were going to object to the invasion. He and his advisors knew that. But most of the objections would be stilled by a quick, surgically neat operation that restored democratic pluralism immediately and was preceived to be that most cherished of American values—effective.

But no one was going to support democracy for Nicaragua if it meant losing several southern states . . . except maybe New Yorkers. Only God knew what motivated them.

Dellman came back in, looking grim. "The *Kirov* just knocked off a Saudi tanker and a couple of smaller ships in the south."

"Are we in position?'

"Almost. Another few hours."

Fletcher thought things over. "We've got to let the British in on this. All of NATO, I suppose."

"Yes, sir."

"Want a sandwich? It's going to be a long night."

"They're on the way. I took the liberty."

Fletcher nodded. "Good man."

They settled down to work.

26

Justine set the breakfast tray on MacKenzie's lap and pulled the bedcovers over his bandaged legs. "How are you feeling, Peter?"

His lips curled. "My legs still hurt. I'm mad I didn't get to sail with my sub and Sebastion left without saying good-bye. Ask me again how I feel."

She leaned over and kissed him. "Don't be petulant. You'll be all healed in a few days." She plumped his pillow and kissed him again.

"That won't work. Officers can't be bribed."

"Children have to be coerced."

He drank some orange juice and mulled that over. "You wouldn't win so often if I were on my feet," he said darkly.

"Consider yourself lucky. If your legs had been broken, you'd be in double hip casts for months. A few days for tendon damage is a gift."

"Wounds received in battle deserve greater respect."

She sighed. "I love you, stupid."

"Gracias."

"Finished?" He was picking at the food.

"Hmmm. Yes. You're learning. The eggs were less like insulation today. I'll demonstrate home fries tomorrow."

She looked dubious. "These cooking lessons, Peter—I don't know. Maybe we could go out to dinner or buy a restaurant. Something simple, you know?"

"Here, help me up."

She bent and got her shoulder under his arm. He was still stiff but improving rapidly. They did a few turns around the apartment.

"Think of it this way," he said, ignoring the painful tightness. "Anybody can be an incredibly beautiful black belt concert pianist who kills alligators with a bare blade. But cook? How many can do that? Besides, my father said a good cook can always find a job. Think of it as something to fall back on."

"I'll risk it," she said, watching his gait. "Try stretching the right a bit more. Yes, like that. You never mentioned your father before. Was he Navy too?"

MacKenzie smiled. "Far from it. He was an English teacher. High school. A good man, bright and dedicated. Heart attack when he was fifty-two. My mother's re-married now to another nice man. Works for the IRS."

"English teacher," she mused. "So that's where you get such a interesting worldview."

MacKenzie limped forward, feeling some of the stiff-ness begin to subside. "I guess. Ideas were always a part of dinner conversation, and I read a lot."

"Why the Navy?"

"You'll laugh."

She shook her head. "I won't."

"The recruiter had no sense of humor."

"Explain, please."

He leaned against an armchair and slowly flexed his legs. "I was in college. All anyone really does in college is talk. Mostly criticize, but always talk. One day I stopped at the gym and there was this Navy recruiter talking about the service. Every time he used the word *action* I felt terrific. What with courses and all, I think I had enough talking to last me several lifetimes. I listened, and after-wards I went over to talk. Some other kids did too. They were clowning and making fun of the pay scale and funny uniforms. The recruiter just kept doggedly trying to explain the purpose of it all, the sense of mission he felt. It was beyond the pay or the benefits or even the see-the-world crap. But they kept on clowning and wisecracking."

"They were just kids, Peter."

He nodded. "Sure, but that's the point. They were, and that's okay, but *he* wasn't. And I felt myself relating more to him than them. So that meant I wasn't either. It was a funny feeling. I felt old and grown-up and shy and frightened all at the same time.

"He took me out for a beer when he realized I was serious and advised me on what courses to take to be eligible for the Nuclear Propulsion Officer Candidate Program. I went directly to OCS after graduation. A year and a half of nuclear power school, then sub school, then my first sea duty as a Division Officer. Later, promotion to department head. The rest, as they say—"

". . . is for another time. Walk's over. You look pretty good."

"I feel good."

She helped him back to bed. The phone rang. MacKenzie picked it up and she heard his tone change almost at once.

"Hello? . . . Yes, sir. . . . Of course. Much better, sir, thank you . . . Will do. Yes, sir. Good-bye."

He hung up. "What was that?" she asked.

"Admiral Garver. He wants me back. Something's up." His disappointment was evident. "Damn it, Justine, I thought we'd have a few more days."

"When do you go?"

"Tomorrow morning. I'll hop a jet at the base."

Justine forced a smile. Sooner or later they both knew this time would come.

"Move over, sailor."

She pulled off her blouse and slipped in beside him.

The next morning she saw him off. It was best, she decided. A summons of her own had reached her. The day was soft and muggy, Florida weather. He kissed her hard and whispered something silly that made her smile. Then he was walking away with his still stiff shuffle, and she wasn't crying exactly, but it was hard to see all the way to where he last waved. . . .

Justine pulled her attention back to the map Terrence Holmes was putting his pointer to. "This area," he said, "this is where the *Kirov* is. We can't attack for fear of a launch. Therefore, no invasion. If the Soviets supply the data we've requested, there's a chance to wind this up quickly. If not, the President will have to weigh the nuclear option. That's it."

Justine saw the implications. And this meeting, held on the heels of MacKenzie's urgent summons back to Guantanamo, explained a lot.

"Then August First is postponed indefinitely," she said, frowning.

"I'm afraid it is. 'It profits not a man to lose his soul for the world—but for Managua?'" He paraphrased the quote from an old movie about Thomas More.

"Sebastion is going to be furious," she said.

"Everybody's furious," Holmes replied. "Your brother will have to accept the leash, like we all have."

"He'd tell you not to knuckle down to terrorism."

Holmes looked annoyed. "Sebastion doesn't answer to an electorate. Come on, Justine. A lot of Americans wouldn't be willing to trade four dollars for your entire country. You expect them to trade Miami or Atlanta? Be reasonable. It's only the Kremlin that can just invade. I presume you're on our side because we're still a place that has people to answer to."

"So you want me to make your case to him."

"Make our case?" There was a look on Holmes's face that she'd only seen a few times before. It frightened her. "More than that, Justine. You're going to have to decide what you want, what's most important to you." He paused. "The invasion to liberate Nicaragua will take place. That's the President's guarantee. But it has to take place according to our own timetable. If Sebastion won't accept that, he can have no place in our plans."

"You'd replace him?"

"Understand me, Justine. I'd kill him. Especially before I'd let him put both our countries at risk. That's why you're going. That's the choice you have to make. Convince him, please, for all our sakes. He's got to hold back."

Justine thought Holmes's words over. If the Sandinistas held off the United States, they would certainly consolidate their regime, and their prestige would skyrocket. That made a successful invasion more imperative than ever. A precipitous move by Sebastion could provoke the U.S. into a hasty, ill-thought-out fiasco like the Bay of Pigs. A worst-case scenario might plunge the U.S. and Nicaragua into the first thermonuclear exchange. This would cause incalculable damage to the American mainland and surely obliterate Nicaragua. Holmes was right, she decided. Sebastion had to see reason. It was best for everybody to hold back until the submarine was put out of action.

"All right, Terry. Even my hardheaded brother should see the logic of it. I'll go."

"Do you correctly understand your orders?"

She looked at him quizzically. "Convince Sebastion to hold his troops. He's not to cross the border into Nicaragua. What more?"

Holmes's face creased. "Please define *convince*."

"Urge, cajole, reason, demand . . . what do you want me to say?"

"Terminate, if necessary."

Justine drew a deep breath. "It won't come to that. I'll stop him. You have my word. But it doesn't have to come to that."

"I hope not. Sincerely. We didn't drag him out of a Sandinista prison just to lose him for being pigheaded. But you must see the necessity of stopping him."

"I do."

"I've been straight with you, Justine."

She sighed. "I know, Terry. Sometimes, though, it's just . . . too much. All our lives, one threat or another . . ."

"I do understand," he said gently. "At least I try to. When *I* was nine my biggest concern was which comic book to buy on the way home from school." She smiled. He was gladdened by it. "Hopefully, the Pentagon boys will eliminate the sub and none of this will amount to much."

Justine reached out and touched his arm in a gesture that said she appreciated his support. She felt tired. Lately it was harder to stay involved, harder to care. Had some selfish streak risen within her, and did MacKenzie have anything to do with it? Or was it just the simple human desire to rest?

"How's your sub captain?" Holmes asked, watching her face lighten at his mention.

"Fine, Terry. Healing nicely. They called him back to Guantanamo yesterday. I assume it's the naval end of the *Kirov* business. Terry?" She stopped for a moment, then continued hesitantly, "Maybe after this is over, I was thinking, maybe . . . maybe it's time to walk away."

"People do."

"But could I? Really?"

He looked at her oddly. "Are you asking me if we'll stand in your way?"

"Will you?"

Holmes's expression surprised her. He looked genuinely shocked. "Justine," he said, "anything you need—anything—it's yours. You want American citizenship? A grant to study? A concert tour? Name it."

"You make me feel good."

He took her hand. "I'm trying to. Look, I know that methods and ideologies can get awfully murky," he said slowly, "and Lord knows we've had enough moral ambiguity since the sixties to last us all several lifetimes, but friendship is supposed to be a constant. You understand? A constant. You remember your friends. It's another difference betwen the sides. You might want to remember it's more than just talk."

Justine came to a decision that had been brewing for some time. "Okay," she said deliberately. "When this is over, Terry, I'm out. You've helped a lot. No more wars for me. Maybe I'll take my sub captain and make us a couple of kids who won't have to worry about anything more than which comic to buy on the way home from school."

"I remember liking Spiderman."

She laughed. "You and MacKenzie. Highbrows. Well, enough soul-searching for one night. When do I leave?"

"Eight o'clock. Flight to San José, then we'll fly you in as far as we can. The rest of the way on foot. Shouldn't be too far—Sebastion's moving slowly for now. We'll alert him you're on the way."

"I'll hold him back. Count on it."

Holmes nodded firmly. "One way or the other."

There was determination on Justine's face. "One way or the other," she agreed, knowing what he was saying.

She wasn't out yet.

27

The plane ride from Florida made his legs stiffen up again, but it was a matter of pride to MacKenzie that he get to his seat in the planning room adjacent to Admiral Garver's office without help. His brother officers would have never forgotten the cane.

He recognized most of those seated. The submarine command was still the youngest of the three Navy divisions: submarine, surface, and air. Most of the WW II captains were retired by now, but it was still a close-knit group. Finally, in recent years enough senior submariners had become represented in the highest echelons to give their part of the service its due—that, and the increasing vulnerability of land-based missiles, which made the far more secure ballistic missile subs even more essential to the nation's defense.

Garver strode into the room and the men fell silent. He ascended to the podium and stuck his bulldog face out, scanning the group.

"Gentlemen, we've got a serious situation and need some solutions to it pretty damn fast. We're facing a scenario unlike any of those contingencies we plan for. The plain fact of the matter is that no one ever envisioned this could happen. Lights."

A map of the Caribbean basin appeared on the wall screen. MacKenzie leaned forward; this was *Aspen*'s last patrol area.

"Several weeks ago," Garver continued, "we were all delighted to watch a disabled Russian Victor Three towed into a Nicaraguan port for repairs. Now we're not so happy. It appears the *Kirov* was deliberately disabled by the Nicaraguans with the ultimate aim of comandeering it for their own use."

Over the next few minutes Garver explained the details of the situation. Coordinates represented by green lines sprang to life on the map.

". . . this trip-wire zone has, in effect, forced us to postpone what I can now tell you but what must remain top secret—the planned invasion of Nicaragua in support of the democratic forces led by . . ."

MacKenzie felt a note pressed into his hand. He unfolded it as Garver spoke. He smiled. It read: *Tapes reviewed . . . Aspen took Phoenix . . . drinks and dinner are on me. . . . Arlin.* Well, that was nice to know. *Aspen*'s crew had performed to the maximum that day. God, it seemed so long ago—the reactor SCRAM, Justine in the water. And now this. How intimately he was connected. What would her reaction be to this?

". . . there doesn't appear to be any easy answer," Garver concluded. "The best military minds in the country are working overtime. Obviously, we in the submarine forces are being looked to with special expectations. This should be our baby. Okay, I'm open to suggestions."

The debate began almost at once. From the thirty or so officers present there were thirty different opinions. Every suggestion had a countervailing argument. Groups began to form. Some wanted a sub sent in right away, arguing that Russian sonars weren't sensitive enough to pick up the quieter American subs. A quick kill was the best chance. Phil Arlin emerged as the spokesman for that idea.

"At low speed," he argued, "we generate an extremely low decibel of acoustic energy. Only a very experienced operator has the slightest opportunity to detect us. One run and we should be able to take *Kirov* out."

"But if they pick us up for even one second, we run the risk of a launch before our torpedoes stand a chance of reaching them," argued another. "And what about torpedo noise itself? It's too risky."

MacKenzie was looking at the map. There was something. He tried to let the thought surface. He was only partially listening to the debate. It wasn't going anyplace he could see. "Low level nukes," someone was saying.

"Too great an area," came the counter. "We'd have to use one so big we'd do to ourselves what we're trying to prevent."

"P-3's?"

"Sonobuoys would alert. The splash."

MacKenzie listened, nagged by something he couldn't identify. Surely these alternatives had already been considered. He looked back to the map and visualized *Aspen*'s last track. There—the Cayman Trench was a dark gash extending well inside the trip-wire zone. . . . Inside? Jesus!

"Admiral!" He was up on his feet before he'd even thought it out fully, and the words poured out. "Admiral, when did *Aspen* sail?"

Garver consulted a printout an aide handed him. "Last Wednesday, Captain. Why?"

"Look at the map, sir," MacKenzie urged. "*Aspen* was sent out on a reconnaissance mission to map the traffic coming out of the Cayman Trench route we found. She sailed Wednesday, sir. Three days before the Nicaraguans set up their zone. Don't you see, sir? *Aspen*'s already inside it!"

Garver turned to his aide. "Verify that."

The aide bent to his computer terminal and punched in the necessary codes. Bright red pinpoints of light began to appear on the wall map, indicating the positions of the fleet in the trip-wire area. One glaring omission was *Aspen*'s location.

"It wasn't entered," the aide said with surprise. He input more codes, studied the result. Finally he resorted to the hand log. "Oh, I see. Your order, sir. No input of Security One clearance missions. They're hand held. *Aspen* isn't in the computer."

"Well I'll be . . ." Garver restrained himself. "Put it in now."

The aide tapped in instructions and a new red light suddenly appeared on the map. "Son of a bitch," Garver said wonderingly. "She's sitting smack dab in the eastern section of the zone, almost two hundred miles in."

"What's this about a new route, Admiral?" Arlin asked.

Still shaking his head with surprise, Garver explained what *Aspen* had uncovered. ". . . so meantime, while all this has been going on and the entire Pentagon has been trying to figure out a way *in*, we've had a 688 class boat there all along. Christ, MacKenzie, somebody should kiss you."

"Try asking for volunteers," cracked Arlin.

MacKenzie grinned but forestalled a reply. There was more, and no one seemed to have seen it yet. "Sir? Unfortunately, *Aspen*'s presence is a double-edged sword."

"How so?"

"Due to the nature of the mission, *Aspen*'s under a communications blackout. She can't call in, even on tight beam, and ELF to her could be picked up by *Kirov*. Besides, she's probably too far down anyway. So *Aspen* sits listening for . . . how long is the duration?"

"Eight more days," Garver said.

"Well, sir, as I see it, the danger is that if *Aspen* moves from her listening post without any knowledge of *Kirov*, she's very likely to provoke a confrontation."

Garver nodded. "I see that."

"Break radio silence," suggested Arlin. "Let the captain know the score. Who's in command?"

"Tom Lasovic," said Garver. "Acting Captain until Mac was ready for sea duty. Now we all know how good a man Tom is, but I can't countenance sending an untried commander against *Kirov*. This isn't an exercise. If we're going to put all the money on *Aspen*'s number, I want to know we've got the best, most experienced man running her. Mac? The floor's still yours."

MacKenzie was thinking hard. "Maybe we're coming at this from the wrong angle, sir."

"How do you mean?"

"Bear with me, please. Maybe the problem isn't getting Tom off Aspen, but getting an experienced commander on."

"But we've already decided that we can't send a second sub in," Garver said flatly.

MacKenzie nodded. "I agree, but if you just look at the problem in a slightly different way. . . ."

Five minutes later Garver had a smile on his face that made him look like a Halloween pumpkin. "Mac, it's the craziest idea I ever heard, but you better get some dress whites on."

"Sir?"

"Come on, damn it, you want to meet the President and the Joint Chiefs looking like you been doing repair work over the side?"

"No, sir. Right away, sir." MacKenzie moved off quickly, only mildly surprised to discover how little his legs hurt.

"And damn it, MacKenzie," Garver yelled at his departing back, "for Christ's sake, will you at least remember to salute *him*!"

28

MOSCOW, THE KREMLIN

There were none of the usual functionaries recording the meeting. Word of it was passed by private line. The Zil limousines that sped through the Borovitsky Gate into the red-brick-walled Kremlin came at staggered times to deposit their occupants at the entrance to the Arsenal, a long, narrow building on the northwestern edge of the pentagonal compound. One at a time the officials ascended the private elevator to the third floor. No aides were present to take their light, summer coats. They draped them over a table in an office adjacent to the meeting room. Fourteen men: the Politburo of the Soviet Union.

Ambassador Belov knew most of those present from long association. He was Gromyko's hand-picked man and traveled in the circles where such acquaintances were made. He'd had a nap since his long flight from Washington and felt rested. His role here should be minimal, he felt, since he was here not as a policy maker, but rather to report and to stand ready as an agent of whatever policy these men decided upon. He took his seat at the far end of the old wooden table and listened carefully.

At the head of the table sat Victor Andreiovich Meledov, General Secretary of the Communist Party and President of the Soviet Union. Arrayed down the sides were the ministers of Defense, Agriculture, and Science; the Foreign Minister, Gromyko himself, now a full voting member; and the Party secretaries. Each had read the documents sent by the Nicaraguan, Barrista. The papers called for the Soviet Union to stand back from events, with an explanation it was hoped would placate Soviet anger over *Kirov's* theft. It was a disturbingly strong motive—the anticipated American invasion.

It was a clever document, manipulating the sympathies. If the theft of the *Kirov* and the subsequent blackmailing of the U.S. were terrorist acts, so too was the "rescuing" of Hungary or Czechoslovakia or Afghanistan. Were not radical actions justified in protecting the motherland?

Colonel Renkov's report was read. The remaining officers and crew were all well provided for. They would soon be on the Soviet guided-missile destroyer *Udaloy*, hastily dispatched to the area. Renkov would continue to provide forward intelligence. The *Udaloy* was equipped for antisubmarine warfare. If necessary it could be sent after *Kirov*.

There were two ways to go then. The American president's request for information was discussed. But what was his counter offer? These were hard men, skilled survivors of the Soviet system of political promotion, which Belov could compare knowledgeably to the American system and decide it resembled more the ruthless advancement of a Mafia chieftain than anything else he'd seen there.

It came down to advantage. The word was used often. Belov was upset by this. When the weapons went off, would anyone have advantage? Yes, it was argued. In a country like the United States, where public opinion mattered, there was great advantage to be gained from provoking the citizenry's fears. If they lost a city or two to nuclear arms, wouldn't the Americans be forced to come to the arms control table with entirely different attitudes— attitudes created by internal public pressure? Advantage.

Loss? One Victor III nuclear submarine, because surely the Nicaraguans would not survive the firing more than a few minutes. Small loss indeed to influence the balance of power and American resolve for generations. The lessons of Vietnam had not been lost on these men. The press would cover the destruction in every last, loving detail, like famished vultures. *Tell us, miss, how do you feel about the destruction of Houston?*

All this without blame to the USSR. The Western

Europeans would face a backlash too. The Green Party would have a field day. See, it *could* happen here. Eliminate the weapons forever. Russians for peace . . .

Belov understood. There wasn't a man at the table who didn't believe that the day the last strategic nuclear weapon was removed from the West's arsenal was the day the Soviet troops rolled across Europe, and Britain had best start teaching Russian in its schools. Advantage.

But there was another faction, more sober and world-weary, that counseled aid. The threat could engulf everyone. There were dangerous precedents here. What if the Israelis or the South Africans unleashed a similar adventure? Did anyone think they could restrain Khomeini in similar circumstances? Belov's heart leaped. Perhaps sanity had a chance. For at least ten minutes this faction held sway and he dared to hope.

It was futile. The hardliners emerged dominant. Fear and power and . . . advantage. Help the Americans? Of course. Belov listened carefully to the list of items he would have to demand in return for the information on the Victor III. It was an impossible wish list. It would strip the West of every tactical—he almost choked on the word—advantage. Alone, he would have cried out in rage. The Americans would never agree.

But instead he spoke. It was risky to expose oneself, even with his record. But he felt he could not let the moment pass without some action on his part. Some listened. Gromyko eyed him narrowly: this was a rare breach. Belov became passionate in his entreaty, almost pleading . . . till he caught the cold, hostile stares. Had the ambassador been in the West too long? Belov was frightened for the first time in many years. He backed off and remained silent for the rest of the discussion.

They reached a decision. Belov stoically accepted his orders. He'd always tried to stand between men of arms; to counsel, to prevent, to soften. There was no possibility of that here. The Americans would never accede to this.

He hoped that in years to come, some historian might come to know this moment for what it was—a time when the world tottered near the brink . . . and was kicked over by blind stupidity.

He felt bitter. We should have helped, he thought. But he rose and accepted his charge.

"I understand, comrades. As you wish. I'll leave in the morning. Good night."

Belov felt eyes on his back all the way out the door. In some ways he felt glad to make it out of the room intact.

That was the saddest feeling of all.

29

COSTA RICA

Justine decided it was the smells that brought the past crashing back most of all. She was following the guide through the dry bush, and every breath of air in the tropical forest seemed to invoke a sense of déjà vu. She'd remembered the way the white buildings in San José reflected the sun and the way the peasants moved in the heat. But it was the impact of a thousand hot and heavy odors in the insect-buzzing air that convinced her she was really home.

She had flown into Costa Rica the previous night and left San José that morning. The Cessna took her as far north as it could, landing on the last airstrip Sebastion's people had trampled into the ground. His camp was about ten miles farther north now and changing too often to continue to build strips. This forced Justine to walk the rest of the way.

She shifted her pack for better weight distribution. The landscape was straight out of her youth, though this region was not as familiar to her as her native Nicaragua. Her Indian guide raised an eyebrow—his way of asking her if she needed help. She snorted haughtily—her way of telling the little, leathery man to fuck himself.

They came over a low ridge that sloped gently down into a valley dotted with brown foliage and cut by a narrow stream. Sebastion's camp was spread out along the southern wall, somewhat sheltering it from the sun.

The camp was similar to that of her northern contras—
there were tents and vehicles and storage dumps—but
this was much more sprawling, less organized. A band,
not a tightly disciplined organization—that was her first
impression.

She followed the guide down into the camp. Passing
through the first group of tents, he simply walked away.
His job was done. Justine walked on towards Sebastion's
command tent, recognizable because of its size and the
Nicaraguan flag flying out front. Some of the soldiers
recognized her and stopped their work to watch her pass.
She heard the whispers. *Doña Justine* . . .

She came up on Sebastion, who was talking animatedly
to an officer she vaguely remembered from when she
fought alongside her brother. The two were comrades for
many years. She unslung her pack and dropped it by
Sebastion's tent. Their voices were rising heatedly. Apparently she'd walked in on a difference of opinions.

"Your way," Sebastion was saying, "we could lose a
whole formation. You don't see that?"

"I see your way we could lose the battle," came the
angry response. "I'm sorry, Commandante. You asked for
my opinion. Why ask if you don't want to listen?"

Sebastion began an angry retort, but Justine watched
the interplay of emotions cross his face unitl what
emerged was a sort of self-effacing snort of bemusement.

"A good point. Why, indeed, Paco?" he said. "What do
you say to putting the radios on the lead jeeps and
sending a spotter across. . . ."

For the next few minutes, they rethought the problem.
In the end, Paco nodded. "All right, Commandante, I can
live with that. It solves my problem."

"Good." Sebastion grinned apologetically. "The heart
of a lion"—he thumped his chest comically—"but sometimes the head of a pig."

Paco clapped him on the back warmly, and Justine
could see the way he regarded Sebastion. She'd never
met anyone better at commanding respect than her
brother, and what always impressed her was that he did it
without sacrificing a personal warmth that convinced
every one of his soldiers that he truly cared about them.
Maybe that was his secret—he did.

Paco walked away, and she came up behind Sebastion. "Still the diplomat, I see."

He turned and embraced her, accepting her presence as if it were the most natural thing in the world. See how he takes me into *his* universe, Justine thought. But she knew his affection was genuine, and she basked in it.

He said, "They told me you'd be coming. I was surprised. Problems?"

"Why do you assume that?" she asked.

"You don't send your big guns for no reason."

"Let's go inside. I'm hot and tired and I need a drink."

Sebastion lifted the tent flap and she ducked inside, savoring the cool shade within. He tossed her pack onto the cot and opened a rope-handled chest.

"This do?" he asked, holding a bottle of tequila.

"Sure."

He took a swig from the bottle, then passed it to her.

"No limes?" she said jokingly.

His laugh was only part humor. "You forget, we're only the number two army. Your friends up north must have gotten the limes. And the salt. And enough ammunition. And—"

She held up a hand. "Enough, for God's sake." She took another swig and grimaced. "That's really awful."

"It isn't that good."

She reached for a canteen and swished the water around her mouth. "How far are we from the border?"

"Less than ten miles. We're stockpiling here."

"You're right on schedule."

His face was serious. "I've worked and waited for this for a long time. You knew I would be."

She sighed. "I knew. One of these days, Sebastion, for your own good you ought to fail at something."

"That's not even good armchair psychology."

"No? Maybe better than you think."

"You're fencing with me, Justine. I worry when you do that. Let's leave my personality out of it, I've managed fine so far. And you didn't come all this way to mend my inner scars."

She looked around the tent. "No, that's true. But you're going to have to swallow a bitter pill, Sebastion, and I'm here to deliver it. Flexibility, Terry Holmes called it. I wonder if you've got any left."

He shrugged. "I make decisions, set goals. I try to get from point A to point B with as little loss as possible. What the hell is flexibility, Justine?"

"The ability to change. To adapt. We've got a serious problem, Sebastion. You're going to have to accept a new timetable for August First."

He grew very still. "Why?"

"The Sandinistas stole a Russian sub armed with nuclear missiles. That makes for nuclear blackmail. It puts everything on hold till the U.S. can remove the threat. Face it, Sebastion, no one is willing to trade Miami for Managua."

Sebastion whistled admiringly. "That is something. Barrista?"

She nodded. "That's the name we have. He's no longer in Managua and is probably on the sub itself. There's one other thing."

"Yes?"

"Miguel isn't in Managua either. We have some information he's with Barrista. One of our locals claims they're using a Cuban captain, but that's not confirmed yet."

"This changes things."

"You understand that?" she said wonderingly.

"Justine, regardless of your opinion as to my 'flexibility,' I'm not an idiot. I can see the U.S. would want to hold back."

She touched his arm. "I'm relieved."

He stood, and that was when she saw that his face was as grim as she feared. "Don't be," he said. "Because the very reason they have to hold back is why I can't."

"Sebastion!"

"Listen to me," he urged. "It's three days to the first. This kind of operation is like a love affair—if you don't go with the immediacy of it, the intensity that propelled you forward grows cold and unwieldy. Plans become overly complex. The fire goes out. It founders, fails. Look at the Bay of Pigs. It went the same way, and somehow the right circumstances just never came together again for another attempt. Grenada was just the opposite. Like a fine affair: brief, to the point, and over."

"This is crazy. We're talking about war, not puppy love."

"Fine, talk war. The logistics of this campaign are staggering. You don't just waltz in and announce, 'Hi, we're here, we just invaded.' There are logistics, advance intelligence officers already inside, spotters, weapons caches, groups set to blow critical installations, kidnap local officials, liberate prisoners . . . need I go on?"

"Call them all back."

"Using what?" he demanded, exasperated. "The phone? You're not that unschooled. I can't call them back. And if I don't move in to support them, they're dead. Then what? Just recruit some more and wait for another signal from you? Maybe I should use up a few dozen teams until you people get it right. What's a few more Nicaraguans more or less?"

Her voice was tight and low. "You've got to hold, Sebastion."

"Look at the logic of it, Justine," he pleaded. "If I stop, all the pressure on the Americans is off. If I refuse, they've *got* to take out the sub pretty damn quick."

"They won't see it that way. You'd be forcing them into precipitous action, one that might lose them a lot of cities. They're sensitive about their cities. They won't allow it."

"Won't allow? That's another one of your euphemisms, isn't it?"

Her tone grew harder. "It means kill, Sebastion. Now you look at the facts. You're not that unschooled either."

"So that's the plan, little sister." His eyes narrowed. "Someone comes in the night and I get a bullet in the head, or my toothpaste tube explodes, or—"

He must have seen something on her face, she realized, because his sudden silence was so abrupt, so . . . pained that she couldn't hold his gaze. She turned away, desperate to conceal, but it was too late.

". . . or you," he said very softly. "They send you."

"Please, Sebastion."

He turned his back on her and stood as rigid as stone by the tent entrance. The light silhouetted his body. She couldn't see his face.

"Sebastion?"

When he turned back, his face was colder than she'd ever seen it. They were suddenly strangers.

"You've got to choose, Justine. Me or them. It comes

down to that as surely as the sun will rise tomorrow. Take all your principles and issues and causes and ideologies and put them on one side of the scale, and then put me on the other. I won't stop you. I won't even defend myself or put a guard on you. Short of taking you myself, there's not a man in this camp who could stop you if you decided to move against me. I could only protect myself by killing you, and that I just can't do."

"I don't know . . . I don't know if I can. Please." She was begging him and didn't care. "Help me."

"Help you?" He seemed genuinely surprised. "To kill me?"

"Help me not to have to," she pleaded, rising and putting her hands on his shoulders.

He shrugged out of her grip. "It's not that easy. You do what you have to do. I won't bargain and I won't stop. You've had it easy, little sister. Poor Justine, terrified while Miguel and I were killing soldiers. Well, stop and think about how we felt. We did the killing! Nobody let me off the hook, and I'm not letting you off either."

His scorn stung her. She reacted bitterly. "You're a cold bastard sometimes."

"That from the assassin," he sneered. "Go somewhere else to feel better. I can't stop you because I already know I can't hurt you. You've got to decide if you can. That's all. I'm moving my troops tomorrow as planned. Comes the first, we'll cross the border. As planned." He stormed out of the tent with a last, "Do what you have to."

Alone, Justine sat unmoving. A fat brown bug crawled up the tent post. She watched it, knowing she could smash it, not wanting to. Same as Sebastion. Had Miguel saved them both that day in Managua just so they could destroy each other now? The wheels turned endlessly. She wished for some music to blot out the noise in her head. She buried her face in her hands.

There hadn't been any music for a long time.

30

THE WHITE HOUSE

MacKenzie had never been in the Situation Room before, nor in the White House, either, for that matter. He was nervous, and the stomach-wrenching flight up to Andrews on the Navy jet hadn't helped. At the Air Force base he and Garver were picked up by an unmarked blue Ford and delivered to an underground garage where Marine sentries checked and rechecked their identification. Then they were passed into an elevator that descended even deeper. A short walk through a series of look-alike corridors, a final guard post, and MacKenzie followed the admiral into a vast, conference-style room with one full wall taken up by a backlit map display.

The room was already filled with top brass from all the services, and MacKenzie felt himself tightening up, intimidated in spite of steeling himself not to be. This was no high school class to be speaking in front of. He spotted Admiral Merton, the Chief of Naval Operations, and Vice Admiral Jack Brisbane, Commander of the Submarine U.S. Atlantic Fleet in Norfolk. Brisbane caught MacKenzie's eye and winked in support. The rest just eyed him speculatively.

Garver must have noticed his tension. "Relax, Mac," he whispered. "In the shower these guys all look just like you do."

"Brothers under the skin, eh?"

Garver grinned wolfishly. "Don't you believe it. Stay awake now." His smile transformed itself magically as Admiral Merton detached himself from a conversation and approached them.

Merton held out his hand. "Hello, Ben. Good to see you."

"You, too, sir."

"This the man of the hour?"

"That he is. Admiral Merton, Captain Peter MacKenzie, skipper of the *Aspen*."

"Captain MacKenzie."

"How do you do, sir."

MacKenzie was aware of the other man's close scrutiny. "They call you Mac?" he asked.

"Yes, sir. Mostly."

"Well, Mac, Ben here seems pretty impressed by whatever you've come up with. I'm looking forward to hearing what it is. Care for some advice?"

"Gladly, Admiral."

Merton gestured around the room. "Most of the Army and Air Force boys don't know a Poseidon from a pop bottle. Now, nobody who's here is stupid, but you won't get hurt proceeding under the assumption that they are. Keep it simple. This is a Navy matter rightfully, and nobody else has come up with diddly squat. Just let your plan speak for itself.

"Okay, sir."

MacKenzie followed Garver and was steered into a seat between him and Merton at the long oval table. He put his notes in front of him and tried to relax. Nothing to it. Sure.

A door opened and the President walked in, followed by someone Merton whispered was Mark Dellman, Fletcher's Chief-of-Staff. They all stood. Fletcher waved them back down and took the chair at the center of the table, facing the map wall. Dellman sat on his right. MacKenzie had a funny feeling in the pit of his stomach. Jesus, this was the President!

"Gentlemen," Fletcher acknowledged the assemblage, "I understand one of our bright lights may have spotted a way out of this for us."

It was Merton's cue. "Mr. President, this is Admiral Benton Garver, the Commander Naval Base, Guantanamo Bay, and Captain Peter MacKenzie, Commanding Officer of the attack submarine Aspen. Captain MacKenzie is the bright light you just mentioned. With your permission, sir?"

Fletcher nodded.

"Captain?"

MacKenzie pushed his chair back and walked to the map display. "Mr. President, gentlemen, the Kirov's zone of interdiction extends from, ah . . . how does this work, please?"

Fletcher's expression was kindly. "Just say what you want, son, the folks in back will put it up."

"Thank you, sir. Okay. The zone extends from these coordinates"—he gave them—"to these." Red points glowed on the screen and lines emanated from them to form a rough square in the Caribbean. "Very nice," MacKenzie said admiringly. "Magnify that area, please."

The genies behind the wall heard his wish and it was granted. The square grew until it filled the majority of the screen. Magically, the focus grew even sharper. "We can't enter this area because *Kirov*'s erected a launch-on-warning trip wire and nothing we have can destroy her without some advance warning. But we overlooked one thing. Several days ago *Aspen* was dispatched on a top-secret mission to monitor the traffic coming out of a newly-found Soviet running route. *Aspen* is presently on station here"—he gave the coordinates, and a bright blue dot glowed into life—"right on the edge of the Cayman Trench. We don't have to send a sub into the zone, Mr. President, we already have one—my sub—well inside it. *Aspen*'s dead silent, not even radio transmission. *Kirov*'s probably passed by her several times already and not noticed her. We build them very quiet, sir. Until she's ready to move, no one's going to hear her."

"Very interesting, Captain. Proceed."

MacKenzie launched into the problem of command, explaining fully Tom Lasovic's strengths as well as his virtual inexperience as a commander.

"So how do you solve your command problems, Captain MacKenzie? I understood you to say *Aspen* is too deep to contact."

"Well, sir, we were all thinking about how to get Tom Lasovic off *Aspen*, or failing that, to contact him and apprise him of the situation. But it hit me all of a sudden that if that was impossible, maybe the reverse wasn't. We can't send in a second sub, sir, but we could send in a DSRV—a Deep Submergence Rescue Vehicle. . . ." He hesitated.

"Go on, son," Fletcher said. "I know what they are."

"The Russians are running the Cayman Trench route at a

depth well below our maximum for attack submarines,"
MacKenzie continued, "and that's the only depth where
we could safely avoid detection by the *Kirov*. But we could
take a DSRV in along the same route the Russians are
using, deeper, in fact, and use it to reach *Aspen*. I can hug
the bottom of the trench at seven thousand feet. The
temperature gradients will mask any leakage. I mate with
Aspen, assume command, and here's the thing, sir—I can
then move very slowly, almost dead silent, waiting for
Kirov to pass by, and take her before a launch is possible.
It's time to put all our theory into practice. Even if we don't
sink her at once, I'll guarantee enough damage to cripple
sufficient systems to prevent launch. That's it, sir. Let me
take a DSRV taxi into my sub and we'll bring you back
Kirov."

MacKenzie looked out at those gathered. He felt good,
certain. "Final consideration. If we leave *Aspen* in place
without warning her about the Zone, we risk provoking a
launch. Any system failure could force Lasovic to move,
any one of a dozen reasons. So we may have to make the
trip regardless of *Aspen*'s use offensively. Let's use the
advantage we have. She's a great ship. Her refit was just
completed and we've got battle engagement tapes that
prove her capability. We can do the job, sir. I know we
can."

Fletcher considered MacKenzie thoughtfully as he sat
down. "Thank you, Captain. Gentlemen, other options?"

Dellman waited a second, then spoke up. "With all due
respect to the captain, I just can't accept the risk involved
in his plan. I did some research, sir. We have an agreement with the Soviets on this type of thing already. The
Standing Consultative Commission, which is the official
U.S.–Soviet body for complaints about arms control treaty
noncompliance, negotiated an agreement a few years ago
to share all information necessary should nuclear terrorism be involved. That's what we've got. I propose as a first
step that we invoke the agreement and demand the
information on the Victor Threes. It has the force of law.
The Russians will have to agree."

"That's going to take some time," Merton objected,
"and who's going to verify that the data they may or may
not give us is correct? The Russians love to negotiate

treaties. They say exactly what you want to hear and then they do exactly what they want."

Merton continued in a stronger voice. "I can see a whole faction of hardliners who'd like nothing better than to see a nuclear accident in this hemisphere. Why should they help us? Frankly, I don't see it, sir."

"It's a more prudent course," said Dellman, pressing his point. "This cowboy mission—no offense, Captain—puts us all at risk. You can't even be sure a DSRV can go that distance."

"The calculations say we can. Extra air and batteries can fit in the spaces where crew is usually placed."

"And what if they fail?"

"I drown," said MacKenzie flatly.

A tight look crossed Dellman's face and he began an angry retort.

Garver broke in. "What Captain MacKenzie means, sir, is that if the worst-case scenario comes to pass, the loss is limited to one Navy captain. We can still be proceeding under the terms of the SCC agreement."

Fletcher nodded. "Mark?"

"It's not the captain's failure I'm worried about, doesn't anybody see that? It's his success. What kind of measured course is based on a duel at fifty fathoms? I'll say it again—it's a cowboy stunt, another shoot-out at the O.K. Corral, and it's just too big a gamble on this level."

Garver leaned forward intently. "Sir, what Mr. Dellman here calls a cowboy shoot-out is in fact what we spend our entire professional lives and a couple of billion of the taxpayers' dollars figuring out how to win. Forgive me, sir, but why the hell else have a Navy if you're not going to let it do what it's trained to do? We're better equipped and more technologically advanced than the Russians. With MacKenzie on board we can take out the *Kirov*, sir. I'd stake my life on it."

Fletcher said quietly, "I appreciate that, Admiral. But would you stake a million lives on it? Because that's really the question. For what it's worth, Houston is no longer the equivalent of Dodge City. Maybe our sub can destroy theirs, but where I sit, I've got to have more than a maybe. Mark's right. We've got to move slowly here, make the right moves. If we blow this, we blow the entire Nicaraguan scenario as well. Our request is in Soviet hands now. Mark will forward them the additional information regarding the treaty. We'll wait for their response."

Dellman began putting his papers away.

"What about *Aspen*?" Merton asked, his tone perfunctory. They had been turned down; move on.

"We have some time before it's slated to move?" Fletcher asked.

"Eight days."

"It's on hold then," Fletcher said. "Anything else?"

"Sir?"

It was MacKenzie. Fletcher had made a move to rise, but he lowered himself back into his chair. "Yes, Captain?"

MacKenzie caught Merton's reproachful stare. As far as he was concerned, the matter was closed. But MacKenzie just couldn't let it go at that.

"Sir, as long as we're being prudent, wouldn't prudence dictate that we prepare for all eventualities anyway? I mean, just in case? Why not ready the DSRV? We may need it, if only to get a message to *Aspen* if our time runs out. The cost isn't prohibitive and, ah, excuse me, sir, but since it's already on its way to Guantanamo . . ."

Merton arched an eyebrow. "On whose authority?"

MacKenzie was way out on a limb. He needn't have worried. "Mine, sir," said Garver simply. "We don't have so many good ideas we could afford to pass this one up. The responsibility's mine."

Fletcher looked at Garver. "You're that sure?"

No hesitation. "Yes, sir."

"Captain?"

"Yes, sir. If you'd look at the battle tapes . . ."

Fletcher smiled. "You don't give up easily, son."

"I was hell in tug-of-war."

He felt Merton's rebuke forming, but Fletcher's laugh cut it off. "I'll just bet you were. All right, continue the refit and stand ready to go when and if. Tug-of-war, eh?"

"Actually, I was better at—"

"Captain!" It was Merton, glowering dangerously. "The President is a busy man."

Fletcher stood, and all the rest did too. He and Dellman disappeared through the same door they'd entered.

MacKenzie felt Garver's hand on his elbow, pulling him from the table. "Nice going, Mac," he whispered under his breath. But MacKenzie had his eye on Merton, who still hadn't seemed to make up his mind.

Abruptly, Merton called to Garver. "Ben? A moment, please."

"Yes, sir." To MacKenzie, Merton said, "Wait here."

The two conferred briefly. MacKenzie couldn't read either's expression. He shifted nervously as the others left. Careers had been derailed for less than going over the Chief of Naval Operations' head.

Garver came back. MacKenzie looked at him questioningly. Merton was now speaking to an Air Force general. Garver was deadpan.

"Iceland?" MacKenzie asked.

Garver shook his head. "Not quite. Actually, he was pretty impressed with you. He was brief and to the point. Glad you spoke up. He feels the plan is as good as we're going to get." Garver grinned. "Also said if you ever embarrass him again by speaking out of turn, you'll relish the transfer he has in mind."

"To where, sir?"

"The Army."

MacKenzie looked sheepish.

Garver clapped him on the back and grinned. "Don't worry. I'm on your side."

"I felt that. Thanks for the support."

"No big deal. I just couldn't let Dellman get away with that cowboy shoot-out crap."

MacKenzie looked at him. "It is, you know. In some ways."

Garver grinned. "Sure, but why tell him? Come on. Let's get back to work."

"Okay, pardner."

In the sitting room next to the Oval Office, Fletcher poured himself a drink. He found the Navy captain's plan appealing. What president hadn't felt the hot desire to react against this kind of terrorism with strong, direct action? Yet, to a man, each one in the end accepted the limits and frustration in dealing with shadowy forces and no-win situations.

Iran, Syria, North Korea and now Nicaragua. He gazed into his scotch. There was a never-ending supply of gnats who bit at the giant's ears. Lately they'd been much too effective at getting the giant to turn its head.

It was exasperating. The Nicaraguan policy had been formulated over months, with all the resources of his office behind it. Now it might all have to be changed because of a few dozen men in a submarine. He put down the drink angrily. He'd chosen the prudent course. He'd had to. Only in the movies did one gain anything from coming out shooting.

"Mr. President?"

It was Dellman. "Ambassador Belov, sir. Are you ready?"

Fletcher looked at his empty drink and wished he could pour another. But that wouldn't do. "Send him in," he said.

Belov had bad news. Fletcher knew that as soon as he saw the Russian's face. Careful, reserved . . . a tinge of guilt, maybe?

"Good day, Mr. President. I have a response from my government."

Belov was wearing a dark suit and white shirt. If the Soviets hate us so much, Fletcher found himself wondering, why do they all wear our goddamned clothing?

"And what might that be, Mr. Ambassador?"

Belov's mouth tightened for a moment. He doesn't like the response, Fletcher thought.

"As you know, Mr. President, military data in the Soviet Union is regarded with a similar reverence as you might hold for religious objects. Our entire history is filled with invasions. To give military information to our, ah . . ."

". . . greatest enemy?" Fletcher supplied.

". . . foremost competitor, might be a better choice, don't you think? Well, for some factions the thought is extremely disturbing, to say the least."

"So is one of your attack subs running amok."

"We're aware of that, certainly. And we want to help. This serves no one. We stand to look like incompetents who can't safeguard their own property. You run the risk of appearing weak if you accede to their demands, or worse, of attack itself."

Belov seemed to be searching for the right words. Fletcher watched him carefully. He saw his inner turmoil. Fletcher had known Belov for years. He'd never seen him like this before.

"Mr. President, we have a very complex situation."

"Swift action can contain it."

"Maybe so, but there's more to it than that. We are aware . . . we are aware that you plan to invade Nicaragua as soon as the threat of the *Kirov* is removed."

The unspoken curses inside Fletcher's head would have made a convict wince. But he held his face expressionless.

"Your information is inaccurate."

Belov sighed. "Of course."

"Look," Fletcher said angrily, "Moscow is obligated by treaty to help us, and we both know it."

"Yes, we know."

"Then I expect assistance to be forthcoming. Any other agendas are irrelevant."

"I can see how you would regard them as such. Would the Nicaraguans?" He held up a hand to forestall Fletcher's angry response. "Very well, I am empowered to make the following offer. You may have the data on the Victor Three and the specifics on *Kirov*. In exchange, we want three things."

"Name them."

"First, the specifications and schematics for your Very High Speed Integrated Circuit—VHSIC—used for ultra-rapid high-speed calculations, especially in command and control mechanisms. Second, the specifications on your Advanced Medium Range Air-to-Air Missile—AMRAAM—and its Stealth characteristics. Third, the specifications for your Anti-Submarine Warfare sonar detection system and the accompanying search/locate Ambient Sound Program—ASP—used in the Cray supercomputer. For these, the Victor Three."

It took a great deal of Fletcher's control to keep from assaulting Belov physically. The Soviets had no intention of helping. No one sane could think the U.S. could give away most of its tactical advantages in one fell swoop, even in a situation such as this. Give them the ASW data, he thought, and the seas would be as transparent to them as glass; the AMRAAM would virtually eliminate American air superiority; and the VHSIC would give the Soviets computational abilities years ahead of their research, saving them billions in research and development costs. The political ramifications of a stalemate in the arms race—and in subsequent global power projection—were as far reaching as WW II.

"No," he said simply. "Even you must know that these demands are out of the question. Follow this analogy. You've just raised the stakes far past what this penny-ante game can tolerate. Not for the Victor Threes. Sorry, we're dropping out of the game."

"Penny ante?" Belov's surprise was genuine. "The *Kirov* threatens several of your cities."

"Before I respond to that, one question, please. You're actually offering us an open road into Managua if I'm reading you right. Yes?"

Belov looked away. "Political realities. It's what you want, isn't it?"

"I wish the Sandinistas could hear how valuable they are to you."

"As I said, political realities. But my question remains unanswered."

"All right, let me give the facts. We can survive the *Kirov*. We can even survive a major nuclear accident. But your 'shopping list' would be a disaster of unparalleled proportions, and the effects would last for generations. The answer, therefore, is no. Not for Nicaragua, not for the *Kirov*."

Belov nodded slowly. "Very well. I understand. I will relay your response to those concerned. I . . . I'm sorry."

Fletcher saw it again then. The slight downturn at the corners of Belov's mouth. He sensed almost a hesitancy to leave. Something more? Fletcher tried to widen the opening.

"Mr. Ambassador, when we last spoke you indicated a willingness to help. Is this all you're capable of?"

"All? Yes, I suppose it is." His hands twisted nervously. Fletcher wondered if he was aware of it. "Yet this crisis, if it escalates . . ."

"It could be disastrous for both countries. Do they see that in the Kremlin?"

"They see . . . yes, I know they see that."

Fletcher probed deeper. "This isn't the way to advantage," he suggested quietly. "A tiger in camp eats indiscriminately."

Belov smiled. "An old proverb?"

"About thirty seconds. Sounded genuine though, no?"

"I felt the sentiment was."

"Then you heard me correctly," Fletcher said. "I hope you'll send it back to Moscow. Do what you can. The Victor Three isn't the newest or the fastest sub in your fleet. The Mikes and Sierras outclass them in quite a few areas. We'll share data on a comparable craft, say the Sturgeon or Skipjack. I'll say it again—no one ought to profit from this."

"And the Kirov?"

"If we take her whole, she's yours. Intact. No tampering. If she's destroyed, one quarter the original cost in grain credits."

Belov thought it over. "Fair. More than fair. But as you know . . ."

Fletcher's face softened somewhat. "You can only report back. All right. Do so. Soon."

Belov rose, hesitated. "You have my sincere pledge to try and broker this agreement as we've outlined. The tiger in camp . . . I hope they see it."

"So do I."

"Good day, Mr. President."

"I'll be waiting, Mr. Ambassador. But, Valery Alekseiovich?"

Belov turned, surprised after all the years at this first use of his given name. "Yes?"

"Not too long. Remember, not too long."

Belov nodded and left.

31

CARIBBEAN SEA

The Nicaraguan officer's Russian was so garbled that Mishkin could only look at him and spread his hands in confusion.

"English?" Mishkin suggested. "I speak a little."

"Bread," the officer said heavily. "Bread . . . tonight. Yes?"

Mishkin nodded. "Bread. Yes, tonight." The officer gave him a resounding clap on the back and left the galley satisfied.

Comrade First Assistant Galley Cook Mishkin bent back over the caldron of soup he was preparing and closed the heavy iron lid. He was a good enough cook to get by in this role, but he was still worried one of the crew was going to slip. He'd stayed in the galley as much as possible and had little enough contact with their new captain, Santillo, but obviously a good number of men recognized him. He'd been able to communicate the idea that he was another secret part of the First International Communist "cruise," and the crew was used to spies among them. Usually KGB. So this new role made less of a ripple than if he'd returned to his regular duties. He suspected some were even comforted, spotting him.

After breaking out of jail he'd made straight for the docks. There he found *Kirov*, but manned by a strange concoction of Cubans and Nicaraguan officers commanding the remnants of his crew which, he decided, must have been selected for its dull-wittedness. It wasn't so difficult to steal in with them, stripping to undershirt, pants, and boots. He looked like the rest after a long, hard liberty.

It hadn't taken him long to understand what was going on. Captain Santillo and his officers made the incorrect assumption that no one spoke Spanish. Well, maybe it wasn't so foolish. None of the crew did, but Mishkin spoke it after years of liberties in Havana. He also spoke English and a smattering of Chinese.

Nuclear blackmail. What a scheme. He had to hand it to the Nicaraguans, even though they must have realized that they were dead meat the instant they fired. This had to be a rogue action, Mishkin thought, certainly not sponsored by the Soviet government. But would his government want it to succeed or not? Of that he was unsure.

He decided he had to do two things. One was to prepare for the possibility that his superiors would want this blackmail scheme not to succeed. The other was to call and ask them.

He made sure the heavy iron lid was secure and lowered the flame. The ball of dough he put in his pocket was certainly not going to cause any comment if he was stopped. He picked up a galley tray he'd prepared and headed for the torpedo room.

There were three crewmen and a Nicaraguan officer in the confined space. Torpedoes were stacked on racklike lifts along the bulkheads, neatly stenciled in white with designations and factory numbers. Political slogans had been affixed also, urging vigilance, sacrifice, and the like.

"Comrades!" Mishkin said, stepping onto the floor grating and holding out the tray. "Breakfast brought to you specially. Sweet rolls." He handed the biggest to the officer. "Yes?"

"Gracias, comrade." He munched on the roll. "Very good indeed."

"You see?" Mishkin said to the crewmen, who were staring at him uncertainly. "The cooking on this boat has improved already."

None of the crew felt it necessary to suggest that their former Radio Officer didn't seem like one of the promised changes, but in fact Mishkin was a better cook, and they accepted his presence, augmented by his cold, stern look when the officer's back was turned. They took the proffered buns and ate silently. Mishkin accepted the officer's compliments and moved off.

Ten minutes later the laxatives in the officer's pastry sent him racing for the head with the speed of one of the torpedoes under his charge. Mishkin stepped back inside. The crewmen regarded him silently, surprised and a little afraid.

"Turn around. Face the wall," Mishkin commanded them unceremoniously. They quickly moved to obey. Gone was the face of the smiling cook. *This* was a Soviet officer.

Mishkin had enough antisabotage courses to know how to prevent it. It was therefore easy enough to do the reverse and cause it. These were the tubes already loaded with cruise missiles. The dough made a perfect insulator between relays. Adroitly applied, the ready lights would still show the tubes operative; however, the relays could no longer transmit a firing signal. He decided not to tamper with the tubes Santillo had been using to fire torpedoes and sink shipping, since Santillo might use them again and Mishkin didn't want his tampering to be discovered prematurely. They were too small for the SS-NX-21's anyway.

"Turn around," he ordered. "A single word of my return visit and you'll never survive the meal after. Think of the officer. You understand? It could have been poison. Remember that. Not a word."

They nodded, not really understanding why he'd come back, and not really wanting to know either. Humping around big torpedoes and eating—that they knew. Mishkin told them they were a credit to the motherland, sighed once, and left the torpedo room.

Mishkin had been watching the radio room for the better part of two hours, passing by as often as he could, delivering food to various sections of the ship. No one had stopped or questioned him so far.

He'd deliberately passed through the control room a few times. Captain Santillo seemed to have things running very smoothly. He appeared sharp and capable, and the crew jumped when he shouted orders. Mishkin felt *Kirov* was every bit as battle ready as it had been under its previous commander. This worried him and made his work that much more important.

Now that the first part was completed, he had to get into the radio room to transmit. He didn't want to use the laxative trick again; word spread too easily in so confined a space. He wanted no questions from the sharp-eyed captain.

But this was taking too long. He decided he was being too circumspect. Returning to the galley, he picked up a pot, filled it with hot soup, and returned to the radio room.

"Yes?" It was the Radio Officer. His two assistants—*my* two assistants, Mishkin bristled internally—looked up, recognized him . . . and turned back to their instrument tables.

"A mug of soup, Comrade Tenente," Mishkin said, smiling.

The officer replied happily, "This is what I like. First class, eh?"

"Absolutely," Mishkin said, and poured the entire contents down the officer's arm.

The scream would have been heard in the forward sonar room were not the radio room soundproofed. The officer leaped to his feet and stumbled out of the room, cursing bitterly. Mishkin looked panic-stricken and kept apologizing profusely, steering the officer towards the storeroom that doubled as an infirmary.

"Ice!" Mishkin yelled after him. "Ice will stop the pain." He turned back to his assistants as soon as the officer was lost from view.

"Comrade Radio Officer Mishkin—" one began.

"Silence," Mishkin commanded. "Listen to me. I am the cook, nothing more, until I tell you otherwise. No rank, no courtesy. Understand? Good. Now you both must remain ready to assist me when I need you. So from now on one of you must stop by the galley every few hours. Do not speak to me or even acknowledge my presence unless I speak to you first. That is very important. You will say nothing to the Radio Officer when he returns."

"Yes, Comrade Radio Officer Mishkin, but—"

"Sorry, no time." He slid into the officer's seat. "Keep watch, let me know if someone comes."

Mishkin slipped the headset over his ears and spun the dial to the constant-monitor emergency frequency. If there were Soviet ships anywhere nearby, they'd receive his signal. He held the codebook on his lap. Encoding faster than he ever had in his life, he prepared his signal for transmission. It was stored in the computers and released in a brief pulse too fast for the Americans to intercept. He hoped he wasn't making too many mistakes. Mercifully, they were at periscope depth with the radio mast up. Probably waiting for the daily communication from Managua, he thought. Very well, it worked both ways.

The message encoded, he sent it forth in a pulse-burst of energy. Finally he instructed his men again and headed back down the narrow corridors to the galley. The soup should be just about ready now.

One did what one could.

Three hundred nautical miles east of the *Kirov*'s position, Colonel Nikolai Renkov stood on the deck of the guided missile destroyer *Udaloy*, staring out over the bottle-green sea, half expecting the black bulk of the submarine to breach the chop and roll to the surface like some giant whale. When he was handed a decoded message sent straight from the ship's captain, he read it carefully, questioned the radio operator for several minutes, then ordered a helicopter readied to take him to Havana.

Returning to his cabin, Renkov carefully checked the *Kirov*'s roster against the list the Nicaraguan officials had provided. Radio Officer Mishkin was indeed listed and supposed to be in transit with the rest of the crew and officers. Could he really have slipped back into the sub? It appeared so. By Lenin's beard, Renkov thought, what a break! An officer capable of communicating, in place on *Kirov*. He checked his watch. Mishkin had been very specific. He could only receive a return message at the same time tomorrow.

"Comrade Colonel? Your transport will be ready on the helipad in five minutes."

"Wait a moment."

Renkov took a few seconds to compose a message. "Take this to the captain. It's to be sent to our ambassador in Washington immediately."

"Yes, Comrade Colonel."

Renkov placed his few things inside his case, slid Mishkin's transmission into a folder and put that in also. He could imagine the stir it would create.

Things were looking better by the moment.

32

MID-ATLANTIC

Ambassador Belov reread Renkov's transmission, which had been radioed from the *Udaloy* to the Soviet Embassy in Washington and then forwarded by satellite link to his plane. He thought over the contents and then looked up at the pilot.

"Can we make Havana?"

"Yes, Comrade Ambassador, but then we run into the problem of returning to Washington. The Americans do not allow direct flights still."

"Your suggestion? I must go to Havana first."

The pilot was an experienced man. "If you approve, we can drop low enough to disappear off their radar screens, fly to Havana to complete your business, then return to our original approach route and continue on in. A convenient fiction for all, and it's usually overlooked if we don't take too long."

"Three hours?"

"Not a problem, Comrade Ambassador."

"Fine," Belov agreed. "Make the adjustment."

Belov had read Renkov's original report. He felt he knew a little about the man. A career officer, not given to rash judgments, careful and ambitious. So if Renkov felt he was in possession of something vitally important, Belov was inclined to accept that.

The Aeroflot jet dipped down, banking sharply as the pilot changed course for Cuba. When it seemed to Belov that the satiny water must be touching the plane's skin, the pilot leveled them off and flew on. For the remainder of the flight Belov contented himself with discovering how close he could come to being very drunk and not showing it.

He called for another vodka from the steward, feeling the familiar despondence settle over him again. When he'd been handed the transmission by the pilot, he'd nursed the brief hope that the Politburo had changed its collective mind. But that was too much to hope for.

They'd turned him down flat. Not him actually, but Fletcher's offer. Belov spoke in favor of it so strongly that he'd come to think of it as his own. In a way it could have been. It was the only rational suggestion to emerge from this madness.

Belov finished the vodka and accepted a refill. It was ice cold and tasted faintly of pepper. An old vice, comfortable and familiar. It helped only a little. Being one of the few people in the world who knew that a nuclear exchange might occur at any moment helped not at all.

He finished the flight in an agitated state of mind. Renkov was waiting for him at the airport. Belov steered him into the section of the terminal reserved for visiting dignitaries, a plush chrome-and-glass complex complete with secretarial services, if required. Belov sat next to a glass wall and could see the jets taking off as Renkov spoke.

". . . when I found out and called you as per instructions, Comrade Ambassador," he concluded.

"You were correct to do so. This Radio Officer's presence is miraculous, an opportunity to end this affair once and for all. I wouldn't have thought it possible only an hour ago."

"End it? But—"

"Of course. A relatively simple act of sabotage and *Kirov* can be forced to surface. We have our sub back and the crisis is avoided. Moscow should be delighted."

"I don't follow you, Comrade Ambassador," Renkov complained. "Wouldn't Moscow be happiest with the Americans and Nicaraguans at each other's throats? That's what I put in my report."

"You've sent this information on already?"

"As soon as I arrived."

"I'm sure your report was excellent," Belov said quickly, "and will be wonderfully received. Have you sent Mishkin's original transmission also?"

"By satellite relay."

"I see." Belov thought for a moment. "May I ask you a question, Comrade Colonel?"

"Of course."

Belov rocked back in his chair. "I'd like a military perspective. Tell me, what would you have Mishkin do?"

"I would authorize him to approach this Captain Santillo directly. Perhaps kill Barrista and his deputy first, to prevent interference. Then offer Santillo a huge sum of money, exalted rank in the Soviet Navy and whatever else he demanded in return for launching the missiles. Offer him also the full protection of the Soviet fleet immediately after."

"But we couldn't protect him. . . . Oh, I see. He launches, the Americans obliterate him, and we have clean hands. Very clever," Belov mused. "You've already suggested this in your report?"

"I have."

Belov stood up. "Very well, time presses me. I also have messages to deliver." He put an arm around Renkov's shoulder and propelled him toward the door. "You've done a fine job, Comrade Colonel. I feel sure the Politburo will see things your way. Return to the *Udaloy* and wait for word from me. Traffic of this level must be handled out of the embassy here."

"But *Udaloy* has—"

"Comrade Colonel, clean hands require a clean record. How would a sudden surge in radio traffic from Moscow to *Udaloy* look immediately preceding, ah . . . such an event?"

"Yes, I see that."

"I've decided not to leave. I can send my message by pouch. Everything may hinge on what we do here next. Return to your ship, Comrade General . . . I mean, Comrade Colonel. Yes?"

Renkov beamed. "As you wish, Comrade Ambassador. Thank you."

Belov watched him go, satisfied. He ran his hands slowly across his scalp, feeling the deep creases over his eyes, the tired folds. Didn't anyone but him want this thing to end? It seemed only he and his enemy, Fletcher, saw eye to eye on things. When had everyone else stopped measuring the lives it might cost?

Belov sat by himself for a long time, watching the planes come and go. The cost might be very high for what he planned. Very high. But the alternatives were unthinkable. In order to execute his idea he had to move quickly. He hoped the office he needed hadn't changed since the years he'd been posted here. Little did in a bureaucracy like Cuba's.

Belov summoned a secretary and dictated a cable to be sent to Fletcher along normal diplomatic channels, indicating the Politburo's rejection of his offer. Then he dictated another to be sent directly to the Kremlin via secure satellite relay. It was a plea to use Mishkin to sabotage *Kirov*, and would follow Renkov's transmission by less than an hour. He'd wait for the response.

He put his pilot on standby and called for a car to take him into Havana.

By a very tricky and circuitous route he had one last message to send.

33

GUANTANAMO BASE

MacKenzie's torch "primpfed" into life when he put the spark to it. He was in the secondary cabin—the second of three internal spheres—of the Deep Submergence Rescue Vehicle, *Mystic*. It was a fifty-foot, thirty-seven ton, cigar-shaped craft whose workings he had come to know intimately.

MacKenzie adjusted the gas flow until the tip of the torch was a blue-white cone and began to weld in the new battery racks to hold the additional power supply. It was an amazing craft, he'd learned, with control panels that looked more like a space shuttle's than a sub's. In fact, *Mystic*'s inertial guidance system was used on the Apollo spacecraft. She had six degrees of motion, which translated into the ability to move at any angle or in any direction, and she was as responsive as a well-bred horse.

MacKenzie kept discovering more and more what a stable craft she was during long hours of practice sessions at her controls.

The hull construction was twenty-six layers of fiberglass, titanium, and a steel alloy designed to withstand pressures up to 3300 pounds per square inch. *Mystic* had already submerged to over five thousand feet and was reputed to be able to go deeper. MacKenzie raised the torch and sat back on his heels to wipe the sweat from his face. The craft's pressurized hull, Doppler sonar system, inertial navigation devices, seven TV cameras, and an exterior mechanical arm were among the most sophisticated in the world.

Mystic was usually manned by a crew of four: a pilot to maneuver the craft and maintain communications; a copilot to handle the sonar, video sensors, and hydraulic systems; and two life-support technicians, who provided environmental control. Since *Mystic* was designed to evacuate up to twenty-four men at a time, MacKenzie knew that oxygen storage with the additional tanks should meet all of his planned needs for the sole two occupants—he and the copilot.

Power was more of a problem though. Ordinarily *Mystic* recharged frequently at the mother sub during a rescue operation. Lacking that "mother," *Mystic*'s hold was being filled with additional batteries to drive her electric motors and twin-ducted thrusters. This was critical. If they ran out of power before reaching *Aspen*, *Mystic* would drop like a dead weight into the depths of the Trench.

Sobering thought. MacKenzie bent back to the work. The Navy techs had done a fine job. The racks fit perfectly. The electricians would be in later for a final wiring. He could have let the techs do this job, too, but it made him feel better to at least do a part of the work himself. It was his life depending on it.

He very much wanted to come back. As a Navy man he regarded the upcoming operation with the importance it deserved. He was certain of its necessity and confident of his own and his ship's ability to meet the challenge. But there was another part, a personal part that wanted Justine and a family and safe haven from danger. That made him not so different from the men with families who served alongside him on a submarine's seventy-day cruise or aboard the carriers or under the ice. Maybe it made this one of the first brave things he'd ever done, putting the first genuine comfort he'd ever known at risk.

He grabbed his balled-up shirt, wiped his naked arms and chest dry, and paused to gulp some cooler air coming in the hatch. He thought about Justine a lot lately. Terry Holmes wouldn't tell him anything more than she had returned to Costa Rica, duration and nature of assignment classified. MacKenzie knew Sebastion was there too. That much one could read in the papers. Some rumblings about a possible invasion were already reaching the media. It wouldn't be secret much longer. And what would happen when knowledge of the *Kirov* blazoned across headlines?

Another day, two at the most, and *Mystic* would be ready. At night, when the crews worked under lights, MacKenzie was studying the Cayman Trench. It was too bad they didn't have a better picture of the terrain, he thought. They were using the best charts available, and the other DSRV—*Avalon*—had already made several runs as far into the Trench as was thought advisable. For the first leg of the journey, at least, he'd have a reliable map.

How many times had he looked at *Kirov*'s Zone over the past few days and wondered where the sub might be at that moment. Several more ships strayed into the area and had been ruthlessly destroyed. MacKenzie interviewed the captain of a Dutch container ship, and a disturbing picture emerged. *Kirov*'s captain gave no warning to allow crew to abandon ship. He made a single run within seconds of his periscope being spotted, and sent in one torpedo amidships. No sentiment, no waste. The CIA said his name was Santillo and he was either a well-trained submariner or a gifted amateur. MacKenzie didn't like that. The first was bad enough, but the second? Who could predict that kind of genius?

He shrugged off useless speculation and continued to examine his feelings as he worked. He wondered if anyone knew that under his professionalism, which concentrated on problems with an almost academic detachment, lay a pulse beat of excitement as hot as any produced by schoolyard confrontations of his youth. Somewhere out there another man waited in another ship and there was going to be armed combat. He felt the visceral, atavistic rush of that. It made his heart hammer as racing on narrow country lanes once had, under a copper-colored moon with the air crystal sharp and the willow trees writhing in the wind like wild, long-haired women.

A long time ago. A lifetime ago.

A wistful smile crossed his face slowly. Old memories. New schoolyards. The boy within the man, always present.

I'm coming, Santillo.

34

CARIBBEAN SEA

Miguel was adamant. "It's got to stop, Phillipe. Santillo's overstepped his authority. One ship, a warning, fine. But these last two? There was no reason."

"They were in the Zone."

"That's not good enough. They were merchant ships, off course by some error or accident. No threat at all."

"You can't know that," Barrista said, angry. "Maybe they were military craft packed with explosives. Maybe they were camouflaged trackers. To maintain our credibility we have to carry out our threats."

"So we turn into murderers?"

"If necessary." Barrista's stare was hard.

Miguel faced him squarely. "Then I want off. You lied to me, Phillipe. Maybe you believed it at the time, but this isn't what it started out to be. We're not deterring anything, we're just killing people."

"We're holding back the entire United States," Barrista insisted.

"With a weapon that's going to blow up in our faces any minute. I tell you Santillo is a killer."

The throb of *Kirov*'s engines was a steady vibration in

the table, seat, and deck. Barrista's voice took on a cutting edge. "When did that ever bother *you*?"

Miguel looked down. "That's a lousy thing to say," he said quietly.

Barrista's tone lost its edge. "You incite me."

"Only so you'll see the truth. Look at what's happened, Phillipe. You've armed Santillo and turned him loose. He doesn't need us anymore. Who is he loyal to now? What are his allegiances? Only to his own distorted vision. Can you honestly believe you can still control him?"

"Of course." But Barrista's tone was less firm.

Miguel pounced on even the smallest doubt. "Prove it. If there is another ship, make him let it go. Shadow it until it's out of the Zone, but let it go."

Barrista looked at him closely. He'd never seen Miguel this shaken before. "There's more to this than just a sudden burst of compassion. What's underneath, Miguel?"

"You can't see it? Look at me, Phillipe. I'm terrified. I can't sleep. My hands are starting to shake." He leaned closer. "One man dies, even ten men, you tell yourself it's war or patriotism or father or whatever you need to get you through it. When the ten turn into fifty, at least you still have the Cause. You sing the strong songs by the bonfires in the hills, the firelight courage. You drink, you follow orders . . ."

"What's so different now?"

"Look around you. Look at this . . . thing. And we're in charge of it. We; us. You and I. This time it won't be a hundred or even a thousand dead if we make a mistake. It will be millions! I tell you it's close to happening, Phillipe. That maniac wants it that way."

"You can't know that."

"No? Just watch him strutting around the control room. Too many people put him down, demeaned him. He's showing everybody now. The whole world."

"But isn't a little of that all right? It binds him to us."

Miguel shook his head in disbelief. "To us? Phillipe, he doesn't need us. He has this submarine and his Zone and his targets, and that's all there is for Captain Santillo except for one last crazy Viking charge and death on a funeral pyre, if he's pushed hard enough. But his pyre will consume half a continent and destroy our country along with it as surely as thunder follows lightning. I won't be responsible for that, Phillipe. I . . . can't. More death on my hands and I think I'll go insane. So let me go, or stop it. If you still can."

"I can't tell you how wrong you are. We're holding the Americans. Everything's working."

"It won't end that way. Believe me."

"I'll show you." Barrista plucked the intercom off the wall. "Control Room, Captain Santillo? This is Minister Barrista. I'd like you to join the Deputy Minister and me in the wardroom, please. . . . Yes, at once." He listened for a moment. "What could be so urgent to . . . But Captain . . . I demand— Hello?" Barrista replaced the intercom. "He cut me off."

"August First is an old agenda now," Miguel said quietly. "Soon he'll tire of it and move off for reasons of his own. We needed this too badly, Phillipe, so we were willing to use even a flawed plan to make it work. Well, it won't anymore. Stop it now."

Barrista didn't acknowledge him. He just pushed back the bench from the table and strode out in the direction of the control room. Miguel saw the big vein in his neck pulsing dangerously. He followed quickly.

The control room was full of activity. Santillo drilled the crew hard, holding them to standards far higher than previously demanded of them. There were constant simulations of attack problems. At that moment sonar was reporting another ship on the edge of the Zone.

"Captain?"

Santillo looked up from the Navigator's table. "Minister, I thought I told you—"

Miguel had to hand it to Barrista. His look of scorn made even Santillo wince.

"In every navy in the world, Captain, there are those who plan and those who execute those plans. This craft belongs to the Sandinista government of the People's Republic of Nicaragua. It and everyone in it are responsible to me. To me, Captain."

The control room quieted. The officers present looked to Santillo. It was clear a crisis point had been reached. The Russian crew, even without understanding the language, sensed the interplay of tensions and made no move to interfere. The cook stopped handing out coffee.

Barrista walked forward, and Santillo looked unsure. "You're tracking a ship," he demanded.

"Yes. One well within the Zone," Santillo said.

"Of what type?"

Santillo shrugged. "What does it matter?"

"*Of what type?*" Barrista's voice held daggers.

"Commercial fisher," Santillo said grudgingly. "Probably crossed the line following a school."

"Let it go then."

"What?"

"I said let it go. It poses no threat."

The stillness around them was fraught with violence. Santillo looked to his officers. "Any ship that enters the Zone resists our authority. That's a risk, Minister. And it's your policy."

"Then it's also my policy to change. Let the ship go, Captain."

"It's a mistake."

Miguel began to move.

"You still don't see it, Captain. If so, it will be *my* mistake. And if I so choose, it will be *our* mistake. Now carry out my order."

That was it then. If Santillo refused, there could be no turning back for either man. Miguel's heart sank. *One more and I think I'll go insane,* he'd said. Oh, Phillipe . . . Music started faintly somewhere. He sidled closer to Santillo. The needle slid into his hand.

"I'm waiting, Captain."

Santillo surged forward angrily. "You dare tell me?"

"Obey your orders, damn you."

"I refuse to . . ."

Barrista saw Miguel rise up behind Santillo like a cobra, saw the needle poised in his hand. *One more and I think . . .*

"Miguel! No!"

It froze Miguel for a split second. The music was screaming. He looked at Barrista wondering. . . . Santillo spun around, eyes wide. Miguel recovered and lunged, but it was too late. Santillo managed to sidestep his thrust and the needle sliced past his head and plunged into

Santillo's shoulder. The control room turned into chaos. Santillo roared. The officers rushed to his aid. Barrista tried to shove past them. He was thrown back viciously and crashed into a steel instrument table. There was an ugly, cracking sound and he slid to the deck limply.

Miguel went crazy. He fought like a madman, breaking one man's hold, kicking another in the groin to get to Barrista. He vaulted the railing around the periscope, slammed into an officer and flung him back, broke free again . . . and staggered back screaming as the galley cook threw the tray with the remaining hot coffees right into his face.

Miguel clawed at his eyes, blinded, flailing around on the deck in a tortured heap. Crewmen grabbed him and hauled him to his feet.

Santillo was breathing heavily, one hand clapped over his bleeding shoulder.

"Pretenses are over," he said harshly. "You and your Minister will be locked away for the duration of this voyage." Miguel started to speak but Santillo cut him off. "You have no authority on this submarine any longer. For our own purposes we will maintain the Zone. It protects us. But I plan to renegotiate with your government. With all the governments, maybe. Directly. No more intermediaries. Villega, take them both to the garbage room and tie them securely."

The Sonar Officer bent down to lift Barrista. A look of distaste crossed his face. "Comrade Captain?"

"To the garbage room, Villega."

"This one is dead, Comrade Captain."

Santillo scowled. "You, Comrade Cook. Come here."

Mishkin was standing back in a corner, observing events. He stepped forward, eyes averted respectfully. "Yes, Comrade Captain?"

"I won't forget your quick action—the coffee, excellent. I am pleased."

"Thank you, Comrade Captain."

"You speak Spanish?"

"Very little, Comrade Captain. Please, thank you, where is the bathroom?"

Santillo laughed. "We'll teach you more. Later. Is there room in the freezers for this one?"

Mishkin's lips curled in aversion. "If you wish, Comrade Captain."

"I do. Come to my cabin later, when you're off duty. We'll talk. Maybe you should aspire to something more than the galley."

"I'm not unhappy." Mishkin shrugged. "But your shoulder, Comrade Captain. The medic. I'll call him?"

"All right. Take the corpse too. Villega, some men. Help him."

Miguel was propelled forward roughly. His vision had cleared sufficiently to see Phillipe's body draped over a crewman's shoulder and taken out. There was a numbness inside him, like a frost had settled over his heart and stomach. He looked at Santillo as he was pushed from the room. The look of triumph was unmistakable.

All the music had stopped.

Back in the galley Mishkin thought over the situation as he directed the temporary internment of Barrista's body.

He'd reacted mostly from instinct, throwing the coffee. He could take no definitive action until he heard from his government, and there was advantage for him in the events in the control room. He'd seen that the Deputy Minister's fight was futile. Where did he think he was going on a submarine? So the coffee hadn't really changed anything but to endear Mishkin to the captain and maybe provide him with some greater freedom at a necessary moment.

Mishkin was worried. The situation on *Kirov* was in flux, and he couldn't let anybody know about it. With Santillo a free agent, who could say what was going to happen? He'd studied the man closely. There was a dangerous instability there, and he was certainly capable of turning *Kirov*'s awesome weapons back on its former owners under the right conditions. Cuba was just as close as the American coast. But Mishkin had received no radio reply to his first broadcast and didn't want to risk another. The best course was to wait.

He thought about the Nicaraguan, Barrista. What a coup to have gotten away with this! He'd stolen a Soviet submarine, blackmailed the United States into submission, and stood the whole world on its ear for a brief time. Now he lay cooling alongside the frozen chickens.

Why had he tried to hold back his deputy? Segurra's small moment of hesitation ultimately cost Barrista everything. Was he hoping to resolve the situation even at that point? Did he think Santillo irreplaceable? Or maybe there was something deeper going on, something Mishkin had no idea of. He shook his head. All this was too labyrinthine. He checked the time.

The return message was only hours away. He began to make plans for several alternatives. In each, his getting out of this situation alive was a clear priority. Lost in thought, he set a caldron of water to boil for the night's soup and began to chop vegetables.

Miguel Segurra didn't know it yet, but he had an ally.

35

THE WHITE HOUSE

President Fletcher nudged the small rectangle of thin, green cardboard with his letter opener, a silver blade which was a gift from his late wife.

"Tell me again where we got this, Mark."

Dellman reopened the folder on his lap. It was yellow with a bright green band, hand delivered from the Department of the Treasury only twenty minutes before.

"It's the damnedest thing I ever saw, sir. Maybe the most clever too."

"If it's authentic," Fletcher admonished.

"Treasury says it is. And State verifies that's Belov's handwriting."

Fletcher lifted the U.S. government check, a standard issue light-green computerized voucher . . . made out to Fidel Castro in the sum of $4085.

"You say the last one he cashed was in 1959?"

"Yes, sir. We've been paying the Cubans since 1903 for the lease on our base on Guantanamo Bay, but except for the 'fifty-nine check, none of the others have been cashed by Castro since he came to power. Maybe he wanted a new car that year. No one knows. But obviously the account is flagged. The check was picked up by Treasury as soon as it came through."

"So the signature isn't Fidel's."

"No, sir. Belov's. And the message to you on the back is his handwriting too. He sent the check for deposit to their Central Bank in Havana. It took about two days to reach us. It's amazing, really. Belov apparently needed to communicate with you and couldn't leave Cuba. He didn't have any means that weren't strictly monitored, so he simply endorsed the check, God only knows where Castro keeps them—probably some government accounting office somewhere—and wrote his message on the back, figuring that such an important event would have to be news as soon as the check reached the appropriate Treasury department. Really, sir, it's so simple it's brilliant."

"Whom do we thank at Treasury?"

Dellman consulted the file. "Man named Rodriguez, Cuban Desk, Developing Nations Section."

Fletcher nodded. "Draw up a commendation. How is security on this?"

"Rodriguez was extremely diligent. Called us direct. We've got a tight lid on it."

Fletcher looked at the check again. His last income tax reimbursement came on one exactly like it. But on the back, under the endorsement, it read:

F,

Send D, Gitmo River Bridge. 2200
7/29. Must talk.

Belov

"So we believe the message is authentic," Fletcher said. "But he should have been on his way here in the first place, Mark. What made him detour to Cuba?"

"There's no way to tell. We have a report that the *Udaloy* dispatched a plane to Havana, and there's been a lot of satellite traffic back and forth to Moscow. It feels like something is definitely up, but what it is? That's anybody's guess."

"You're willing to go then?" Fletcher asked.

Dellman looked surprised. "Of course. We can't pass this up."

"It could be dangerous."

"I'll accept my Purple Heart graciously." Dellman smiled. "You want to start on your presentation speech?"

"Not without your help. Seriously, Mark. You're an academic by profession, shanghaied into politics for the chance to test your theories. I don't want you alone. There's a Marine contingent on Guantanamo. They'll accompany you. Belov doesn't say you have to be alone."

"It might be better."

"Absolutely not," Fletcher said.

"Yes, sir."

"Mark, this is a major crisis. The *Kirov* sank two more ships yesterday. I've got to do something very soon. Belov presented my deal to the Kremlin. I'm betting his lack of an answer means no. But there may be something else. Belov sees the dangers. He's worried, just like I am. See what he's got, Mark, and bring it back to me."

"I'll do my best."

Fletcher nodded. "I know. You always do. By the way," he added, "you're not to be armed. That, too, is an order."

"But I thought—"

"No way, Mark. In and out quietly. The Marines are there for anything else. Wasn't it you who called that Captain MacKenzie a cowboy?"

Dellman grinned ruefully. "Poor choice of words. It seems a bit smug now."

"It was. I'm putting MacKenzie and the DSRV, *Mystic*, on standby. I want to know what Belov says as soon as you can get it back here. Anything else?"

"No, sir. I'll make the arrangements." Dellman turned to go.

"Mark."

"Sir?"

Fletcher was looking up at the picture of his wife.

"Millicent would like it very much if you'd bring your ass back here in one piece."

Dellman was touched. He understood who was doing the asking.

36

GUANTANAMO BASE

MacKenzie was alone on the beach. The night breeze had cleared away most of the humidity as well as the insects, and the sand under his shoulders was warm and supportive. He stared into the night sky, thinking about Justine, hoping she was looking at the same stars, as if that alone would provide some metaphysical connection.

He liked to come here after the day's work, shucking off his sweat-drenched fatigues and plunging nearly naked into the bay. A long pull across the cove and back to loosen knotted muscles and empty his mind of the thousand details of the upcoming operation, then, finally emptied, he'd sprawl in the sand, look up at the heavens, and tend to inner balance.

The work in *Mystic* was done. It had mostly been hump work—big air tanks and heavy duty batteries, cramped spaces that led to sore arms and bruised shins. But now *Mystic* had the power and the air to get him to *Aspen*, according to the calculations. He thought about Tom Lasovic waiting so patiently at full fathom, listening intently for passing Soviet subs. Did the lack of traffic in recent days worry him? Was he contemplating leaving his position or breaking radio silence? Either would be disastrous. The doubts were fierce, MacKenzie knew. But Lasovic was a fine officer. MacKenzie decided he'd stay put.

A funny thought struck him. Could he sneak a pizza on board *Mystic* and pop through *Aspen*'s escape trunk yelling, "Delivery!"? He chuckled at that, then reminded himself to be properly serious and filed the thought under the heading, Good Ideas That Aren't.

A jeep came to a stop up on the rise. MacKenzie reached for his clothing as someone approached. He left his reverie regretfully.

"Mac?" It was Garver. He squatted alongside him in the sand and passed over a cable. "Just got this."

MacKenzie read it in the moonlight. Devoid of the signal traffic codes, it read:

MYSTIC CODE YELLOW. STAND BY IN PLACE.
                                                    MERTON

He looked at Garver. "Timing couldn't be better. We're ready, Ben. Only going to get older and tireder from here on."

"I know. I checked with your crew chief. He says you've been working in *Mystic* yourself, the time you're not at the controls or in the trainer. You're a good officer, Mac. I'd like to see you make it."

"I'll make it."

"Never say die, eh?"

"I'm not saying I'm not full of fears and worries, but it's sort of self-defeating to say anything else."

Garver picked up some sand and threw it over the water. It sounded like weapons fire. "Sure, Mac. But down that far under, where you're taking *Mystic*, well, it's a different world. You won't be in a three-hundred-foot submarine that's filled with a hundred men and room to stand and a cup of coffee when you call for it."

MacKenzie grinned. "All the comforts of home."

"Not in *Mystic*. She was never designed for this kind of run. You'll be piloting by instrument in a pitch-black crevice over a mile down, using every trick you know to cover your sound. There are rocks on those walls like spikes and currents that could toss that fifty-foot cigar right onto them. And getting through that isn't enough. If you miss *Aspen* or she's moved, well, you've seen the figures. All out, nothing to get back on. Makes a man think, Mac."

MacKenzie watched the interplay of emotion on Garver's face. "You're pretty philosophical tonight."

Garver thrust his chin at the silver band of light that lay on the ocean like a road. "Maybe it's the moon." He shrugged.

"Sure. I understand. And thanks."

"For nothing."

"For the way out. I hear you. I appreciate it. But, well . . . what the hell, Ben, you know?"

Garver smiled. "I know. It's just what we do." He stood up. "Nice beach."

"You should get down here more often."

"I should do a lot of things."

"Who's taking us out?" MacKenzie asked.

"*Mystic* is being mated to *Phoenix* right now. Arlin will take you to station at the point the Trench is closest to the Zone. If we get the green light, you'll launch from there."

"Right."

"By the way"—Garver lowered his voice—"the President's aide, Dellman, the one who torpedoed you in the situation room . . . ?"

"I remember him."

"He's here. Very secret. Some kind of meeting."

"Something to do with us?"

"It wasn't handled through me directly so I wasn't told. If it is, we'll know soon enough. Coming?"

"I think I'll just sit for a while." He lay back. "Sand feels good on my toes."

"Good night, Mac."

"Night, Ben."

Garver's feet made soft padding noises. His jeep started, revved up, and dropped into gear. He drove off with a squeal.

MacKenzie studied the stars for a long time before turning in.

Most borders exist only on maps. Few are marked by anything more than a river or a road. Sebastion was moving his forces steadily northwards, and Justine couldn't be certain if they'd entered Nicaragua yet or not.

She was sure of one thing though. If they weren't in Nicaragua now, they surely would be by August first.

Sebastion hadn't said anything to her since their argument in his tent. He steadfastly refused to listen to her pleas to hold back for a while. So she hefted her pack and the rifle she'd been issued and trudged along in line with all the others—men and jeeps, command vehicles and supply trucks, rolling kitchens and camp followers.

She wore a .45 on her hip and carried a knife in her right boot. Sweat stuck the green fatigue shirt to her back. There was fighting up ahead. She could hear sporadic retorts of fire carried back on the warm breeze. Her stomach knotted at the thought. Sandinista troops. More borders. She thought of old Lucho, who had tended to their instruments in the old pickup truck. She hadn't thought of him for a long time. He was killed only weeks after her father. She cried for him too. No more music, not then and not now. Only walking . . . and anticipating the day's first kill.

Light aircraft circled several times during the day, observing the troop movement. Each one sent Sebastion's army scurrying for the forest. But reports would flow back to Managua that Sebastion was on the move. The lines to Washington would be ablaze with threats. The pressure that put on the situation would be almost unendurable.

What to do? It remained the central question. Holmes had sent her because she was the most likely person to convince Sebastion. But did he really understand the position it put her in if she failed to do just that? Killing your brother. Fratricide. She felt a sickness in her gut that was deeper than any conscious *knowing* could fathom.

Was Sebastion's life more important than the millions who might die? No. But was it more important to her? That was harder to answer. Much harder.

Up ahead they were breaking for camp. Soon wood fires were lit and food smells began traveling on the air currents. Later the singing would begin. Firelight courage, Miguel always called it; the songs and the strong drink. She wished she could tell Miguel what saving her and Sebastion had led to—on a grand scale, the destruction of two countries; on an individual one, the destruction of a brother and sister, for Justine knew she could not live if she killed Sebastion.

She walked to a group of soldiers knotted around a fire. They made a place for her. She accepted food and drink. These were the faces she knew so well; broad planed and brown skinned, shiny with sweat in the firelight; thick black hair and features that could look Asian. Front line troops didn't talk about ideology. They talked about the weather and the march, old friends and half-remembered lovers; the sister of one in Argentina, an uncle in the United States; and as time passed, they talked about food and shoes.

Someone passed Justine a guitar. "Tonight, Doña Justine. For luck?" She pushed it away politely. Others protested. They clapped her about the shoulders.

She took the battered instrument. Firelight songs. She remembered them. She took a long pull on the liquor bottle. Soon she wasn't singing dispassionately . . . or alone.

Once, through the fire, she saw Sebastion watching her. His face was set in hard lines, but she saw a mixture of love and pain in his eyes. She wanted to cry out to him. She understood. Love and pain had been inseparable all their lives. Instead she played . . . and prayed for a reprieve.

She thought about Peter MacKenzie while she played. Her last conversation with Holmes indicated Peter was a part of the effort to destroy the Russian sub. Could he know how much more he would save if he did destroy it? Surely not.

She played far into the night. Dusky halos surrounded the moon when she finally put the guitar down, exhausted.

Maybe MacKenzie was looking at the same stars, far away under his own night sky. She hoped so.

In many ways she was still depending on him.

37

GUANTANAMO BASE

Mark Dellman saw the Naval Air Station on the leeward side of the bay as he flew over it. Just north of it the southern tip of Mahamilla Bay elongated into a stomach-like appendage which connected it to a winding river that ran down from the mountains. That was the Guantanamo River, and it marked much of the eastern border of the American property, running north directly into Castro's domain.

The River Bridge was the north/south boundary of the two realms on the leeward side, and it was there that Dellman was going to meet Belov. He was less afraid for his personal safety than about his own lack of experience in such matters, augmented by an academic's constant worry about details. The Marines who flanked him now, in the small boat they'd boarded at the Ferry Landing, seemed from another world—burly, fit, visceral, and active. Dellman felt like a freshman history major thrown into a varsity football game.

The River Bridge was now used almost exclusively as a foot crossing and connected only the most rudimentary of roads. It was thus assumed that Belov was coming by boat, and a small one at that, as the river there was very shallow. There were four Marines in the Navy launch besides him and their commanding officer, Colonel Orobello, a well-built man in his mid-thirties with sun-lined eyes and forearms like varnished oak. All were dressed in full jungle gear and carried automatic weapons.

The launch moved upriver with a soft putting from its silenced motor. Marsh sounds were loud—croaks, buzzings, and sudden splashes. Reeds along the bank swayed with the chop their passing created. Dellman pulled his windbreaker more tightly around him. How far from ivy-covered halls . . .

"Mr. Dellman?"

"Yes, Colonel."

"We're close, sir. Another mile or so. I'd like to put two of my men off here to come up on the bridge on foot. If all goes well, we'll get them on the way back. If not, we have a crossfire position."

"As you see fit, Colonel."

"Yes, sir."

It was becoming more real to Dellman. It took only moments to let the two Marines off, and then they were heading upriver again.

A few hundred yards farther upstream, Orobello

stopped the boat. The other two Marines went over the side and crawled snakelike up the banks. Dellman heard the soft snipping of wire cutters.

"Castro's little traps," Orobello explained. "A few listening devices too. Nothing really sophisticated. We'll be done here in a few minutes."

Dellman peered into the gloom. There was a dark smudge up ahead. "Is that the bridge?"

"Yes, sir. That's it. Like to have a look?" He passed over his night scope. "Could be your man just beyond."

Dellman squinted through the scope. Sure enough, sitting in a small motor boat very much like the one Dellman sat in, was Belov. He was wearing a kind of angler's hat, complete with hook imbedded, and he held a fishing pole dipped casually over the side.

"That's Belov," Dellman confirmed.

"Good. It's all clear, Mr. Dellman. But just in case, if anything does start, just drop to the ground and my men and I will get you out. No heroics, okay?"

"That suits me fine, Colonel. Ready now?"

Orobello's men slipped back into the launch and they passed under the bridge. Shore sounds grew closer, more compressed. A sudden splash made Dellman start, but beyond, in the open again, sitting as comfortably as a fisherman off his home dock, Belov raised a hand and tipped his hat.

"Good evening, Mr. Dellman. So kind of you to come."

The two boats touched, and Dellman scrambled into Belov's. Orobello backed off a polite distance. Dellman extended his hand. "How could I refuse, Mr. Ambassador, with such a novel summons?"

Belov seemed pleased. "You liked it? I'm glad. It was clever, I thought. But also a move of desperation. This isn't Washington or my embassy. I had no other way."

"You managed fine. Now please, I'm here as you asked. What is this all about?"

Belov touched his pole lightly, running a finger over its line. "I'm a fairly old man, Mr. Dellman. I've seen a great deal. But in all my years I've never seen either your country or mine this perilously close to using nuclear weapons. Maybe I value peace more now. Maybe I'm just worried by the new players in the nuclear game. I don't really know. It could be just fear. But I can't allow this . . . this terrible disregard for international conventions to continue."

Dellman waited. Belov would tell him in his own way.

"Did you know I was a fisherman, Mr. Dellman?"

"No, I didn't."

"I am. a very good one too. I fish every opportunity I get. At home we cut holes in the ice and fish through them all winter. It's my sole remaining passion."

"Are there no others?"

Belov adjusted the pole. "Peace, maybe. But before you scoff, I'm not talking about some naive 'everybody loves everybody' nonsense. I've always worked for a much simpler idea. Let us just permit each other to live long enough for the race to grow and mature and iron out its differences. That's all. Just to survive. The differences needn't consume us. There're not so many, you know."

Dellman was moved by the simple speech. He said honestly, "Most of the time I think they're insurmountable. Human history is a history of war."

"True enough. But things change. One of those changes is that we can't afford war any longer. Not in this day and age. Too many will die. Too much will be lost. The post-nuclear age would be a horror."

"Yes, I believe that, but—"

Belov's voice was very low. "We have a man aboard *Kirov.*"

"Say that again."

"We didn't know about him. The radio officer escaped from the Nicaraguan jail and slipped back onto the submarine. He is pretending to be a cook. He managed to send out a transmission with a request for orders. I've been awaiting Moscow's orders to pass them on to him."

Dellman saw the possibilities at once. He couldn't keep the excitement out of his voice. "For Christ's sake, you'll tell him to sabotage her, won't you? We'll bring her up and she's yours, intact, no questions asked."

Belov's mouth tightened. "You think it's that easy?"

"Why not? No one could possibly want this to escalate into . . . wait a minute. That's what you're saying, isn't it? A nuclear accident of this type would profoundly alter our public opinion on nuclear weapons. It could be to your country's advantage to let it happen!"

Belov nodded sadly. "That's the truth of it. Shortsighted, maybe, but how many of your leaders have been blessed with great wisdom?"

"Precious few," Dellman admitted. "What are you going to do? If what you say is true, I don't see any way out."

"There is one. When the signal comes in from Moscow, regardless of what it says, I'm going to transmit a sabotage order to our man. His name is Mishkin, by the way."

"You'd do that? For us?"

"Not for you!" Belov's voice was harsh. "Not for you. For the kind of world that I just talked about. For a few more years to grow, to increase the chance for race survival. For that only."

Dellman sat back. "What can I say? I feel humbled by you, Belov. Mean and cheap-spirited by comparison. Does my thanks mean anything?"

"Oddly, no."

"It's purely personal then," Dellman observed.

Belov considered that. "Yes, I suppose it is. Call it consistency if you like."

"What do you want us to do?"

"Just one thing. You must destroy *Kirov* completely. It's the only way to cover up my treachery. If any one of the crew returns to the Soviet Union, my superiors are bound to find out I changed the order."

"How will we know you've sent the sabotage order?"

"First contact was made two days ago at seven A.M. local time. We were to send a reply at the same time yesterday. But Moscow had not reached a decision yet, so I managed to forestall any contact at all. The next contact is at seven A.M. today. That's less than seven hours from now. I will relay my message at that time. Plan to send in your sub anytime after that."

"You're asking for a lot of trust."

"I'm asking nothing. Do as you wish."

"Like you, I can only report—"

"I understand," Belov said tiredly.

Dellman was silent for a long time, just looking at the

man in the angler's hat sitting so quietly in front of him. "The Kremlin's taking a long time to answer. What if they're voting sabotage?"

"If you believe that anything but self-interest rules there, you're unspeakably naive. There will be no such vote."

Dellman said with regret, "No, I'm forced to agree. Advantage governs . . . Maybe for reasons that I agree with more here in my country, but there, too, nonetheless."

Belov pulled his line on. "That's all, Mr. Dellman. Call your boat to take you back."

Dellman signaled, heard the response. "Mr. Ambassador, we would welcome you if . . . if anything . . ."

"Thank you, but no. Leave it at this. I can't be pressured or put to use. One time we come together. That's all. After this I retire."

"And fish?"

"Where the ice is so thick we cut it with a saw, and the vodka stays cold enough to burn your tongue without help." He sighed wistfully.

"Good night, Mr. Ambassador."

"Good-bye, Mr. Dellman."

Dellman transferred back to his boat. The gulf between them widened. Belov started his motor and within seconds was lost to sight upriver.

"Back to base, sir?" asked Orobello.

"As fast as we can, Colonel. Son of a bitch." Dellman whistled. "Looks like it's a whole new ball game."

Belov fingered one of his lines as he traveled upstream. His other hand was on the tiller. It was done now. One more transmission to send at seven A.M., and then *Kirov* was doomed. Oddly, he had few regrets about the hundred men he'd just sent to a watery grave. Not all were Russian, the rest were thieves, and he'd done a balancing act all his working life with greater and lesser goods—since that day Gromyko first called him into his office.

The humidity was worse now, it seemed to him. His collar was wet with perspiration. Maybe it was tension too. He loosened his shirt. The feel of the line was pleasant in his hand; a continuous cord, like life itself, he mused idly. Always we're brought back to the beginning.

To prevent powerful nations from resorting to arms, he'd told Gromyko that day. Very well. It would be his first and last act. The loop again. God, this humidity!

He was puzzled when the line dropped from his left hand. Had he released it unconsciously? He leaned forward . . . and felt the first crashing pain in his chest like a hammer blow, slamming him over the seat backwards. He sprawled in the boat, unable even to reach the tiller. The boat slid into the reeds on the riverbank, tangling the prop. It stalled.

Belov lay there, unable to move. The moon was up. He watched it for a long time. He was trying to reach the tiller when the second hammer blow came and shut his eyes in agony. He clawed at the air. The pain subsided after a while. Slower, this time. He understood. The third would kill him.

He began to compose himself. Not so bad to die here among the reeds. A fish splashed in the distance. The sound brought a smile to his face, and tears. The *Kirov*! He suddenly remembered. Too bad. Just not enough time . . . not enough.

His hand dropped from his chest and by accident fell on the tangled line in the bottom of the boat. He looped it gratefully around his fingers, imagining the gentle tug of something under the water so very far away, this time pulling *him* down deeper and deeper. . . .

The motion of the boat loosed it from the reeds. It began to drift. Clouds crossed the moon. The third attack killed Valery Alekseiovich Belov with a suddenness that allowed no pain. The line still entangled his fingers.

Local fishermen found him that way in the morning.

38

Fletcher listened to Dellman's story and measured it against what he knew about the Soviet ambassador. It was just possible, he supposed, that Belov could do such a thing. Dellman obviously believed him; that counted for a great deal. He was still out of breath from the night's exertions and the hasty trip back.

"I wish we had a way to verify his actions, Mark," Fletcher said when Dellman finished. "How far do you think we can count on him?"

"I'd say all the way. I believed him."

Fletcher got up to pace. He wore a robe over an old gray sweat suit and hadn't bothered to change. "Assume Belov is telling the truth. First, he makes it very clear we're on our own. The Soviets won't help. So much for your treaty gambit."

"Sadly."

"Second, it raised the odds very much in our favor. We could be going after a crippled target."

"Or not, if he's lying."

Fletcher looked pensive. "The pressure to act is building anyway."

"I can list our options," Dellman said. "A low-yield nuclear strike, with all the consequences. An attack by a squadron of our attack subs. The plan of one Captain Peter MacKenzie to use the DSRV."

"Frankly," said Fletcher, "I wish I could just order the first and be done with it. But the use of nukes would create just the kind of repercussions we're trying to avoid. A fleet of attack subs multiplies our power but also multiplies the chance of alerting *Kirov* of our presence in the Zone."

"Does that lead us to MacKenzie?"

"Well, as Garver put it, it's what they do. More subs than MacKenzie's don't really give us more advantage. Plus he's got stealth on his side. If Belov is lying, that's just as necessary today. More so—it could be a trick to lure us in."

"I believed Belov, sir. It's no trick."

"I'm going to proceed on that assumption. Call Admiral Merton. Give him the green light. Explain the time frame."

"On my way."

"And Mark? To MacKenzie . . ."

"Sir?"

"Tell him, Godspeed."

A good distance south *Kirov* lay at rest. Santillo liked to bottom her out, lie silently, and extend the sonars as far as they were capable. This left *Kirov* almost invulnerable. Nothing yet designed could locate a sub lying that quiet that deep. So far it had also allowed *Kirov* to pick up two more ships close enough to the Zone to qualify for extinction. One was a pleasure craft heading south. The other was an old freighter, a drug smuggler probably, ignoring the warnings about the Zone and hoping to slip through with its illegal cargo.

Santillo sank her, then turned back and rammed the pleasure craft, sending it and the family on board to the bottom.

Perez, the navigator, was concerned. Little was to be gained from such actions. But Santillo stormed about the control room like an angry bull, brushing aside any suggestion to let even the most minor craft pass. Perez had no desire to end up in the garbage room alongside Miguel Segurra. He backed off. The other officers did, too, but the grumbling continued.

Mishkin saw all this and logged it carefully in his mind. The ship had a strange feel. The crew went about routine tasks, the officers watched the captain warily, and Santillo discharged angry energy like a power station gone awry. The situation was increasingly volatile.

This made Mishkin even more concerned about the failure to respond to his signal the day before. Could he have failed to raise anyone? He had to accept that possibility. Or were his superiors just being cautious? It was frustrating not to know. He came to a decision. No response today meant none was coming.

But if none were coming, then what?

Get the hell out of here, was his first response. The sub was a pressure cooker, bound to burst. Barrista's death was the first shock. There were bound to be others.

The Nicaraguan government, President Ortega specifically, had refused to deal with Santillo directly. He demanded to speak to Barrista or Segurra. Santillo refused. An uneasy state of tension existed as to who would break first. Santillo was threatening to break off contact, but feared to go completely rogue. The Nicaraguan council was desperate to resume control, frantic to keep the loss of control from the Americans. Santillo pressed even harder, demanding to assume Barrista's title and position within the government.

No, Mishkin decided, things were not going to get better.

He made his way back to the trash room. Sealed bags of refuse were stacked against the bulkheads. The smell was rank, but trash was rarely released. It, too, contained secrets. Miguel Segurra was tied to a pipe crossing the starboard bulkhead. There was an air of despondency about him, and he barely moved when Mishkin slipped in.

"Segurra?" No response. "Segurra!"

"What do you want?"

"Say hello to your savior. You want to get out of here?"

"I don't believe in saviors."

"Start. I'm sorry about your Minister. He was a good friend, no?"

Miguel looked up, and Mishkin saw the confusion in his eyes. "If he hadn't yelled, he'd still be alive. It makes no sense. I've been sitting here just trying to figure out why he yelled."

"If he hadn't, you would have killed Santillo."

"I would have, yes."

Mishkin shrugged. "Maybe he didn't want you to."

"But why? Santillo was clearly defying him. There was no way to go back once that happened. You didn't know Phillipe. He would have seen that at once."

"You were that close to know him so well?"

"Yes," Miguel said. The one word spoke volumes.

"Then maybe what I said was correct. In this language,

forgive me, maybe it wasn't clear. Maybe he didn't want *you* to do it, to have to kill him."

Miguel pondered that. *More death on my hands and I think I'll go insane. . . . Oh, Phillipe!*

"The needle." Mishkin shuddered. "Santillo would not have been the first, right?"

"No, not the first."

"Maybe your friend knew you were . . ." He searched for the correct idiom. "Worn out. Inside. Yes, that's how you struck me."

Miguel eyed Mishkin curiously, "You see a lot for a galley cook. I remember, the one who threw the coffee in my face. Why?"

"You were being foolish, and they would have hurt you, like your Minister. Where did you think you were going?"

"You're no cook. Who are you?"

"Radio Officer First Rank Vyachslav Pytorovich Mishkin. I got out of your jail and sneaked back on board. Cooks can move around. I became one."

Miguel's eyes showed some signs of life. "What do you become next?"

"Hopefully, an ex-cook. Look, half the American navy must be encircling the Zone, waiting for Santillo to make a mistake. I think he's already made one, cutting himself off from your government. Now he's just a rogue. *No one* can afford that. No one's going to let a rogue with a nuclear submarine survive long."

"He can still launch any time he . . . why are you smiling?"

"Cooks deliver to torpedo rooms too. I fixed the tubes for the cruise missiles so they won't fire."

"That's wonderful! Mishkin, I—"

"Look, no more now. If you want to get off this ship, trust me. I need to gather the necessary equipment. We'll store it in here. It's the only place. You'll keep quiet?"

"Of course."

"Okay, I'll be back."

Miguel felt his spirits lift for the first time since Phillipe died. To save him? Maybe, if Mishkin were right. Mishkin, who'd removed the threat of the missiles too.

He felt a funny feeling in his chest, unfamiliar. It took him a while to realize it was hope.

* * *

The Soviet Ambassador to Cuba was frantic. He held the Kremlin's response to Renkov's and Belov's transmissions, and at this very moment Belov should have been sending it on to *Kirov*. It was fast approaching seven A.M., but Belov had disappeared. Gone fishing? His propensity for the sport was well known, but now? How did he dare? But the fact remained: no Belov, no codes. The paper in the ambassador's hand was just a meaningless string of letters and numbers without Belov.

He recabled Moscow as soon as it was clear that Belov wasn't going to make the seven A.M. deadline, but given the secrecy of the entire affair, could a secondary transmission be arranged in so short a time? Fallback positions always decreased security. He could take matters into his own hands, he supposed, and send his own message of support to Comrade Mishkin. A phrase from Lenin, perhaps. Something to help him hold fast. Should he? His hand poised over the message pad. The Communications Officer waited. . . .

Where the devil was Belov? The man should be hanged for such lack of responsibility. Fishing? Heads were going to roll over this. It suddenly occurred to him that his own might be in jeopardy. He came to the decision to distance himself as much as possible. Inaction was never as dangerous as action. If he tried something and fouled up the works, he would never be forgiven.

He turned to the Communications Officer. "No sending this morning, comrade." The man turned back to his console.

It was 7:05. The time for contact passed. The ambassador felt better.

Mishkin waited until seven-ten, when the return of the Radio Officer from his daily trip to the head forced him out of the radio room. A daily laxative in the man's morning coffee guaranteed the scheduled rest stop.

So . . . no response. He reaffirmed his decision to leave the sub. But the tubes he'd sabotaged worried him. What if he was doing the wrong thing? Maybe removing his handiwork was best. After all, protecting Americans was certainly not Soviet policy. The more he thought about it, the more sense it made. He started forward.

Returning from the torpedo room, Mishkin stopped at the captain's cabin and rapped sharply on the door. Santillo opened it and stared at him for a full second until recognition dawned.

"Comrade Cook. What can I do for you?"

"Excuse me, Comrade Captain, but you said if anything . . . come and see you."

"Yes, what is it?"

"Forgive me, it's a small matter. But some room, in the galley, for storage . . . I need additional space. With your permission I would like to store some things in the rear equipment lockers. No interference, I promise. Plenty of room."

"What's in there now?"

"Air tanks and ropes and things. Gathering dust, mostly."

Santillo mulled it over. "Comrade Cook, I like your initiative. You may use the space."

Mishkin turned to go.

"Comrade Cook!"

Mishkin froze.

"Send me some coffee and bread."

"Yes, Comrade Captain. At once." Mishkin let out a sigh of relief and trotted away.

The equipment locker was a small room with scuba tanks, wet suits, and life rafts arranged along its walls and secured by metal clips. Mishkin cleared a space and put down the heavy flour tins, ostensibly, the things for which he needed room. He pulled down two complete sets of scuba gear and wet suits along with one raft and stuffed all the things into two big canvas garbage sacks. One at a time he dragged them forward.

Miguel watched him hide the sacks under others filled with garbage. His surprise and respect for the man increased with each trip the Radio Officer made.

"Mishkin, you're quite something," he said when the task was complete.

Mishkin grinned. "I had the captain's permission, re-member."

"When do we go?"

"We'll be at periscope depth again in the morning to receive any incoming traffic from Managua. Very shallow, very slow. Then."

Miguel fixed him with a hard look. "I don't know how you're going to feel about this, but before we go I'm committed to sabotaging the cruise missiles. Santillo will want to launch them before this is over, and I just can't let him."

Mishkin looked chagrined. "But I just *unsabotaged* them."

"You mean you fixed them not to fire and then returned them to normal? Why, for God's sake?"

Mishkin shrugged. "It's not my country Santillo's threatening."

"You saw what he did to me," Miguel said grimly. "You and yours could be next. We're very close to Cuba, too, Mishkin."

"True enough. But I have no orders. How can I know what to do without orders?"

"Look, I know that individual initiative is not looked upon with much favor in your navy, but this once you're going to have to think for yourself. Do you feel safe with *Kirov* armed as she is in Santillo's hands?"

"No. Admittedly, that's true."

"Mishkin, you wouldn't give a loaded gun to a disturbed man. Santillo is even worse. You must return the tubes to inoperative."

"I . . . I have to think about it. Tomorrow at seven, Miguel. I'll come for you."

"Mishkin!"

"We'll see. Tomorrow at seven."

"Please, let me—"

"Shhh, someone comes."

The hatch closed and Mishkin was gone.

39

Phil Arlin's sub, *Phoenix*, roamed slowly under the seas off Cuba, the much smaller DSRV attached to its aft escape trunk like a pilot fish to a swimming shark.

MacKenzie was in the wardroom studying the best available charts of the Trench when Arlin came in and dropped the VLF transmission onto the table.

"Just in, Mac. Code Green as soon as we're on station."

MacKenzie felt a lurch in his stomach and a sudden prickle up his spine. "Anything else?"

"From the President: 'Godspeed.'"

"I appreciate that. What's transit time, Phil?"

"We're entering the Trench in about ten minutes. The charts for this part of the run are already in the computers. Say two hours at reduced speed. That's as far in as we're allowed to go."

"Plenty of time. I'm going to recheck *Mystic*'s power levels."

Arlin put a hand on his friend's shoulder. "Mac, they'll be as fine as the last time you checked. Why not get a hot meal, take a shower, and get suited up? We'll be ready when you are."

MacKenzie thought it over. "Okay, Phil."

Arlin left the wardroom. MacKenzie knew *Phoenix*'s captain wanted to take his sub right down the Trench after *Kirov* and to hell with all this DSRV tricky shit. Always the direct way, that was Arlin. It was the quality that allowed MacKenzie to take *Phoenix* that day, however. Taking *Kirov* required more stealth.

MacKenzie picked up a tray of food in the galley. As always, the food was outstanding, one of the compensations to the crew for spending seventy days in a three-hundred-foot tube. Dinner that night offered veal Parmigiana, potatoes, two vegetables, salad, three desserts, and assorted breads and beverages. Passing on most, however, MacKenzie took some bread and salad and poured himself a cup of coffee. He ate alone in the wardroom, feeling a bit withdrawn, knowing it was the usual inward resource building that preceded action of any kind.

In the head adjoining Arlin's cabin, so tantalizingly similar to his own on *Aspen*, MacKenzie stood in the hot shower and thought about the upcoming operation. It could be done, he told himself again. Soon enough he'd be on *Aspen*; twelve, maybe fourteen hours. He got out and pulled on a pair of coveralls. The mirror told him nothing he didn't already know.

Arlin and the technicians were gathered around the aft trunk when he arrived.

"All set," Arlin offered. "Johnson's already in, and we're running the check list now."

Lieutenant Lucas Johnson, "Luke" to MacKenzie for the past week, was his copilot. A wiry southerner, he was a fine mechanic and had a touch at *Mystic*'s controls or at her hydraulic arm that was smoother than a silk glove. Johnson would also double as life-support technician, and in a pinch was a competent pilot.

Arlin offered his hand. "Good luck, Mac. Come on back."

"You still owe me dinner. I plan to collect."

"Sure. In the best place we can find." He lowered his voice. "Look, I'll be waiting here until you pass the point of no return, and maybe then some. If you do have to come back, just get close enough to yell and, well . . . screw *Kirov*, we'll come running. Okay?"

"Thanks, Phil."

"I'll be in the conn. Good luck, Captain."

MacKenzie clambered up the ladder into the tube, not much wider than his shoulders. He secured the hatch from above. Passing through the bell-shaped skirt that connected *Mystic* to *Phoenix*, he secured *Mystic*'s hatch as well. When, as now, it was pumped free of water, the pressure created a leak-proof seal.

"Nice to see you, Captain," said Luke Johnson as MacKenzie pulled himself into the front compartment— the forward "sphere," actually—and slid into the pilot's chair.

"How are things, Luke?" In front and all around

MacKenzie were banks of knobs and switches. A small television screen was mounted into the dash on his right. The rolled wire cords of radio mikes dangled down from the cabin ceiling in between the padded arm rest chairs for the pilot and copilot.

"We're all powered up, sir. Take a look."

One of Johnson's skinny arms reached out and punched in commands to the on-board computer. A curve flowed onto the screen, steadied.

"Looks fine. Captain Arlin told you we got the go? No more drills, Luke."

"Yes, sir. All set."

"Good. As soon as we get the okay from the conn, we'll launch. Meanwhile, when you checked the hydraulics . . ."

For the next hour the two men ran through every system in *Mystic* that could be checked. Finally satisfied, MacKenzie took up the radio mike and called Arlin.

"Conn, *Mystic*. MacKenzie speaking. Position?"

"*Mystic*, Conn. This is Arlin. We're there, Mac. Sonar reports all free and clear. Gonna take you in just a little bit more before we drop."

"Mama always told me to date gentlemen," MacKenzie said with a smile. "Appreciate it."

"Five minutes to disconnect. Conn out."

MacKenzie touched the pilot's stick, feathered it lightly. He could almost feel the water surging past *Mystic*'s skin. But the layers of hull made it quieter than a church at midnight. Around them, though he couldn't see it, the walls of the Trench were starting to tower hundreds of feet above them. The bottom here was over eight thousand feet.

"Like flying though the Grand Canyon, if they ever filled it," Luke said, mirroring his thoughts.

"*Mystic*, Conn. Station plus twenty miles. Course steady on two-two-five. Depth one thousand feet. Ready to disconnect."

MacKenzie checked his own guidance system. The data matched. "Luke?"

"All set, Captain."

"Conn, *Mystic*. Ready to disconnect. Many thanks."

"On your mark. Good luck, *Mystic*."

MacKenzie hit a switch. Pumps began shooting water into the bell housing, equalizing pressures. He felt *Mystic* shift slightly as the seal loosened.

"Breakaway!" Luke called out.

MacKenzie fed power to the electric motors. *Mystic* began to rise, taking her head. Simultaneously Arlin dropped *Phoenix* down a few feet and severed the final connection. MacKenzie brought *Mystic* up sharply to avoid *Phoenix*'s sail, increased power, and suddenly they were free of any encumbrances and moving under their own power.

"*Mystic* to *Phoenix*. Commencing radio silence."

MacKenzie brought *Mystic* on course. He could visualize *Phoenix* slowing to almost a full stop with barely enough lift under her planes to hold her position. Here Arlin would wait till MacKenzie made it to *Aspen* . . . or till there was no more sense in waiting.

He flicked on the powerful floodlights. They cut a swath in the gloom. Luke scanned the screen.

"Midnight in a coal yard," he muttered. He reached down and pulled out a thermos. "Coffee, Captain?"

"Luke, you're a wonder. Love some."

The copilot passed him a no-spill plastic mug. "Commuter special, sir."

"Any other tricks of the trade?" MacKenzie inquired, sipping gratefully.

"Sandwiches and fruit, gum and a flask of brandy."

"I admire preparation."

"I've been working with *Mystic* for a long time, sir."

MacKenzie flexed his arms. "She feels fine. All systems show green. You ready for some real depth?"

"Down is my business, Captain."

"Mac, for the duration."

"In that case, basement please, Mac."

"Press B."

MacKenzie pressed forward on the control yoke and *Mystic* began a slow descent. As they dove deeper the canyon walls began to narrow. Finally, at over five thousand feet, both walls were visible on the screen at the same time. MacKenzie piloted smoothly in between.

"One mile," Luke said.

"Water temperature?"

Luke read it off the gauge. MacKenzie dropped *Mystic* lower. "And now?"

Again Luke read it out.

For the next half hour MacKenzie raised and lowered *Mystic* like a slow roller coaster. Luke read out the temperatures in a constant stream. Finally MacKenzie steadied them out at 5500 feet, far deeper than he'd ever been in a conventional submarine. It was an eerie feeling.

"May I ask what the temperature readouts are for?" asked Luke.

"Sure. You're trained to operate sonar, aren't you?"

"In a rudimentary way. All we've got to do is locate a sub, and we usually know where it is because it's sending out a distress signal."

"This is a basic antisubmarine warfare tactic," MacKenzie explained. "Remember your high school physics? When the teacher put a stick into a pail of water if looked bent, right? That was the refraction of light thrugh the different medium."

"I remember."

"Sound works the same way. You can bend it, make it bounce, or avoid it. In this case I was looking for a thermal—a current of water with a different temperature than the water around it. The Gulf Stream is a good example. To an ASW man, that's just a river in the ocean."

He brought *Mystic* up a bit, following the thermal.

"The Gulf Stream is warmer than the surrounding water. If you ride the edge, where the two temperatures meet, sound will bend away just like the light coming from the stick in the water. Useful, if you want to remain as undetectable as we do."

"We're riding a thermal now?"

"Yes. Cold layers above the bottom. Slightly warmer at this level. Could be volcanic action or a warmer current from elsewhere. The currents are tricky as hell down here as it is, but we're on the edge in between. Couldn't find us now even if they thought we were here."

"More coffee?"

"Thanks, no. Settle down, Luke. We've got a long way to go."

He increased power to the motors and *Mystic* sped on its way through the chasm.

* * *

Sebastion had marched them all day. They followed his trucks, convoy style. Justine only saw her brother once. He gave her a hard look and said simply, "We're over the border tomorrow. Probably have to engage Sandinista troops. I can't be looking over my shoulder. Decide."

Justine felt bone tired and the .45 at her hip was like a nagging question. Sebastion wouldn't hold. He was under a death sentence. Waiting for MacKenzie to ride in like the cavalry was just prolonging her agony.

What mattered most? she asked herself. She no longer knew.

Justine picked up a blanket and draped it around her shoulders. She went out of her tent under the back edge, close to the dirt, unseen. Her knife was in her left hand, concealed by the gathered folds of the blanket. The .45 was in her right.

She flowed through the brush around the camp, coming to Sebastion's tent from behind. She drew the blanket over her head like a shawl and sat down cross-legged against the coarse canvas. In the dim light she was nothing more than a hazy gray lump, indistinguishable from the swaying, broad-leafed vegetation. She felt for the outline of Sebastion's cot. There. With the light on or off she would know where he lay.

She settled in to wait.

Mystic suddenly lurched wildly.

Luke started. "Mac, what?"

"I don't know!" He fought the controls. *Mystic* was like a wild stallion bucking underneath him. The buffeting continued unabated.

"Rocks, Captain. Big ones," Luke shouted. "Hard starboard!"

MacKenzie understood at once. "Rock slide," he shouted, veering hard to starboard. In a space this tight they were almost sure to get hit by boulders cascading off the Trench walls.

"Can't fight these currents. Too strong," he said through a clenched jaw, rolling aside from the shower. "Got to find some cover or we'll take a hole sooner or later, Luke. Either way, smashed into the walls or hit and holed. Either way . . ." He dove hard, twisting and rolling through a sickening curve.

Luke searched the screen, jumping from camera to camera to find something, anything to hide under. A loud crash against the hull felt like it was right over his head.

"Over there, Mac. Look!"

MacKenzie could barely hold *Mystic* steady. He glanced at the screen for a split second and saw the overhanging ledge at once. It could protect them, but there were dangers too. Another rock clanged off the hull. At this depth the pressure was over 2500 pounds per square inch. A single crack in one of a thousand seams and they would implode in an instant. But the overhang could fall and crush them, or break off and drag them down. . . .

"Anything else, Luke? Anything?"

"That's it, sir. That one or make a run for it."

MacKenzie struggled against the currents. *Mystic* couldn't take much more battering. A surge here—hard rudder. Slow. Drifting. Sudden force, faster—hard again. The chasm walls loomed closer. He came to a sudden decision. Wait . . . power! Hard against the force of the swirling water. This deep there were no rules. He was piloting on reflex alone. Feel it. Let the current push you . . . there. Power now! Slow . . . slow . . . let the water take you. . . . The walls loomed up . . . turn!

Mystic slammed into the ledge under the overhang with a crash that jarred their spines. The current rammed them up against the overhang, wedging them into the juncture between the massive rock formations. MacKenzie fought to hold them there. They bobbed up against the overhang again and again until MacKenzie thought they must burst from the buffeting alone.

All of a sudden he heard a sound that for a moment he couldn't identify . . . until it came to him.

"The overhang! It's collapsing."

He poured power into the motors in a desperate attempt to slide out from under the crashing projection, but it was too late. The overhang broke off from the weight of the rock smashing into it and slipped downward, trapping them in between the ledge and the chasm wall. The motors began to whine in protest. He had no choice but to shut them down.

Over a mile under and they were pinned to the jagged wall, unable to move.

Luke recovered his composure. He scanned out through their cameras. The rearview showed their predicament. They were sitting on the ledge, pinned under the overhang which extended over them like the hypotenuse of a right triangle, extending from the chasm wall to the ledge. The overhang seemed to have broken off completely. It was just bad luck it hadn't fallen past the ledge into the depths below.

"Only some small stuff now, skipper," Luke said, watching pebble-sized rocks fall like rain. "Current's abating too."

MacKenzie felt weak-kneed. He tested the controls. "We've got about ten degrees of upward motion left," he announced. "Then the overhang stops us. Nothing lateral or forward and back at all."

"Just lovely," Luke said disgustedly.

MacKenzie looked at the TV picture unhappily. "This is usually the time captains look around and say, 'Gentlemen, I'm open to suggestions.'"

"You going to say that now?"

"Will it help?"

"No."

"Then you say, 'Let me get back to you on this one, sir,'" MacKenzie explained with great patience.

"Do that, sir."

"Do what?"

"Get back to me. Coffee?" Luke asked politely.

"Love some."

MacKenzie studied the screen. "We gotta get out of here."

"I knew I could count on you, sir."

MacKenzie reangled the cameras, studying the ledge. As before, he saw that the overhang and the ledge formed a right triangle, with *Mystic* sticking out slightly, like a hot dog from a bun. Particles of sand floated off into the darkness beyond the floodlight's range. But from what he could see . . .

"I think there's a way," he said finally.

Luke turned serious at once. "Yes, sir."

"The only motion we've got is straight up. With a little

bit of room we could get a good shot at the overhang above us. Can you use the hydraulic arm?"

"Yes, sir. It's free except for overhead. You're planning to dig at the base?"

MacKenzie smiled. "Smart boy. That's the idea. Let's clear anything that would prevent the slab over us from sliding off the ledge, and hit it high with everything we can muster. Hopefully we can knock it loose."

"Or down on top of us."

"Pessimist."

"No, sir," Luke said dryly. "You're too kind. I'm sure it won't work."

MacKenzie ignored him.

The digging went slowly. It was hot in the seven-and-a-half-foot diameter sphere, because they were preserving power. Though the hydraulic arm had been designed only to clear debris from a downed sub's escape hatch to permit mating, Luke Johnson was using it like a spade, thrusting it into the rough boundary between the overhang and the ledge.

MacKenzie watched with admiration as Luke manipulated the arm. Using a joystick kind of lever and a series of buttons to control the opening and closing of the "hand," Luke painstakingly cleared a series of channels under the overhang and pushed rock after rock over onto the chasm.

Suddenly, "There!" MacKenzie exclaimed. "Did you feel that?"

"My hand's cramped and I can't see from the sweat. All I feel is bad, sir."

"Almost there, Luke. Work on that section over to the right." The copilot complied. "And Luke?"

"Sir?"

"Love the up attitude."

The copilot grinned and bent back to work.

MacKenzie looked at the gauges. He was going to blow all his ballast at once to give *Mystic* the maximum lift if could generate. That was going to take a lot of air. It could leave them short later.

It was an odd feeling. *Phoenix* had turned back to wait at station hours before. They'd passed the point at which it was closer to *Aspen* than turning back. But Arlin had promised to come running. . . .

MacKenzie explained that to Luke Johnson. "Want to scrub?" he asked finally.

"Nope."

MacKenzie couldn't help but smile. "Me neither. Ready?"

"Yep."

"What happened to 'Yes, sir'?" MacKenzie inquired casually.

"I'm waiting to see if this works."

MacKenzie nodded. "Me too. Ten seconds, Luke."

"Yes, sir." He was Navy again.

MacKenzie flipped every pump switch in rapid-fire succession. There was a series of loud whooshings, and sudden streams of bubbles shot up all around them.

"Hold her back," he ordered. "Use the arm, Luke. Careful! Don't let go yet."

"Can't hold much longer, sir," the copilot said. "She's bending. . . ."

"Hold, damn it!"

"I can't. . . ."

"Hold, I said."

"Captain, I—"

"*Now!* Let her go now, Luke!"

Mystic shot up like a helium balloon and smashed into the overhang. MacKenzie yanked her into the juncture at the wall. It sounded like a thousand razor-sharp teeth were grinding at the hull.

"Use the arm. Lever it out," he commanded.

Luke manipulated the joystick madly. "It's going!" he shouted. "I can feel it."

Mystic lurched upwards. The awful grating sound continued. In the TV screen they could see the huge slab over them sliding down a few feet, then a few more. MacKenzie prayed for the hull not to puncture.

They broke free. The overhang was lost to view as it tumbled end over end in slow motion down into the chasm below. MacKenzie reached over and clapped the copilot happily on the shoulder. The other man was grinning from ear to ear. He raised his coffee cup in a salute.

"Nicely done, Captain."

MacKenzie breathed in air that suddenly tasted very sweet. "You, too, Luke," he acknowledged.

They cleaned up and ate the rest of the food Luke had brought on board. Then MacKenzie slid back into the pilot's chair and flexed the controls in his hands. He fed power to the motors. *Mystic* shot forward.

It was time to find *Aspen*.

40

THE WHITE HOUSE

In his long and varied life Fletcher had never actually seen the blood drain from anyone's face, as the metaphor suggested, until Mark Dellman picked up the phone and listened to the voice from the State Department. He literally turned white and sank weakly into a chair.

". . . Yes, I understand. He must have been there all night. . . . No, I saw no signs of it. . . . How about verifications? . . . All right. Let us know." He hung up.

"What is it, Mark?"

"Belov, sir. We just got a report that he's dead! They think heart attack. Some local fishermen found him and brought him to the town doctor. He took one look in Belov's wallet and called Havana. State just picked it up."

"Did he send the message to *Kirov*?"

"I don't see how he could have if he never got to his embassy."

"Recall MacKenzie," Fletcher said without hesitation.

Dellman was on the phone to Admiral Merton within seconds . . . and put down the instrument almost as quickly.

"Too late, sir. *Mystic* was launched hours ago. There's no way to recall it."

Fletcher swiveled his chair around and looked grim. "Then we've sent him after a fully armed enemy sub, not the declawed version Belov promised. Shit, Mark. That's a worst-case scenario."

"I'm afraid so, sir. I consider myself responsible. I'll—"

"Cut it out, Mark. It was a good bet, and I backed it. All the way. No one could have predicted this. What was it that Carter discovered during the Iran crisis? Whatever you're least prepared for, that's what you can depend on happening. My main concern is, do I send a squadron in along with MacKenzie?"

"You may want to now. If he doesn't make it, you'll have to anyway."

"If he doesn't make it," Fletcher mused out loud. He turned away and looked out the window at the gardens, so bright this time of the year.

"But he might make it," he said. "And if he does, we've got the best submarine in the world in perfect position to make the attack, with an experienced captain on board. Another bet, Mark?"

"I'm not very hot on my luck, sir."

"No? Maybe Belov did us a favor after all. It's a new situation." He turned back to Dellman. "When I was a school kid I used to have a terrible problem changing answers on tests. I'd make a choice, then change it two or three times till I'd so confused myself I didn't know what was right anymore or what I remembered studying. Invariably my first answer was correct. Taught me a lesson—after all the preparation you can do, rely on your instincts. I think I'm going to remember that lesson now. This is no time to start changing my answers."

"You're staying with MacKenzie?"

Fletcher nodded.

"I feel terribly responsible," Dellman said bitterly. "I've got a pain in my chest that feels like I swallowed a table."

Fletcher's expression was kind. "I know it well."

"How do you stand it?"

"You try and cultivate a deep down feeling that the other guy wouldn't have done as well, even with all the mistakes."

Dellman filled two tumblers. He didn't say anything as he poured.

"Something else, Mark," Fletcher said, accepting his drink. "Most men with responsibility learn it."

"Sir?"

Fletcher looked over the liquid's amber depths. "You've got to have a little faith "

The night sounds surrounded her. Cicadas screamed in the trees. Justine had been sitting motionlessly against Sebastion's tent in the darkness for over two hours. Now the tent lit up and she heard him saying something to one of his lieutenants. She waited.

The tent flap slapped shut. She heard/felt the creak of his wooden cot just inches from her as he lowered himself onto it. They were separated only by the thin wall of cloth.

He was breathing heavily, mumbling to himself. When the canvas bowed out toward her suddenly, she realized he was sitting, leaning back against the tent wall. She could make out the ridge of his spine. She transferred the knife to her right hand. Could he have made it easier?

"Our Father who art in Heaven . . ."

Sebastion. Praying?

"Thy kingdom come, Thy will . . ."

She froze in disbelief. Unshakable Sebastion?

". . . Forgive us our trespasses as we forgive those . . ."

Did he know? Could he somehow sense her near? She listened . . . and every word was a knife twisting in her guts.

". . . so very tired. Help me through tomorrow, please. I know more people are going to die, but I don't seem to know any other way."

She felt embarrassed and perverse, listening. Embarrassed, because no one else should hear such private things. Perverse, because she was about to kill.

". . . I'm so unsure these days, God. Justine's hatred for me is torture. Miguel will never come back. What am I supposed to do?"

Justine felt the first warm tears slide down her cheeks. Never hatred, she wanted to cry out. Oh, Sebastion, never hatred.

He went on hoarsely, "How can I stop? I'll let so many down if I don't have the will to finish it. . . ."

His voice was very low. "I don't know what to do, God. I can't stand the loneliness anymore."

Justine put the knife away.

As she crept back into the woods she realized she would never be truly certain that he hadn't known she was there. An act? There was always that chance. But it didn't matter. He'd shown her things she'd needed to see all her life: Sebastion in doubt, Sebastion in pain just like her own, Sebastion needing her as she needed him. Mac-Kenzie knew. He'd seen it from the first. He'd even tried to tell her.

In her tent she wet a cloth with cold water and draped it over her forehead. She stripped off her clothes and lay silently in the darkness.

Miguel couldn't let her die that day, and neither could she harm Sebastion. Some things were larger than sides. They would probably send someone else to kill Sebastion when they found out she hadn't. She'd have to watch for that.

She tried to sleep. She needed the rest. Tomorrow the real fight began.

Again.

The hatch to the trash room opened. Miguel looked quickly to the place Mishkin hid the gear. Nothing showed.

"Miguel?"

He let out a sigh of relief. "Mishkin! Where have you been?"

"Things to tend to. Ready?"

"Just cut these wires."

Mishkin produced a cutter and snipped the coils from Miguel's limbs. "Get into a wet suit. Put your coveralls on over it."

Miguel did as he was instructed. "How do we survive once we get off?" he asked. "Aren't we in the middle of the ocean?"

"The lifeboat has a week's provisions and a transmitter. Once we get out of *Kirov*'s Zone we'll turn it on. Somebody should hear us fairly quickly." Mishkin slipped into his garment. "That's all. Grab a bag and follow me."

They padded down the narrow corridor. Twice they ran into crewman, but each time a stern order from Mishkin was enough to send them away blank-faced. Mishkin stopped at the aft escape trunk hatch cover. Producing a small packet of tools, he began to pry off an electrical cover next to it.

"What are you doing?"

"Killing the circuit that lights up on the main board in the control room when the escape system is activated. Otherwise they'll come running."

Miguel looked down the corridor. "The torpedo room is down here, right?"

"Yes, but—"

"Wait here for me."

"Miguel!"

Miguel dropped his bag and ran forward. Mishkin called after him hoarsely, "Miguel!"

The torpedo room was unmanned when he slipped in. Miguel knew the tubes were already loaded with the cruise missiles but had no real idea how to sabotage them surreptitiously. Dials and gauges stared at him defiantly. To hell with caution, he decided, and looked for a hammer, a screwdriver, anything he could do damage with.

"Comrade, what are you—"

Miguel hit the crewman once, a sharp blow that dropped him to the deck helplessly. *No needle* . . . Miguel rendered him unconscious with a second, precise blow. It was enough.

He looked around. Time was pressing. There would be others coming. What did he need to do?

"Here. Let me."

He looked at Mishkin's resigned face gratefully. In a few moments Mishkin had the missiles rendered harmless.

"Now let's go," he demanded. Miguel followed eagerly enough.

They helped each other into the scuba gear, and Mishkin tied the raft bundle to his wrist. Miguel turned his air on and then Mishkin's. They climbed into the escape trunk and Mishkin shut the hatch underneath them. He hit a red button and water began to filter in, replacing the air. It swirled around them in the tight chamber and passed over their heads. The sounds of the bubbles obscured the pumps.

A ready light glowed. Mishkin spun the release wheel of

the overhead hatch and pushed hard at it. He encountered resistence, like trying to open a car door against the wind. But *Kirov* was moving very slowly. Together they opened the hatch.

They swam out onto *Kirov*'s deck, holding themselves on by the railings. Mishkin closed the escape hatch. The sea was bright green. Sunlight filtered in from overhead. The current was as mild as a sea breeze.

Mishkin gave Miguel a quick nod and could see the other's look of appreciation through his face mask. Mishkin pointed to their rising bubbles. Miguel understood—don't outpace them.

They released their holds and kicked up into the open sea.

Kirov's black bulk slid by beneath them and was soon lost to sight.

41

CAYMAN TRENCH

"What's our depth, Luke?" MacKenzie asked.

"Twenty-eight hundred feet, sir, and still rising."

At this depth there was more maneuvering room in between the chasm walls. MacKenzie increased *Mystic*'s up angle. The air supply worried him. They were lower than he'd planned.

Aspen's theoretical position was already locked into the computer guidance system, but that only assured them of the general area. Final placement was Lasovic's decision, so it might vary as much as a mile or two. At this depth finding a 360-foot black tube on the dusky, shifting bottom within an area of ten to fifteen square miles was not going to be an easy task.

Mystic's floodlights were picking up marine life that was more familiar than the creatures who inhabited the chasm's perpetual night. Some of these higher layers were rich in nutrients, the result of life in the waters above dying and drifting down to the colder, denser layers below.

"Two thousand feet."

He had to be very careful about their sound this "high" up. He slid *Mystic* along every temperature gradient he could find, and piloted as close as he dared to the precipitous walls. Every few minutes he came to a full stop, hoping to fool any sonar operator into thinking they were just a freak signal. He found icy currents and rode them like a raft over a frigid stream.

"Fifteen hundred feet."

This was it then. They were well inside *Kirov*'s Zone. *Aspen* should be within a few miles. Another two hundred feet up and *Mystic* would be over the chasm walls, out of the Trench. Emerging into open water carried with it attendant dangers. *Kirov* might be a hundred miles away . . . or just over the edge.

MacKenzie cut power and blew more ballast. They drifted upward slowly. "Sonar?"

Luke Johnson was listening intently. "Nothing at all. Eight hundred feet. No contacts."

"Be certain, Luke."

"I am."

"Must be a nice feeling," MacKenzie said dryly, adding power. *Mystic* shot forward. "Put the grid on the screen, Luke. We're as close as we're ever going to be."

"Yes, sir."

The copilot punched instructions into the computer. The TV screen shifted suddenly, glowing with the hydrographic chart of the sea bottom. Luke input additional commands. A lighted green grid began to crisscross the map. Linked to the inertial guidance system, like the one used in ICBM's, *Mystic*'s position was a bright red dot in one corner and changes would show up on screen as they moved. MacKenzie could begin his search pattern and not waste time or oxygen in aimless pursuit or going over the same territory again. An area that was fully covered turned dull gray, those yet to be explored were yellow.

"Beginning search pattern," he told Luke. The copilot was watching the TV screen that showed the sea bottom. His eyes would never leave it till they found *Aspen*.

Due north to the top of the grid, then turn due south to

the bottom. MacKenzie made his course adjustments, preparing to zigzag across the first section of the grid.

Feeling as if the critical part of the voyage were just beginning, MacKenzie brought *Mystic* up and over the chasm walls and began the search.

Four hours later Luke's eyes were red-rimmed with strain and MacKenzie was running a desperate race between caution and their almost depleted oxygen supply.

"Grid 13 complete," Luke said wearily. That left three.

MacKenzie flicked his eyes to the screen. The bottom was mostly silt, easily stirred up by *Mystic*'s prop if he got too close, out of the range of his lights if he got too far. His arms ached from the strain of constant maneuvering. His mouth was dry. They'd finished the last of the provisions hours ago.

"Mac? I think I . . . naw, forget it. Just a shadow."

"You're sure?"

"Yeah. Sorry. Damn."

"We'll find her soon, Luke. Don't let it get to you."

"Sure. Okay. That's the next one. Head north." MacKenzie could hear the effort it cost him to control his disappointment.

"On course. Here we go again," MacKenzie said. On his board the oxygen reserve light began to flash a warning. The main supply was exhausted. He pushed the power to maximum. The race was tighter now.

Tom Lasovic handed the auxiliary headphones back to the Sonar Officer. "Sounds like it's going away," he said, "whatever it is."

"Yes, sir. Same pattern. If it wasn't so odd a signature, I'd say it was a search."

"For us?"

The officer shrugged. "No way to tell."

"But you're certain it's not a sub?"

"Yes, sir. This is much too small. Propulsion sounds like electric motors. No cooling system or I'd be picking it up. I couldn't even be sure it *was* a craft till it was just about overhead. A lot of the time before that it just faded out. Now I'm sure."

"How big is it?"

"Maybe fifty feet."

"Too big for a torpedo," Lasovic mused. "A deep sea explorer like the NR-1, maybe?"

"Or a DSRV. But what the hell would either be doing out here?"

"And without a mother sub," Lasovic added. "I don't know. Continue tracking it and let me know if there are any sudden changes."

"Yes, sir."

Lasovic walked back down the short passage to the control room. What the hell was going on? Was this some kind of test during his first assignment? The sudden falling off of Soviet traffic in the past few days had already worried him. Now this?

Best to be prepared. "Maneuvering, Conn. Prepare to power up on very short notice. Stay as quiet as you can, but I may want to take us out of here in a hurry."

"Maneuvering, aye, Captain."

He looked to Lieberman, acting XO. "Keep on top of the men, Frank. We're still full silent. Not a peep from anyone."

Lieberman nodded and trotted off.

"Attack Center, this is the captain. Prepare a firing solution for that contact of Sonar's. Arm torpedoes one and two."

"Aye, sir. One and two armed and ready."

Lasovic felt better. He could run or fight, whichever was necessary. He settled in to wait for a clear signal to do either.

"Grid 16 completed. That's it, Mac," Luke said despondently. "No sub. Nothing at all but a lot of mud."

MacKenzie let his hands fall from the controls. "We better retrace," he said. He was physically depleted and the thinning air only made it worse. Several times he'd had to shake Luke from a head-lolling drowsiness. He understood it. He wanted to sleep also.

"I feel funny, Mac. You?"

MacKenzie grabbed the control. Had to stay awake. They were so maddeningly close.

"Luke, I . . . Luke? Luke!"

"Sorry, Captain. I just . . ." The rest was lost to mumbling. His head drooped. "Almost . . ."

MacKenzie let him sleep. Pointless to suffer. He bent back to the search. Starting again, he'd never get through the entire grid. Where was it that Luke thought he saw something? Ten. No, thirteen. That was it. He spun the craft around.

His eyes felt heavy. He wanted to sleep . . . wanted to . . . wanted . . . He jerked *Mystic* back on course. The course tracing looked like a seismograph reading. His lungs hurt. A wave of panic tightened his throat. Wait, it's only dry. Relax, he told himself. Nothing gained unless he was under control.

He continued to pilot. Breathe slowly, he reminded himself. Don't stop. Forget about goals, just don't stop. There is no success, only not stopping. The screen! Remember the screen! Watch carefully. Don't stop. Never stop.

Look at the screen. There—that object. Remember! Why is it important? Remember. Keep awake. Don't stop. Never stop. Fight the fog. Forget about winning. The key is not stopping. Remember why that object is important. . . .

The realization penetrated in a sudden flash. *Aspen!* Where? He'd gone right past. Slowly now. Turn back. Don't make the same mistake. There's no time for another mistake. Pilot. Check the course tracing. Follow it. Control. Breathe. Pilot . . .

The sleek black submarine swam into view on his screen. There was the sail. Keep going . . . bring *Mystic* down. He needed help. He shook Luke but there was no response. Please live, he prayed silently. He fed more power to the motors and slid by the sail with only inches to spare.

One eye on the screen and one on the controls, MacKenzie knew he was going to get only one try at dropping *Mystic*'s hemispheric skirt over *Aspen*'s aft hatch. There were black spots swimming in his eyes. Pressure wrapped around his head like a bandanna. Slowly, deliberately, he pumped in ballast. *Mystic* dropped.

The aft hatch was a hazy target twenty feet away. *Mystic* drifted down. Currents sent silt in between them. He

couldn't see! Wait . . . there. Ten feet. He corrected a
wobble, straightened out. His hand hovered over the
ballast pump switch. One try for all the money. He cut the
engines. Closer. Five feet . . . three . . . His hand
flashed out. . . .

Lasovic wheeled around as Sonar's voice came over the
intercom, filled with alarm, "Captain, it's right over us and
coming in!"

Lasovic hesitated. The thing was too close to torpedo. It
had surprised him, coming to a new course so suddenly.
What was it and why was it here? The computer now
identified it as a DSRV. But how?

"Conn, Maneuvering. Ready to power up if you need it,
Captain."

"Hold, Maneuvering."

"Captain?" It was Lieberman raising an inquiring eyebrow. It was now or never.

Lasovic came to a decision. "Let it in, Frank. Take the
conn. I'm going aft to see who's come all this way to see
us. Chief, break out some sidearms and meet me."

"Aye, sir."

"I have the conn," Lieberman announced.

Lasovic felt the clang of contact as he slid through the
engineering-room hatch. The chief was already there with
a squad of sailors, all armed and ready. Pumps began to
dewater the skirt between Aspen and the DSRV. When the
ready light went on, two crewmen swung the heavy wheel
on the hatch around. It opened with a rush of seawater.

"Tom . . ." MacKenzie almost fell through the trunk,
taking in air in great, heaving gulps.

"Mac, what the hell . . . ?"

"Inside . . . no air . . . copilot," he managed weakly.

Crewmen went in and handed Luke Johnson's unconscious form down and out. Lasovic ordered him carried to
the medic. They put MacKenzie on the deck and propped
his head up. His color was returning slowly. Lasovic bent
down beside him.

MacKenzie reached up. "Whatever you do, Tom"—he
had to stop to breathe—"don't move Aspen an inch until
we've talked. Ultra-quiet. Got me?"

"Sure, Mac. But what's going on?"

MacKenzie wanted to tell him, but oxygen starvation and fatigue sent him careening over the edge, into a distant place where everything, including *Kirov,* was lost in the darkness.

42

CARIBBEAN SEA

Kirov's torpedo-room crewman was nursing a severe headache, made worse by the captain's incessant questions.

"You're certain it was Segurra?"

"Yes, Comrade Captain."

"He was alone?"

"I saw no one else."

"Not the cook?"

"You mean Radio Officer Mishkin?"

"No, no. I mean . . . why did you call him that?"

The crewman looked like he wanted to hide. "But Comrade Captain, that's what he was before we became the First International Communist Submarine. He told us to say nothing. Was that not right?"

Santillo stared at him. The cook was one of *Kirov's* former officers! Mishkin, in charge of the radio room. Now it made sense that he had the skill to get off the ship. With Segurra's help too. How far back? That was the question. The crewman had been discovered less than an hour ago. They couldn't be far.

A sudden thought struck him. The torpedo room . . . the cruise missiles!

"Cordova. Quickly. I think the SS-NX-21's have been tampered with. Check every system."

"Yes, Comrade Captain."

Santillo's rage was almost overwhelming. How easily he'd been taken in. Mishkin must have stored the missing raft and scuba gear in with Segurra. They left together, probably heading for the edge of the Zone, hoping to be picked up. Well, he was going to see to it that they died together. Segurra couldn't be allowed to speak to his council. Ortega was balking as it was, and Barrista's death would be the last straw.

He felt hemmed in suddenly, and that only fueled his anger. Why were things so difficult? He fulfilled his promise. No matter—he held back the United States, he could hold back the world if necessary. Independence was the answer. No allegiance to anyone but himself. He was invulnerable with *Kirov*. An island of his own, perhaps. But he needed time to plan. The Zone had to stay intact for a while longer. After that, to hell with Nicaragua and its petty problems. He just had to stop Mishkin and Segurra first.

"Helm, right full rudder. Steady on course oh-nine-oh. All ahead full."

The intercom squawked. "Captain? Cordova. You were right. All the missiles were rigged. Someone crushed the relays. It's going to take a little time to make the repairs."

"Fix them!"

"Yes, Comrade Captain."

That was the problem, Santillo realized. Everyone had begun not taking him seriously. They needed a practical demonstration. No more words. No more hesitation. One missile, one city. It would be an excellent beginning to negotiations; just the right tone.

Fire and destruction. It was time.

Lasovic shook his head in rueful disbelief. "And we've been here all this time without knowing? Jesus, Mac, the bastard's probably been by here a dozen times. Close enough to blow him out of the water."

"That's why I'm here," MacKenzie said, finishing toweling himself off after a shower. "We're going to nail him." He paused. "You understand, Tom, this is no reflection on you."

"Mac, in five years, when I'm as experienced as you are, I'll mind. Till then it's the best man gets the job. Give the orders, skipper."

MacKenzie pulled on a clean uniform. "Thanks, Tom. Captain's brief in ten minutes."

* * *

MacKenzie briefed his officers in the wardroom. They listened intently, each one a member of a crack team whose entire training and career had been to prepare for just such a moment as this.

". . . so it's got to be a quick kill," MacKenzie concluded. "If Santillo has any chance at all to launch those missiles, we can depend on him taking it. We're not protecting just a convoy, gentlemen. This is Houston or Miami or Atlanta in a nuclear firestorm. We're the defense. One good, clean shot may be all we get."

"What's maximum launch sequence time?" asked Fire Control Officer Sam Talmadge.

"Less than ten seconds, Sam. That's the time it takes to launch the cruise missiles."

Talmadge considered that. "What do you think of setting the torpedoes to magnetic proximity rather than contact? Cut a few seconds off run time."

MacKenzie understood what he was suggesting. Setting the torpedoes to explode when they were close enough to the *Kirov* to register her huge magnetic bulk, rather than having to explode on actual contact, would trigger them that much sooner. The explosion would be enough to hole her hull.

"I think that's wise, Sam. But only the fish in tubes one and two. The rest we may need if we have to make a second pass to be sure of a kill."

"Aye, skipper."

"John, what do your tapes show?"

Sonar Officer John Gonzalez passed a computer printout over the table. "We ran all our contacts through the computers and separated out the Victor Threes. Looks like our boy passed this way at least four times, we figure. Repeat signatures every twenty hours or so."

"When was the last one?"

"Nineteen hundred hours yesterday."

MacKenzie did some simple calculating. "That should give us about five hours minimum. We'll go on standby in three. What about course and speed?"

"Always comes at us from the west, usually about ten to fifteen knots. Depth varies though. Anywhere from three to six hundred feet."

"Good work, John. Let's hope you're close. We're going

to be at battle stations for a long time as it is, just waiting for *Kirov* to poke her nose into our area."

"The crew is up to it, skipper. I think they'll welcome the activity after days on watch."

MacKenzie nodded. "Okay. But impress this on every one of them, on yourselves too: We have to get *Kirov* with our first shot. If he's not sunk or severely crippled, we've as good as failed, no matter how close we come. So nothing cute or fancy. We lie in wait dead silent, track him with passive gear only as he comes in, and fire at minimum range with a spread of two MK-48's."

"Torpedoes have failed to detonate before, skipper," said Talmadge. "What if ours misfire?"

"We'll be right in on their tails, Sam," MacKenzie explained, "from the time we shoot till the moment she's destroyed. Harass her, shoot again, ram her if we have to—anything to keep her captain too busy to recover. He's got to be sure that the second he slows to launch, we'll be roaring in to put another torpedo down his throat."

There were more questions. Strategies were discussed for the better part of an hour before MacKenzie finally said, "That's it then. You all know the stakes. Just one last item. A little insurance if we need it. Tom and I already talked this over. It will take a little bit of jury rigging, but I have faith in our Electronics Section. Here's what we have in mind. . . ."

The meeting broke up half an hour later. One by one Division Officers returned to their respective sections. Word began to spread through the ship like a brushfire: Action. Soon.

43

Santillo swung *Kirov*'s periscope through a full turn. Nothing. Where were they? Mishkin and Segurra couldn't be out of the Zone yet, and no one could have slipped in and gotten them.

"Comrade Captain, we're receiving a low power radio distress signal. It could be from the life raft."

"Direction?"

"East of us. Approximately thirty miles."

Santillo slapped the scope. He had them!

"Navigator, give me an intercept course. All ahead top speed." He called down to the torpedo room. "Cordova, how much longer?"

"Another hour or so, Comrade Captain. That's all."

"Excellent. Let me know as soon as repairs are completed."

Kirov raced on under the waves, her engines turning at high speed. Santillo thought over the terms he would dictate to the superpowers. Things were going his way again. But first Segurra and Mishkin. He pictured bursting up under their fragile raft like the great whale pursuing Ahab. He savored that vision of himself, allied with *Kirov*'s power. The avenger—an unstoppable force. *Kirov* was more than a weapon—it was his will incarnate.

He felt his own power. This kill was going to be a pleasure.

On *Aspen* MacKenzie took over the conn with a feeling akin to coming home.

"Welcome back, Captain." It was Randall, the Diving Officer.

"Thank you, Mr. Randall. I can't tell you how nice it is to be back."

"Must have been quite a trip in *Mystic*, sir."

"Let's just say it will never replace docking at port," MacKenzie said dryly.

The intercom buzzed. "Skipper? Maneuvering. Cardiff here."

"This is MacKenzie, Jake."

"All set on what you ordered, sir. Mr. Lasovic and I can't really test it, you know, but we're pretty sure it will work fine."

"That's damn quick, Jake. Good work."

"Thanks, skipper."

So the hardware was in place. Now for the crew. He planned to run a few drills, gradually increasing time and tempo until *Aspen* was humming like a well-tuned engine. A few more dry runs and then battle stations till *Kirov* showed. He had at least three more hours at a minimum if Sonar's calculations were right. Planning to move the—

"Conn, Radio. Skipper, we've got something odd here. A distress signal. Russian style. Very faint."

"Kirov?"

"Not likely. One of her life rafts, maybe."

What was this all about? he wondered. "Sonar, this is the captain. What the hell is up there?"

"Whatever it is, sir, it's got no engines. We're picking up something that could be a paddle slap, but that's open to interpretation. Nothing else in the area."

MacKenzie was bothered. *Always the things you didn't prepare for* . . . "Mr. Randall, make your depth five-nine feet."

"Periscope depth five-nine feet, aye, sir."

"Very, very slowly," MacKenzie ordered. "Take her up with care. No noise. Minimum plane movements, Mr. Randall."

Aspen began to rise.

Mishkin lay back weakly against the life raft's rounded black side and cursed Miguel soundly.

"You're a fool, Segurra. Let me die. You'll only call Santillo back with that."

"You are the talkingest Russian I ever met, you know that? Do us both a favor and save your strength. Move over a bit, if you can. I want to get you out of the sun."

Mishkin shivered violently. Blood was still seeping from the terrible rows of punctures on his arms and legs.

Miguel wrapped some more gauze from the first-aid kit around them. There was blood mixed with seawater pooling on the raft's bottom. He moved the makeshift umbrella of wet suits to better shield Mishkin from the hot sun.

"Stupid fool. You could make it alone," Mishkin said bitterly.

"Probably. And that barracuda would have probably taken off half my skin, too, if you hadn't gotten in between us and . . . cut it out, will you? I've got to stop the bleeding."

"Turn off the radio. What's the sense of us both dying?"

"Too late now. Saltwater activates the battery once it's immersed. Look, we were almost at the edge of the Zone anyway. *Kirov*'s probably a hundred miles away. Couple of hours, someone will pick us up."

Mishkin shivered again, and Miguel covered him as best he could. God, what a horrible creature that barricuda had been, all teeth and evil eyes flashing again and again even after its own flesh was in tatters. Mishkin had only a knife but he'd never relented, pushing Miguel out of the way and tearing at the darting menace till the water was filled with blood and pieces of rent flesh. He was a brave and resourceful man. Miguel wanted him to live very much.

I'm sorry, Phillipe, he prayed silently. *You were very brave, too, in your own way. I'm sorry it didn't work . . . so many things I'd change. But at least I understand why you stopped me. Poor Phillipe, will saving this man repay at least some of my debt to you?*

"Miguel . . ."

"Yes?"

"I'm cold. Thirsty. I—"

"Shh. Here, let me help."

Miguel pressed against Mishkin and put the water bottle to his lips. The man drank greedily till there was almost none. Miguel was thirsty, too, but he didn't drink. He capped the bottle and put his arms around Mishkin till the shivering stopped.

Mishkin fell into an uneasy sleep. Miguel pulled the rubber jacket over him.

The sun blazed overhead like a torch. They bobbed silently on the bottle-green sea, waiting.

Several hundred yards away, MacKenzie peered at the life raft through his periscope. "Could they be from *Kirov*?" he wondered out loud. The high-power lens made him feel as if he were on the raft with the two men. "Take a look, Tom."

Lasovic hunkered the scope around. "It's definitely Russian, skipper. Where else could it be from?"

"One of the ships Santillo sunk?"

"None of them were Russian, and besides, there'd most likely be others."

A life raft off *Kirov*. Why the hell was it here? "We've got a real problem," MacKenzie said grimly. "I can't risk surfacing. We'd be a sitting duck for *Kirov*."

"There aren't any other ships close enough. They'll die if we leave them," observed Lasovic quietly.

MacKenzie peered through the scope again. One man down low. He looked hurt. Were those bandages? It might explain why they'd use the radio. He could see the second man clearly. Oddly, something was familiar about him—the bone structure, the hands too. Why did the man remind him of Justine?

His inability to pick up the castaways ate at him with a physical pain. It went against every sea law and every moral code practiced by seagoing men for centuries. Could he just stand here and watch them die? He slammed his fist into the steel railing in frustration.

Miami and Houston . . . nuclear fires. He kept recalling the balance. What were two lives against so many? Trade-offs. But it ate at his guts like acid.

"Conn. Sonar. Contact, skipper! Bearing two-six-nine at about sixty thousand yards, closing rapidly. I'm certain it's a Victor Three, sir. Turn count indicates a speed of twenty-five knots, course oh-nine-oh. Coming right at us, sir."

Too soon! That was MacKenzie's first thought. He didn't have enough time to prepare the crew. Not enough time to drill them and raise them up to a fine pitch. It had to be *Kirov*—but she was three hours early!

Santillo had to be after the two men on the surface. He

was heading straight for them. Evidently they'd escaped from him and he'd retraced his course to find them.

Mission imperatives ran through his mind. Santillo's early return changed nothing for the two men on the surface. Logic still demanded that they die. MacKenzie's best bet was to back off and wait for a better opportunity, when the crew was fully ready. Tomorrow. Be certain, an inner voice prompted. Be certain . . .

He was. A feral look crept over his features. It had been Santillo's day too long. His hand hit the General Quarters alarm soundly.

"This is the captain. Battle Stations. This is no drill. Battle Stations."

Aspen had to take *Kirov* now. It was a little early, maybe, but if he waited, another opportunity might be too long in the making. And the two men above would die. Here, at least Santillo's attention was focused on other targets, his senses preoccupied.

"Sonar, Conn. Your best range."

"Conn, Sonar, fifty thousand yards and closing fast."

"Torpedo Room, conn. Flood all tubes."

"Flood all tubes, Torpedo Room, aye."

All around MacKenzie, men were racing to station. The atmosphere in the conn grew as taut as a bowstring.

"Mr. Lasovic, rig ship for ultra quiet. If it so much as hiccups, shut it down. We'll open the outer doors on tubes one and four in thirty minutes."

"Aye, sir."

"Maneuvering, Conn. This is the captain. Jake, this will be a test of wills. We need to keep Santillo on the defensive. I may need you to give me everything you can, but keep the plant on the line. We can't lose her this time."

"No problem, skipper. She's ready to run."

"Attack Center. Mr. Talmadge, keep tracking her now and be certain you have a firing solution. He's coming at us from the west. I figure him to come up under the raft like a killer whale and ram them. He's a real bastard, this one. I intend to shoot the first unit from tube one and shoot from deep while he is in the shallows."

"Aye, skipper."

"Helm, right five degrees rudder, steady course two-

two-oh. All ahead one third. Nice and easy, everybody. As he gets closer I'll want to keep pointing him as he passes close to the raft. We'll fire immediately after he crosses our bow. Got it?"

"Steady two-two-oh answers ahead one third, aye, sir."

Lasovic came back into the conn. "All quiet, skipper. The men are ready. Any other plans for the attack?"

"Santillo will probably stay on this heading so he won't run into the sun," he explained. "I plan to take him from the south. We'll use as many torpedoes as it takes."

"You want me aft?"

"I do. If we need our little surprise, we're going to need it in a hurry. By the way, how's Luke Johnson?"

"Just fine. Wrapped around a hot meal and out of the way. Good luck, skipper."

MacKenzie clapped him on the back. "To us all, Tom."

Lasovic hurried aft, and went back to the task at hand.

"Fire Control. Range?"

"Twenty thousand yards and closing. Still holding course, skipper."

MacKenzie brought *Aspen* around in a wide, slow turn to keep pointing the target. Speed meant noise, and that could give *Kirov* warning. The moment her captain realized *Aspen* was stalking her had to be the exact moment he had to defend himself. Only the most urgent need for self-preservation would keep him too occupied to launch. In the best case he'd never know *Aspen* was there until the torpedoes exploded.

Slowly, almost silently, *Aspen* slid through the sea. The days of flashing out at top speed to outflank an enemy were long gone. Stealth was everything and surprise was the classic strategy. But with ASW systems and sonars as sensitive as these, surprise meant quiet.

"Make your depth four hundred feet, five degrees down bubble, Mr. Randall."

"Four hundred feet, aye, sir."

"Conn, Sonar. Range ten thousand yards and closing."

MacKenzie pictured the two men above, unaware of death approaching like a stalking shark. "Sonar, Conn. What's her course, speed, and depth?"

"At the speed she's making, she's kicking up quite a fuss. Course oh-nine-oh, speed twenty knots, depth

approximately two hundred feet and coming up slowly.
We can hear the hull popping."

MacKenzie nodded to himself. The faster the better. At
twenty knots *Kirov* was close to deaf. Santillo was careless.

"Fire Control. This should be a passive sonar approach.
I do not intend to go active unless we need a second
pass."

"We've got an excellent tracking solution, skipper."

"Keep it refined. Maneuvering, prepare for all ahead
flank any moment now. Immediately after launch, if she
counterattacks I want a damn big knuckle to pull off his
sonar."

"Aye, sir. We'll be ready."

"Frank?"

Lieberman looked up from his chart table. "Begin your
turn now, skipper. Minimum range in three minutes."

MacKenzie took a slow breath. "Helm, right ten degrees rudder. Easy son, that's it. Settle down."

One hand on the column housing the periscope and
one on the steel railing, MacKenzie felt the emotional
surge in every fiber of his body as *Aspen* moved to his
commands. Nerve cells carried sonar signals, muscles and
sinews reacted; *Aspen* came into position.

"Conn, Sonar. Course oh-nine-oh, range three miles,
speed twenty knots, depth one hundred feet and rising.
You called it, skipper. Straight at the life raft."

"Fire Control, Firing Point Procedures."

"Ship ready. Weapon ready. Tubes ready. Solution
ready, sir."

The computers were tracking well. *Kirov* drew
closer. . . .

"Torpedo Room, stand by tubes one and four."

"All tubes ready to fire, sir. Standing by one and four."

Kirov was coming at them. She was rising towards her
prey, two helpless men in a life raft. MacKenzie felt a hot
anger inside him. Not yet though. Not yet . . .

"Conn, Sonar. Range two thousand yards."

MacKenzie felt the blood drumming in his head. Men
leaned forward. *Kirov* was almost across their bow. . . .

"Match sonar bearings and shoot."

"Set—standby—fire tube one!"

MacKenzie felt the brief surge as the MK-48 torpedo burst out from amidships. This was it, the one good, clean shot he'd promised. Miniature sonars in the MK-48 fixed on *Kirov*'s noise. Thirty-five hundred pounds of lethal missile speared through the bright waters.

"Conn, Sonar. Unit running hot, straight, and normal."

"Sonar, Conn. Keep tracking. Match sonar bearings and shoot tube four!"

"Closing on target, skipper."

MacKenzie launched a silent prayer along with the torpedo. Someone was thumping an involuntary drum beat on the deck. One good, clean shot for all the money.

"Closing, skipper. Closing . . ."

Kirov's Sonar Officer suddenly clenched his headphones and called out in a voice filled with shock and fear, "Torpedoes, Comrade Captain! Closing on course oh-nine-oh. Comrade Captain!"

"Impossible!" Santillo roared. "From where could . . ." He realized they had only seconds. "How?" he gasped.

"They are bearing down on us. Range closing rapidly."

There was no time for questions. Segurra and everything else would have to wait. "Dive!" he yelled stridently, leaping over the railing and grabbing the controls from the planesman. He rammed them forward. *Kirov* answered with a sickening groan and shot downwards.

Santillo prayed the hull would stand the strain. "Engineering, all ahead full power. Keep this all the way down," he ordered the planesman.

"Comrade Captain, torpedoes closing."

Santillo heard the fear in his voice. He cursed the heavens and poured ballast into *Kirov*'s tanks, hitting switch after switch on the control board. They shot downward like a stone.

"Depth?" he bellowed.

"Six hundred feet . . ."

"Keep it coming, damn you."

"Six-fifty . . . seven hundred . . . seven fifty . . ."

It was a race now between the speed of the torpedoes and *Kirov*'s rate of dive. The Russian sub could dive far deeper than the American. If it had room enough, the torpedoes might run out of fuel trying to follow. Try to outrun them, Santillo thought. Outrun the torpedoes. First that.

"Cordova, launch the decoys," he ordered.

"Decoys away!"

From the aft pod miniature charges blew decoy sound generators into the water to fool the "smart" torpedoes and confuse the Americans' sonar. From the beginning Santillo *knew* it had to be the Americans. Outrun them . . .

"Attack Center. All tubes. Fire back on their course track now. Fire at will."

The Soviet computers read the incoming torpedoes' track and returned a firing solution for the American submarine. Santillo felt his ship surge as a salvo was fired from the rear tubes.

"Prepare to fire the cruise missiles," he ordered. Ten seconds . . . give me just ten seconds, he thought. Fire and smoke . . .

"Fourteen hundred . . . fourteen fifty . . . fifteen hundred . . . fifteen fifty . . ."

"Missiles ready, Comrade Captain."

Santillo felt the hot breath of pursuit on the back of his neck. It had to be now.

"Comrade Captain, they are still closing!" yelled the Sonar Officer in panic.

"Seventeen hundred . . . seventeen fifty . . . eighteen hundred . . ."

"Torpedo Room. Cruise missiles—"

The explosion shook *Kirov* like a child's toy. Santillo pitched over the railing. Water burst from ruptured streams hard enough to flay off skin. Somewhere men were screaming. The lights went out, went on again weakly as emergency batteries cut in. Sparks cascaded from short-circuited boards, and acrid smoke from burning insulation filled the control room.

Then silence.

Santillo picked himself up gingerly. Dead men in blue wool uniforms lay face down in a foot of water. His wound had reopened. Blood merged with the sodden cloth of his tunic. But *Kirov* held.

He hauled himself back to the Diving Officer's chair and

pushed the former occupant's prostrate form away. He flipped a switch and circulating fans began to clear the air.

"Sonar?"

Weakly, "Comrade Captain?"

"Engine Room."

"Badly damaged, Comrade Captain. One-third power at best. Many men dead, but we're holding."

It would have to do. "Torpedo Room," he continued his roll call.

"We're still here. Damage to tubes one, two, three, and four, Comrade Captain. Only rear five and six operative."

Damn! That was an end to the cruise missiles. Santillo grimly sent a silent compliment to his unknown adversary. No fire and smoke would come from *Kirov*. Not unless he escaped and could make repairs.

It was far from over yet. The decoys must have pulled off one of the incoming torpedoes, and the one that exploded must have been on magnetic proximity fuses. Only the desperate dive saved them. They were damaged surely, but they still had teeth.

He checked the depth. Far deeper than the Americans could follow. Grabbing the helm, he began to bring *Kirov* around.

MacKenzie said in his mind, Now!

"Conn, Sonar. Explosions, sir! Very deep. *Kirov* was diving hard."

Smart captain, MacKenzie conceded. He had abandoned the raft the second he picked up the incoming torpedoes. Dove straight down to avoid them, and managed to launch decoys, probably. But he had to be hurt. At least one of the fish must have gotten to him.

"Sonar, what are you getting?"

"Noise, Captain. The explosions are still blocking everything. Reverberations, white noise, some odd rebounds, echoes."

"What kind of echoes?"

"Probably from our torpedoes. High cycle, intermittent bounce off—"

Torpedo! MacKenzie knew it as certainly as he knew *Kirov* had escaped destruction.

"Helm, right full rudder. Ahead flank. Attack Center, launch decoys in a full pattern. Emergency Deep."

They'd fired back along the incoming track. He only hoped they hadn't time to program properly. If he got enough distance between *Aspen* and her last position, the decoys might confuse the torpedoes enough to set them off. *Aspen*'s nose dropped and he grabbed the stanchion.

Another sixty seconds and it would have worked.

Kirov's torpedo was activated by a decoy only a hundred feet from the hull, and *Aspen* rolled as if she'd been struck by a giant hand. Nothing could totally withstand that sudden burst of pressure. Metal buckled and systems failed. Seams split and delicate electronics systems shorted out, making manual control, not computer, the order of the day.

MacKenzie directed damage control action and bulkhead hatches slammed shut. A crew less disciplined might have panicked, but one by one compartments contained their damage and reported.

The crew got the main and emergency drain pumps operating. "Maneuvering, Conn. Are you there, Jake?"

"Cardiff here, Captain," came the voice, tight with pain. "Steam leaks . . . caught us, but they're isolated now."

MacKenzie pictured the compartment. It would be like a sauna by now. "What's the situation there, Jake?"

"I can keep us moving, Captain. But only single turbine and about thirty percent power. We won't be as capable as I'm sure you'd like. Lots of damage, but she's hanging together damn well."

"Repair what you can as soon as possible, and keep me cut in, Jake. Out."

That was it. They were badly damaged but still watertight. Weapons systems were limited to the torpedoes already loaded in tubes two and three, and the computers were down to basic-solution shots.

"Sonar, anyting indicating cruise missile launch?"

"Nothing, sir. No launch."

MacKenzie mentally scored that one for *Aspen*. If Santillo hadn't fired by now, he couldn't fire. The major part of *Aspen*'s job was accomplished. Now the rest was to stay alive.

"Can you fix the computers, Mr. Talmadge?"

"I don't see how, sir. Not in less than a week."

Two torpedoes, only basic computer capability and barely enough power for propulsion. "Welcome to World War Two." MacKenzie grimaced. "Rig ship for ultra quiet," he ordered. It was time to play the timid mouse again and hide. "Mr. Randall?"

Mr. Randall was wiping the blood off his face. He'd been thrown face first into the control console. "Sir?"

"I'm sorry, son. You'll have to take the controls yourself."

Randall looked over. The helmsman was still at his station, but his head lay bent back at an impossible angle and his wide eyes stared lifelessly upward. Gingerly, Randall pulled him from the seat.

All over the ship men did the same, replacing dead or crippled shipmates. Systems were jury-rigged as fast as possible. The ship's condition was serious. MacKenzie had doubts they could survive even another close call.

Of one thing he was certain though—Santillo was still out there and planning to come at them again.

Santillo brought *Kirov* up to eight hundred feet and leveled her off.

"Sonar, anything?"

"We heard the explosion, Comrade Captain. Now it's quiet. I think we hit them."

Santillo frowned. "It would have been almost an impossibly lucky shot to do so. Stay quiet. We'll see."

He made the crew changes, ordered the dead taken to the trash room, and retook his position in the control room. Soft beeps from Sonar filtered in; a burnt smell hung in the air. He was reminded that any of his systems could fail any second.

"He's out there, our quiet friend," he said softly. "The trick will be to get him to make some noise."

He thought about that for a long time. Finally the beginnings of a plan began to form.

"Cordova, Villega. Come up here. I have a list of things. Listen to me. . . ."

Half an hour later the two officers met Santillo by the aft escape trunk.

"You have what I asked for?" Santillo demanded.

"Here, Comrade Captain. But why do you want these things?"

Santillo smiled. "Because we need to be in two places at once, Cordova, and this is how we accomplish that. We're going to make our silent friend think he knows where we are so he will come at us and reveal his position. Then we'll take him once and for all."

"But scuba tanks and canvas bags?"

Santillo produced two timed detonators he removed from the now useless cruise missiles. "Along with these, yes."

Villega shook his head. "Forgive me, Comrade Captain, but—"

"It's simple, really," Santillo began. He was enjoying his own cleverness. "The detonators are attached to the valves on the scuba tanks, and both tanks are placed in the canvas bag."

The men complied as Santillo continued. "We will set the detonators to sixty seconds, enough time to rise well away from us once filled with air and released out the escape trunk. When the detonator goes off, the tanks will rupture and create a mass of bubbles just about equal to a sub's propeller cavitation. The escaping air should also propel the bag forward, like air escaping from a balloon. With the bubbles and the velocity and the metal tanks to reflect sonar, I think they'll go after our little present thinking it's us. If they do, we'll go right in after and finish them."

The officers eyed Santillo respectfully. "Brilliant, Comrade Captain," said Villega. "This is genius."

"Wait for my command. Cordova, put on a tank and enter the trunk. Arm the detonators only when the outer hatch is open. Let the bags rise freely after you inflate them and push them out."

Santillo left them and went forward. "Soon, my friend," he muttered. "Very, very soon."

MacKenzie passed the word for Lasovic over the sound-powered phone. "Tom?"

"Here, skipper."

"What's the condition there?"

"Jake says we're closer. Still about twenty minutes though."

"And the rest of the system we rigged up?"

"I'd be lying if I told you I was sure of anything."

MacKenzie grinned in spite of things. "That makes two of us, pal. Get ready, Tom."

He settled in to wait.

Santillo took the conn.

"Helm, steady on course two-six-oh. All ahead one third. Make your depth three hundred feet."

Kirov began a slow turn and ascent. Santillo's face was set in hard lines. Only one of us leaves here, he swore silently. The last run.

"Villega, is Cordova in the trunk?" he called down.

"He is, Comrade Captain."

"Have him release now."

Santillo looked to the console of gauges. There the hatch was open. He counted off the seconds. The light blinked off.

"Comrade Captain? Package away."

Santillo felt his spirits rise. Very soon now.

"Torpedo Room, prepare to fire locally."

"We're ready, Comrade Captain."

"Sonar, after the detonators fire and the tanks shatter, we're going to hear our friend move in for a firing position. Compute a firing solution quickly. Be ready.

"Yes, Comrade Captain."

Slowly he increased their speed. "Right ten degrees rudder. Bring us about carefully. No noise," he ordered. "Make your depth one hundred feet."

"Depth one hundred feet, Comrade Captain."

Santillo ticked off the seconds in his mind. Now!

"Comrade Captain, the detonator has activated. Cavitation noises . . . moving . . . moving . . ."

Santillo leaned forward eagerly. "And the sub?"

"No."

"It must be!"

"No . . . wait. There! Bearing one-eight-oh, rough course two-seven-oh, speed four knots, estimated depth one hundred feet. There she is."

Santillo was on his feet. "Torpedo Room, set those parameters as inputs and prepare to fire."

"Torpedo Room, Aye. Inputs set."

"*Fire!*"

The seconds were like heartbeats. One . . . two . . . three . . . Soon, very soon. Six . . . seven . . . Closer and closer . . .

"Sonar?"

"Bearing of torpedoes and . . . contact match! Explosions."

Santillo's fist struck the railing joyously.

"No noise, Comrade Captain. No noise at all. Congratulations."

Santillo accepted his due. A fine enemy. But the gods had chosen.

"Helm, come left to course one-eight-oh. All ahead full," he ordered, returning to his deserved throne.

Aspen's Sonar Officer removed his headphones quickly. "There goes *Mystic*, skipper. They blew it to hell and back. And there's *Kirov*. Bearing oh-one-oh degrees. No doubt, loud and clear. All caution thrown to the wind."

MacKenzie experienced a moment of elation and sadness combined. The trick worked. But *Mystic* had been one hell of a fine craft.

His face like cold steel, MacKenzie ordered, "Open the outer doors, tubes two and three. Fire Control, compute a basic, simple, straight-running shot. Firing point procedures."

"Ship ready, solution ready, Torpedo Room ready."

"Helm ahead two thirds. Right full rudder, steady oh-three-oh degrees."

"Ahead two thirds. Steady oh-three-oh degrees, aye."

Kirov drew closer, blind and deaf at such a high speed.

"Bearing oh-one-five degrees. Range three thousand yards. Steady oh-three-oh degrees, sir."

"Very well," MacKenzie acknowledged. "Match sonar bearings, and shoot tubes two and three."

"Set—standby—fire! Tube two unit away. Set—standby—fire! Tube three unit away."

MacKenzie gripped the handrail. All on one bet. No more torpedoes, no more loaded tubes. He had almost fallen for Santillo's decoy. Instead he'd launched *Mystic*. Now Santillo was coming to him.

"Torpedo and contact bearings are merging," Sonar called out.

MacKenzie willed the torpedoes in, got behind them with every ounce of mental energy he possessed. The crew were up on their feet, holding back, waiting. He held his breath.

"Explosions!" Sonar yelled. "We got her, skipper. We got her!"

They pounded each other on the back, unmindful of rank. Lasovic pumped MacKenzie's hand. "Nice work, Mac. You did it."

Someone thumped him soundly. For a long moment chaos reigned. Then men began to return to their positions.

MacKenzie felt the aftermath of battle drain him. "Prepare to surface, Mr. Randall. We've still got those men up there. Let's not forget them. Antennas up as soon as we surface. Tom, see to the pickup."

"On my way."

"Conn, Radio. What do I send, sir?"

MacKenzie thought it over. Then, "From *Aspen* to COMSUBLANT, etcetera . . . you know, I don't even know the date."

"It's August first, sir."

"Thank you. Send this: Clean Sweep. *Kirov* destroyed at sea. All hands performed as warriors. *Aspen*."

When *Aspen* was holding on the surface, MacKenzie proceeded to the bridge and watched as the two men were brought on board. He savored the sun and the sound of the sea lapping at the deck. It was a warm day, forgiving.

Lasovic had the two men on deck. The unconscious one was immediately lowered inside.

"You there," MacKenzie called out to the other. "Your name, please."

The man looked up to MacKenzie. His gaze took in the United States emblem. "What about the *Kirov*?" he asked.

"Done."

The man nodded. "That's good to hear. My name is Segurra. Miguel Segurra."

MacKenzie smiled.

"Am I under arrest, Captain?"

MacKenzie shook his head and felt the first release of tension since he'd left *Phoenix* what seemed like so long ago. A grin spread over his face. After all, how could he arrest his future brother-in-law?

"Set a course for Guantanamo, Mr. Lieberman," he ordered as soon as they were below.

Moments later *Aspen* slid beneath the water and the ocean above it returned to a plane of unbroken glass under the sun.

EPILOGUE

They made the pickup at night. MacKenzie remembered the beach. He could see it clearly in the moonlight. So many rules had been broken to give him command of this particular mission, he thought it better not to list them.

Almost a year had passed since he was here last. Ten months since they'd taken *Kirov*. He now wore the single two-inch gold stripe of a Rear Admiral, and *Aspen* was firmly in Tom Lasovic's competent hands. She had been repaired at Norfolk's yards and was on cruise in the Mediterranean at this moment. Tom swore she was even better than before. MacKenzie reflected that it was hard to improve on a ship like *Aspen*.

"There's the signal, skipper."

It broke him out of his reverie. "Thank you, Mr. Randall. Send the boats."

Randall was a fine Division Officer. Phil Arlin spoke well of him here on *Phoenix*. MacKenzie had been rotated to squadron commander almost four months before. It came with his promotion. So did the desk. It was steadier, more in line with his ultimate goals. But sometimes . . . God, how he missed the action.

"First one off the beach and on the way back, sir," Randall said, peering through the night scope. "And, ah, sir?"

"Yes?"

"I think this is the one you, well . . ."

"Thank you, Mr. Randall. Still the soul of discretion, I see."

"But sir . . ."

MacKenzie smiled. "Help them up, will you?"

"Aye, sir."

He felt a flood of memories as he watched the boat unload. So long, it seemed, since he was here. Not so long at all, really. He waited. Emotion caught at his chest and tightened his throat.

Justine was thinner than he remembered, and the gaunt planes of her face pained him. But if anything she was more beautiful than even the picture his mind's eye had painted, and something in him clutched when he saw her, just as it had almost a year before.

But a year was a long time. For a second he hesitated. She came up on deck and looked around.

"Peter!"

She ran to him, and he moved forward in a rush with his arms wide open. There were tears filling her eyes. He crushed her against him till neither could breathe.

"How did you manage this?" she demanded happily.

"They owed me one. I'll tell you about it later."

"Never again, Peter. I promise."

He held her at arm's length and looked at her lovingly. "Why is it you always look so lousy when I come to pick you up?"

Justine plucked at her bedraggled clothing and felt her sopping wet hair. MacKenzie's uniform was creased to a knife edge. "Contrast?"

He smiled brightly, but turned sober when he remembered her loss. Word had come through Holmes.

"I'm sorry about Sebastion. Truly. I liked him very much."

She nodded tightly. "One fight too many. We were very close at the end. In a way it made it . . . easier. You understand?"

"I will. Later. There are other things too. Later."

Randall was at the hatch. "Topside is secured and last man is down, skipper."

"Prepare to dive, Mr. Randall. We'll be coming in a second. Justine?"

"I'm ready, Peter. Darling."

"Hmm?"

"Nice car," she said, grinning.

MacKenzie led her down the hatch. He looked up at Randall and said within Justine's earshot, "Home, James."

Justine laughed at the odd look Randall gave him as he secured the hatch.

Home sounded right.

ABOUT THE AUTHOR

A native New Yorker, Bart Davis is a graduate of the Bronx High School of Science and of the State University of New York, Stony Brook. He holds a brown belt in karate and is a licensed hypnotist, a reasonably good shot, and a seasoned European traveler. He taught English in the public school system for eleven years, specializing in disruptive students, has traveled extensively through the United States; and has lectured frequently on education, social work, and writing.

Married to an attorney, and the father of a young son, he resides in New York, where he is working on his next novel.